D1098454

Night Calypso

a&b

Night Calypso

LAWRENCE SCOTT

First published in Great Britain in 2004 by
Allison & Busby Limited
Bon Marche Centre
241-251 Ferndale Road
Brixton, London SW9 8BJ
http://www.allisonandbusby.com

This is a work of fiction. While, as in all fiction,
the literary perceptions and insights are based on experience,
all names, characters, places and incidents are either products of the author's imagination
or are used fictitiously. No reference to any real person is intended or should be inferred.

A catalogue record for this book is available from the British Library

ISBN 0 7490 0663 3

Printed and bound in Wales by
Creative Print & Design

LAWRENCE SCOTT is from Trinidad and Tobago. He is the author of the much acclaimed novels *Witchbroom* and *Aelred's Sin*, for which he received a prestigious Commenwealth Writer's Prize, as well as the short-story collection *Ballad for the New World* which contains the award-winning short story "The House of Funerals". He lives in London where he combines writing with teaching English.

Contents

"The true stories of our time have to be able to reconcile a pile of clothes in a drawer with world historical upheavals."

John Berger *Afterword, Nineteen Nineteen*

For Jenny

Porta España
1983

Iguanas and Orchids

Come on in.

It's the stories that I remember, the telling of stories.

Yes.

On returning, I'd come upon it much as it had been left. The doors were hanging off their hinges. The windows banged in the breeze. The fire had not taken all the buildings. Collapsed jalousies allowed the light to paint in broader strokes. There were shards of shattered glass on the floor. The weather had since intruded on the rooms and corrupted the papers, damp and mildewed, lying on desks and in drawers, dusty with wood-lice. Rain and light had done their work. The surfaces of windowsills and tables were sticky and grainy with salt. Cupboards still held bottles and vials of medicine. The contents had spilt, or evaporated. Others were still there, lurid and labelled. *Chaulmoogra Oil.* Filing cabinets had been rifled, thrown to the ground, with their personal records pulled out and strewn on the floor. Syringes were now glass dust. It crunched under my feet on the pitch pine floors.

Was this the way of the exodus, or had this happened in its aftermath? A bit of both, I supposed. This was the kind of thing I saw in the offices and the stores.

Scraps of bandages, like cotton on the cotton trees outside, hung in the fetid air with the dust.

A net of mosquitoes festered like the noise of discordant violins.

On the wards, the iron beds were upended, some had had their springs knocked out, their struts and posts collapsed. Fibre from the disembowelled mattresses was sodden and rotting. Feathers from gutted pillows stirred in the air, floating in the light. Despite this almost total exposure to the elements, a lingering hospital smell filtered through the scent of decay. Human residue and chemicals. Faeces were smeared on the walls. There was the stench of urine.

Somewhere, still, there was that other smell, creeping out of everything.

Two iguanas scuttled among the dry leaves beneath the old almond tree. The mauve mimosa, *Ti-Marie*, crept to the door with her thorns, closing her leaves to our passing touch.

The bush had encroached on what had been the clean yards around the huts. The pink coralita vine scrambled over broken-down, rusty galvanise fences. I could see broken crockery and corroded pots and pans. The gardens had joined the wild, but their purple, red and orange bougainvillea, the chalices of yellow allamanda, still broke out, overburdening the other bushes in the enamel-like jade which was the green of this place.

Butterflies hovered and attached themselves to the wild flowers. The garden ticked with insects. It screamed, the *cigales'* scream, that incessant pitch of the cicada's sawing whine. It rustled and creaked. In the breeze, it scratched at the wounded galvanise roofs which bled their rust.

A wild, white orchid exuded its perfume.

The place was unusually still. Then, there were the gusts of wind, the soft touch of sea-breezes, and the waves breaking repeatedly, with their particular monotony, on the beach below, where I'd left the pirogue. I wandered back to the boatman on the jetty.

In the distance, the ocean was swollen and smacked against rocks on the point beyond Salt Pond and Bande du Sud. It rolled on in an unstoppable tide, coming through the *bocas* between the islands and the continent.

I felt that much had been preserved in the camphor of time, but time had also picked holes in the fabric of this place; a place which had been home for each of us for a period which had seemed as if it would never end.

Leaves fall from a library of leaves in a dry season.

And, now, I think, why do the stories repeat themselves? Where do they really come from, anyway? What really lies in them for me, the stories about the doctor, the nun, and the ones of the boy who keeps interrupting? There are those about Krishna Singh, Jonah the boatman, the other boy Ti-Jean, and the crowd from Galilee congregating under the almond tree, waiting to be healed. What is my interest in them? Was it fear, gossip, adventure? Was it the stories they all told me? A fascination with an island: its geography, its dangers, its mysteries, its history!

It was where I became what I am, asking the big questions about love and death.

An island always blazing in my mind.

And the time, that particular time we all lived through! We must not forget that. It's that time which lays down a challenge to me to be imagined, urgent with its danger, its unspeakable cruelty. And, there were.

Yes, you were saying.

Well, there were always the iguanas and orchids.

And the stories.

Yes, of course, the stories, what they reveal.

They may hide more than they reveal.

What do you mean?

We must stop there today.

Ah.

El Caracol
1938-1939

The Doctor's House

The boy was still sleeping. The door of his room was open. Vincent noticed him as he came out onto the landing and walked over the creaking floor-boards. 'Theo.' He was dead to the world.

Dawn had broken in his room at the back of the house. The light created a shadow-play of leaves and branches of leaves. It flickered upon the white muslin curtains, throwing its magic-lantern show upon the walls and bed. The bush at the windows, with the incessant ticking of its teeming life, pressed against the wooden house.

At intervals, the scream of the *cigale* filled the brightening distance outside with its detonations and decibels high above the island. Water, water, the cicada cried. Rain, rain! This was a dry island.

Vincent noticed, as he stared at the boy, a strip of bright, hot light pick out a spot on the pitch pine floor at the side of Theo's bed and dazzle it. As he watched this, his mind was lost in the frightening events of the night before.

A soft, cool breeze lifted the curtains, and a more neutral, yellow light flooded the floor, showing the grain of the bare wood on which the small iron bed stood, holding the sleeping child.

Theo moved his brown legs and arms, lying beneath the mosquito net, scratching with his toes the white cotton sheets, dishevelled on the fibre mattress. He kicked the feather pillows to the floor. Shadows of leaves tattooed his skin and mottled the canopy of net above his sleeping body. Vincent continued to stare at the child, sleeping among the shadows of leaves, trapped in a net.

'Theo,' he called again. The boy did not stir. He wanted him awake, the assurance that he was all right.

He lay curled on his side, with his back to Vincent. At some point in the night he had shed his blue and white striped pyjamas which were now stuck down at the bottom of the bed.

23

Along his spine were stitches: a suture, a stitched wound, running from the base of his neck to the coccyx. The engine of his breathing caused a sense of rippling along the spine. Vincent could feel each of his separate vertebrae under his fingers as he ran them along that ridge in his imagination. He had touched them in the night, when the boy had turned away from him, as he lay across the bottom of Vincent's bed on his stomach, exhausted from his tale.

IS MY calypso, you know, doctor?

The boy had whispered a question which was a statement. His night-time voice still echoed into the morning.

The sea muttered beneath the window on the pebbled beach, sucking its teeth, *cheupsing*, shifting the pebbles, sifting the sand.

'*Adolph Hitler, Adolph Hitler, how you looking at the Bntish Empire?*' The fishermen were singing their calypso, hoarse with bush rum, beating bottle and spoon, coming over the water after their night-time trawl off Point Romain. Their songs mocked the time.

As a child, Vincent had rolled his rosary beads through his fingers. *Aves* and *Pater Nosters*. Each of the boy's vertebrae had felt like each bead on his chaplet, rolled between the thumb and index finger, while he had meditated on the mysteries, catechised by his devoted mother. Prayer had been her remedy. Something now reminded him that that instrument might have worked last night. But, it had not suggested itself either to him or to the crazed boy. There was no return to those childhood mantras, once a sceptical adulthood had emptied them of all their innocent faith, passion and meaning. They would not do now. They could not, he told himself. No, the way of the friars had not worked. The boy had had enough of prayer and exorcism. It would have to be reason and love now.

Vincent could not pull himself away from his sentinel's post, and yet, he would not have wanted the boy to wake and find him. He might be embarrassed and feel that Vincent had betrayed his privacy as he lay there, naked. It might startle him, bring on some deeper fear.

Theo turned again in his sleep. Vincent could see his face. A slight frown crinkled the already pronounced scar on his forehead, just above the nose bridge.

I GET IT from a stone Jai throw in the yard when we climbing the water tank. Mama say, it need stitches, but I never go and see no doctor. So it heal up so. All crooked. So.

He had put a finger there, pointing at his childhood scar. He had retraced it on his brow as he frowned in the night, rewriting a boy's adventure, a fight with a *pardner*. It was a childhood accident, told in a voice that had come to haunt the night. A flood of words.

RIVER come down.

A voice like a drum, but it had not told the story of the scar on his back which had also healed, *just so*. Vincent wondered if a doctor had ever attended to the original wound.

The perspiration on the boy's upper lip and brow glistened like small crystals. His slightly reddish hair, the colour of Demerara sugar, glinted in the light which flooded the room under the billowing curtains.

Vincent could not stop staring and wondering. He noticed Theo's slight frame, small bones. He was eleven going on twelve maybe, and young for his age. When the doctor had first seen him, he had thought immediately that he needed to put on some weight. But he was a strong boy. He had noticed the strength in his feet, as they gripped the boards of the deck on the journey over, balancing himself, and pulling on the rope which held the pirogue moored to its anchor about twenty feet off the jetty. He saw the muscles in his arms, calves and thighs tighten. He was a bare-backed, country boy, in khaki pants, like a boy from the estates Vincent had known as a child; one of those who played cricket in the savannah and lived in the barracks beneath the house at Versailles.

He was a child abandoned now to the innocence and demons of sleep. His legs stretched and fell apart, his pubescent penis was slightly erect in the bush of his newly sprouted reddish pubic hair. Vincent's doctor's mind said, a full bladder.

'Doctor, doctor!' A cry, stuck in the throat filled the whole house. It ripped through the floor-boards and walls. It seemed as if it echoed across the bay. 'Doctor, doctor!' Rows and rows of beds along an interminable ward, each ringing with an agonised cry came before Vincent's mind. But, it was only one cry from a young boy, on a single iron bed in front of him.

Vincent stood at the door and watched Theo writhe on his bed. His small, brown body twisted and arched as he cried out in his sleep. This was what he had been told about by Father Dominic at the friary of Santa Ana. This was Father Dominic's devil, he supposed. He pulled up the mosquito net and lifted it over the boy's naked body and dragged him onto his lap. 'There, there. Is okay now, boy. Is a dream, a bad dream. Is all been a bad dream.' He patted his back, stroked his shoulders, pulled his fingers through his hair. Then his fingers travelled the ridge of the boy's spine. 'Sleep, sleep, go back to sleep.' The childhood song of Vincent's own nurse, Sybil, came to his mind. '*Do Do, petit popo.*' He heard Sybil, her plaintive tune, as she swung the hammock under the house at Versailles, and with her voice in his, he found a fathering to comfort the boy. '*Do do, petit popo.*'

It was a tune the boy recognised and hummed. Accustomed to comforting himself, he sucked on his thumb. Vincent's fingers read the braille on his back. It was a story for those who were blind. 'Who did this to you, Theo?'

Theo opened his eyes and looked up. 'Mama?'

'Doctor Metivier, Theo.' He did not think his answer, framed as a question, was the boy's accusation. It was, rather, a desire for his mother, on opening his eyes.

The boy closed his eyes again. Who and where was his mama, Vincent thought, that she did not want this beautiful boy, had not come, asking for him?

How had this started? It started the day that Father Dominic's letter arrived from The Priory of Our Lady of the Rosary, Santa Ana, Porta España, February 12th 1938. "Dear Dr. Metivier, You'll remember that Mother Superior asked me to come and bless the foundation stone of the new hospital you want to build at Saint Damian's. I'm writing to ask a favour of you. I was very taken with your attitude to healing, how you worked with children at the leprosarium.

"There's a young boy in our care. He came to us a year ago from one of our missions, where our Father Angel de La Bastide is the parish priest. Father Angel sent him to us. There was some trouble and we were prepared to help. But, it has not worked out. The trouble gets worse every day, with serious consequences.

"We need the boy out of the island for a number of reasons. There's little money. Then, I thought, ah, Dr Metivier on El Caracol, just the man.

"He's a very intelligent boy. He's had a thorough and sound elementary education. He was to make the Exhibition Class, but that had to be terminated abruptly. He has told me part of *his* story.

"When he first came to us, he would not talk at all. He was practically dumb. 'Struck dumb, by the devil,' is what Father Angel de La Bastide said. That's the parish priest's explanation, with more lurid accounts about his mother Emelda, and a man going under the name of Spanish. Is he the father? Who knows, with these people. We coaxed. We worked together. He has been sacristan. Dresses like one of our lay brothers. We thought it best to do that. His hair was shorn, but has begun to grow again.

"Truly, it has not worked out. Then I thought of you with your attitude to healing, to healing and the stigma of disease, healing the whole person. That was the subject of our conversation on your delightful verandah looking out onto the beautiful bay. Such a good rum punch, Doctor! Remember?

"By the way, give my kind regards to the chaplain, Father Anscar Meyer. I remember his Wagner.

"The boy does not talk anymore. He will not talk here. He cannot stay here. I believe that you can get him to talk. When he does, his story will go in fits and starts, wander here and there, but it will return. It does return to the main road, if you see what I mean. He'll repeat so that you can hear, and remember. It is too much for me now.

"Please get in touch with me when you next come to town. Come and have *le déjeuner*. I shall endeavour to get this to you by the next steamer.

"Greetings to the community on El Caracol from all of us at Santa Ana. My best wishes to you. God bless, Sincerely, Father Dominic Le Febre."

Vincent had been struck by the statement that he had to get the boy off the island, that he would not be able to stay at the friary. There was an urgency in those words.

A week later, he went and had the priest's lunch. Then, they went to the guests' parlour to where Theo was brought. Just before the boy was introduced, Father Dominic said, 'Remember, he's dumb. Cannot get a word out of him for weeks. We've tried everything.'

The door opened a crack and a slender child dressed as a novice of the friars of Saint Dominic entered the parlour. 'This is Dr. Metivier, Theo.'

Vincent put out his hand to shake the child's, 'Hello, Theo,' but there was no response. The boy kept his hands under his black scapular.

Father Dominic looked embarrassed and irritated. 'You see what I mean,' he said, under his breath.

What were they doing, these friars, hiding this boy? What a crazy idea. His shortened hair gave a pronounced distinction to his features: his high cheekbones, his slender nose, slightly flared, his determined chin, his full lips. He was a handsome boy. Vincent studied him. He needed some feeding up.

He did not answer any of Vincent's questions which were polite pleasantries. 'Theo, are you enjoying your work? Are you keeping up with your reading?'

He kept his eyes downcast. It was either shyness or religious training. Only once did the boy look up and glance at the doctor with his green eyes. This was when Father Dominic, amidst many patronising statements, said, 'But Doctor, Theo's a very bright boy.'

Vincent could see in the boy's eyes that he had looked up to see what the reaction to that statement would be. But it was as if he could not wait to see. The shutters came down as quickly as they had been lifted.

But he noticed him scratch his left leg with the sandalled foot of his right, lifting his habit indecorously to show his naked legs, which made Father Dominic fidget with his rosary beads hanging down his side, muttering, 'Coco, Coco.' The boy winced at the name.

Vincent thought it odd that the priest should be calling him Coco. Was it a nickname?

The boy's actions showed him that he had also relaxed, and that he had found in the twinkle of Vincent's eyes, and in the smile on his lips, a response to the mention of his intelligence that he had been looking for. 'That's wonderful Father, I'm sure Theo's a bright boy. You are, aren't you, Theo?' But there was no reply.

Vincent concluded the painful interview, trying to avoid the friar's patronising tone, by asking 'Theo, would you like to come and stay on El Caracol?' He risked this invitation, but was almost sure that the boy would say yes. He turned smartly on his heels. They could hear him, the clatter of his sandals, pelting down the corridor.

Father Dominic looked at Vincent with raised eyebrows. In no time at all, Theo had arrived back at the parlour door and stood waiting impatiently, holding a bulging brown grip, which seemed about to explode at any moment.

28

His eyes darted Vincent a glance which said, Get me out of here, explanations will come later. Vincent noticed all these signs.

As they were leaving the friary, Father Dominic said to Vincent, 'Doctor, there's more to this than meets the eye.'

'Oh, I'm sure there is, Father. Would you like to tell me the relevant details?'

'See how you get on with him. We've tried everything, all the might of Mother Church and the Grace of God.'

'I see. You're admitting failure in this regard.'

'It's not for us to question the ways of God.'

'Far from my intentions.'

'We know about you, Doctor, your free thinking. But I was struck by the way you were with your patients on El Caracol. Miserable souls.'

'Sick people, Father. Of their souls, I've no idea, having not yet discovered them.'

'And the boy, what do you think?'

'He seems to know what he wants when he's given a choice.'

'Well, you must wait.'

'Yes. But I don't think it will be the devil that I'll be encountering. I feel there must be causes other than such outrageous suggestions. Your exorcist has probably terrified the wits out of the mite. I'd like some history, where and with whom this boy has grown up. I hope you're not keeping anything from me that I should know.'

'Would I do that? You've got my letter.'

'Yes. Anyway, I'll listen to what he tells me when he speaks.'

'You'll be lucky.'

Soon, they were at the wharf. Vincent had got the car from the District Medical Officer in Sainte Claire to wait for them. Luckily, there was a boat leaving for El Caracol, one of the *bumboats*, collecting the new patients to take them to Saint Damian's.

A young girl was giving trouble to get onto the *bumboat*, like a wagon behind the launch, looking like Marine landing craft. Here the patients were kept separate from the other passengers. The girl was being forced out of her mother's arms. Other patients were being herded in after her.

Theo had gone straight to the bow of the launch. Vincent noticed him

29

looking at the struggle between the young girl and the warders who were dragging her forcefully. Then one of the women patients comforted her and calmed her down. This was often the case with some of the children. They did not want to leave their relatives. The girl screamed, 'I don't have nothing. What you sending me away for?' The mother, left on the wharf, could not be consoled.

Theo was taking it all in.

The family waved as if the girl was going on a vacation. They were trying to hide their shame. The warders did their job, making the separation business-like. The children did not know where they were going. The *bumboat* sat deep in the water on the voyage, so the patients got properly drenched by the spray.

Vincent remembered Theo staring. The mother on the wharf cried out, 'Christiana!' But there were no questions. He saw Theo and the East Indian girl lock eyes. She was a girl that he might have known in the country. He saw him taking it all in. He looked ahead, but then kept looking back at the girl.

For the rest of the voyage, he stood in the bow, looking ahead. The spray drizzled his cheeks. Vincent came and held on, close to his shoulder. 'El Caracol,' he said, pointing to the island in the distance. 'The Snail. It crawls out of the sea. It crawls out of the slime of the waves.'

The boy was poised for his future, as they gazed at the island ahead which was to become his new home.

'Look, the feelers of the snail. See how they reach up to the summits, one to La Chapelle, and the other climbing from Perruquier Bay. To the left is Salt Pond, behind the cocorite palms and the blue-green agave.'

Vincent did all the talking. Theo's face was stoic before his future. 'So, El Caracol. You know who gave it that name?' Their eyes were close and they looked together. 'Columbus. Great Navigator! He was so great that he got lost here. But you know your history, your geography.' Theo turned and looked at him quizzically. 'Father Dominic says that you are a bright boy, yes?' There was no answer. Vincent talked for both of them. He took a chance and ruffled the boy's hair. Vincent noticed the slightest wince, the slightest pulling away of the shoulder. Too close, too soon, he thought.

Then they were passing the *bocas* on their right. Vincent enumerated and named them for the boy: 'Boca de Monos, Boca de Huevos, Boca de Navios

30

and then, beyond El Caracol, Boca Grande. All make up The Dragon's Mouth. Monkeys, Eggs, and Ships!' A geography lesson became an adventure story. Beyond was the Caribbean Sea, the Atlantic Ocean.

The boat entered the wide embrace of Chac Chac Bay. 'It's the sound that the birds make, like *chac chacs.*' Vincent spoke into Theo's ear above the drone of the motor launch. 'Or, it may be the monkeys. But, then again, it could also be the name for cotton on the cotton trees, in a Carib language only the parrots still speak.'

The water here was the colour of the Orinoco. Silt and algae from its deep upper reaches were emptied through its wide estuary from as far as The Serpent's Mouth at the southern entrance to the gulf, staining the water around the islands with the yellow and green of *callaloo.*

It had been a long first day, the boy not talking at all. Vincent had decided that he would not return to the hospital that evening, despite the new patients. He would leave that to the sister on duty. He felt satisfied, as he knew it would be the impressive new sister from France, the one with the dark eyes, Sister Thérèse Weil.

He spent his time talking to Theo, who followed him around the house, taking in everything he was saying, but never himself saying a word.

That evening, Beatrice, one of the patients who had become a helper, when she had overcome the disease, brought food from the hospital kitchens. She came on the back track from Sanda's Bay, over the hills, on the donkey, Cervantes.

'Evening, Doctor.'

'Hello Beatrice. This is Theo. He's staying with us for a while.'

'Hello, young fellow.' Theo stared. Beatrice had lost two of her fingers. 'Cat bite you tongue?'

'He's shy,' Vincent explained. Theo darted a look, then lowered his eyes.

'I bring some nice dumplings. He go like that.'

'Yes, Beatrice, he will. I would like you to stay with him tomorrow when you come over to make breakfast, stay till I return in the afternoon.'

'That's fine, Doctor. I go be here on time. But that donkey slow for so.'

After eating their dumplings, Vincent and Theo sat on the jetty till it got dark. The boy watched Vincent fishing off the edge. 'Fish not biting tonight.'

Vincent waited for a reaction. Not yet, he thought, take it easy, he said to himself. Then they went off to bed.

Vincent woke to a soft voice. At first, he thought it was a dream and could not make out where the voice was coming from. Theo was sitting at the foot of Vincent's bed. The mosquito net had been pulled out. He was in the bed with his legs stretched out facing sideways. Vincent was astonished. He sat up. Theo was talking to him but not facing him.

'Doctor, doctor. Sleep, sleep. *Do do, petit popo,*' he sang. He rocked himself back and forth. But it sounded like he was trying to put Vincent to sleep. Vincent lay back and closed his eyes. He played the game.

Then, it started. He had never heard anything like this before. He lay unmoving, hardly opening his eyes, as if the least distraction might stop what was going on. Was this Father Dominic's devil?

MAMA SAY, that Mister know about history, that this kind of thing happen before. She say, we go be safe, even if them coolie in the sugar and nigger in the oil field make trouble.

When Mama speak like this, she sound just like Mister. Not up here, in the sweet cocoa hills, where the red skin *'panol* and our good old negroes know on which side their bread is buttered. None of that confusion will come here, Mama say, speaking just like Mister. Not looking at her nigger self neither.

Who say that? Not me that say that.

Her black skin smooth like the moss rock down by the river, but full of the light that break through the trees. Yellow light on the yellow hog plum.

My Mama, she could talk! She could talk, *oui*!

What was this drama? Vincent listened, terrified. Was he talking about his mother, Emelda, whom he had heard of from Father Dominic. Mister? Who was Mister? Was he talking about the recent labour riots on Sancta Trinidad? And who was he talking to? To Vincent, himself, yes, but to who else? It was the voice of a smaller child at times. But, then, it was a voice as deep as a gully. It was the voice of a child who was a woman with the voice of a man, an accusing voice at times. It found its timbre in a village. Was he speaking in tongues, with an adult's voice?

YOU WANT me to tell you how it is, when it happen? Where it happen? You come like a detective, like an investigator? This is inquisition, and me, like a criminal. Who is criminal? Like you don't believe me, Father?

Something had happened. Who was the investigator? Not me, Vincent thought. He had hardly pried. Maybe, at first. He became guilty about any questions he had asked him in the day, on the journey from the friary. Was this poor Father Dominic? What had he done? Why really had he got to get rid of the boy?

Vincent now felt that he had made so few investigations. Something had clicked and he had decided there and then to take him, seeing him standing there with his little, bulging, brown grip. He could not resist him. He felt that he knew him immediately. His instinct told him that the boy had wanted to get out of that friary. What had Father Dominic said in his letter? 'We need the boy out of the island for a number of reasons.' Why? He had never asked. These priests!

YOU HEAR Radio say:
They want to licen' me foot they no want me to walk.
They want to licen me mout' they no want me to talk

Theo sang a calypso of the day.

AND YOU KNOW is this very island, blessed by the Holy Trinity, Father, Son and Holy Ghost moving over the hills down by Moruga. I learn it all from Father Angel. Columbus!

He intoned like a priest at the altar, then, like a schoolmaster on his dais. What had Father Dominic done? Vincent was all ears, sitting bolt upright in bed, listening to the boy at the foot of his bed. Who were these people who had had the care of this boy? What had happened to launch him onto this compulsive nocturnal tale? Now he mimed his story.

HISTORY and geography scratch on my slate. Spit and wipe off. Scratch it again till you learn it all. Watching from under my eyes for Father Angel wiry tamarind switch, lying there on the desk. *Bois,* wood, a real snake with venom

33

in it. My blood crawl with scratching the chalk on the slate, crawl with the learning. Chalk on my fingers.

You want dates Father Dominic? Is not long since I is a small boy. Shock you? All that I know? All that I come to know, so early? Father? Birthday? Birth certificate? Mama say she get Ramdaou the messenger man from the estate, to take the news by the registrar. She want it register proper. But, Ramdaou come back, and say he don't know who to say the father is. They write down, *Il-le-gi-ti-ma-te*. But, he put his mark, his cross on the paper, that *coolie* man. Them old *coolie* can't read and write, you know. That's to say, he sign it. Mama say to hell with the father. Then she say, they go know in good time who the father is.

Baptism certificate? I go tell you, because you asking me everyday to tell you. Yes. I christen by Father Angel in La Divina Pastora church. The little wooden church with the cemetery, La Divina herself black like we people black. She dress up for a fine party, dress in satin and lace with necklace and bracelet. *Ave, Ave, Ave Maria.* Father Angel know everything.

Vincent tried to keep up, as the story moved between different characters and places, in different voices.

YOU COMING everyday swish swish along the corridor, knock knock, *Benedicamus Domino, Deo gratias.* And you don't care where I start?

Where I go? I know at first I don't want to talk. Like cat bite my tongue, like fish bone stick in my throat. I choking. I know all that horrify you, to see me choking on my own words. Till one day you find I speak with the force of the waterfall, drum on the rock, drum in the hills, *Pampadam* But you don't like what I say.

Even I, Father, with this blood running in my veins, can hear those drums. I don't have to cut myself to show you the blood. You see it in my face, in my brown skin arms, in my legs like red mahogany and my eyes like green glass-bottle at the bottom of the river.

This was a story for Father Dominic. It was a night-time confession accompanied with laughter and scorn. It was the continuation of something. Vincent kept his eyes shut and listened. He dared not move in case he interrupted the flow.

34

But too, is because is words that make me from small. Is words that tell me everything I know. Every touch he touch me with, was with a word. You hear the calypsonian, Caresser. Always, a whisper in my ear: *Coco, Coco, Cocorito.* Bird language and all! Trying to fool me.

In my Mama's bed. Smell my Mama. Onion on her fingers, vanilla on her tongue, ginger between her breasts, sweat from big house under she arms. Smell my Mama when she move and change her bloomers. Like salt fish that need some lime. Eh eh. You want me to stay there, eh, Father Dominic?

You say, Theophilus, because you call me Theophilus, Stay with it *mon garçon*, stay with it, *mon petit garçon*, stay with your pain. Pain? Pain yes, Father, and then a funny kind of pain that was a funny kind of pleasure. Nice, nice. Nice eh? Pain, a funny kind of shame. Nice shame. Me, shame?

Stay with it, *mon petit garçon.*

I carry it always, his voice. You-want-to-see-it-you-want-to-see-it? Whispering all the time. Like a lizard in my ear.

Then I hear you, Theophilus. Theophilus, be still. Brother Theo, be still. Together now, *Je vous salue Marie pleine de grâce, Le Seigneur avec vous, vous êtes bénie de toutes les femmes. Le Seigneur...*

Theo bound his fingers with his black rosary beads, lifted himself from the bed and then collapsed exhausted. Famished, ravished. Like a spirit had entered and then, was gone.

Then he rose from the bed like a sleep walker, rose from the foot of the bed and left the room. He left with his *Hail Mary*, the French priest's prayer, his, *Je vous salue Marie pleine de grâce...* His chaplet knotted around his fingers slipped and dropped onto the pitch pine floor, rattling like beads in a calabash.

Here, now, sitting at the edge of the boy's bed on the morning after, Vincent wondered what he had heard. What had he listened to in the night? A child remembers, a child forgets, a child remembers and reinvents, he thought. Theo was slowly coming into consciousness, and Vincent left him to doze while he got dressed for work and went downstairs.

Beatrice had just arrived and was tethering Cervantes in the grassy patch behind the house to graze. 'I preparing breakfast for both of all you,' she announced as she came through the back door. 'Morning, Doctor. Where the child?'

'He's still sleeping, Beatrice. You must be soft with him.'

'If he sick, you mustn't keep him here. You know what Mother Superior say.'

'No, Beatrice, it's not like that. He's not sick.' Vincent smiled at Beatrice reprimanding him with Mother Superior's orders.

'Not sick with *cocobay.*' She used the local name for leprosy, because of the name of the bay on the island to which the patients were brought.

'No, Beatrice. He needs love.'

'All of we need that Doctor, all of we.'

'Yes.'

'And is you giving him that?'

'With your help, Beatrice.'

Beatrice prepared some breakfast for Vincent. 'Is cassava bread this morning, and hot cocoa. And I leaving some aside for the boy to eat when he get up. I better clean the house one time for you today, as I here whole day.'

Beatrice talked on. Vincent had been thrown by the night. How would the boy cope with the day alone? He suddenly wondered whether he could swim. With the boy here, the house seemed full. His life seemed full of responsibilities, the like of which he had not felt or experienced before. He did not know what it was to have children like this.

He left a note for the boy to read on the kitchen dresser. *Theo, ask Beatrice for anything you want. I'll see you this afternoon. Doctor Vincent.* How was he to do this, if he did not talk. Maybe Beatrice would perform a miracle. 'Beatrice, the boy must not go in the sea till I get back. That's my one demand.'

'This boy need to be in school. Take him into the school with you.'

'Not today, Beatrice, not today. Look Jonah is here.'

The put-putting pirogue came around the point from Sanda's Bay. Vincent was on the jetty collecting the rope. 'No whales today?' Vincent shouted his absurd question.

Jonah laughed. It was the ritual greeting. 'I keeping a lookout, Doc.'

'Don't get swallowed up.'

As they pulled off from the jetty, Vincent looked back at the house. The morning sunlight was now catching the faded red roof. The salt in the sea blast had rusted the nails and hinges in the doors and windows. The spouting was perforated where the rust had disintegrated altogether. Vincent often wondered what was holding the place together. How would it withstand its newcomer?

Theo appeared at the window in the gable of the house. It was odd to have someone looking out at him. He waved, but there was no response from the boy. He just stared. Vincent turned to face the open bay. He hoped that the boy would be safe.

The Convent

'Are you all right, Sister? I heard a noise. You weren't at Matins.' Sister Marie-Jeanne put her head around the door of Sister Thérèse's cell.

'The window is shattered! There's glass everywhere!'

'Yes, for about ten minutes, just before Matins, there was a sudden squall off the gulf. You know how they rip up the coast. I was awakened and closed my windows in time. It's died down now.'

'I was in a deep sleep.'

'*Mon Dieu*! You're bleeding. Your face.'

'Am I?' Sister Thérèse put her hands to her face. Her fingertips were pierced with splinters. 'I feel quite faint.'

She then realised that she was standing on broken glass, sharp shards around her feet. In the dawn light, at the window, she saw her hands were cut. She could feel the glass dust encrusted on her palms as she pressed against the sill. The two glass windows must have become unhooked by the wind, then banged shut and shattered.

'My hands.' She held them up for the other nun to see.

She leant out of the window to secure the shutters once more. There were daggers of glass sticking out of the window frame. She saw that her hands were bleeding. There was blood on her white cotton nightgown, on the sleeves, and down her front. It was only as she began looking for something to stop the bleeding on her hands, that she felt the extent of the broken glass. Glass dust was all over her bed and the floor of her cell. She could feel the soles of her feet pressing on splinters.

'The windows must've crashed repeatedly. Why didn't I wake? The force must have thrown the glass into the cell, scattering itself everywhere. I must've fallen into a very deep sleep before that. Not to have heard the impact!'

'It's extraordinary how the glass is everywhere, like shattered crystal. I'll get a broom.'

In no time, Sister Marie-Jeanne was back from the end of the corridor where the brooms were kept, sweeping up the glass in the cell.

Sister Thérèse was at the window looking out. 'Have you seen...' Then she broke off.

'What?' Sister Marie-Jeanne came and stared over Sister Thérèse's shoulder.

'Nothing. Must've been a dream.'

'Come now. Yes, you've probably had a bad dream, what with the window shattering. You're in shock. The squall was very powerful, like one of those small hurricanes we had last year.'

'Can't you see it?' Sister Thérèse insisted.

'What?'

'Nothing.'

Sister Marie-Jeanne was sweeping up the last of the glass and shaking out the sheets from the window. Then she went out of the cell down the corridor to the laundry room.

As Sister Thérèse stood alone in her cell, the mood of the night came back to her; what was dream, what was real, still indistinct. An insistent voice returned.

What is your name? The voice of her dream had woken her. And then, falling back to sleep, she was being instructed. Your name is Madeleine Weil. She woke again startled, hearing the harsh voice which came from her dream, but sounding clearly in the cell, awake, like her. She was being interrogated. She could not remember by whom. No, she insisted. 'I'm Sister Thérèse of the Order of Martha and Mary.' She answered the voice repeatedly. 'I am Sister Thérèse from the convent at Embarcadère Corbeaux on the island of El Caracol. Then the questioning was terminated. She listened attentively again. She thought that what she heard was thunder, and she waited for it to sound again.

'Are you all right?' Sister Marie-Jeanne entered the cell without knocking. She did not know what to make of the accident. 'Let me just finish sweeping up all this glass. And this blood! Where is it coming from? I need to wipe it up.' She left the cell again to go and fetch a mop, saying, 'When I return, I'll get you to the infirmary.' She tried not to raise her voice as she entered the silent corridor, because of the other sisters at *Lectio Divina* in their cells.

39

* * *

Sister Thérèse was in her own world. The night returned to haunt her. She remembered the salt breeze lifting the rough, white cotton curtain at the jalousies. The sound in the wind was, *Weil.* The sea sucked at the rocks beneath the cliff. The sea too, she thought, said, *Weil.* A sheet of galvanise banged, dislodged from its nails on the roof of the small cloister below, shouting *Weil! Weil!* Under the lifted curtain, moonlight lit the pitch pine floor. The glow of the dim night light in the corridor, outside her cell, slid under the door. The shadow of the curtains rose and fell. Far away, again, there was that sound like thunder; like the thunder that followed long after she had seen the sheet lightning opening up the sky all along the west coast of Sancta Trinidad, beyond Gasparee, the island of centipedes. The thunder echoed *Weil, Weil, Weil,* in her still-dreaming ears.

'Sister Thérèse!' She turned from the open window. Sister Marie- Jeanne's voice jolted her back to the early morning. 'Where were you?'

'What?'

'You seemed in another world.'

'Did I? Let me help you.'

'All done for the moment. Come with me to the infirmary and let me make sure that all the glass is off your hands and face. Maybe we'll find one of Sister Luke's remedies for shock.'

In the infirmary, the morning sun lit the glass cabinets and sparkled in the vials of medicine. The sinks and enamel bowls gleamed. The scrubbed floors were smooth beneath Sister Thérèse's bare feet. She had left bloody footprints on the clean floor. She had not seen her tracks on the corridor.

'Here's some Arnica. Let it dissolve on your tongue,' Sister Marie-Jeanne whispered.

'I've left blood on the floor.' Sister Thérèse stood in her bloodied night gown. She felt faint. 'Papa.' Then, she fainted.

The seconds seemed like the whole night before.

The wind had picked up and was howling in the caves on the insides of the cliff below the convent. *Weil!* She was standing at the window of her cell, as she used to stand at the window of her bedroom in Provence, looking at the full moon and the orange tree in bloom. The moon was right overhead now, bathing the bay with its white light. As she stared at the open Chac Chac Bay, the rippling tide, phosphorescent beneath the moon, she could not believe what she was seeing. She thought it was a *trompe-l'-oeil*. It lay on the green surface, as slender as a pencil, gun metal and gleaming. It was quite still, not making a sound. She still could not actually believe that she was seeing what to her eyes was a warship. The small waves broke along the clean lines of the vessel, scalloping the edges with shinning white, watery lace.

The beam from the lighthouse above Monte de Botella passed over the bow and deck, on which she could see two prominent guns. She stood and stared. What was she looking at? Her heart was in her mouth. Was it actually there? Her eyes became accustomed to the darkness. The warship was a kind of apparition. It had slid into the bay, soundless in the dead of night. Then she realised that the ship was closer to the cliffs than she had first thought. It was tucked into the bay, hidden.

She had always been told that the water was many fathoms deep off the rocks. The wind had died down. She thought she could hear singing. It was ever so quiet. Then she lost it with the surf's percussion. There it was, unmistakable, a man's voice. She picked out the figure of a sailor in a white uniform, standing in the stern. With repetition, she caught the tune and the words. *'Ja, ja, die Liebe ist's allein, die Liebe, die Liebe ist's allein!'* It was then that the beam from the lighthouse lit up the *Swastika* on the bow, and on the pennant which flew at the stern beneath the sailor. The tinkling of the rigging, the knock of metal on metal, a jangle in the breeze, accompanied the song.

Sister Marie-Jeanne was kneeling beside her. She had the smelling salts under her nose. Sister Thérèse revived with the inhalation. 'Sister, you fainted.'

'My foot, my foot. I've cut myself.'

'You cried out for your father.'

'He's a doctor.'

'I see. Of course.' Sister Marie-Jeanne examined her foot. There was a large gash near her ankle, now bleeding profusely. No wonder there had been all that blood. She worked fast with bandages. She tore strips of cotton from old sheets, like they used to when they had to staunch the flow of blood with the patients at the hospital.

'This may need stitches. We'll have to get a message to Doctor Metivier. I'll have to speak to Mother Superior. Let us bandage it tightly. See whether there's any glass visible. Use some disinfectant. The doctor can examine it more thoroughly when he comes.'

'It's more shock than anything.' Sister Thérèse tried to strengthen herself.

'If you're sure, Sister.'

'My father. I fear for my father.'

'Your father? Why this morning?'

'There's going to be a war. I'm sure. They hated me. They'll hate him.'

The nun did not want to pursue Sister Thérèse's fear. She did not fully understand it. She guided her back to her cell.

Sister Thérèse stood at the window in her bloodied nightgown, with her cropped head and with her scars on her feet and hands. The wind had died down. But, there, still testament to its own reality, was the German destroyer, gun-metal grey and gleaming on the lit sea, its *Swastika* appearing and disappearing as the wind tore at the pennant in the stern. She turned from the window into her cell. 'Have you seen the boat, the war ship in the bay?'

'What?' Sister Marie-Jeanne exclaimed.

'Look. It's German. See the *Swastika.*'

'No?'

'Last night, there was a sailor singing a love song.'

'No.'

'He's not singing now. If you had been here and stood long enough for the beam from the lighthouse to fall on the bow, or where the pennant flutters in the stern, you would've seen the ensign of the *Swastika*. The sailor has probably changed his watch. The new watch does not sing love songs.' Sister Thérèse smiled with her explanation.

'Sister? Part of your nightmare?'

'Yes, *die Liebe ist's allein.*'

'What?'

'Nothing. Love, it is love alone, *c'est l'amour seul.*'

Sister Marie-Jeanne continued tidying the cell.

Next to the rough wooden bed with the fibre mattress was the *prie-dieu* with a small wooden crucifix on the wall above it. The Jew who had died for his people. Sister Thérèse saw it like that now. There was a bare table with two books: *The Imitation of Christ* and *The Lives of the Saints.* She had hung her habit over the chair at the table. Her spare one hung from a nail behind the door.

She surveyed her small private world from where she was standing as Sister Marie-Jeanne restored order. This was all that there was. There was not even a mirror. But she used to steal a look of herself in the glass of the window, and even once in the flat surface of the water in the bucket when it was her turn to do corridor duty, sweeping and mopping. 'Sister Thérèse Weil! Where are you, my girl, with your head in a bucket? My child!' Mother Superior seemed to be there whenever she was performing some transgression.

'You have a rest now, and I'll go and inform Mother Superior of your accident before she leaves for Saint Damian's.' Sister Marie-Jeanne closed the door quietly behind her.

When she had arrived from France, a year ago, Sister Thérèse had come straight from the Porta España harbour to Saint Damian's, on El Caracol, in Jonah's pirogue. When she woke in the night she often went back to her departure from France and her father, then to her arrival in the *Antilles*. It shocked her at these moments, what she had done. She was sick for home and her Papa.

Before leaving France for the mission she had been made aware, by her father, of what was going on in Germany. From this distance, she ran over in her mind the escalating danger that he had described in his letters since Adolf Hitler became Chancellor in 1933. Over the last five years, he had kept her in touch with what he saw as having a long history in Europe over the centuries. 'Anti-Semitism,' he had said, 'is deeply ingrained in European Christian culture.' He explained it to her carefully. It was a wonder that he had married a Christian, and a Catholic at that, who prayed during their Good Friday services for heathens and Jews to be converted.

In the novitiate, at Tulle, she remembered the other novices and her novice mistress playing down the significance of the anti-Jewish laws in Germany. She was more than once cautioned about the contents of her father's letters, censored by the novice mistress. 'You must remember, Sister, that we are taught to render unto Caesar the things that are Caesar's.'

Her father's visits alarmed her. His stories of how Adolf Hitler was building the German army frightened her, no matter what the novice mistress said about Caesar. There was the movement of the German army into the

Rhineland, Adolf Hitler's treaty with Mussolini and the fascists in Italy. And, the year that she had left for the mission, Adolf Hitler's withdrawal from the Treaty of Versailles. A good history student, she could work out the significance of that event. Her father's letters filled the gaps made by the absence of newspapers in the cloister. Mother Superior and the novice mistress were the only links with that kind of information. She depended on their transmission, however censored it was. When her father came to visit she found herself torn. 'But Papa!'

'What do you expect?'

Then she thought that it was part of her father's anti-Catholic feeling that he had at first not wanted her to join the convent, and after she had, had wanted her to leave.

Sister Marie-Jeanne had been dispatched by Mother Superior to send a message via the nuns' boatman to Jonah to bring Doctor Metivier to the convent. Sister Thérèse was to be examined by Dr Metivier in the infirmary. She waited there for his arrival. She sat in her bandages, wounds on her face, hands and feet. The infirmarian, Sister Luke, was there to witness the examination.

Vincent received the news with interest, he had not been called to the convent before. He had hardly begun his duties at Saint Damian's when Jonah found him in the pharmacy. 'They want you in the convent, Doc.'

'What, now?'

'Message from Mother Superior!'

'Well, it must be now.'

On the way over to Embarcadère Corbeaux, they saw the German training ship leave the bay. Their pirogue rocked in the wake. These events distracted Vincent from the apprehensions he continued to have about Theo, since leaving him with Beatrice. From this distance, he thought he saw the figure of the boy at the end of the jetty in front of his house. But then, he could not be sure.

'Good morning, Sisters. You've been to the wars, Sister Thérèse?' Vincent Metivier smiled as he entered the infirmary and found the two nuns. 'Now where are all these cuts and abrasions? Can I have some warm water? Lint, clean bandages, cotton wool and disinfectant.'

The infirmarian put the kettle on the small kerosene stove. She began tearing an old sheet into strips. 'We're very short on lint and cotton wool, Doctor.'

'What you can spare.' Vincent held Sister Thérèse's face, turning it sideways, so that he could have a better look at her cuts. 'There are still little splinters of glass. I'm going to swab the small cuts on your face. Anything in those dark eyes of yours?' He smiled. 'Let's get that glass dust out. What on earth happened?'

'The window shattered in my cell.'

'Must've been an almighty crash.'

'Yes, the squall. I was in a deep sleep.'

'The sleep of someone with a quiet mind.'

'No.'

'No?'

'I mean, yes. I usually sleep well.'

'But, not last night?'

'No, yes. Yes and no.'

Sister Luke held the enamel basin under Sister Thérèse's chin as Vincent soaked some cotton wool in the warm water, clouded with Dettol. He worked the splinters of glass out of the cuts and abrasions on her forehead and cheeks. 'Can you remove your veil?' Sister Thérèse looked at the infirmarian, who nodded her approval. 'I'm sorry to have to ask. But you may have been cut on the head which would be dangerous. I need to check. Any pain there?'

The infirmarian helped to unpin her veil and remove the tight skull cap to reveal her cropped head of black bristle.

Vincent examined the skull expertly with his fingers. 'That seems fine. Nothing to worry about there. Thanks. Now, if you could roll up your sleeves, so that I can have a good look at your arms. Let me have your hands.' He held her palms in his. 'Swab.'

Sister Luke held the basin, while Vincent worked on the cuts on the arms and wrists. 'This is a nasty one. You must've put your hand on a sharp splinter. Painful. You're not aspiring to the Stigmata are your Sister?'

The infirmarian coughed disapprovingly at Vincent's sarcastic teasing. Sister Thérèse looked up and smiled. She knew what he was like in the hospital, teasing and always on the brink of impropriety; like her Papa, when she had witnessed him with his patients. It was his bedside manner.

45

'I can't have you off work, holding up the research.' Vincent pretended to be stern.

'No, Doctor.' She heard her Papa's voice. 'You concentrate on your research. Be a good nurse.' And, that is what she had become. She hoped that he would be proud of her. She tried now, not too proudly, to let him know this in her letters home. In his last letter, he hinted that he might make the transatlantic trip. But then he described everything as so troubled in Europe.

'Now let us see to the serious matter of your foot. Let's help her up to the examination table. Just lie back. Can you arrange her skirts?' Vincent indicated to Sister Luke. 'I need to see the ankle and the surrounding area. The cut is close to a main artery. More warm water, cotton wool, Dettol. Ah, this should have stitches. Sister, in my bag.' The infirmarian threaded the needle with gut. 'Now you can have a little chloroform or we can proceed?'

'Proceed.' Sister Thérèse was being brave.

'Are you sure?' The infirmarian looked worried.

'Yes.' Sister Thérèse was insistent.

'Very well done. You will be half way to canonisation after this.' There was a cough of disapproval from Sister Luke again, to get things back on the right track. Vincent began the stitching.

Sister Thérèse had assisted him at the hospital. She had noticed his gentleness; his way with the patients which put them at their ease, how they relaxed with his jokes and so dealt better with the pain; those who felt pain. He was particularly good with the children.

Sister Thérèse closed her eyes and bore the pain. She winced and then screamed.

'Chloroform!' Vincent ordered. 'Don't jump and yell. Won't be good for my sewing.' He stitched her wound.

The last words she heard were Doctor Metivier's voice 'There'll be a scar. But who'll see it?'

The voices disappeared into a tunnel.

The distant thunder broke into Thérèse's chloroformed sleep. The anaesthetic intensified her unconscious retrievals, echoing from afar. It scared her, as she lost consciousness and re-entered her dream. The whole room was moving to the rhythm of the lifted curtain, to the swelling sea below the cliffs. Light, then shadow, sliced through the jalousies. She dozed off. Then there was that thunder again, and a word, one of her father's words, in Doctor

Metivier's voice. *Pogrom*. Her father had told her about the *pogroms*. And, now, here it was on her lips, the word which meant thunder. *Grom, Grom, Grom*. It travelled down through the ages, now under the cliffs in the caves, in the thunder over an island.

The waves had changed their rhythm now. She heard them sounding like rain lashed by the wind, slapping the rocks. The interrogation began again.

Sea crabs scuttled on wet rocks as bright as magenta.

She had to defend her name. Yet, she was hiding it, insisting on her religious name instead. She had been part of a long queue waiting to be interrogated. She needed to show papers. She had no papers. She had her name. They did not like her name. It was like in the novitiate at Tulle.

There were looks and sniggers at the novitiate at Tulle. It was the colour of her skin, the shape of her eyes, the darkness of her hair.

Was it the novice mistress interrogating her in her dream? Yes, that cruel joke she overheard in the laundry about her nose. 'Something indefinable,' one sister had intimated, 'makes you different from anyone I've met before.' Different? 'Do you feel different? It must be so odd to be you,' the sister had added.

She felt that they were jealous of her because of how well she had done in her exams; how she was complimented by Doctor Rothmann, a friend of her father's at the Tulle teaching hospital, who had praised her ability to notice mutations in her cultures that the others had not. 'Your father's daughter,' he had said out loud. 'Natural instincts.' She remembered that phrase and, 'Born looking into a microscope,' so that the other sisters looked up at her, and then buried their eyes in their own microscopes again. She did not want it this way. She closed her mind to these irks. She convinced herself that they were petty. She escaped into her training, into medicine.

The world that moved beneath her microscope obsessed her: *mycrobacterium leprae*. It was part of her reason for choosing the mission at El Caracol when she was given the choice. There was the persistent thought, Get away from it all. There would be an opportunity to carry on her research in the field. But it meant leaving her father, leaving him in a dangerous world at a troubled time. The doubts about her decision grew each day. His parting gift was his microscope which she had been allowed to keep.

She had his letters. Every month or so, the mail came with the ships of the French Line which sailed from Le Harvre to Southampton, then embarked on the transatlantic voyage. Or, there were the banana boats, Elders and Fyfe, bound for Kingston via Porta España. She lay awake, imagining her father's letter in the mailbag, crossing the ocean next to a giant tarantula, making the return journey. News grew more and more alarming.

In the day, she threw herself into the present. With the new Doctor Metivier, there was more work to do, research to pursue. He valued her work like Dr Rothmann did. Dr Metivier was a doctor like her father. He was dedicated to his work. But it was never just research with him. She had found that out soon after meeting him for the first time. It was always linked to the practical care of the patients. 'We do it for them,' he had said, leaning over the bed of a patient to take off a bandage. Yes, she thought, he has the priorities: care and research, hand in glove.

But she was not permitted to have conversations with him. She could not depend on him for praise. He was not supposed to be talking to the sisters about their work in that way. He reminded her of her father and how he sometimes talked when he came to visit her at the novitiate. 'Research, research, research.'

Mother Superior had warned her only the other day, outside the pharmacy. 'Dr Metivier has his own ideas, Sister. You, on the other hand, must follow the ideals of our Order.' Now, she was not at all sure what Mother Superior meant by her precise remark. She supposed that it was Doctor Metivier's, 'Eyes to your microscopes. That's what you're here for.'

When Sister Thérèse came out of the anaesthetic, the first face she saw was that of Doctor Metivier. 'It's taken five stitches,' he was saying. 'Not many, but needed.'

Vincent left the infirmarian to clear up while he washed his hands at the sink. 'I recommend a day of rest.' Vincent turned from his ablutions, pouring the rest of the warm water from the kettle into an enamel bowl. He noticed that there were no towels. 'Towel, Sister?' The infirmarian realised that she would have to go to the cupboard in the corridor. She clearly did not want to leave the doctor alone with Sister Thérèse. 'Clean bandages,' Vincent added, as she left on the errand.

Sister Thérèse sat up on the examination table. 'Doctor?'

'Yes, Sister.' He could see that she was troubled. 'Pain?'

48

'No. Not this. When you crossed the bay early this morning, did you see the German destroyer?'

'Yes. It was a surprise to see it. Extraordinary. Jonah tells me it's a training ship. The fishermen know everything. He went alongside and talked to one of the sailors who spoke fluent English. They're training in the South Atlantic. Had to stop to do some repairs. They were leaving as I came across. Why do you ask?'

'I saw it last night from the window of my cell. There was a sailor singing a love song.'

'A love song? What kind of love song?

'*Die Liebe ist's allein.* I think it's from Mozart's *The Magic Flute.* Just two lines over and over, Yes, yes, it is love alone.'

'I see.' He smiled at the pretty nun.

'Then my window shattered.'

'There was a squall, high winds. I slept right through it. I needed to.' Vincent did not tell his story of Theo.

'There was thunder. I heard it repeatedly in the distance. They'll kill my father. *Grom...*'

At that moment Sister Luke re-entered the infirmary. Vincent changed the conversation, but was inwardly alarmed by Sister Thérèse's mention of her father, and her startled use of the word, *Grom.*

'Now let's put some fresh bandages on your wound. Then you must get some rest. You make sure you're out tomorrow. We can't do without you at the hospital.'

'Yes. Thank you, Doctor.'

Sister Luke was out of the room again for an instant, clearing up.

'I must tell you about my father. Something happened in my cell. They don't listen here.'

'Tomorrow. Get some rest. She needs a good breakfast,' Vincent said, as the infirmarian re-entered. He smiled as he finished his cleaning up.

As Sister Luke stepped out of the infirmary with the soiled bandages and the debris of the little operation, Sister Thérèse grasped her moment again. She began hesitantly. 'I'll be there for research.'

'Good.' Vincent Metivier dried his hands again as he turned to face her.

'Doctor?'

'Yes.'

'Can I talk to you when we're at Saint Damian's?'

Vincent noticed his patient's hesitancy. Yet there was an undertone of urgency.

'Yes, of course.' Then, the infirmarian re-entered the room. He respected his patient's confidence and left.

Sister Thérèse stood at the window before returning to her cell. She stared out onto the convent's garden with the nun's cemetery. It was one of the first places she had been taken when she first arrived, in order to see the grave of Sister Matilde, who had been one of the original sisters. She remembered being moved to tears on seeing the name inscribed on the pitted stone over the grave: Sister Mathilde Le Clercq. Born, Clermont Ferrand, France, 1850. Died, El Caracol, 1935. Was this to be her own future? she had asked herself, learning that Sister Matilde was one of the few nuns who had eventually succumbed to the disease. Had she, Thérèse, herself, escaped one danger only to be exposed to another?

Saint Damian's

Theo had kept Vincent awake again with another tale. He was exhausted after another week of his crazed calypso. He did not know how he was going to continue to care for the boy. He did not want to believe in possession. What had Father Dominic landed him in? What had he taken on? The boy was wrecked by his tale. He needed to tell his story. He had had to lift him from the floor and take him to his bed last night. In the morning, Vincent knelt beside him. 'Theo, come boy, is time to get up. Remember, we going to Saint Damian's today.' Vincent did not want the boy out of his sight.

After breakfast, they waited on the jetty for Jonah. They watched the put-putting pirogue come round the point. Jonah looked surprised. 'Like we have an extra passenger today, Doc.'

Vincent looked at Jonah. 'He's shy.' He spoke under his breath. 'You take a seat in the bow, Theo.' He sat in the middle.

Jonah crouched in the stern with his hand on the tiller. The pirogue cut out from the jetty.

Vincent watched the dark green mirror of the bay crack and ripple away from the sides of the pirogue. Far above them, a frigate bird soared, a cross in the sky. On the other side of the wide Chac Chac Bay, Vincent could see that the nuns' launch was leaving from their jetty at Embarcadère Corbeau.

The tiny, black specks in the far blue above were vultures. When some dead thing in the bush, or on the shore, alerted them, they spiralled down, turkey buzzards, intent on the dead.

The nuns' launch, *Maria Concepción*, sat deep in the water, churning away at the *callaloo* of green, the Orinoco's stain. The squat bow ploughed ahead, not like the pirogue's chevron, raised in flight, now that Jonah had it at full throttle. The speed did not last. The engine spluttered and had to be started again. A whiff of gasoline from the motor mixed with the salt air.

Jonah stood now, firmly balanced, with a hand on the tiller, the engine racing again. 'We go beat them today, Doc!' It was his little game to reach the Saint Damian's jetty before the nuns.

Vincent held onto his Panama. He smiled at Jonah's enthusiasm. 'Take it easy, Jonah. Mind, Theo,' he called out.

'We go reach, Doc. Hold tight, boy.'

Would Sister Thérèse be on the launch today? She had had something to tell Vincent. *They'll kill my father.* Her words echoed even now from the nuns' infirmary a week ago. He still saw her cuts and bruises, the wound on her ankle. She should be in today for him to take the stitches out. He had been missing her, his best nurse, all this week on the wards. The enclosure of the convent had folded about her. 'She's resting, Doctor,' were Mother Superior's words when he asked why he had not seen her.

Theo was staring resolutely ahead. A flotilla of pelicans, disturbed by the pirogue's roar, rose from the choppy waves, then plunged as suddenly back into the sea. Vincent leant over and touched his shoulder. 'Look.' Theo winced.

Vincent looked back at Jonah. He was beaming, braced by the dawn, and the fact that he was winning the race, as usual. 'We go win, Doc!'

Vincent waved. 'You always do,' his voice made inaudible by the racing motor.

He crept up to Theo at the bow and knelt behind him, looking over his shoulder. He took care not to touch him. How was he going to tackle the difficult subject of Saint Damian's itself? 'Over there, Theo, to your right, is the leprosarium.' Vincent looked for a reaction in the boy's face. He knew that he was good at his vocabulary, Father Angel's bright boy, so the chances were that he would know the word leprosarium. 'You see the hospital? Go up so from the jetty, the low building with the long verandah. That's the chil-drens' wards.' Vincent saw a twitch on his face at the word children. What was he imagining? He realised that this talk was more his nervousness than a real need to inform Theo.

Theo was humouring him. Did Vincent really think he did not know what was happening on the island? He had seen the new patients, the girl Christiana, brought over the day he arrived. He had seen her crying. He maintained his usual mute self. 'Then, over here, see.' Vincent continued pointing. 'Those are the huts, where some of the adult patients live who can take care of themselves. The lower row is for the women, the ones on the higher terrace over there are for the men.' Vincent looked for a reaction.

'Not long again, Doc.' Jonah was guiding the pirogue. Just then, the *Maria Concepción,* was gaining on them.

'Like the nuns late this morning, Jonah?'

'Everybody late. Storm last night.'

'That's the boat belonging to the nursing sisters, Theo. They work at the hospital with me, looking after the patients.'

Jonah had trouble navigating the pirogue this morning, because of the wind and the choppy waves out in the bay.

'You know about leprosy?' Vincent asked the question directly. 'It's in the gospel. Remember, Jesus heals the leper. *Cocobay.* You hear that expression from the calypso, *cocobay.* Well that is Coco Bay where the jetty for Saint Damian's is. That is how leprosy here get that name. This is where they bring those who have leprosy.' Vincent hummed the calypso tune, '*If a man has money today.*'

With a small voice, under his breath, Vincent heard the completion of the couplet. '*People do not care if he has cocobay.*'

'That's it, Theo.' He's engaging, Vincent thought. 'Yes, my patients have *cocobay.* No money though. Leprosy, and I'm trying with the sisters to heal them. We look after them. And some of them are children. I want you to meet Ti-Jean. He's about your age. But remember, *cocobay* is not a nice word. There's no need to be scared though.'

Vincent carried on talking, trying to allay the fears he imagined the boy must have. He was sure that he must have heard descriptions in the country. He might even have seen someone with the disease, with blanched skin patches, without fingers or toes, or, at least, heard of the fear which the presence of the disease in the village would cause.

As Theo crouched forward on his seat, Vincent saw again the scar down his spine. It looked like a raised welt now, blistering the length of his back. He was marked with his own blemish. What was the tale there? 'Here Theo, put on your shirt now for school.'

As they neared the shore, the rusty galvanise roofs caught the sun. The leprosarium looked like an abandoned fishing village where the huts were being encroached upon by the bush, entangled by wild vines. The pink coralita, running riot, embroidered itself onto the decaying wood.

Vincent continued to point out the landmarks to the boy. Just up from the jetty and in the valley under Monte de Botella, the small, wooden Roman

Catholic Cathedral, dedicated to Saint Catherine of Alexandria, an echo of the original evangelisation of the island, spired between the *mahoe chardon* and the *gommier* trees. Next to it was the Anglican church, in colonial gothic, with its wooden fret work. Pinnacles of a Hindu Mandir, turrets and dome of a Muslim mosque shone white. Stuck in the muddy shore, the Hindu *jhandis,* saffron and white prayer flags tied to tall bamboo sticks, fluttered in the morning breeze, catching the light, taking prayers to Hanuman, the monkey god. The white statue of the Virgin Mary, *Stella Maris,* kept guard at the end of the jetty, gazing implacably out to sea. An abundance of faith! What could they do for his patients, these faiths? Vincent always asked himself.

As they drew nearer, they saw the old people on crutches, leaning on each others' shoulders, descending from the huts. He would have to introduce Theo to this reality. He was nervous. Theo stared, unmoved. The patients were coming down the red dirt tracks to the meeting place under the large, shady almond tree outside the stores. Already, the boys and girls were hanging out on their verandahs in front of their wards. Theo was now all ears and eyes. Vincent noticed his sudden agitation.

Suddenly, a squall swept off the gulf. Torrential rain burst down, fighting with the burning sun, clattering on the leaves. The hills steamed. The wet leaves shone like green enamel. The parrots screamed.

Vincent noticed the nuns huddled under the dripping canvas roof of their launch. Theo and himself were soaked, but already drying off in the hot sun.

'We well baptise,' Jonah laughed.

Jonah had won his race again. He and the boatman of the *Maria Concepción* promised each other another challenge.

'You need to learn how to drive boat, man,' Jonah boasted.

While Jonah steered the pirogue deftly alongside the jetty, Vincent stretched out for one of the rubber tyres which were slung along the side to prevent the boats being scraped. He tried to see if he could glimpse Sister Thérèse. Bowed heads, wimples and veils sheltered her from his view, if she were there at all.

'A safe delivery, Doc.' Jonah steered the pirogue alongside the Saint Damian's jetty.

Vincent threw the mooring rope to the boy hanging over the edge, supporting a crutch under one arm, the other stretched out to take the rope from Vincent, and crying out, 'Here, here Docta.'

'Okay, Ti-Jean, take care.' Vincent waved.

Ti-Jean was always there, waiting with a group of the more able children who loved to come down to the jetty to meet the boats in the morning. They wore their ragged khaki pants, bare backed, or with torn merino jerseys, part of the jumble sent by a nuns' charity from Sancta Trinidad. They showed their open sores. Vincent put his hand on Theo's shoulder, wanting to protect him.

Ti-Jean was ready to give his doctor a hand up onto the jetty. Having tied up the rope, he was standing on one crutch and waving the other dangerously. He was jealous of this role and would not allow his position to be usurped by any other boy, or for that matter, any girl on the children's ward. He was fourteen, bursting with life, but handicapped by the disease. There was a bond between the boy and the doctor. It had to do with his stumps, his hands and his feet. Vincent was determined to save them by repeated bandaging, except for the first joints of the fingers and toes. Disease and injury had taken those before Vincent had arrived.

Ti-Jean represented Vincent's great hope for his other patients. It was the spirit which Father Dominic had seen in the doctor, and which made him decide that Theo would be better off at Saint Damian's. 'Come, Theo, hold on to me.' Theo held fast. How was this going to work with the two boys?

'Here, here, Docta, take it, take it.' Ti-Jean's art was to stick one of his crutches out as a helping arm while he dropped the other and held on with all his young life to the mooring rope knotted to one of the pylons on the jetty. He was the great trickster.

'Thank you, Ti-Jean. What would I do without you, boy?'

'Fall in the water.' The idea always wreathed Ti-Jean's face in smiles. His laughter coincided with the disapproval of Mother Superior who did not take the chivalrous crutch, but chose instead the arms and shoulders of two of her nursing sisters to hoist herself out of the launch onto the landing stage, then up the steps to the jetty.

'Ti-Jean, you should be in line for school. Doctor, you encourage this boy,' Mother Superior said censoriously.

Ti-Jean lowered his eyes, and then smirked mischievously.

'I do. I do, Mother. Look how well he is,' Vincent protested.

'You know what I mean. You know exactly.'

'I do. I do, Mother.'

'You are incorrigible. And who is this boy?' She looked at Theo.

'This is the boy that Father Dominic has sent to stay with us.' Vincent put his hand on Theo's shoulder. He was not sure what details Mother Superior had had.

'Oh, yes, I remember. Well, I hope you have him in hand. Let's hope he can teach Ti-Jean some discipline.' The two boys eyed each other. 'And we've got a meeting today, Doctor.'

Ti-Jean was quickly saved from Mother Superior's admonishments by Sister Thérèse. 'I'll see to him, Mother.'

'Good morning, Sister.' Vincent had not noticed Sister Thérèse on the launch in the confusion of disembarking and the sudden rain. 'We've got an appointment this morning to take those stitches out.' Vincent tilted his Panama hat and smiled at the young nun. He could seem a dashing figure in his white shirt, khaki pants, and his Panama, shading his dark brown hair and wide dark brown eyes.

'Good morning, Doctor Metivier.' Her dark eyes shone.

'I hope Sister Luke has been keeping that wound clean and dressed. We don't want tetanus or septicemia spiriting you away. We must take the stitches out today.'

Sister Thérèse looked at Mother Superior as if for permission to speak, and then answered. 'Yes, Doctor, once I've seen to the children.'

'Then you'll see to me? I mean, I'll see to you.' Vincent liked to tease the young nursing sisters. He felt that this troubled nun needed some humour in her life. It was also a way for him to get along with the nursing nuns. The doctors always teased the nurses at University College, where he had been a houseman.

This kind of banter got Vincent a severe, reprimanding stare from under Mother Superior's eyes, while Sister Thérèse was tugged away by her sleeves into the procession of nursing sisters; she in turn, tugging Ti-Jean along.

'Sister!' Vincent called her back. 'Theo, come, you go with Sister Thérèse and Ti-Jean. Is that okay, Sister?' Theo was hesitant.

'Come, Theo.' Sister Thérèse put out her hand. 'Let me show you our school.' The boy relented, looking over his shoulder at Vincent for reassurance.

'Go along, Theo. I'll see you later.'

'You not hear the trouble, Doc?' Jonah stood by Vincent after tying up the pirogue. 'You know Singh talking to the people. Singh think he is Uriah Butler. They say he walking barefoot all over the place. Like the Creole, Cipriani, he rousing the people.' Jonah was alluding to the French Creole and the black labour leader, Butler, who had been imprisoned for inciting riots in thirty-seven down South, on Sancta Trinidad. The riot which had caught like a cane fire had not burned out. He knew that it still caught fire in the mind of Theo at night. It was also burning in the mind and heart of Krishna Singh, the pharmacist.

Vincent made his way to Mother Superior's office between the rows of huts which reminded him of the dilapidated barrack rooms on his family estate at Versailles. On the right of these, in a cluster, were some which Singh was asking to be made available for the married quarters. Mother Superior was resisting. Singh had taken it upon himself to represent the demands of the patients, or the people, as he called them.

When Vincent entered Mother Superior's office, Singh was already there and in full flow. 'Mother Superior, you can't have people living in these hovels, these barrack rooms. You can't have men living away from their women. These people are people, you know.' Vincent let Singh talk. He was saving his powder for later.

He watched Mother Superior's eyebrows arch as Singh went on. She began with, 'Mr Singh,' in that sardonic tone. 'I'm running a hospital and a convent. You seem to be starting a revolution.'

He came back at her. 'Mother Superior, I with the people and we asking for some basic human rights.'

'Mr Singh, we're talking about poor, ignorant people who have an incurable disease!'

'Where we agree is that they poor. Where we differ is that they are ignorant and incurable.'

He would not leave it alone. Vincent found himself an unlikely, momentary, mediator.

Singh was pressing for change. Vincent wanted it too, but done differently. 'Use your scalpel, Doctor. Is an operation we need here.'

'That's not the only remedy a doctor has at his disposal,' Vincent answered. 'With many of my patients disintegrating before my eyes, the lancing of wounds is the last thought on my mind. It is more a question of education in hygiene, awareness of their conditions and the truth about their disease.'

'Doctor Metivier, I agree. We're just putting it differently. But as the pharmacist here, I'm frustrated by how few drugs we've got at our disposal to administer.'

'I agree with that. We've got to press the authorities for this.' Singh was schooled in the politics of protest and struggle. He had noticed. He had come from the labour riots in the cane fields. He had had his education at the university of hunger as he called it.

'Gentlemen. We don't have the drugs. But what we've got is prayer and faith,' Mother Superior interjected.

'Prayer and Chaulmoogra oil. Dr Escalier's way.' Vincent was never too sure that his new appointment had met with Mother Superior's approval. He was appointed by the government, she by the church. This was an old battle. She had been very fond of his predecessor, the old Frenchman, who had retired and wanted to return to France before the outbreak of the threatened war, to be with his family. He had been a firm believer in the repeated injections of Chaulmoogra Oil.

As Singh and Vincent left Mother Superior with tempers boiling, she interrupted their departure. 'Doctor Metivier.' Singh left the room. 'Remember your vocation, Doctor.'

'I've not heard any call, Mother. I'm motivated by justice and wanting to heal patients, rather than faith in God.'

'Well Doctor, that's what you call it. But I know that it must be God that has called you here or else you would fail.'

'Krishna, Hanuman the monkey, which one? Which pantheon are you using? Is it your Triune god? Or is it the prophet Mohammed's Allah?' He could not help it sometimes, provoking Mother Superior. 'Are you talking about Shango?'

At this she fumed. She might as well know his true colours. There was no arguing. Why get into these discussions? Vincent thought. She might have the power to get rid of him.

'Which drums should I listen to? Those that beat for Legba, the Prophet Mohammed or, the Messiah?'

'Doctor, you run the risk of blaspheming?. And you know I would not be paying any attention to drums. You shouldn't encourage these people in their superstitions.'

'You can only blaspheme if you are a believer, Mother. Superstitions? Me? Encourage? Who is more superstitious? The drums at least have some life in them. You can't live on El Caracol and ignore the drums.'

'You think intellectualism will save you. You're a young man. You'll learn. You'll see, one day you'll reach the end of your endeavours, and there'll be someone else you'll have to call on.'

'When I reach the end of what I know, Mother, I'll say I don't know. I'll wait. I'll wait. I'll search. I'll research, and I'll keep observing.'

'Wait for whom, for what? Search for whom, for what?'

'Facts. Knowledge. And there is beauty.' Vincent looked to the hills and then over the sea, stretching out his hand.

'A poet as well, I see, Doctor?'

They always agreed to differ. But he heard her sigh and bemoan the fact that she had lost Dr Escalier.

Singh was waiting outside. 'We want you on our side,' he said to Vincent as they walked down from the verandah.

'I'm always on the side of my patients.'

'On the side of the people?'

'What do you mean?'

'I know you is a doctor. But...'

'But what?'

'And is up in Gran Couva you come from? Versailles, big cocoa estate? All you French creole! We know all you, you know.' He turned away.

'Singh, don't turn from me like that. I know what you mean. But you're going to have to trust what I do, even if you don't like what I sometimes say. And you're going to have to mistrust appearances. I am who I am. But what do you see?'

Singh turned back and smiled. 'Okay, Doctor.'

From the verandah, Vincent watched the light play with the trees, with the water and with the sky above. In the shimmer, the separateness of everything was diminished. Returning, after his seven years of training in England, had given him a transfigured vision of the place, the land and its history. Its hope was in this mingling of people, a shocking idea for some, he knew; as the trade unions pressed for their rights and the old planter class and the new import-export businesses resisted. He would have faith in the people and in the endurance of the place. Yes he did believe in the people.

Each day was like he had arrived yesterday. 'This is beauty, boy!' He turned towards Singh. 'Just ordinary beauty.'

'What you say, Doctor?'

'Ordinary beauty!'

'We place.'

'I think it should be.' There was pride in Singh's voice which delivered his words with the timbre of a labour leader.

Coolies in the sugar and niggers in the oil fields. Vincent heard Theo's voice, ringing the bitterness out of Mister's words in his night calypso. The child was reading the time.

Parrots, in pairs, screamed low across the sky above them, splashes of green; minnowing shadows skimming over the surface of the sea, hysterical.

'Docta?' Ti-Jean had escaped again from the nuns and the classroom and was tugging at Vincent's arm, while balancing on his crutches. 'You day-dreaming again!'

'Just the man I want. Let's make our rounds. Where's Sister Thérèse and Theo? I need them too.'

'Them in the school. How old he is, Doc? He quiet quiet. But he could read. He could read pappy! He read from "The Royal Reader" to all the children. But I know that story already so I come to look for you.'

Vincent winked at Sister Thérèse as she joined them. She had a soft spot for Ti-Jean as well. Theo had elected to stay in the classroom. Sister Rita had chosen him as her assistant. He was reading and doing sums with the small ones.

'First, I want to see the patients who came in recently on the boat from Porta España. That girl, Christiana. Did you notice any bad cases?' Then he remembered that Sister Thérèse had not been at the hospital for the last week.

'When they meet you, Ti-Jean, they know that there is hope. I want you to organise a football match in recess. And I want the teams mixed. No more of that bad cases in one team, good cases in another. Let the girls play too if

60

they want. I know Monica will take on any of you fellas. Ask Theo to play and Christiana, the new girl.'

'He could play football? He quiet quiet!'

'Well, you'll have to see.'

They began their rounds in the infants' ward. Ti-Jean and his irrepressible talk and humour kept everyone amused and distracted from the horrors which were the inevitable object of the doctor's rounds.

'So, spirits high today! But first let me see your wounds. Are they healing? Ti-Jean, what's this sore? And this on your toe. Come, come! How can I take you onto the ward as an example of how the others must look after themselves, if you let me down. Sister, come, let's get this boy cleaned up.'

'I sorry Docta. I don't know how this happen. I sorry, Docta.'

'We'll have you cleaned up in a jiffy. Don't say sorry. Say, I'm going to be more vigilant.'

Sister Thérèse watched Vincent at each bedside, his hands always reaching out to the children. These were the ones who moved her the most, and he was particularly good with children. 'Touch.' He had taught her that. 'You must touch your patients, not only professionally, but as a friend. And these little ones, pick them up, hug them, caress them.' She knew that his advice was not Mother Superior's which spoke of decorum. She was of the school of thought who believed, despite the evidence, that infection was easy. She believed in quarantines. Vincent's new regime meant increasingly open nursing and proper education in hygiene. 'We have to understand this disease. We don't believe in Medieval plagues.' He spoke like her father, Sister Thérèse thought, both as a doctor and as the free-thinking Communist her father was. Both he and her mother had joined the party.

Even with the windows open to the sea breeze, there was that pervasive smell of rotting flesh mixed with the smell of Chaulmoogra Oil when they peeled off the used bandages. Sister Thérèse was at hand with new dressings, the lint falling through her fingers.

'I want all these wounds dressed today. We must have fresh dressings everyday. I insist. Even if it means they have no cotton bed sheets left in Sancta Trinidad to sleep on. Strip them and tear them into bandages.'

Vincent turned to Ti-Jean, took him by the shoulder. 'Stand straight, boy.' He smiled at Ti-Jean. They alone knew that they had just got him ship-shape for this exhibition. 'This boy is not a miracle,' Vincent announced. 'He's a trickster, yes. Stand straight boy. But no miracle.' Ti-Jean was giggling, trying to balance straight, playing tricks with his crutches like a performer in a circus. He was enjoying the attention and the prominence on the ward.

'There are no miracles here. Only common sense and hygiene. Medicine is reason and science. Keep your bandages on. Watch yourselves as you move about. Watch for rats!' The small children screamed. Rats were an endemic problem in the night, nibbling toes and fingers. 'You must divide up the time to keep watch at night. Those who spot a rat and chase it off get a penny from me.' Vincent continued down the ward on his rounds, giving instructions, examining, making the children smile and laugh. He was speaking to the staff more than to the children. He believed in the repeated insistence of his theories which he was developing. 'You may think you have been trained. Well, you have to retrain.'

'And love, Docta. You know is love too.' One of the old ward assistants was mopping down the floors between the beds. She had lived her entire life on El Caracol.

'Yes, Ma Rosie, there's love. Yes, sweetheart.' She beamed. He bent and kissed her on the cheek. She beamed again.

'Is faith that heal me,' she proclaimed to the ward.

'Don't believe a word,' Vincent echoed, 'Hygiene and common sense. But, have your faith as well, Ma Rosie, if it makes you look after your sores and wounds. Have your faith.'

'Thank you, Docta.' Ma Rosie beamed again. 'Is love, I mean.'

'And what about the prayers the chaplain does say with we?' Sybil Goodridge, who had been at El Caracol since she was a baby, declared. She was one of Mother Superior's spies, Vincent calculated.

'If prayers help, pray. But don't forget what Dr. Metivier tells you.'

'Yes, Docta.' There was a chorus across the ward.

Sister Thérèse knew that when Vincent lectured he was not ordering her or his patients. He was speaking out against the imposed economies, the lack of rations. He was talking out for the Colonial Office in Porta España to hear. She had overheard the loud arguments in Mother Superior's office.

She tried her best. She was his ally. 'Yes, Doctor.' She winked at Ti-Jean and they moved on. She liked this conspiracy of three.

'You have a story to tell me.' Vincent spoke directly to Sister Thérèse as he leant over to take a clean bandage from her hands.

'Doctor?'

'Your father?'

Sister Thérèse's eyes filled with tears. 'Papa.' Her voice betrayed a guilt, as if she had been caught not keeping vigil over his memory. 'Not now. Not here.'

'Later, then. Yes?' He smiled, not teasing this time, respectful.

She continued to hand him clean bandages. Then she said, 'He's a doctor too.'

'Ah.' 'Why will they kill him? And who are they?' Vincent asked directly.

'I know it sounds wild. Well, the stories you hear. He's Jewish.'

'Your surname, yes, Weil? What about your mother?'

'She died five years ago.'

'I'm sorry. A Jewish Catholic?'

'Me, yes. My mother was Hélène du Bois. They fell in love at the Sorbonne. She was brilliant.'

'And you are a brilliant nurse, right across from the other side of the world.'

'Yes. I mean...'

Vincent smiled. 'We'll talk later.'

Ti-Jean amused the patients with his jokes and tricks, dropping his crutches and then crashing to the ground after them, or keeping his balance and proclaiming a miracle. 'See what Docta do!'

'No, Ti-Jean, you can perform your own miracle. So can you all.' Vincent looked back at the ward as he left. 'Next ward.' Sister Thérèse and Ti-Jean followed.

'You're right to be worried about what is going on in Germany. But France?' Vincent continued as they walked along.

'My father always maintained that the bigotry was European. He says it's a matter of time.'

'So, you lost your mother recently. I was the same age when my father died.'

'Oh.'

'This will take up all our time and all our thought.' Vincent looked down the ward.

Nothing he had experienced before had prepared Vincent for this work. They were exhausted by the time they had finished with the mens' ward. 'Run along to school now, Ti-Jean, and bring Theo back with you.' He and Sister Thérèse crossed the yard to the pharmacy.

'I wonder what I'm doing here sometimes.' These were the moments when Vincent was tempted by the thought that he should have chosen a private practice in Porta España.

'It's a vocation.'

'You have the vocation. This is my job.'

'I don't think you mean that, from what I can see. You talk as if it's a vocation also. It's what my father believes.'

'Yes, but you know what I mean. How did your father feel about you joining up, coming out here?'

'He wants me to be a good nurse.'

'Well, you are that.' Sister Thérèse bowed her head. 'No, I mean it. But a nun?'

'It happened when my mother died. I was drawn to the sisters.'

'I see.' He had cousins who had entered the priesthood and the religious life. He remembered the fathers at college trying to encourage young fellas to join up. He knew how it happened.

'I'll scrub up now.' He watched her at the sink. She was young to be experiencing all the change she had undergone. She was right. It was a vocation.

He knew he had been sent to El Caracol because he was young, he had concluded after his interview, or, at least, younger, twenty-eight, straight back from university, needing a job. He would have the latest experience, the knowledge, they thought. He had enthusiasm. But Vincent felt that he was being tested. If he got through this appointment with success, any job might be open to him in the colonial structure of appointments. But, now, just inside a year, he had fallen for the challenge.

He had not started his study straight out of school. He had had a bout on the Versailles cocoa estate straight after the accustomed education at the college of the Immaculate Heart of Mary, in town, Porta España, built in the nineteenth century by the Catholic priests for the sons of the cocoa planters.

But while he had wanted to help and please his mother after his father's death, he knew that life on a cocoa estate was not for him. The job had then fallen to Bernard, his younger brother.

Vincent and Sister Thérèse watched the life of the yard from the verandah of the pharmacy. Life on El Caracol had congregated under the almond tree outside the main entrance of the outpatients' ward which was for those who came from the huts on the hills. 'I'm not Jesus of Nazareth,' Vincent laughed, pulling Sister Thérèse into conversation again. She had been instructed to use her spare moments between tasks for meditation, or as an opportunity to recite a decade of the rosary on her beads. 'I cannot say, take up your bed and walk. Drop your crutches and run. I cannot send them into the yards shouting that they've been healed.' Sister Thérèse was pulled between Vincent's musings and her prayers. 'They look in all their disarray and disfigurement like a congregation of sick on the shores of Galilee, wanting to be healed by the Messiah.'

Sister Thérèse smiled, trying to be polite to her doctor, but also trying to keep her religious observances.

Krishna Singh was holding forth. Jonah was adding his bit under the almond tree. He watched the two men, the East Indian and the Negro. They represented the enforced migrations which had peopled this place. They represented the great mingling of peoples. Vincent wanted to be part of that. The older people sat listening. 'Bread, Justice, Rights, Wages,' punched the air. Then there was a mumble of agreement.

'My father is a Communist. If he was younger he would have fought in Spain.' Vincent realised Sister Thérèse was taking in everything, despite the evidence of the rosary beads passing through her fingers. She was a strange mixture, he thought, more than met the eye. He could see that she had been well trained. Visions and science were mixed inside of her reason and faith.

'They are looking for a Messiah, for a Moses. They are looking for someone to take them out of the land of Egypt into the Promised Land.'

This would not be his own language now, but maybe the end was the same. There were those with crutches, but mostly they were without, walking hip hop on the stumps of legs, and sometimes, on all fours, with the stumps of hands. Some of the more adventurous propelled themselves along on pieces of board and galvanise, tobogganing themselves over the grit and gravel of the paths from the huts. A dangerous journey. More adventurous boys made box carts, and their journey to the clinic or school was like play. While the descent could be exciting for the young, the ascent back for the elderly was very hard work.

'There is a spirit in these people,' Sister Thérèse added.

'See these people, Doc, they not go take anything, you know. Not any more.' Jonah came and stood beneath the verandah. 'Morning, Sister. Things go have to change. Come and talk to them.'

'I've just done my rounds of the wards, Jonah. That's my pulpit. That's where I give my sermons on hygiene. Where I talk about nourishment.'

'Each of we, go do we own thing, Doc.'

Vincent relented and left Sister Thérèse to her meditation, and walked over to the almond tree with Jonah. He looked at his patients, or at the people, as Krishna Singh addressed them.

'People of El Caracol.' Those with tuberculoid leprosy were the least disfigured. They carried noticeable blemishes on their skin, both on their hands and faces where the skin had died. But there was no major external disfigurement. But there were those poor wretches who were covered with nodules, whose features had caved in to give them that proverbial lion-face look, with their flattened noses, the absence of eyebrows, foreheads and cheekbones which had thickened. This was *Lepromatus* Leprosy.

Vincent had discovered, from his examinations and observation, that these patients had little control of their facial muscles, and that it was often difficult to tell the difference between a smile and a grimace. Joy and sadness presented themselves with ambiguity.

Vincent stood with Jonah and listened to Krishna Singh putting the case for better conditions. 'He should've been a lawyer.' Jonah leant over Vincent. 'His father dead. They ent have enough money save to send him to London. He have to support his mother and sisters.'

During applause, Jonah carried on with the story of Singh. 'He make Exhibition Class, try for School Certificate, get a training as apprentice pharmacist. The best job they give him is here.' Vincent looked at Singh anew. 'Law was his first ambition. But now is people. We people,' Jonah concluded.

Vincent looked back at Sister Thérèse. She was still on the verandah, looking on, distracted from her meditations, caught by Krishna Singh's speeches. He noticed that Theo was standing by her side.

'Jonah, make certain Singh keeps this thing under control. I don't want my patients risking their health for his revolution.' The crowd under the almond tree had doubled in numbers since yesterday. Word was spreading.

'Trust them.' Jonah pointed at the crowd.

Vincent paused on the verandah. Sister Thérèse looked up and smiled. He stood at the balustrade and gazed out to sea. Theo and himself watched Ti-Jean swing his way on his crutches into the yard to hear the old fellas under the almond tree. 'I play football, you know.' Vincent was astonished at Theo's spontaneous remark.

'Good.'

Theo jumped down from the verandah and ran over to join Ti-Jean. Then he saw the girl Christiana join them.

'They're doing well.' Sister Thérèse was looking over to where Ti-Jean and Theo stood at the edge of the crowd.

'Yes, Ti-Jean's learnt about his illness. He's active in his recovery. We can see the signs in the body. It's different with the mind.'

'The mind?'

It was out before he had time to think whether it was the right thing or not. 'Theo. Something is not right.' Vincent told Sister Thérèse about the nocturnal tales.

'Frightening. His mother and father?'

'Yes. Well, there's a mother. The father? It seems less clear who he might be.' Vincent did not reveal his suspicions. It seemed complicated at the moment to go into those details, to divulge a history when he was not sure of her, how intimate he could be with her. He should not be talking like this to a nun anyway.

'You're worried about the state of his mind?'

'Well, he does seem a troubled boy. Troubled by his past. He's clearly not dumb. He speaks eloquently.'

'Bring him to school again. Good for him to be with the other children.'

'I'll see what he's thought of today.'

'I'll keep an eye on him. And Ti-Jean. Ti-Jean will be his friend.'

'Well let's not rush. Otherwise Ti-Jean might well wonder why he can't live in my house as well. We need to get those stitches out. I can see you are not putting the usual pressure on your ankle.'

Having embarked on the story of Theo, Vincent did not then want to continue with the intimate details.

While Vincent prepared to take out the stitches from the wound above Sister Thérèse's ankle, Sister Luke hovered. He was getting used to working with nuns.

At a moment when the infirmarian was out of the clinic disposing of the old dressings, Vincent said, 'Let the boy's stories be our secret for the moment.'

'Yes,' she looked at him, realising that he was expecting her to hold some knowledge confidential between them, knowledge which she was being invited to keep from her sisters, and in particular from Mother Superior. She had entrusted him with a confidence of her own about her father, her fear for her father. Maybe it was because of that that he felt that he could exchange a confidence with her. Without immediately answering about the boy, she returned to her father.

'I've got a letter from my father, Papa. It came yesterday. He tells of the mounting tensions on the streets in Germany. Then I saw the headlines in the local papers in Mother Superior's office. It happened the night the German sailor sang a love song under my window.' She hummed the tune. '*Die Liebe die Liebe ist's allein.*'

'Yes, there were terrible attacks on Jewish establishments.' He watched her eyes, he heard her tune.

At that moment, Sister Luke re-entered the room. Vincent and Sister Thérèse looked at each other, sealing their secrecies. She brought her skirt down over her ankles and stood up.

'I'm better now. Thank you, Doctor.'

'Now, you take care.' She still limped a little. He watched her leave the room with her anticipation of pain.

When Theo joined Vincent to return to the doctor's house they met Mr Lalbeharry.

'Is your son, Doctor?' Theo could not stop staring, so that Vincent hoped that Mr Lalbeharry was not hurt and embarrassed.

'No, Lal, this is a young friend of mine staying with me for a while. Have you not seen him about the yard? Theo, meet Mr Lalbeharry.' Vincent held

Theo's head, his fingers in his sandy hair. Mr Lalbeharry put out his claw hand for Theo to shake.

'Hello, young fella.'

Theo did not respond. He kept his hand behind his back. He could not take his eyes of the face of Mr Lalbeharry who had the classic lion-face look, with the collapsed nose bridge. He had the shortened fingers giving him the claw hands. There were blemishes and patches on his skin. His speech was impaired, because of his nasal disfigurement. Theo continued to stare.

'The little fellow not accustomed to us yet?' This was typical of Mr Lalbeharry's openness. He was one of the most confident of the older patients, despite his considerable disfigurements. He patted Theo on the shoulder. Theo froze. 'We don't bite,' he said, and smiled.

'He's a shy boy, Lal.' Vincent, using his affectionate name for Mr Lalbeharry, came to Theo's defence.

Theo tugged at Vincent's hand. 'What's it, Theo?'

Then the boy slumped to the ground. Vincent knelt next to him.

'I feeling bad,' Theo whispered. Then he fainted.

Hiding

The house was again rocked by the boy's calypso in the night. Theo's fainting, the fear generated by seeing Mr Lalbeharry, had precipitated a night of sleep walking. Vincent was kept up, wandering about the house, having to comfort the boy as he sobbed his heart out. There were no words, only the music of tears. In the morning, Theo refused to go to the school. He had had a fright. This was a child with extraordinary sorrow.

Vincent had to arrange again for Beatrice to spend the day at the house.

'I go cook him something nice, Docta. Come boy, stay with me,' Beatrice comforted him.

Vincent waved to them on the jetty from the pirogue.

Jonah had the boat at full throttle.

When Vincent and Sister Thérèse met again, they were taken up in their work. There was no time for teasing this morning, as Vincent donned his white coat. There was no time for the nun's tale, for their shared secrets. They were busy administering the dosage of Chaulmoogra Oil, the interminable injections under the skin, to the long queue of patients who had come down from the huts in the hills. Some had come from Indian Valley beneath the lighthouse on Cabresse Point, others came from the terraces built into the hills above the hospital.

There were some *tapia* huts, some of the original wattle huts of the nineteenth century, which were even more remote, ruins of the original leprosarium. No one came from there. Vincent had never ventured there on his rounds. He trusted the older nurses, who said, 'No one live there now, Doctor.'

'What good does this do?' Vincent dumped a broken syringe into the rubbish bin. He washed his hands at the sink in the clinic, then sat at his desk, taking a rest from this painful routine, lighting up a cigarette, taking a long draw and exhaling as he leant back in his chair. 'What possible good?'

'Doctor, you must not let them doubt their recovery.' Sister Thérèse was preparing the new batch of injections. 'They think it does them good, particularly the older ones,' she argued.

'But at what a price!' Vincent was thinking of the sores the injections themselves could create. 'Escalier's cure! Between the Chaulmoogra and the putrid stench, I don't know which is worse.' In the old Frenchman's time some of the patients had had more than a hundred injections a week.

Indeed, it was the common treatment of the time. In the absence of the new Sulfa drugs they had heard about, it was all they had.

'You see, this is where Singh is right,' Vincent argued. 'We should be trying those new drugs. Our patients have a right to them. Anyway, they don't prevent the infectious sores, the loss of joints and limbs, their inability to feel pain.'

'Doctor,' she tried to calm him.

'They think they can just throw people off Sancta Trinidad into this backwater, give them the free nursing of nuns, one misled doctor with fantastic ideals, and that's their problem solved.'

'You're not misled. Just frustrated. Your ideals aren't fantastic. They're the right ideals.' She left the room, tossing her veil from her face as she walked into the sea breeze blowing onto the verandah. The routine got to her as well.

Vincent watched her through the mosquito screen as she went along the line, preparing the patients for their injections, accompanied by Sister Rita. There was more independence in her today. He noticed that her body still anticipated the pain she might feel if she put full pressure on her sore ankle. She expected the pain to send its signal, but she was getting better. Her wound had healed. Her wound had not rotted. She was well. She had the natural gift of pain. How could he get his patients to feel pain, or at least to compensate for the fact that they did not? Chaulmoogra Oil was not the way.

Later that morning, Vincent prepared to give the first of a series of lectures to all the nurses and their assistants. A lecture might have been too grand a title. This was a new idea. Another of his fantastic ideals, he thought. He wanted his hospital, no matter in how small a way, to be a teaching hospital.

Mother Superior was the first, at the front, in the row of chairs arranged on the verandah outside the nuns' common room. She had eventually relented, giving her permission. Between Mr Krishna Singh with his political speeches under the almond tree, not to forget Jonah Le Roy, the tall black man, as she always referred to him, looking more like Moses than Jonah, and now this new, free-thinking doctor with his lectures, she wondered where she could make her impression, except in the Chapter House of her convent.

She invited Father Meyer, the chaplain, to come along, as a kind of inquisitor, Vincent thought. Maybe he would be taken out and burnt at the stake afterwards for heresy.

Sister Thérèse sat with Sister Rita at the back. Those other nuns who were not on duty filled up the other seats. Krishna Singh was at the front. Jonah was standing at the back, near the steps.

Vincent placed a small table in front of his audience, laid out his papers, securing them from the relentless wind with a stone. Sister Claire brought him a chair from the common room

The gist of Vincent's lecture was education. The stigma, as old as the disease, making outcasts of the lepers; the image of people bandaged in rags, shunned, forced to ring a bell to announce their arrival, so that others could get out of the way, had to be resisted. 'We've got to educate the public and the authorities.' Vincent looked up from his paper. He saw anxiety and disapproval on the faces of Mother Superior and the sisters near her. But he continued. 'We're quarantined here. Our patients are exiles in their own home. We must change that view.'

He needed to catch some other eyes. 'There's the shame our patients feel when they first come to us. We see it whenever the *bumboats* arrive. There's the loss of self brought by this disease. It's as if their very history has taken their self-esteem away.'

Before he moved on from the social stigma of the disease, he looked up and thought he saw the faintest glimmer of a smile on Sister Thérèse's lips. Her bright eyes encouraged him.

Singh looked ahead proudly, sitting next to the chaplain and Mother Superior. Jonah was beaming from the back, ushering in some of the older patients, like Mr Lalbeharry, who sat on the steps. Vincent gained in confidence.

'Where the infectious, incurable form of the disease exists, there is relentless deterioration. It can seem an endless task: suppurating sores, joints that rot away, faces which collapse. Yet shining through, like in some of our boys, Ti-Jean, for instance...' Vincent looked up and smiled proudly. Everyone knew that the boy was his hero. 'Or, take Ma Rosie! We see the individual no

72

matter the state of their body.' He paused to mention other particular patients, to drive his point home. ' You, Lal.' Mr Lalbeharry smiled from the back. 'We can get depressed that, after all our advice, we see the little care some of our other patients take of themselves. Why is this? They burn themselves. They stump their limbs. They cut their skin. We need to remind ourselves that this is not the disease itself. Yes, it's a job of clean bandaging. It's a matter of looking after wounds and sores. But, there's more. There's understanding the complexity of this disease. What can we do to heal? What can we do to prevent deterioration?'

Lastly, Vincent said, 'A bit of love, sisters. Let them experience that. And, dare I say it, a bit of pleasure.' Jonah stamped his feet with approval. Singh applauded. Mother Superior moved her chair deliberately as if to get up and leave, then remained sitting, bolt upright with an unflinching face. The chaplain coughed profusely. Vincent had noticed that this was a nervous reaction on his part throughout the speech. 'The general well-being of our patients, the opportunity for a full life.' Vincent caught Sister Thérèse's eyes. 'By encouraging full relationships, sisters, we can bring happiness amidst so much sadness.'

Mother Superior came up to Vincent when he had finished. 'I'm glad that you appreciate the individual soul, Doctor.'

'Soul? Who said anything about the soul? I mentioned the individual. It's their mortality I'm interested in improving. I know nothing about immortality. I leave that to you, Mother, and Father Meyer here. You deal with the invisible. I'll deal with the visible, even though I may need your entire community looking into a microscope to find it.'

'You think words will heal. You joke. You charm. But you don't charm me Doctor.'

'Just the opposite. Understanding what the disease is, how it works, how it's prevented. We know more than we did. This is what lies behind research. Research and education is allied to treatment. That is the valuable work your nuns can do. Meticulous, relentless research in order to extend our understanding helps us prepare our treatment.'

'They're just poor people. They know more than any of us, how to suffer and to accept the cross Christ has given them to carry. We can assist in that.'

'I see no cross. Poor, yes. But that means they deserve even more, surely. Even your religion teaches us that.'

'The poor will always be with us, as Christ says in the gospel.' Father Meyer, within earshot, contributed.

'Well, yes, if you think that way, we can then rely on the poor always being with us. My work is to help them, so that they can work themselves out of poverty.'

The other sisters moved away in embarrassment, their loyalties stretched.

'Don't underestimate the gift of patience which they have, and what it allows us to witness. Suffering, Doctor, is the way of the Lord.'

'I admire my patients' endurance. Don't get me wrong. But I want to harness it to improve their health, their self-esteem, not remain silent receivers of charity.'

Father Meyer smiled. He preferred his battles over a few rum punches and Wagner on the gramophone. He patted Vincent on the shoulder in order to quieten him. He patronised both him and Mother Superior with his smile, as if their discussion was beneath him. Seemed to Vincent that his philosophy was that charity was to keep the poor poor, even if not expressed so bluntly. 'They allow us to advance in virtue, as they themselves grow in that very same virtue.'

'And don't forget, Doctor, that my nuns are brides of Christ.' With that parting salvo, Mother Superior turned her back and walked away.

Singh, leaning up against the balustrade of the verandah, caught Vincent's eye. 'I see you on our side now, Doctor.' He patted Vincent on the back.

'I hope we're on the side of our patients.'

'People. People, Doctor.'

'Words, Krishna. You heard Mother Superior.' Vincent smiled. 'How many brides does Shiva have?'

'And Mohammed?'

'Religions! They'll keep the poor poor.'

'Opiates!' Singh proclaimed.

Later that afternoon, finishing his rounds, Vincent turned to Sister Thérèse who carried a tray of bandages. Resting it down, she passed the lint through her fingers, snipping with her scissors. He knew she was one of the best on the wards. She was firm in her purpose, but delicate and gentle. He watched her hands turn in the light. He watched her fingers in the strips of cotton cloth and muslin lint, a gold band on her marriage finger. She was Christ's bride. He watched her wash wounds and clean suppurating sores. What had brought this young girl to El Caracol?

'*Le village*. The village.' She spoke phrases in simultaneous translation. It was a kind of nervousness, a kind of being in two places at once, being in two minds at the same time. After her doctor's lecture, and the public response from her Mother Superior, the air was tense. She spoke in her French accent, opening conversation on something other than their work as doctor and nurse. She talked about the place from where she had come. 'We went to Provence in the summer and vacations. Otherwise, we were in Paris.'

They were not supposed to have personal conversations. When Vincent had first arrived, Mother Superior had always insisted that Sister Gertrude, a woman of nearly seventy, should be his ward assistant. Then he used to look at the young sisters giggling together, catching them in an off-guard moment in the pharmacy.

He had requested Sister Thérèse Weil because of her research experience. He was getting used to her as his best assistant. She was looking up at him from where she bent over her work. 'What's it, Sister?'

Her eyes were always being lifted from below a bowed head, an irritating gesture of humility, learned in some spartan, Jansenist novitiate in France. Not her natural demeanour, he thought. She extracted from her copious sleeves an envelope which was as blue as the Antillean sky. 'A letter from Papa.' The paper had faded with its passage, and was creased with its secrecy, secreted into the folds of her habit, now withdrawn between the tips of her fingers. Once read, already censored, it should have been destroyed. That is what Mother Superior would have wanted.

'You've not given up the world, Sister, that you long for its news so,' Vincent teased.

'Papa, you know. I've told you of his letters.' She smiled, refolding the letter, indicating its author, putting it back into her sleeves, secreting it further, somewhere deep in all those folds. He could not imagine where it eventually encountered her flesh.

Women who had worked in his mother's house lifted their blouses and inserted money and keepsakes in the depths of their bosoms. Hers were flat. She seemed like a boy in girl's robes. What had she done with her breasts? 'No, go ahead, Sister. I would be delighted to share your news. I'm of the world. I long for its news.' Vincent smiled.

75

'Papa is worried. He hears from friends, *les amis*.' There were tears in her eyes. What was he to do with a crying nun? He moved to comfort her, then stopped, folding his arms. Better to keep those out of the way.

'What does your father say? What has he heard from a friend?'

'Events in Germany will encourage ideas in France. It's a long history. *Kristallnacht*. It sounds pretty. Like the name of an opera, or a piece of music.'

'Yes Sister, it was in the local paper. It was on the radio.'

'*C'est dangereux*. For France.'

They talked about the report which had come through on the BBC, again reported in the local papers. A high-ranking remember of the German embassy in Paris had been shot. A seventeen-year-old young man had been detained for questioning. He was a Polish Jew, Hershel Grynzpan. The man was reported to have said that he shot the official, Ernst Von Rath, to call attention to the fate of Polish Jews in Germany. He died on the afternoon of November 9th.

Vincent and Sister Thérèse exchanged these facts. Between their exchanges were long silences.

'There were riots by the National Socialists right across Germany,' she continued to read from her father's letter.

'Yes, Sister.'

'Acts of revenge.'

Vincent remembered Theo glued to the radio, fiddling with the knobs to try and tune in the reception more clearly. '"*Kristallnacht*", new vocabulary, Doctor.' Words excited the boy.

'*It's been reported that SA men in uniform, some in civilian clothes, rioted in the streets of many German towns across the country, destroying Jewish shops, synagogues, attacking Jewish citizens. Many are seeing these riots as a direct result of the killing of Ernst Von Rath in Paris, but others are seeing it as a pretext for what is now National Socialist policy, as expressed recently by Herman Goring. He has called for all available resources to be brought to bear on a final solution to the Jewish question. They have no place in our economy.*'

Sister Thérèse folded her father's letter over and over till it was as slender as a needle, which she then again inserted into her sleeve, as if she were administering herself an injection. She looked up. 'They'll kill my father.'

Vincent listened.

As if to distract herself from her real pain, she spoke quickly of other reports in her father's letter. 'News coming through says that the riots were supposed to appear as a spontaneous outbreak by the *Volk*. Leaders of the Jewish community are calling the attacks a *Pogrom*.'

'Your father is very detailed.'

'Witnesses in the city of Aachen have reported that the firemen, responsible for putting out the flames to the burning synagogue in the city, were seen spraying chemicals which contributed to the destruction.'

'I can believe it.'

'He says the smashing of windows with bars, sledge-hammers and picks have inspired commentators on major newspapers to call the night of destruction, *Kristallnacht*, describing the broken glass in the streets, in many cities, across the country.'

By now, Sister Thérèse had unfolded the letter once more, like some piece of espionage.

'Sister, I'm sorry, try not to disturb yourself.'

Tears wet her cheeks. She paid no attention to Vincent's caution.

'"It is reported that there are thousands wounded, and a hundred people have been killed. The events are said to have caused concern in many European capitals, though there are no official statements, which other commentators are seeing as the delicate caution with which the government of the National Socialist Party is being treated."'

'It's terrible. You're not helping yourself.' He put his hand on her shoulder. 'Come, sit. Don't read anymore.'

But now, as if to heed Doctor's advice, she switched to the news of developments in Sudetenland since the recent agreement in Munich between France, Britain, Germany and Italy to concede the province in north-west Czechoslovakia to the Germans. She read blandly, emptied of emotion.

Sister Thérèse's hands were full of the sodden bandages taken off from Ma Cowey, whose feet were worse than ever. She and Vincent were both thankful for the sea breeze. The stench of putrefaction and ulcerous sores was overwhelming.

'Ma Cowey, you are not using the crutches we made for you. That was a good piece of cyp that Singh cut for you from the forest. *Bon Bois*.' Vincent registered Ma Cowey's name in his ledger. Two hundred injections this week.

'Docta, you know how it is. I not accustom to crutches. And I not feel nothing. I not feel nothing happening. I surprise myself to see it so.'

Sister Thérèse helped Ma Cowey down the steps to the yard after completing her bandages. 'Come again tomorrow at the same time.'

She returned, wiping her hands on her apron. She went to the sink and scrubbed with carbolic soap. 'Scrub hard, Sister.' Vincent tried to clear the air of emotion.

She returned with her hands in a towel, then unbuttoned her sleeves and rolled them up her arm. She wiped her naked arms. '*Il fait chaud.*'

'You're right, Sister. It making hot, as the old people say.'

She smiled. Then she became serious again. 'She's not using the crutches.'

'What do you deduce from that?' Vincent interrogated his assistant.

'She talks almost as if she doesn't see the need for them.'

'Why?'

'She doesn't realise what's happening. She forgets she needs them, because nothing reminds her that she does.'

'Nothing? Why?'

'She cannot feel. She cannot feel pain.'

'Exactly. Pain should remind her. Pain is the message that we hurt. Pain tells us that we need healing. They're not getting that message. I was looking at you limping this morning. Even after I'd taken out the stitches, you had patterned yourself to limp, just in case. You were getting compensatory messages.'

'Pain is a gift.'

'Well, it's our protection. We're wired that way. Something has gone wrong with their wiring. I want to carry out those nerve experiments. But I need a cadaver. I need the conditions in which to work on it.'

They completed their rounds by seeing how a new boy had settled in. Christiana, the new girl, had shown no signs of the disease so far.

Already, Ti-Jean had taken the boy off to school, to play football, getting himself another holiday from the classroom by being legitimately let off by the doctor, but having to avoid Mother Superior nonetheless.

Suddenly, it was overcast. Coming up from the gulf was a hard rain. A dark gloom settled over the yards. There was a serrated flash, followed by deep thunder and a downpour which had everyone scuttling for shelter under verandahs and doorways as rain, like rock stones clattered on galvanise roofs. Children bawled with excitement and fear on the wards. The drains gargled and pelted down the hills to the sea, in runnels of brown water. Then it was over. The clouds had blown off to the Atlantic. The sun baked the wet yards dry. The scent of hot steam filtered through the humid air, like on ironing day. Children played in the water-filled drains.

From the path, going up to the huts, there was a wide view of Chac Chac Bay and the gulf beyond. It was strangely empty. Recently, they had become accustomed to seeing the trading ships which came up from Brazil and Argentina. They sailed along the coast of Cayenne and the Guyanas, sheltering and refuelling in the safe embrace of the Golfo de Ballena.

A lone frigate bird soared high above the island. There always seemed to be this crucifixion in the sky.

The breeze lifted Sister Thérèse's veil. It wrapped her white cotton habit around her legs and hips. She laughed, disentangling herself, bowing her head to her knees, keeping her skirts down over her ankles. She was like a giggling schoolgirl.

Vincent and Sister Thérèse stood and surveyed the bay. They looked at each other and smiled and then continued on their walk. He remembered to respect the sisters' silence, their proper decorum.

They reached the very last of the huts, calling in and checking on patients who had not managed to get down to the clinic. Neither of them had come this far in their rounds before. There was still much of the island that they both had to explore, and there were stories that some patients had escaped from the compound, and were hiding in the hills like maroons.

At the end of the track, they could see a hut set apart from the rest. As they walked towards it, a bent figure covered in rags crossed from the bush to the hut. Vincent was immediately reminded of such a figure shuffling away from behind the stores, near the jetty one afternoon, when he was leaving Saint Damian's. He had meant to inquire the next day, but it had slipped his memory. There were, periodically, reports of food stuffs missing from the stores, depleting the already meagre rations.

Vincent and Sister Thérèse approached the hut into which the figure had disappeared, then recoiled from the retching smell which they recognised from their work on the wards with the most deteriorating patients. Dead flesh!

They dreaded the worst. The door of the hut was jammed. They had to push hard, at the same time calling out, if anyone was there.

In the gloom of the hut, the smell was so intense, that Sister Thérèse turned away. She had to go outside and bend down at the side of the track and vomit.

Vincent noticed several figures who had retreated far into the corners of the hut, covering themselves, hiding in the gloom, not wanting to show themselves. He steeled himself, holding back his feelings, his instinct to be sick.

'There's no need to be afraid. I want to help you.' He repeated this phrase. 'Help you, help you.'

Sister Thérèse, now recovered, echoed her doctor antiphonally.

There was heavy breathing, but no words came from the gloom.

The figures began to stir. They moved towards Vincent together. When they were on their knees they extended what was left of their arms. Some, who still had fingers, clasped them in a prayer. Claw hands were raised in the gloom.

'This is the bad leprosy,' Sister Thérèse whispered as Vincent knelt to be at the same level as the patients in front of him. The sight which met his eyes at such close range was horrifying because of the disintegrating faces. He had to fight against his revulsion. This was *Lepromatus* Leprosy at its worst, unattended kind.

These people had retreated here out of shame. It was a shame which had started in some village when they were first detected with the disease. They had had to come on the enforced journey to El Caracol. It was a paradox. Some had wanted to come because of the pain of being shunned. They welcomed their exile. Others wanted to hide.

'This has to change,' Vincent whispered to Sister Thérèse, trying to observe all the worse signs of the deteriorating condition before him. Then he spoke to the patients in front of him again. He had now worked out that there were at least six of them. He was not sure, as yet, who were men and who were women. 'We want to help you. We will help you. You mustn't stay here.'

They unlatched the wooden shutters of the hut and secured the door open. Light shone in like a searchlight, and frightened the huddled mass of six back into the corner, with their backs turned, their faces against the walls.

The wind moved dry leaves and newspaper on the floor. 'You must allow air into the room. You must wash yourselves at the stand pipe. Later, we'll bring up new clothes, as well as dressings for your wounds.' Vincent could see that one of the patients was only a torso in a bundle of rags. This person was being carried by two others. He thought it was a man, but could not really tell. He hated to think how this situation had arisen. How had this been allowed to continue?

Dr Escalier had grown old and not been able to cope. That was clear. But also Vincent continually found, in the older religious, a resignation which depended on prayer, not on science, as he was fond of repeating. He looked at the young sister at his side and hoped that she was the beginning of new blood among the nursing nuns. He hated to think of the worse stories of the marooned groups in the hills. He had his work cut out for him, as Jonah was so keen to remind him.

In the late afternoon, the rooms were smoked and disinfected. The patients had to be deloused at the stand pipe outside. Vincent and Sister Thérèse came back with fresh bandages. They made a record of those for whom a treatment by Chaulmoogra Oil injections would be suitable. They knew that they were working in a potentially infectious area, because of the long-term neglect. Vincent watched the nun's young hands, her young face. His concern was more for her than for himself. They both registered the other's battle with revulsion to the sores and the disfigurements. The next day they would begin a gradual rehabilitation of the patients onto the different wards.

Coming down the stairs, to the clinic, Vincent turned towards where the light poured through an open window onto the counter. Sister Thérèse was standing with her back to him, preparing medicines, so that all he saw of her was the white cotton veil which fell wide over her shoulders, halfway down her back. It was as if she was behind a screen. She turned, as the staircase creaked. He suddenly saw her differently.

He concentrated on her face, her dark eyes peering out of the tight under-veil, taut beneath her chin and stretched over her forehead. It was damp with perspiration. The full veil fell from the crown of her head over her shoulders forming a tight cocoon. Her face peered out of a hole, as if cut in a sheet. Her skirts fell to below her ankles, just above her sandals and stockinged feet. Her arms were covered in full sleeves to her wrists. A scapular fell loose from her shoulders, over her flat chest and down her back. She was girdled with a leather belt and a black string of rosary beads, the Fifteen Mysteries, hung at her side. The sleeves were folded back from her wrists, to prepare the drugs on the counter. But, beneath these full sleeves, and cuffs, were other tighter sleeves and cuffs, buttoned down at her wrist. Her face and her hands were her only exposed skin. Her eyes were black. They shone.

All of her presence came up into those two eyes, peering out of that face. Her skin was creamy, but cinnamon with the sun. Her cheeks were raddled, like rouge. She smiled. Her skin was pulled back by the tight veil. There was nothing to distract from her face, her eyes, except her hands which she wiped on a blue apron. She put her arms away, folding down her sleeves, hiding her hands. She lowered her head as Vincent stood at the bottom of the stairs staring at her. He noticed the slightest wisps of jet black hair escaping from beneath her taut veil near her temples.

He had just recently attended to her as her doctor, lifting her skirts above her ankle. But now, suddenly, he was looking at her differently. Had it been the shared intensity of their earlier experience, finding those abandoned patients?

The afternoon sunlight was a halo behind her. 'Sister?' he exclaimed. She was both holy looking and ravishing.

'Doctor?'

She reached out and touched his hand. She had not done that before. He saw that her eyes were full of tears. Something was the matter. They had not completed their chat about her father and her worries. He had not listened to the news that day. The BBC's World Service was their life line. She was seeking reassurances. 'I'm sorry, no news, not today, Sister.'

She began again. 'So far away. Yet, so close.' She pressed her hands on her heart.

'We must wait for letters.'

'I think news will become even more difficult now than ever to get.'

'We'll see. My brother, Bernard, he's over there. Somewhere in England. My mother has not heard much. We don't know what will happen.'

'Yes, I must not think just of myself.'

'We've got our work. We're lucky,' he said reflectively.

'Yes.'

82

She held onto his left hand. He put his right one over hers. They stood alone in the clinic.

The last couple of weeks had been too intense. He put it down to that.

They both seemed shocked at the same time, as they looked around them, standing alone. 'Here we are,' Vincent said nervously. The realisation of what was afoot in the world was creeping closer, staggering them, as they stood together and looked out of the window and saw the fragile huts, the rusting galvanise roofs of the hospital and the stores down by the jetty. It was a strange encampment.

There was the congregation of patients under the almond tree.

A group of girls were skipping on the verandah. The two holding the rope had one leg each. One balanced herself on the bannister of the verandah, the other held onto the door. The girl who was skipping had no arms below her elbows. Her face was pure joy. She screamed with laughter.

'There's the new girl, Christiana. How pretty she is. How long will it last? You say she's not got the disease.' Sister Thérèse folded her arms away into her sleeves.

Vincent watched the children playing. 'We don't know.'

'I must return to Theo.' Vincent interrupted their meditation. 'Beatrice will want to be leaving.'

'Theo, Lover of God. God has come to live with you, Doctor.'

'Just a boy with a lot of needs.'

Vincent headed for the jetty. He turned. Sister Thérèse was still standing at the door of the clinic. He waved. She waved back.

As the pirogue rounded the point into the next bay, Vincent did not feel his usual elation on arriving home. He had grown fond of the place very quickly. After a day at the hospital, he was more than delighted for the peace of the empty house, the jetty, fishing on his own. The pink and white house wavered and fractured, reflected in the yellow and lilac water. But because Vincent anticipated his meeting with Theo, the house appeared sinister, holding the boy's presence. There was no sign of him or Beatrice.

As they drew close to the jetty, a figure looked out of the upstairs window, quickly vanishing, then reappearing on the verandah downstairs. Vincent waved. But Theo stood and stared without response, then disappeared.

'Okay man, see you tomorrow.'

'Watch yourself, Doc. You sure you don't want me to stay?' Jonah had picked up Vincent's anxiety about the boy.

'No, Jonah. Is fine.'

The two men waved goodbye. Vincent pushed the pirogue away from the jetty.

Theo was not on the verandah, or in the drawing room. The kitchen was cleared from the night before. The wares, pots and pans washed. There was no Beatrice either. 'Beatrice.' There was silence. The house was dead quiet.

The stairs creaked as they always did when he climbed to the bedrooms. Theo's bedroom was empty. Vincent went into his own room and found that the bed had been made. The dressing table had been tidied. The floors had been swept. 'Theo!' he called again. 'Theo!' There was no reply.

As Vincent descended the stairs, he heard a creak, which was not one of the usual creaks, the music of the house, the tune it played as he walked about on the pitch pine floors, its expansions in the heat of the day and the contractions in the cool of evening.

As he stood listening, the sea breeze banged the bathroom window. It unhooked the latch on the kitchen door and entered. It got wild. He had to dash about closing the windows which faced the sea. The waves rose and rushed the small beach at the side of the jetty, sucked back out by the tide.

A percussion of pots and pans falling off the shelves in the kitchen alarmed him. Loose sheets of galvanise banged on the roof. The wind whistled through cracks in doors and windows.

Vincent called, 'Theo,' and listened again to the particular creak near him. It came from under the stairs. When he opened the door, it was dark and smelt of mildew. Vincent could not see anything unusual, at first. But when he bent down, to look into the furthest recesses under the slope of the stairs, he discovered the crouching boy in the gloom. He was bare backed and wore only his short khaki pants. He crouched with his back to Vincent, his head between his legs.

'Theo. Come, boy. You don't want to be sitting in here, alone.' The boy did not move. Vincent touched his bare back and read the same story he had read earlier. 'Come Theo, I can't leave you here. Let's go out and catch some nice sea breeze. What about fishing? We could go on the jetty and fish.'

Theo did not speak, but he allowed the doctor to coax him out of his hiding place into the glare of the verandah, into the astonishment of the setting sun. The wind had died down.

Why had the boy been hiding, when only a moment before he had seen him on the verandah? He wanted the doctor to come and find him, a small child's hide and seek.

That evening Vincent and Theo fished together from the end of the jetty, but the fish were not biting. They only got two *crapeau* fish. They threw them back into the water. But, with a last try, Theo landed a small red fish. As he unhooked his catch, Vincent thought he saw a smile, not quite, but a flicker in the glow of the kerosene lamp.

Vincent made hot cocoa for them both. They went to bed early after fried fish and bake. Sleep seemed the best way out of their wordless communications. The windows at the front of the house facing the bay let in the moonlight.

Vincent woke to the voices as insistent as the sea.

MY EYES get big big. My ears nearly drop off with Mama talk, hot from big house. I on top the bed jumping up and down. Mama brisk brisk, taking off she dress, standing in front the window in she white silky petticoat, Mistress give she. She drop it on the floor. It look like a pool of milk for Curly, the cat, to lap up.

Mama caress she self in panty and brassiere. Mama gaze out the window. Breeze rustle the sapodilla tree. It go quiet. Fowl peck the soft dirt under the window. Now and then, cluck cluck.

Stop that jumping. All the coconut fibre busting out, already. Who go bring mattress for Mama? Who go make feather pillow? Look at the bed. Straighten up the counterpane.

Mama gaze. I look up at she. She gaze out the window. Gaze at the blue hills. The sweet breeze move the curtains.

Mama talking talking all the time, talking, talking, talking.

No one go stop Mister, walking in Esperance. Or, stop Mistress and the children take a train into town from Pond Road Station, to stand on the station and wait for a train in the afternoon.

That is what Mama say. Mama say it like, she is Mister. Like she is Mistress self.

* * *

It was like many voices all at once. Vincent was frightened by the strange lucidity.

AND THEN, Emelda say, No one going come with hoe and spade and big stick to march up into Mister yard. No one going come with iron and rock stone to pelt this house. She raise she self up. Big house on the hill. This is a house that hide secret in turret room. Is a house that have cellar for the best wines bring from Burgundy and Beaujolais. I see the label them. Special room with special aquarium for crab, for the special crab and *callaoo* soup that every Monsieur Marineaux like to suck.

Trouble go come, Emelda say, with a look in she face which say that she know more than Mister. She feel more than Mister. Emelda know more than Mister. All know, all who in the yard, all who meet under Chen shop, that these people who Mister call *niggers* and *coolies* on the march from Fyzabad to San Fernando, go reach town with their noise and demand. They go out do Mr A. A. Cipriani in town which still echo with the 1919 calypso.

Gal, who you voting for?
We don't want Major Rust to make bassa bassa here.
Cipriani
We don't want no Englishman, we want Trinidadian
Cipriani.

One good apple in a rotten barrel. Captain A. A.! Mister say he gone England and come back with Labourite ideology. Now he walk barefoot with *coolie* and *nigger*. He own people self watch him, and know that this kind of thing dangerous. Even if they feel is from inside their own house he come out. They have him down as a mad man.

Like they have Butler down like a mad man too.

But they bound to think he mad. Buzz!

Mama boy read the news, cut out the picture and writing from *The Gazette*.

Mama, you see Butler! They take out he picture in San Fernando band-stand, Harris Promenade. She boy read like an Exhibition Class boy, who never go in San Fernando, or move from Pepper Hill self, but plenty time get a promise to go town to ride tram and trolley bus.

Child what nonsense you reading, and messing up the house with all this cut up newspaper? Is that they does teach you in Exhibition Class?

All the time Mama talk, she look over her shoulder and pretend to read the news. Mama can't read.

'Theo. Stop now.' The boy was in a sweat, as if wakened from a fevered sleep, thrashing around, gesticulating, inhabiting now this voice, now that, himself a character in his own story. Vincent understood Father Dominic using exorcism. But of course it had not worked. How could it?

'Come, Theo, let's get you to bed.'

The fluency of this night-time tale, this calypso, as the boy had called it in the nights before, was as if it were written down. Indeed, it did go here and there and then come back to the main road, as Father Dominic had said it would.

What was the drama between Mister and the boy's Mama? How had he imbided the Labour riots of the last few years so clearly? Butler and Cipriani, political figures entered as principal players of his drama. Vincent marvelled at this orchestration of voices, this recall, this living history.

But the engine which drove this story was fuelled by something else. Why was he so full of it? Why was he mute in the day, talkative at night? For Theo, to come again tonight, and perch at the end of his bed, startled Vincent.

Early the next morning, the fishermen came close into the bay. Vincent heard them under his window, with bottle and spoon, and hoarse rum-stricken voices, reach their *do re me* with:

'What does the Austrian corporal expect to do
His plan for invasion must eventually
End in the ruin and destruction of Germany.'

Versailles

'You feel time could stay so sweet, Doc?' Jonah asked, beaming. The sweet season of Christmas, with its soft breezes, brought 1938 to an end. Jonah strummed his cuatro, playing *parang*. '*Maria Maria Maria, Maria Magdalena.*'

Singh and Vincent joined in with their own more raucous song. '*Drink a rum and a puncha creama, drink a rum, on a Christmas morning,*' beating bottle and spoon, trying to sink their differences with the spirit of the season and the rum.

From Saint Damian's came the sound of bamboo bussing. 'Young fellas having a good time,' Singh relished the cannon shots echoing across Chac Chac Bay.

They all wondered if time could stay so sweet.

Across the gulf, the ships in the harbour off Porta España blew their hooters and sirens, announcing the New Year of 1939. They could hear the oil tankers as far down south as Pointe-à-Pierre. Vincent called for a toast. He, Jonah and Singh drank in the New Year, Jonah sprinkling a libation of rum on the ground for the ancestral spirits, before filling their glasses. 'You have to remember those who gone before.'

Singh called out, 'Theo, come boy, come and have a nip for the New Year.' The boy sat unmoving at the end of the jetty. He did not know Singh like he knew Jonah.

Vincent rested his hand on Singh's arm, restraining his invitation to the boy. 'He'll come in his own time.'

'Is the rum, Doctor,' Singh explained.

The men drank and talked, while the boy stayed out till well past midnight, watching the flares from the fireworks in the Porta España harbour.

Let the boy have his freedom, Vincent thought. He wished for new things for him in this new year. He had not as yet opened his present. Remembering his own childhood, Vincent was playing daddy. He wished the boy had opened it, to find the new fishing rod. But he had left it, from a week ago, at the bottom of his bed, still wrapped in the red crepe paper.

Across the bay, the convent lights were on for midnight-mass. Sister Thérèse was again in Vincent's thoughts, her hand on his, his on hers.

'Things looking peaceful and happy tonight, eh! But it not going to stay so, for long,' Singh said. The light was the colour of the rum they were drinking.

'I feel so too.' Jonah joined in, pouring himself another drink and striding out onto the verandah. His shadow filled the walls as he moved, a kind of colossus, overwhelming and enveloping them in his open arms, as he spoke and declaimed, 'I feel so too! I feel so too! It not going to stay so. It can't stay so, when the things that going on, going on.'

Vincent listened to the two men, who had been at Saint Damian's longer than himself and had a closer feel for the patients, when they were not being respectful to *Docta*.

The three men were a map and a history of these islands. But, they could not be described just by their ancestry. They were who they were in them-selves. Despite all the sympathy for his patients, his socialism, his member-ship of the Fabian Society when he was a student, Vincent wondered at times how Jonah, and particularly Singh, who had already voiced his distrust, viewed him. How did they see these colonial divisions, these histories of skin? He wondered whether they thought he belonged here. His family went back to 1840 on the island.

On returning from university, he had not re-entered the world of the cocoa hills, the houses with the turret rooms, among the tall teak and the *immortelle*. He had not been down to the Union Club, on Porta España's Plaza de La Marina, with the sons of the white, linen-suited planters, stand-ing on the balcony above the square, looking down onto the promenade, eye-ing up the young mulatto girls strolling down Almond Walk under their parasols.

He was not going to the Country Club, the old de Boissiere estate house, Elyseé, a heaven in the imaginations of its founders, on Saturday nights to drink and dance, or play tennis in the afternoons. No, he had not dropped in at Casuals and Tranquillity, or the Sainte Claire Club, on the Maraval, for the *fêtes* and balls.

'How you going to meet a nice young girl, darling?' his mother would ask with prayers in her eyes, with rosary beads entangling her fingers, with novenas in her thoughts, and whispered ejaculations to Saint Jude, or whoever was the patron saint of pure love and marriage for hopeless cases. 'You know is better to come home and find one of our own girls from one of the good families, than come home with an English girl, not knowing what kind of people she has come from,' was how his mother had put it in letters received by him in London.

When he visited her, on his days off now from his work at Saint Damian's, she invariably had some suggestion, some Chantal or Nicole, some little Corsican butterfly, who had just disembarked from a ship of the French Line and fluttered ashore, back from finishing school in France; some countess even, from the Parisian cousins; some de Noirmont, some de Pompignon, some d'Origny, some Boisluisant, some Lahens.

His mother had a list. Increasingly, he did not go to Porta España, or up to the house at Versailles, on his days off, to have lunch, to meet aunts who smelt of *vertivert* and held his chin in their arthritic fingers, as if he were a boy of twelve, and been naughty for staying away so long. 'Vincent, *le petit garçon.*'

After a priest in the family, he was the next best thing, a doctor. If not the consecrated fingers to bring Christ down upon their altars, at least a physician, to keep them in good health, to do some good for *these* people. They were always referred to in that way, *these* people, separate, and ultimately unsaveable, kind of diseased.

The look in his aunts' eyes, when he talked about Saint Damian's, was of thoughts that one day he would be canonised, become Saint Damian himself. 'Don't know how you do it, Vincent,' they would say. 'But, darling boy, for how long? Surely soon, you'll want a practice of your own?'

They leapt ahead. His whole life was planned out on the verandah before lunch. 'Come, come now darling have some nice *callaloo* and crab.'

'We can work together, Doc.' Jonah drew Vincent from his reverie. 'Singh, what you say, boy?' Jonah was the optimist.

'I say it depend on we working together. That's where the hope of the people rest. But...'

'But, what Singh? What you mean, but?' Jonah interrupted.

'Wait nuh, man, let me talk. I know where *I* stand.'

'What? Like you don't know where we stand?'

'Who is we, Jonah?' Singh came back.

'We, you and me and the doctor. Doc, what you say?'

Vincent winked at Jonah. Still there was tension between him and Singh.

'Jonah, you and me come out of a village.' Singh continued. 'I see you. I definitely see you. And you, you see an Indian boy. You know me? I think so. But the doctor here?'

'Singh?' Vincent questioned Singh's tone.

'Let me finish, Doctor Metivier.'

Vincent sipped his rum and walked to the edge of the verandah and stared at Theo at the end of the jetty. What would the new year bring for the boy?

He turned back to listen to Singh. The rum was going to their heads. But, Singh was right.

There had been one or two Indian fellas and negro boys, like his *pardner* Jean la Borde from Arima, who boarded across the road from the college, before Vincent went away. Unlike Bernard, his brother, he had close friends among them. But, in the afternoons after school, they went their different ways home, into different kinds of homes. He saw the houses on the side of roads, down in a gully, perched on a hillock, when he passed in his father's car. They lived in barrack rooms on the estate board houses, which were skeletons of their hoped-for selves, ribs of wood through which he caught glimpses of interiors, shadows of the people of the house, with the light leaking through at night from the kerosene lamps. They were half-finished houses, for lives which, he now began to feel, were half-lived lives. But who was he to say? They might be full lives, lived against all odds! Maybe he had lived half a life.

These men had emerged from these houses. Their journey to their ideas had started there. They had responded to a politics forged in the fire of poverty and history. They had been nurtured in that university of hunger, as Singh liked to lecture. They had gone on the hunger marches out of the cane fields and oil fields, from South to North.

Now, in this work here, there was an acceptance of him, because he was a doctor. He had something crucial to offer. But he could not do his job without them. An unconscious alliance of sorts was being formed. Though they were also suspicious, particularly Singh. Doctor Escalier had been the villain in the past. They did not automatically trust a doctor.

So, as the rum worked, the talk got better between the three men.

'Singh, how you get into this business boy?' Vincent was more relaxed. Singh, normally reticent in conversation, saving his words for the platform under the almond tree, got up and walked out to the edge of the verandah.

'How you mean, Doctor?' He spoke with his back to the two other men, looking into the darkness and the flicker of the *flambeau* next to Theo fishing on the jetty.

They listened to the sea breathing.

'Well, I know very little about you,' Vincent answered.

Singh turned back, looked at Jonah and Vincent and laughed. 'You want to hear story? Jonah is the one with the stories. He have big history and thing from his grandfather and grandmother, who was a big *Shango* woman in Moruga. His father was a stick fighter in the *gayelle*. That was his arena.'

'Don't worry with he, Doc. He have story. Singh know well the story that driving him. Tell him the story, nah, man. The white man need to hear this story.' Jonah laughed and winked at Singh, and then looked at Vincent, with his smile.

The rum was working. It was Old Year's night. Vincent, again, noticed the hunched back of Theo on the jetty, intent upon his fishing. The *flambeau* bowed in the breeze.

The nuns' Compline chants came across the silent waters of the bay. Their sombre night prayers were accompanied by the antiphons of the waves. The face of Sister Thérèse, cocooned in white, was there in Vincent's mind.

'This island is full of stories.' Vincent lit a cigarette. 'Now is a night for ghost stories.'

'Not them kind of story Doc, not them kind of story, not the story about the nun who make baby with a fisherman and then drown she self. They say they does see she walking on the jetty at La Chapelle Bay, crying for she baby. Not them kind of story. Is not ghost, Doc. Is spirits. Yes, is spirits, *oui*. Hmm! Take another drink, Doc.' Jonah handed the rum bottle to Vincent. 'Tell him, Singh. Tell him the story of how your grandfather reach all the way here into them barrack room. Right up so, in Golconda on the way to Barackpore. How he reach there. How you come out of there. Tell him that story.'

'The doctor know them kind of thing already, Jonah. What you talking about tonight? Like the rum really get inside your head tonight, boy. You want me to tell this story, so that you could tell them story about Africa.'

'I go tell my story when I ready. Is your turn. Talk, man. I don't need you to tell the doctor anything, so I could talk about Africa. When you look out across the Atlantic ocean, you not meeting any land till you reach Africa. You know that, you know that, man.' Jonah knocked back his nip of rum. 'Africa!'

Vincent turned to Singh. 'In one way, I know the story Singh, but in another way, I know nothing.' Vincent looked at Singh intently as he said this. Then he winked at Jonah.

'You never wonder about the people in the barrack room on your father estate?'

'Of course I have. But. You know...'

'But what? You watch from the outside. You sit at at your table and you hear man beating woman. You hear baby cry. You hear someone get chop with a cutlass. Man beat he wife, he chop she and she bawl. You hear that? You is a child. Them is noise, noise you can't properly understand, but it terrify you. It terrify you, what you hear coming out of the one room barrack room in the gully below the white bungalow, with the palms swaying with its plumes. Royal palms! Hmm! Royal palms! I watch that dream from inside the barrack room. I watch you. I watch all you good.'

'You hear the story, Doc. Now he telling story. Take a next another rum, nuh, Singh? It go sweeten you mouth.'

'Doctor, don't worry with Jonah, nuh. Tell your story Jonah.'

'Man, you only now start. You not even start.' Jonah laughed.

'I want to hear it as you tell it Singh. Take a smoke,' Vincent encouraged.

Singh smiled. The rising anger and mockery slipped from his tone now. 'It start in Calcutta. It end in Golconda. See how they call the place, making an India of *Chinitat*. It cross the *kalapani*.'

'*Chinintat, kalapani*?' Jonah echoed and beamed. 'You hear words boss! That is words, pappy! Is how he does mix them medécine.'

'Is so the ancestors first pronounce Trinidad. They cross the Black Water, the passage from Calcutta. Right so, 'Singh pointed to the Boca Grande, 'We would've see she, the Fatel Rozack, coming through the Boca Grande, in the early morning.' Then Singh pointed across the bay into the gulf. 'Nelson Island, where them Jews in quarantine now, is there self, they drop the first load from Calcutta. Disinfect, delouse, this lot for Reform, that one for

Retrench, another lot for Harmony Hall, hear the name. That one for this sugar estate, this one for the other, and so on. Right on these little islands, these things happen.'

'You hear music, Doc. Hear that with a *tassa* drum coming out of Caroni. All of we have a calypso to sing. Indian have a calypso to sing.'

'Jonah, you *mamaguying* me, boy. You making joke of me,' Singh complained.

'Come, Singh, tell your story, don't bother with Jonah.' Vincent was getting into the spirit of the men. Of course, they were all fuelled by the spirit of the bottle.

Jonah walked off the verandah down to the jetty and stood behind Theo, watching him fish. He knelt next to the boy and leant over and gave a little tug to the line. Singh and Vincent watched from the edge of the verandah. Jonah called up to them, 'Red fish biting, red fish biting good.'

'It mean something to me what I hear my father and my grandfather say. The way they tell we coming. The way we tell our arrival.' Singh drew on his cigarette, inhaled deeply, and then blew the smoke slowly into the air.

'Sure. I understand that.' Vincent leaned towards him, lighting another cigarette.

'Yes, I believe you.' Singh softened with his own story. 'You and me here. But our people...'

'Our people?'

'White people, East Indian people.'

'Yes?'

'We looking at each other. We just looking at each other.'

'History delivered us here. The British Empire put us here together.' Vincent was deeply involved.

'Yes, Jonah people and my people, and we meet your people here. The first ones, they done kill out. You does only hear them in the language the parrots speaking,' Singh laughed.

'That's true,' Vincent agreed.

'But, I mean it don't have to stay so. Take you and me. Why you here, Doctor? Why I here?'

'Medécine.'

'Come. We don't have to practice our respective skills here. You know that.'

'Leprosy. The challenge, the interest,' Vincent added.

'Yes, of course. But I watch you. Is more.'

'My patients,' Vincent asserted.

'People. They part of something bigger than themselves. They're at the extremity of their own people. Shunned by their own.'

Vincent watched Singh. He saw him in a new light. He began to understand the man.

'So, you and I here Old Year's Night talking. An Indian and a French Creole. You not over there and I over here. We here.' Singh reached out and put his hand on Vincent's arm. 'And Jonah, the black man. He not over there. He here. We three. That have to make a difference to the people, than if we apart, if we continue watching each other from afar.'

Vincent was following intently, pulling on his cigarette.

'It make a difference for us, but above all it go make a difference for people. If, when we speak, we speak for all people. For the humanity of all people.'

Jonah had climbed the steps from the jetty. 'That boy can fish, *oui!* Red fish, biting yes. How he coming on, that boy? He talking yet, Doc?'

'He catching fish? No, not yet. He talks and then he doesn't talk.'

'Catching, for so! He already have three red snapper and some carite. We talking, he fishing.' Jonah walked over to the table with the drinks. 'Like you need to bring a next bottle, Doc.'

'You know Doctor, the story Jonah want me to tell you is our history. You have yours, and sure as hell Jonah have his. He go get into that. Them is good stories and we go have to keep on telling them because that is how we reach here. But now, you and me on this jetty, right now, and Jonah there. Our patients with their big big needs, and we have to ask ourselves what we going to do about that. Is not we, is them.'

'You tell him the story yet, Singh?'

Singh did not pay attention to Jonah.

'Now that Escalier gone, we have a chance. I see you pressing the Mother Superior.' Singh was looking intently at Vincent.

'I'm doing what I can.'

'Sure.' Singh lit another cigarette, slipping his fingers into Vincent's pack on the arm of the Morris chair. He was intense, his white cotton shirt tight on his arms. His thin moustache and a wisp of a beard made him look older than he was, a young man of twenty-five. An earnest man. Vincent now saw his sensitivity, as he had before noticed his fastidiousness. 'I determine we go see this thing turn out good. But there might be some hard things too.'

'But Mother Superior catch between what she must see as the devil and the deep blue sea.'

'Who's the devil, Doc?' Jonah laughed.

'Well, let's take the devil to be the Colonial Office,' Vincent argued.

'We is the deep blue sea, then? That okay with me,' Jonah boasted.

'You see, on the medical side, these Chaulmoogra Oil injections have to stop. They not doing any good. Not in the long run, anyway. They have more side effects than people want to admit.' Singh lectured the two men now.

'I agree,' said Vincent. 'You know the position.'

'The position is, that they don't want to spend money on the new Sulfa drugs which they could import.'

'Escalier love to give people them injection, three hundred a week, yes. Poor people,' Jonah threw in.

Singh continued, 'There's the business of accommodation. Men must be able to visit the women, have relationships. Married men must be able to live with their wives. We'll have to work out what we do with the children. There are different theories about this infection thing, you know. Different theories about contagion.'

'Krishna,' Vincent used Singh's first name now. 'Krishna. You know I lectured about these very same things. You were there. Where is the big difference between us?'

'You see Doc, these things gone from bad to worse before you reach,' Jonah contributed. 'They making the people work for nothing, a few cents a day. I mean to say! They sick for one, and then they have to keep the place going for nothing. I don't blame the nuns them, in a way. They in a fix too because the Colonial Office getting them on the cheap. The Governor say, call on the nuns. It suit them. They capitalising on their good will, their vocation as nursing nuns. But in the end, they does side with the authorities, rather than with the people, when it come to the crunch.'

'Is so the church is. They'll go with the government, against the people, when it come to it,' Singh added.

'What you mean, come to it?' Vincent asked tentatively.

Jonah and Singh looked at each other. Then Singh spoke. 'They can't blame the people if they take things into their own hands, you know.'

'What do you mean, into their own hands? They're not capable...'

Singh cut Vincent off. 'They capable alright. Don't underestimate the spirit in these people. You must know that, Dr Metivier. You must know. Anyway, Jonah, we must get back. We go have to leave you. Happy New Year. And, take care of this boy. How you come to look after this boy?'

Theo was, just at that moment, coming up from the jetty with his catch.

Jonah was as friendly as ever. 'Boy you catch fish for so. You and Doc, go have a New Year feast.'

Theo remained mute and passed them on his way into the kitchen only with a quick glance at Jonah.

'Ei, boy, you ent see me?' Singh tried again. 'Send him by me, Doctor, I go give him a little training in science.'

Theo turned for an instant at the kitchen door and took in Singh on the verandah, in the dim glow of the kerosene lantern. The men did not understand the look on the boy's face. They looked at each other when he had passed into the kitchen. They smiled at each other.

'Like you have your work cut out, Doctor,' Singh said. He and Jonah looked at each other again. 'That boy don't have mother and father?'

'Mother, yes, the father is a mystery,' Vincent said.

'Mystery? There's never any mystery about fathers. They does just get up so and go.' Singh watched Jonah.

'Boy, why you watching me so? I does go and see after my children. Is up here I get a work, but I does carry them things. I does carry their mother things,' Jonah argued.

'Come boy, let we go. I only giving you *fatigue*. The doctor want to sleep. Put that child to sleep. You sure you not pulling a fast one on us, Doctor?' Singh would not leave the subject of Theo alone. 'You past catching up with you?'

'Singh boy, what you telling the doctor?'

Vincent laughed. 'Come, all you need to go.'

'We go see you, Doc. A happy New Year to you, Doc.' The three men shook hands, and then Jonah and Singh went down to the jetty and rowed away.

Theo went up to bed. 'Goodnight, Theo. A happy New Year.'

There was a faint reply. 'Happy New Year, Doctor Metivier. Thanks for the present.' The reply startled Vincent.

'My pleasure, Theo.' Vincent had one last drink on his own at the end of the verandah.

Out in the gulf, the kerosene lamps of the fishermen were a constellation. There was one in particular winking at him, right in line with the Boca Grande, Vincent thought, as he stood and stared and lost himself in what seemed like signals being transmitted to him personally, a kind of Morse. He did not have the code to decipher them.   .

It reminded him of how, as a young boy, he would sit on the verandah of the Versailles Estate house and stare at the fireflies out on the pasture, wondering at their signals. Matches being struck in the darkness. Candleflies. He did not know then what they meant. Though, he remembered desiring a message, an answer to something. He and Bernard went out and caught the pulsing insects between their fingers and put them in a glass jar. They winked and winked, green light, codes at the nerve end of their fingers. Each pulse had a message.

The Versailles house rose before him now, out of the pasture and above the wide saman trees near the low cocoa houses. It rose to be as high as the palmistes where its turrets and topmost balconies reached the great flowering of the plumes from the heart of the swaying palms. He remembered now that behind the house, where there were always some goats tethered on long chains, was his favourite guava tree. You had to jump from one soft grass patch to another, in this part of the pasture, because of the *Ti-Marie,* soft name for the mauve mimosa which grew close to the ground with her thorns and leaves, which closed to their touch. He could smell the guavas when they burst open on the ground, yellow with ripeness, sticky with their pink flesh and seeds.

It was the green guavas they liked best, Odetta and himself. The ripe ones were collected for his mother to make guava jelly; peeled and boiled with sugar, the pulp squeezed and strained through a thin gauze for the syrup to boil and thicken for her jelly. It became a clear glaze of crimson held in the small globes, which she then let drop into a saucer of water to test with her fingers, rolling the syrup into a ball, her touch testing whether it had formed to the consistency that she wanted. Then the warm syrup was poured into jam jars, stood on the windowsill to cool in tins of water to ward off the ants. The crimson glaze caught the morning light. The stained muslin was rinsed and hung out on the line in the sun.

He counted the ants crawling back and forth along the windowsill.

His father was in the war.

Odetta and himself loved to climb the trees for the green guavas. She was Sybil's daughter. She climbed the smooth guava trees in a white cotton chemise. He could see her brown legs and more, as she shinnied up the smooth trunk, gripping with her knees. When she was much smaller, she called him to come and peep at the spider between her legs. Then, he was frightened. He was always bare backed out on the estate. Just in his short khaki pants. Running about bare-foot. His mother said that he was getting to look like a *coolie* boy. 'Playing with Odetta again,' his mother's voice followed him.

Odetta hammocked the guavas that they had picked in the skirt of her chemise, stretched between her knees. She held them there, securely, in a bundle, between her legs. They climbed the stairs fast to the top turret, bursting into the room, where the breeze whistled and from where they could see the world, or at least the gulf, the Golfo de La Ballena. 'You see a whale?' He remembered pointing out of the turret for her to see. She did not believe him. Odetta emptied out the green guavas onto the floor. A balcony ran all the way round the outside of this small room, the walls panelled with jalousies. It was empty except for a hammock. And the floor was bare, plain, scrubbed, white pitch pine.

The fishermen had stopped signalling. Maybe, they were on their way home after their catch, could be even Jonah by now. He used to meet up with some fellas from the Carenage where they went to meet women, *Dorothy went and bathe...* Caresser's words caressed the night.

Then that thought left him and the others returned. Vincent listened out. The boy was still sleeping.

The white, scrubbed, pitch pine floors, the empty room, the hammock, the afternoons, disappeared when he and Odetta climbed into the turret room with their horde of guavas. 'Don't get belly ache,' was what Sybil her mother used to shout up to them, when she saw the children climbing the stairs furtively. But what he remembered more, now, were his mother's words: 'You still playing with that girl, Vincent? You too big now,' when he was older, after Confirmation Class. But his lips were already sore. They were almost blistered, with his kissing. Odetta's were red with the blood that rose and pulsed. Blistered lips and bruised knees, from rubbing on the bare floor! He could not stop, once she had let him kneel over her, pulling her cotton chemise over her head and showing him. 'Let me show you,' were her words, soft, almost unspoken, peeping from behind the raised hem of her soft cotton chemise. The light through the jalousies sliced her with its lances. What did she show him? Her small breasts, pinky, puckered and brown. He wondered how they appeared to rise out of her, his, small brown sunburnt nipples, flat and tight, hers to fit the palms of his hands, small round sapodillas. He held them. She left the rest to him. There were no words yet, only smells and taste. Later, it surprised him how he needed his handkerchief. She watched him wipe the *break* from his khaki pants. It smelled like the jelly of kimeet fruit, leaving a stain like starch. She watched him wipe himself. In the silence, he watched the woodlice eat away at the floorboards.

They did not talk then, nor afterwards, when they left the turret room. Those ceremonies were left to the turret room, among the scratching palms, up in the indigo sky. Quiet like confession. It was a time when innocence and experience did not jar, when one fed the other in an idyll, till his mother's voice, speaking to Sybil, sounded a voice of caution and warning. 'Sybil, I think that child is too big to be playing with Master Vincent.'

Afternoons! Afternoons and scratching palms! Hot afternoons and the smell of guavas! The pastures rolled away to where the khaki river chuckled under the cocoa. They ran down by the river to bathe and let Sybil catch them in her brown arms in the green light. The great shadows of the saman trees on the pasture moved like great clouds over the grass as the branches swayed in vast undulations in the breeze.

Vincent left the verandah and the sea and went to bed. What thoughts to be having now, at this hour! Odetta? Where was Odetta now? He had not even thought to go and look for her when he came back from England.

The following morning, Jonah arrived in a sombre mood. He was earlier than usual. 'They need you quick, Doc,' he shouted up from the jetty.

Vincent did not inquire why immediately. He shouted up to Theo. 'Tell Beatrice I had to leave in a hurry. Take care of yourself.'

On the journey over, Jonah told him that a body had been washed ashore. 'Two fishermen coming in early this morning, notice it. Nearly run it over in their pirogue. They think is one of them big *gommier* logs that does float out and get bring back in by the tide. When they get close they see is a man body. When I leave they still have the body on the beach. Fish start to feed on it. Must've be in the water since last night. Lucky them sharks and barracuda didn't get to it. Tide low at the moment, current not running, so it not get take out into the gulf. Policeman come and ask question.'

'Any idea who it is? Is it one of the patients?'

'Must be, Doc. You know them young fellas. Is the same problem we talking about. Nothing go stop them trying to swim the bay at night to get to the women huts.'

'They'll be a lot of sadness today.'

'Yes, Doc. For sure.'

Jonah kept his hand on the tiller, one eye ahead. He listened intently. He slackened his hold on the throttle.

When they pulled into the jetty, they could see a crowd collecting on the beach a little way off. 'Jonah, I'm going down there right away.'

Already the recriminations had started. 'See Doctor, see what they do the young fella!' The body was that of Sonny Lal, a young man who lived up in Indian Valley. His girlfriend lived in the huts along the shore in Sanda's Bay. The quarantine had kept them apart. But Sonny had found a way, like many of the other men in the past, to swim the length of the bay at night to see Leela.

It was Leela who knelt next to Vincent now, as he inspected the body. She cried quietly, moaning and repeating the name of her lover and the father of her child. 'Oh God, Sonny, Sonny, Sonny, look what they make you do. Kill your self. For me, Sonny.'

Vincent put his arm around Leela's shoulder. 'Come girl. He's not here anymore.'

'Oh God, doctor,' the young girl cried.

'Yes, come, we must see that this never happens again.'

Vincent accompanied the men who lifted Sonny Lal's body to take it to the mortuary room. At the bottom of the steps, he met with Singh and Jonah. Vincent left the procession to talk to the two men.

'This have to stop, Doctor.' Singh could hardly suppress his anger.

'I know the problem, Singh. But not now. Leela needs our comfort at this moment. Let us deal with it later.'

'Later. When is later?'

'He right, Doc,' Jonah argued.

'I have a job to do now.'

'We know how he die, Doctor.'

'There are procedures, Singh.'

'Fock procedures!'

'Come, Singh. Come man. We go deal with this later.' Jonah put his arm around Singh's shoulder and led him off.

Vincent felt himself torn between his duty as a doctor, as a comforter of Leela, and as one who wanted something done about the reasons this tragedy had happened. As he left Leela, in the arms of other women who had accompanied her from the huts that morning, he went back to a moment at Versailles when he was a boy, when he and Odetta watched a young man taken down from a mango tree, who had hanged himself. 'He hang himself for *tabanca*,' he heard a man from the yard tell his father. 'He hang himself because of the love of a woman.' Sonny had not hung himself, had not taken his life in that kind of way, but had risked and lost, and proved to Leela that she meant all that he loved. Vincent had wondered, looking at the hanged man, whether he himself loved Odetta in that way.

As he turned on the steps to tell Leela that he would come and see her later, he saw Sister Thérèse crossing the yard towards the mortuary. She was coming to assist him. He waved. She waved back.

He remembered that they called that place near Versailles, with its avenue of mango trees, Hangman Alley.

At three o'clock that afternoon, a crowd descended from the hills to collect under the almond tree. They began to shuffle on quietly, everyone in their own thoughts, along the paths, down to the beach where the Hindu Pandit and his assistants were performing their *pujahs* and reciting their mantras, as the body of Sonny Lal was laid on top of the pyre which had been built earlier that day. Then, at the appointed moment, the wood was lit. Leela, the young pregnant girl, whom Sonny Lal had died in his efforts to reach by swimming across the bay, circled the burning body, feeding the flames with *ghee* butter. All stood quietly and watched the fire consume the pyre with its load.

White egrets settled on the nearby mangrove. Then suddenly, unsettled, they ascended in their flight across the bay. ' Watch he soul, fly away,' one of the old women cried quietly, confirming the belief of many.

Pyre

The sun rose raw and burning into a vault of blue emptiness. The dry season had the island in its tight grip this morning. The bush near the house ticked. The *cigales'* screaming decibels reached out into the blue nothing. The sea in the bay lay flat and blistered. Vincent shut his eyes against the burning glare. His fear this morning was bush fires, that they might leap the yard's perimeter and attack the house.

Jonah had not yet arrived. The bay was deserted. There was no Beatrice with breakfast.

The news on the BBC was that Germany had invaded the rest of Czechoslovakia. 'Where this going to end, Theo?' Vincent asked, trying to engage the boy. There was no answer. Theo pressed his ear close to the radio to receive the news through the crackles and humming. He was getting an education in geography and contemporary history. He had found an old atlas under the stairs and had been busy drawing and tracing maps. This absorbed him more than anything else now.

Without Jonah, Vincent decided that he would get to Saint Damian's along the track which ran behind the house into the hills. In the dry season it would be clear of bush. 'Come Theo, hurry boy.' Vincent had packed some bread and cheese to eat on the way.

The pouis and *immortelle* ignited the hills, the yellow and orange petals covered the paths with flame.

As they neared Saint Damian's, they could see the old people on crutches leaning on each others' shoulders, descending from the huts below them. There were far more people up and about than usual. Vincent wondered what was afoot.

When his patients saw him, they called out, 'Good morning, Docta. God bless you, Docta.'

Others put out their hands to touch Theo. 'The boy nice, eh?' Theo pulled away and walked ahead.

The warmth of his patients always moved Vincent. He admired their endurance. 'It's okay, Theo. They're just being friendly.'

'What happening? So many people out so early?' Vincent inquired of one of the women.

'Young fellas knock us up, moving about quick, quick. They telling people to come. I myself, not get some green tea to drink this morning.'

'Thank you, Mistress Maude.'

'You remember my name, then, Docta?'

'Of course I do.'

'The other docta don't remember my name, you know? I could be anyone. With my face changing so, who could blame people.'

'We'll fix that soon. How is the burn on your leg?'

'I taking good care of it, Docta. This morning self I going by the surgery to get the dressing change.'

'You do that, Mistress Maude. Excuse me now.'

'God bless you, Docta.'

Would Sister Thérèse have got the news about the invasion of Czechoslovakia? Probably not, Vincent thought.

He was late for his clinic.

Seeing his patients like this, as they were this morning, in their masses, he almost despaired. There were over two hundred in the leprosarium now. They were always there to meet him, at the opening of the surgery; more in need of a kind word than a remedy. What real remedies were there anyway?

But today, it was different. He could not figure out what had happened to create all of this confusion. 'Theo, wait for me.'

There was a noise like rain coming down from the hills, like a river flowing over rocks, pelting down. The noise was like gargling drains in the wet season. But this was not rain in the hills.

The sky was a tight blue drum.

Vincent could see people coming down from Indian Valley, the place they called Fyzabad.

They had reached the lower huts on their descent. Here as well, everybody seemed to be out at the same time, and marching with the same intent. From out of the other valley, beneath Cabresse Hill, more patients were emerging out of the crowded huts; one room barrack rooms, housing at least twenty patients each. This had to change; the discussion with Singh and Jonah on Old Year's Night was going through Vincent's mind.

Young boys dragged each other along on pieces of rusty galvanise. Some pulled the aged and infirm in box carts. Their grating on the dirt tracks added to the great noise of their arrival at the meeting place under the large, shady almond tree outside the stores, where people were protecting themselves from the hot sun.

Already the boys and girls were hanging out on the verandahs in front of the children's wards, mimicking the marching cries of their elders, 'Justice and Bread!' Their singing soared in their high, shrill, children's voices.

A group of fellas called out to Vincent as they passed him. 'You with us, Docta?'

'Look, the Docta boy,' some of the girls called out who had met Theo in school.

Patients from the hills who had not seen Theo before asked, 'Is your son, Docta?' He drew close to Vincent, away from the outstretched claw hands trying to touch him on his arm, take his hand.

When they arrived at the almond tree they saw Singh, standing on a box. 'We demanding Justice and Bread, brothers and sisters,' he proclaimed.

It seemed that nearly all two hundred patients were shouting, 'Give us justice and bread.'

Others shouted, 'Give us fair wages.'

Vincent, with Theo holding his hand tightly, could see that Jonah was on a box as well. What was going on? Why had they not told him about this? Questions boiled up in him.

Singh and Jonah were both leading this grand meeting. But Vincent could see that it was Jonah who was the real leader of this crowd, towering above everyone else.

Singh lit the fires with his persistent and unrelenting argument. He had the contacts with the young fellas who had rallied everyone this morning. He had the detail. Jonah had the vision.

It was then that Vincent saw and heard Ti-Jean hanging over the banister of the boys' verandah and crying out, 'Docta, Docta, you see Jonah! You see Jonah!'

Behind Ti-Jean were the small community of nursing sisters as if they were standing for a formal photograph, or before a firing squad. They were unrecognisable from each other. Sister Thérèse was lost in the anonymity of her community.

Then, like the sound of Hosay, a Muslim group had started up the beating of the *tassa* drums. Suddenly, the place was electrified as people picked up anything that they could find. They beat anything: wood on galvanise, stones on dustbin covers, old pans filled with gravel. They made an orchestra out of the refuse and decay strewn around the yard. They made a music of protest, a symphony of demand.

Vincent did not know where to stand, where to take up his position. This crowd on the move was like wildfire in the cane fields, like bush fire in the hills, this dry season. 'Theo, stay close to me. Eat this bread and cheese.'

Suddenly, a hot wind swirled through the yard tearing into the roofs, almost ripping them off. The sea pounded the shore. 'This is a sign,' an old woman standing by Vincent keened. 'Docta,' she pulled on Vincent's sleeve, from where she was crouching, brought low by one of her amputated legs.

Vincent stooped down to her height. 'This is something, yes,' he agreed. A few had parasols, protecting them from the relentless sun. The hot wind tugged at the fragile frills. The drumming and the chanting came from the crowd collecting under the almond tree. Theo held onto Vincent.

This whole scheme of Singh's had jumped ahead without Vincent realising. His head was buried in his research, his responsibility for Theo and, he had to admit, with Sister Thérèse. But now, he had to talk to Singh and Jonah. How could they be encouraging this without consulting him?

The wind was tearing into the crown of the coconut palms. It was twisting them and then letting them go in a furious flurry. The wind ripped the palms to tatters.

The crowd under the almond tree were attentive to the speeches. Singh was talking to small groups now, going around from one to the other. They were mostly men, but there were some women. They were a mixed group of negro and Indian. Vincent could see that Jonah was also working the crowd.

He joined them and was greeted warmly. He was their doctor. He was the one who could help them. He would cure them. This would not cure them, Vincent thought. Their hope overwhelmed him. He could see that they knew that there was something that Singh was telling them. He could tell from the talk, that they wanted him to join them in their demands.

'You can see what we saying, eh, Docta?' they chorused.

'I know what you saying.'

'So, you with us, Docta?'

'I with you, of course, I with you,' Vincent said easily, moving further into the crowd, careful to pull Theo along into a clearing within. Then he felt scared by what he had just said, so easily, shaking hands, touching heads. 'I with you.'

He lost Theo for a moment. Then the boy grabbed his hand again.

'The docta with us,' Anetta Pleasant shouted to those around her, as Vincent made his way through the crowd.

He noticed that a small dais from the schoolroom had been set up near the trunk of the almond tree. Some of the women were hanging ragged bits of red cloth to the low branches. A table with three chairs had been placed on the small dais. Above it, hanging between the branches, was a banner. The words bled the red of sorrel. BREAD and JUSTICE, it proclaimed. Singh mounted the dais. 'Comrades!

He had gone beyond what they had talked about on Old Year's Night. Vincent felt he had to see him before the meeting got out of control. He had to protect his patients. It would be so easy to rouse them. And he had wanted to take up Singh's suggestion to leave Theo with him at his pharmacy. How could he do that now?

Vincent was struck by the use of the titles, Brother and Comrade. He remembered the meeting in London recruiting for the Civil War in Spain. He felt worried for his patients.

Voices from the crowd joined in with, 'Speakers on the stage.' Jonah clambered aboard. He towered over Singh.

'Well, I think we can start comrades, friends, brothers and sisters,' Singh continued.

Someone at the front near the dais shouted out, 'And what about the Docta?' It was then Singh and Jonah seemed to notice Vincent for the first time.

'The dais not too big, you know, boy,' Singh quickly rejoined.

Vincent heard the doubt in Singh's voice. He saw him look at Jonah and raise his eyebrows in apprehension. But he also saw Jonah smile with encouragement at the suggestion. He knew that Singh wanted him as the doctor to be on his side, as he had repeatedly said. But he also knew that Singh had suspicions about him, because of his French Creole background.

Then a couple of fellas started to clap, and others picked it up with the chant of, 'Docta, Docta, Docta.' Singh looked uneasy. Jonah beamed. Vincent dismissed the idea at first, but was then pushed from behind and moved towards the dais. He tugged Theo along.

In the end, he went with the movement. By now, almost all the adult patients had collected. He turned as he left the edge of the crowd and looked across the yard to where he glimpsed the nuns on the verandah of the children's ward. He looked for the face of Sister Thérèse. He needed to see her face. Once under the almond tree, he lost sight of her, her frozen apprehension.

He took his seat. Singh, Jonah and himself were crammed on the small stage. Theo was standing at the front just beneath him, next to Christiana. Singh began his speech.

'Tell them Singh. You hit the nail on the head, boy. We asking to be recognised as human,' Mr Lalbeharry shouted from the crowd.

The crowd began getting worked up and shouting, 'Human, human, human.' Singh looked relieved that he had managed to carry the crowd. Vincent began to look uneasy. Jonah beamed his approval. Some of the people had shifted, coming in closer, and Vincent caught another glimpse of Sister Thérèse on the verandah. He could not see her face plainly, but something in the gesture, the way she moved, assured him that he had recognised her. He had to tell her the news about Czechoslovakia. How was she going to be included, he wondered. How would the nuns be included in this struggle?

Mother Superior was one thing, but the other sisters who worked day and night, giving their labour and sacrifice, had to be part of what it means to be human, part of this struggle. Even Mother Superior must be human too! Jonah would understand that, and when he could talk to Singh more privately, he would see that they had to carry everyone, to carry the best in people, to get what they wanted for their patients,

As Singh continued to outline the main demands for a minimum wage, better living conditions, improved working conditions, more effective distribution of drugs and other remedies, Vincent wanted to stop the big speech to the people as a crowd, and get Singh to look into the faces of the individuals at his feet. He preferred the Singh on the jetty talking on Old Year's Night, someone who was becoming his friend.

Vincent noticed Beatrice at the back of the crowd. He waved. At first, she did not seem to see him. Then she smiled and waved. He now understood why she had not turned up this morning. Some of the women had rosaries entwined around their fingers and stumps. Beatrice joined in these prayers.

Singh was winding up, trying to be heard over the screams of the parrots. 'Keep up your spirits. Comrades, we'll meet here tomorrow at the same time. I'll have seen the Mother Superior. By then, myself and Doctor Metivier will have talked to her.' He sat down, wiping his brow with his handkerchief. He looked relieved. He turned towards Vincent.

'What the hell are you doing?' Vincent blurted out. 'Why whip up all this anger, this rage?'

'I born angry. I born in a rage.' Singh stared Vincent down. His discipline had snapped for a moment. Then they both controlled themselves up on the stage. Vincent looked down and smiled reassuringly at Theo.

Jonah stood up tall and broad. The crowd shouted and clapped. Vincent watched the stumps and clawed hands beating against each other. 'Brothers and sisters. Brethren.' He spoke now like a priest. 'Let us join together. Let me teach you this, if you don't know the words.'

Then Vincent noticed three of the policemen that were resident on the island standing at the edge of the crowd, looking in, surveying the meeting. Two were new officers, and one had been stationed on the island for many years.

Jonah continued, 'I will not cease from mental strain, nor shall my sword sleep in my hand till we have built Jerusalem in Empire's broad, fair and pleasant lands. Brothers and sisters!'

It was like a litany in the church, with the congregation repeating Jonah's words. A hot wind took hold of the branches of the almond tree and the red banner with its words, Bread and Justice.

'O Lord, Our God, arise, scatter our enemies, and make them fall. Confound their politics, frustrate their knavish tricks. On thee our hope we fix.' Vincent listened to the familiar words that Uriah Butler had used over and over again at meetings. Butler had come back from the First War, as did Cipriani with an education in liberty. He had seen the British working people fighting for their rights and he wanted the same for his people. He did not see why they should be second class citizens here on this island colony. Jonah relished the words and repeated them once again. The crowd were fired. He was not giving them facts like Singh. He was giving them passion, a vision. 'I will have built Jerusalem in Empire's broad, fair and pleasant land.' He declaimed the poetry out beyond the almond tree.

While Singh's voice was a shrill whistle, a flute, Jonah's was a bass drum. He was speaking not only to the crowd below the almond tree, but also to the sisters on the verandahs, to Mother Superior locked in her office refusing to come out, but hearing each and every word that was spoken at the meeting. Jonah was speaking to be heard in Porta España, to be heard by the Governor, to be heard across the ocean in the very British parliament itself. He was speaking to the world.

He was Moses, as Vincent watched him, his head almost touching the branches of the almond tree. But he was also Jonah, hungry for conversion, but doubting his efforts. And for this, he had had to endure three days and three nights in the body of the whale. Vincent watched the dilemma in the boatman, between the Moses who wanted to lead his people into the Promised Land, flowing with milk and honey, and Jonah who doubted he could have an effect on the people of Niniveh. He had grown fond of this man who brought him across the bay each morning.

The strong winds had freshened the stale, pervasive smell of the Chaulmoogra Oil and the smell of rotting flesh. There was a feeling of resurrection in the air, of the coming Easter in the breeze, after this Lenten heat and fast. Jonah was indeed the son of a *Shango* woman from down in Moruga.

Those orange lilies which burst straight out of the parched earth in the dry season, sprouting in clumps in the yard, seemed now, as the hot sun caught their petals, brought forth by the words of Jonah. The place could suddenly seem miraculous: yellow pouis and flaming *immortelle* in the hills.

This was Vincent's awe. He culled from the remnants of his Roman Catholic liturgy the sense of the sacramentality in things. Things represented some other reality. It seemed so now, at this heightened moment, with the up-turned, hopeful faces of the congregation. It did seem like a church under the spreading almond tree. Vincent let it happen. He did not resist it with his reason, not altogether, at least, not emotionally.

While the policemen watched Jonah rousing the crowd, they also knew that this was Jonah the boatman who they *blagged* with on the jetty, Jonah, their *pardner* who they played cards with. Now, he was speaking as the leader of the people. They were taught to take note of that on behalf of the Colonial Constabulary.

'Brothers in arms. Brother Singh give you the facts of the case. Is left to me to say one thing. Is not a question of dermatology. You know what I talking about. Is no big word for big word sake that I get up here to speak to you today. You know what I talking about. Is not the disease of the skin. Is the disease of the mind that I worry about. Is a matter of philosophy, is the politics of the matter. Tell me, if it was a bunch of white people down here, practically in Venezuela, you think they would treat us so? No brothers and sisters! Is because of the dermatology business, but is also because of the colour of this skin. I going to let the doctor talk to you about these things, because he is a white man. But you know he is your doctor who has your best interests at heart. We are citizens, brothers and sisters of the Empire. We demand the right of citizens of this Empire. We might be at the farthest reaches, on the periphery, as they tell us. We deserve the same treatment as if we at the centre, in London town. We must organise ourselves. Those of you who work in the laundry and kitchen, in the gardens, growing food for the benefit of all of we, going to have to down tools until they listen to us about the matters that Brother Singh speak to us about.'

Everyone cheered this suggestion with, 'Strike.'

'Brothers and sisters. I go introduce your docta to you. Docta Metivier.' Vincent had been carried along by the rhetoric. Swept along, his anger with Singh was subdued.

The nuns were still on the verandah having a grandstand view of the proceedings.

Vincent waited for the cheering to die down. He smiled at Theo whose eyes were as big as saucers. He had been looking onto the crowd for almost an hour now. Vincent was so accustomed to dealing with his patients individually, that looking at all of them in a crowd, right there in front of him, was shocking. While he had grown accustomed to their individual ailments, no matter how advanced the illness in some, he did not always see them as a whole, as a community of sick. He was shocked now to look at them. Now he saw the stumps and the claw hands, the shortened fingers and the lion faces, the collapsed noses, joints jutting at awkward angles, faces disfigured with nodules. They were close to him on the stage, so he could see all these details as they hung onto crutches and each other, a ravaged group of people, decimated by an illness which instilled fear in others. Vincent rose to his feet.

'Friends, I speak to you as your doctor. I speak to you as one who wants the best for your health and happiness. That means I want the best for you physically, but also, psychologically; for your peace of mind, for the comfort of your hearts. I don't want you to be afraid. I don't want you to be sad. You need to keep your spirits up to fight this disease in its many guises. You know that I have spoken to you about that. You must have confidence in yourself to live with your illness. You must not be allowed to live in isolation from each other, in your exclusion, in the prejudice which, centuries old, have made you do.'

The crowd listened quietly. They were accustomed to being soothed by the doctor and his words. Vincent looked across to where the nuns were on the verandah, including Mother Superior now. They were listening more intently than ever, because they would be most concerned as to where Vincent would place himself in the discussion.

'Friends, we must look together at what is the best understanding of your disease, what it tells us about infection, contagion. We all want to be responsible about that, as you know. You know that's what I tell you about everyday. Look after your habits of cleaning, personal hygiene. I know you do your best. We must help with that. These things touch on all that Singh and Jonah have been saying. Together we're going to sort these things out.' He wanted to display a united front despite his difference with Singh.

'You talking positive, Doctor. But what if it don't happen?' This was young Christian la Borde.

'Strike, strike.' Some of the fellas began to shout. The language of the Labour riots on Sancta Trinidad in the recent past, led by Butler, Rienzi and Cipriani in their different ways, had not been lost on the patients of El Caracol. Those events had inspired them then. Now they saw their own black man, Indian and French Creole up on the stage giving them a vision of how things might change for them.

'Burn the place down,' some the other fellas shouted.

Vincent ignored the shouts for strike and fire and spoke directly to Christian. 'Christian, I tell you, I'm going to do all that is possible to make things better. Let us try. Let us come back to you after we have spoken to Mother Superior. Then, you can judge.'

Vincent spoke these last words with his head held high, so that his voice could carry beyond the shade of the almond tree, as far as the verandah where the Mother Superior was standing with her nuns. So, now, everyone would know where everyone stood.

The crowd applauded and shouted warmly. But, after Singh and Jonah's rousing speeches, things had subsided with Vincent's carefully chosen words. Vincent noticed that Singh looked as if he wanted some more fire in his words.

But Jonah patted him on the shoulder with, 'Wise words, Doc.' Vincent was glad for the warm approval from Jonah. Singh avoided him and lost himself in the crowd.

Then he realised that Theo was no longer where he had been at the front under the stage. He could not see him anywhere in the crowd.

Sister Thérèse was on her own on the verandah. He walked towards her. Before he reached the verandah, she had disappeared into the children's ward.

He did not know where to turn. Why had she moved away? He wanted her to help him search for Theo. He stood for a moment looking at the crowd get into a march, the cries of, 'Burn, Burn, Burn' alternating with the chant, 'Strike, strike.'

The police were manhandling some of the more exuberant, young, able-bodied fellas.

Singh and then Jonah took up positions at the head of the crowd. Vincent wondered if he should join them. Where were they going? Where was there to go? He had to find Theo. He was sure the rhetoric would simmer down. He decided that this was a demonstration of force to gear up the people, but then everyone would return to their usual tasks. Then he and Singh could meet up with Mother Superior. He turned to go inside to look for Sister Thérèse. Maybe Theo had gone to the school.

He found her in the pharmacy. She was alone. He shut the door quietly behind him. She continued with her work. He stood at the door. She turned. 'Doctor?'

'Good morning, Sister.'

'Non, non, not a good morning.' She looked weary and worried.

'Have you seen Theo?

'No. It's a worrying morning.'

'Yes, yes, it is as I...'

114

'I understand. But is this the way?' She was earnest.

'Who knows?'

'You were on the stage with Singh and Jonah. I saw you.'

'You saw me? Yes, I was asked by the patients, to join them on the platform.'

'Patients? I don't see patients when I see them like that.'

'Yes, mine and yours. They're our patients,' Vincent insisted.

'You're their doctor, not a politician. Look at them. What can they do? When they are like this they frighten me.'

'They have an illness. But they have rights. They've entitlements, even more so because of their disadvantages. We must not forget that.'

They both stood and stared out of the window at the sea, as if there was an answer there.

The noise was coming from the yard in bursts. The marching and demonstration had not ceased as Vincent had expected. In fact, the chanting had got louder. 'Burn, Burn, Burn,' was accompanied by the drums, the percussion created out of the debris of the yard. Sister Thérèse turned towards the noise.

Vincent tried to change the subject by getting onto their work. 'What are the results of your investigations? What've you seen below that microscope of yours?' He tried to lighten things.

'I think it's as you've been suspecting. The paralysis is caused by damage to the nerves. This accounts for the anaesthesia. Why they forget their pain.' She was impassioned.

'It does not register,' he added. He needed to find Theo.

'So we can conclude our observations as to why they keep opening their wounds without knowing, or, why they can hurt themselves, and each other,' she continued.

'Yes. This should encourage us to work on the orthopaedic aspects. Not dermatology. That's secondary, in this case. The real problem is beneath the skin,' he argued.

'We must continue work on the hands,' she said intensely.

'We need to do an autopsy. We need more than the cultures.'

The noise outside could not be ignored. Vincent and Sister Thérèse went to the window which gave onto the yard where the demonstrators' chants were coming from. Suddenly, there were screams, screams that signalled danger.

'Theo! You know I've lost Theo. I must go and see where he is. Come and help me,' Vincent pleaded.

They were stunned by the sunlight as they came out into the yard from the pharmacy. There was still a crowd under the almond tree, Singh and Jonah might be in there, but Vincent could not see them anywhere.

They noticed another part of the crowd who were circling an even smaller group, from where the chant of 'Burn, Burn, Burn,' sounded, infectious in its repetition. Even the children, the small children hanging over the bannisters of their verandah, were chanting the rhythmic, 'Burn Burn, Burn.' Something else was going on here.

'Come with me.' Vincent took hold of Sister Thérèse's hand. 'Fire. We can't have fire, otherwise we're going to have multiple injuries in no time at all.'

It was then that the first whiff of gasoline came on the breeze from where the smaller crowd was gathered between the stores and the Anglican church. People started screaming and scattering to reveal the group performing a ritual with fire.

Two of the policemen were trying to disperse the crowd. Their presence was enraging them more.

Vincent and Sister Thérèse were terrified, seeing not only some of the able bodied patients, but some of the more infirm, screaming and scattering as they threw the fuel over their shoulders. Gasoline flames flayed out of the cans they carried. The fuel had fallen on their shoulders and their backs, catching fire. They were unaware. They could not feel the pain.

Sister Thérèse and Vincent ran towards the flame-throwers, trying to beat the fire down with palm branches which they tore from nearby trees.

This was when Vincent saw Theo. He was standing, staring at a flaming crumpled heap, which was revealed as the dancing crowd scattered. What was it?

Some other children were screaming the chant, 'Burn, Burn, Burn!' Then they ran off with flaming cans of gasoline. Vincent hoped that Ti-Jean was not among them. He could not see him anywhere. He ran towards Theo, who was still standing, transfixed.

The small band of warders were trying to control the crowd. Vincent could hear the crowd even more clearly.

'Burn him! Burn him! Burn him!' The fire throwers shouted, circling throwing their tins of gasoline from a distance now. At one point Vincent lost sight of Theo in the flames. He noticed the girl, Christiana, standing near him.

Vincent then caught a difference in the chant. Sister Thérèse joined him, running towards Theo. He ordered people as he ran to bring water. He was surprised that his voice still carried some authority. Where were Jonah and Singh?

'Theo, what are you doing standing here staring? Don't you see what's happening?' Vincent grabbed hold of the boy, lifting him over the flames.

The body of a man lay on the ground very badly burnt.

When Vincent knelt next to him, beating down the last flames, he realised that he was already dead. He had suffocated from the smoke and the gasoline fumes. His clothes had gone up quickly in the flames. The body was burnt all over.

Theo stood and stared. He seemed unable to react.

The body was charred. What had happened here?

Singh and Jonah were nowhere to be found. In a remnant of clothing, Vincent noticed a piece of a police uniform. One of the three policeman had been burnt to death.

Vincent and Sister Thérèse were now alone in the yard with Theo. She held the boy who now clung to her skirts, burying his head in her lap. Christiana had run off.

The community of nuns had come out onto the verandah of the hospital. Jonah and Singh emerged from the crowd under the almond tree. The dead body still lay where it had been doused with gasoline. Vincent shouted at Singh. 'Look at what you've done. Watch your words!'

Everyone was standing around the edges of the yard silently looking at what had happened. Vincent and Sister Thérèse stood together with the stunned Theo.

A small band of children, led by Ti-Jean, entered the yard with their own music made with tin cans, old galvanise, thumping bamboo on the ground, like in a *tamboo bamboo* band. They had their own calypso. Ti-Jean on his crutches, came to the centre of the yard singing. His young boy's voice was shrill on the air. He was like a young calypsonian.

'Everybody rejoicing,
How they burned Charlie King,
Everybody was glad,
Nobody was sad.
When they beat him
And they burn him in Fyzabad.'

Everyone stood still, dazed and shocked, looking at the young boy on his crutches, performing his macabre dance, followed by his small band of other children, beating their biscuit tins, chanting 'And they beat him and burn him in Fyzabad.'

Very slowly, Ti-Jean's calypso became hypnotic. From the large ragged circle around the yard, the tune was picked up. Words of protest were uttered. There was a tinkle of sound which then died out. One by one the patients began to drift away. In the end the reality of what had happened took the heart out of the protest. There was the sound of box carts and galvanise grating on the gravel paths.

Two male ward assistants came over to where Vincent and Sister Thérèse stood with Theo, next to the corpse. They removed the body of the policeman, Michael Johnson on a stretcher.

'What has happened here?' Vincent asked, not sure to whom he was addressing the question. Singh and Jonah had walked away. Who would have the answer?

By afternoon, the routine of Saint Damian's had regained its normality. The event had kept a lot of patients away from the hospital. Some of the regulars discussed the matter under the almond tree.

'Boy, you wouldn't think people could do thing so again,' Mr Lalbeharry reflected, remembering the burning of Corporal Charles King in 1937, in Fyzabad on Sancta Trinidad during the Butler Riots.

But most of the patients stayed in their huts with their own thoughts and their silence. There seemed to be a desire for time to be turned back to before all of this had happened, yet there was a knowledge that things would never be the same again. The two remaining policemen began to make investigations. They made it clear that there would have to be an inquest.

El Caracol
1939-1941

Rites of Passage

Singh and Jonah stood by the door of the nurses' common room, listening to the crackling news together. The voice of Mr Chamberlain announced that England and the British Empire were at war with Germany. New Zealand, Australia and France were also at war. Two days before, Theo had run out onto the verandah at the Doctor's house with the news, 'Germany invade Poland!' The impending war had loosened his tongue.

Vincent, Mother Superior and the nursing sisters stood in the common room. He looked across the room at Sister Thérèse. They caught each one looking at the other. Their eyes held all they wanted to say. They had not yet found words for these feelings, nor the opportunity to express them. He saw the terror on her face. Her fear and imaginings were becoming reality.

Later that afternoon, Vincent watched the island steamer depart. There was now ice and new provisions. The water boat also, at last, arrived. It filled the tanks and was now leaving. The daily routines of the day unfolded in their usual way. Vincent and Jonah followed behind the fishing boats as they left Perruquier Bay. Their elegiac calypso, beaten with their bottle and spoon, came across the water: *Chamberlain say he only want peace*

Please hold your hands. It is time to cease. The words of Beginner's calypso faded as the fishermen entered the gulf. *Chamberlain tell them to realise, these are the days we are civilised.* Vincent smiled at the irony.

The island steamer had also brought the late mail. A letter from Vincent's mother told him that Bernard, his brother, had been called up. He was stationed near Steyning in Sussex. He would be flying with the RAF. The English place name, in his mother's hand, opened up the scorched Sussex downs, one hot summer above the town, which he had visited as a student on vacation. He and an English girl had found different histories: standing stones, an Iron Age fort. In the distance, they had looked out on the haze and the sea of the South Coast; the English Channel, France. Now, Vincent saw his brother's helmeted head in the cockpit of a Spitfire. He heard the hum of a *Messerschmit.*

But, against these big events, far away, it was the inquest into the murder of the policeman, Michael Johnson, who all now called 'Charlie King', which had dominated life on El Caracol over the last six months. The tension between Vincent and Singh over the criminal investigation often erupted into the open. 'Criminal? Who is criminal? Is a kind of war here, you know,' Singh argued. 'This too is a war, if they go keep people so.' His position was becoming more extreme. He openly accused Vincent of trying to frame him for incitement with his evidence to the inquest.

It had taken the police and the authorities three months to gather their evidence, and the inquest itself, held in Porta España, had taken the other three months. It had involved transporting to Sancta Trinidad a selection of patients who were prepared to give evidence. The newspapers had concentrated on the pathos of children being involved. Their evidence was held *in camera* at the Casa Rosada. Vincent and Jonah went with the patients, and Vincent was present during the *in camera* sessions. This inflamed Singh.

Some of the patients still carried scars of burns they had not felt. The anaesthetic of their condition represented a kind of amnesia. The scars told of something which they had not suffered; could not remember. They all wanted to forget the incident, but it hung over them, brought back by the questioning, representing the fact that, despite all that was learnt from suffering, or not, all were capable of inflicting it. The communality of the act made it difficult to ascribe individual guilt, or guilt to any particular group. Less, of course, all were guilty. Too many of the patients, both children and adults, maintained their silence, claiming that they had not seen anything.

From the talk under the almond tree, Vincent, Jonah and Singh knew, like everyone else, the prime movers, those who had flung the flaying kerosene.

While Father Meyer maintained the secrecy of the confessional for those who were Catholic, it was hoped that he had at least advised the young ones to confess themselves.

Nothing which would hold up as evidence at the inquest came forward. It rested on intention. What had been the intention of those who had fed the fire, dousing the body of the fallen policeman? What had they realised when they were doing so? Vincent could never bring himself to question Ti-Jean. He did not want the boy to lie to him, nor did he want the truth, and have to live with it.

The suspected action of the children, the presumed innocent, the holy innocents, which had caught the imagination of the newspapers, was in the end what prevented further investigation into Mr Krishna Singh, Mr Jonah Leroy and Doctor Vincent Metivier, and the part they might have played in the incitement to violence. It prevented the unearthing of all the evidence there might be, and the bringing of charges. Nevertheless, the judge concluded with a degree of censure for the three men and their political activity, as it was described.

Ironically, despite the tension and accusations during the inquest, Singh and Vincent were brought closer by the common censure. Singh felt vindicated. Vincent, linked now publically with Singh and Jonah, though privately outraged, felt he had achieved an equality. Singh could not now accuse him of privilege, and he now saw Singh's view differently. At no point did the inquest censure the authorities for the state of poverty and deprivation which it maintained by its policies. This omission from the verdict was a turning point for Vincent.

It seemed to Vincent at this moment, these thoughts running through his mind, this afternoon, in the pirogue with Jonah, that the war was not a part of this world. The truth of these events on El Caracol was greater. That bundle on the ground, the pieces of police uniform he had fingered in the embers of the fire, were a more staggering fact of what human beings could do to each other, than the war in which his brother was now involved.

The verdict of accidental death had come through yesterday.

'So, what you think about the verdict, Doc?' Jonah broke the silence.

'What you think, Jonah?' Vincent could see that his friend was eager to have some word about the matter before they parted this evening.

'Well. Is what I tell Singh. Is not they didn't have the evidence, but we wouldn't give it to them.'

'I think you might be right, Jonah.'

'What that make you feel, Doc? '

'It makes me very uneasy, but...'

'What I say, Doc, is that you can't divorce what happen from this place, from what happening to people. You can't divorce that from what happen to the corporal. Look at this place.' Jonah was pointing at the empty sea, but he really meant the leprosarium and its poverty.

'A kind of rough justice?' Vincent asked.

He could not get out of his mind the picture of Ti-Jean with his macabre calypso leading the small band of children into the arena of the yard. He saw Theo staring. Christiana watching.

'Remember what Pilate ask Jesus. What is truth?' Jonah quoted the New Testament.

'Yes, what is truth? What is history?' Vincent added.

'History, Doc?'

'Yes, history.'

He pulled his Panama over his brow and looked into the far distance, the western shore of Sancta Trinidad. The coast was a faint pencil line, a trail of grey smoke. He surveyed its contours, as if tracing his finger along a map. His eye travelled from the mouth of the Caroni River where Walter Raleigh had once entered, and much earlier, the conquistador, Antonio de Berrio, had taken his ships, under the swaying bamboo, to the founding capital at San Jose de Oruñya, the site of the hanging of twelve Caribs in the sixteenth century, a rough justice in retaliation for the crucifixion of twelve Spaniards. Here the caravels of Europe, their charnel galleons, their slaving ships, arrived on their Middle Passage, from the coasts of ivory and gold, or, later, when that enterprise had foundered, brought those others in bunks upon bunks in the holds from Calcutta and Uttar Pradesh, for the business of Empire, sugar.

The gulf, now that Vincent could see more of it, was stacked with tankers and merchant steamers. These were part of the transatlantic convoys which came up from Brazil and Argentina, along the Guianas through the Bocas, stopping here to refuel. The tankers were here to collect the oil for the war from the refinery at Point-à-Pierre.

'See, history.' Vincent stretched his arm wide, pointing into the gulf and beyond. When he turned towards the house, he saw the figure of Theo. Theo was at the end of the jetty, sitting on his own. Vincent's heart rose with anticipation, with apprehension. Jonah pointed, 'Watch, the boy, Doc, he waiting for you.' Then he added, 'You ent think the boy need a mother?'

I could have a son that age, Vincent thought. Then he smiled to himself ironically. The figure of Odetta fleeing through his mind, he answered Jonah.

'A boy needs a father. A father needs a son. What about your children, Jonah?'

'I does look out for them. I does carry their mother things for them in Moruga. But is here I get a work.' It was Jonah's common defence.

As the pirogue neared the jetty, Vincent could see Theo more clearly. So slight. He sat resting his chin on his knees, peering over the end of the jetty. From further out, Vincent had thought that he was fishing, remembering that he had said that he would fish with him this afternoon at four. There was a rod by his side.

'Hi, Theo, catch this.' Jonah coiled the rope at the bow to throw to the boy to tie up. The motor idled as they neared the jetty. At first, Theo did not show any recognition of their arrival, but when Jonah called again, 'Boy, what wrong with you, catch the rope,' he stood up and faced the two men. He was stark naked. He stood facing them directly, then turned and ran, as fast as he could, up to the house.

They saw him climb the steps to the front verandah, two steps at a time, then disappear; a naked child in the glare of the afternoon sun, running.

The two men looked at each other in astonishment. They did not speak. Vincent raised his eyebrows in alarm. He took the rope from Jonah, who went back to the stern and steered the boat alongside the jetty for Vincent to clamber off and tie up.

'I better go and see what's the matter,' Vincent said to Jonah.

'You want me to remain, Doc? In case there's some trouble?'

'Yes,' he reflected. 'Hold on a moment, Jonah, if you don't mind. I'll let you know if I need you. If I do, I'll call from the window upstairs. He's probably in his room at the back. Not himself since the burning. That's why he's not been at the school.'

Vincent was a while. Then Jonah received the signal that it was fine to go. 'See you in the morning,' Vincent called. The echo came back from across the bay.

'Right, Doc.' Jonah cupped his palms around his mouth like blowing into a conch. The boatman's voice came back from the hills. He waved from the jetty, undid the rope, got back into the pirogue, started up the motor and set off.

Vincent stood for a moment watching him from the upstairs window. He looked across to the convent. The figure of a nun was standing on the cliff overlooking Embarcadère Corbeau. The skirts of her white cotton habit ballooned in the breeze, her veil fluttered like a white flag of surrender. Thérèse? Vincent asked himself.

He turned back into the house. The stench was overpowering. As soon as he entered the house, he could smell the putrid odour. The wind had died down, so there was not the usual sea breeze to dispel the awful retching smell.

Vincent heard only his own heart beating hard in his chest, as he walked about downstairs, looking into the kitchen, which was spotlessly clean, as was the drawing room and the verandah which he had walked through earlier. Theo had swept, mopped and dusted. He wondered whether he had gone out the back door to his perch on the wall by the water tank. Vincent could see from the kitchen window that he was not there.

Far in the distance, he caught the dying sounds of Jonah's *put putting* pirogue arriving at Embarcadère Corbeau. There was the sound of Jonah's conch and the echo of it in the hills across the bay, as he announced his arrival.

Vincent knew now where to look, having discovered the boy's hiding place under the stairs in the past.

But no, Theo was not there, not even in the deepest recess. So, then, his first thought that Theo would go to his room must be correct. He climbed the stairs. It was obvious that this was where the smell was coming from. There were more flies than usual, even downstairs. But, on the stairs and on the landing outside Theo's room, they buzzed and flew off and settled again, particularly near the crack at the bottom of the bedroom door.

His first thought, on entering the house, had been that one of the lavatories had been blocked again, because of the lack of water. The tanks had been running dry until the water boats had eventually arrived earlier today.

The house was still and hot. The heat worsened the pervasive odour of human excrement. The door knob was smeared with dried faeces. Vincent took out his handkerchief and used it to open the door.

Even before he had fully opened it, he heard the low moaning sound coming from inside the room. But with the door fully open now, the full blast of the stench which seeped through the house was unbearable. He had used his handkerchief to protect his hands, so now he had to bury his nose in his shirt sleeve, as he entered and looked around the room, whose floors and walls

126

were smeared with shit. The bed sheets and the mosquito net had been painted with the excrement. There was a strong smell of urine now as well.

Vincent wondered in what place he was. He could not see Theo, but he continued to hear the low moaning sound. There was an old, wooden, varnished Victorian press in the corner of the room, behind the door. The low moaning sound was coming from inside the press. He went over and opened it. Under two shirts, hanging on wooden hangers, one blue, the other a white school uniform shirt, was the naked Theo, curled up like an overgrown foetus. Vincent could now see what he had not seen outside, that his skin was smeared with his own excrement. The body paintings were on his face and arms, and in long streaks across his chest and stomach.

Vincent was retching. He now had to tolerate the smell as best he could, as he tried to attend to the boy. He had learnt to deal with the stench at Saint Damian's: the smell of rotting flesh, the putrid bandages, the Chaulmoogra Oil. He had to bear this. He was a doctor, after all.

'Theo. Theo, come boy, come.' Vincent put out his arms to lift the boy out of the press. He did not help Vincent. He was a dead weight. His head was bent between his legs. His hands were tucked beneath his buttocks. Both his hands and the cheeks of his buttocks were caked with his faeces. While Theo continued to moan, he swayed back and forth. Vincent wondered at the old press not collapsing. 'Come, Theo, let me lift you. Help me.'

Then he recognised the moan. It had words. Two words with two syllables, each said deliberately, issued from the buried head, the hidden lips of the foetus. These were then followed by a kind of trill. The moan wanted to be a song. 'Coco, Coco, Cocorito.' Vincent remembered Father Dominic in the convent parlour in Porta España, calling Theo 'Coco'. He wondered at the friar using what seemed a pejorative nickname at the time. When had Father Dominic first heard that name, in what circumstances? It did not seem to be a name to trifle with. It had not cropped up in any of Theo's nocturnal stories. Not as yet, at any rate.

There was a visible relaxation, as the boy let himself be coaxed out of his curled up shape, and made to stand on the floor. Vincent lifted him into his arms and took him downstairs, outside, down the short, pebbled path to the beach, across the stretch of ochre sand. He walked straight into the sea with the naked boy, Vincent himself still fully dressed. He squatted in the shallows and small waves. Holding Theo in his arms, like a baby, he bathed his head and wiped off the faeces from his face. The boy allowed himself to be administered to in this way, without any objection. Vincent looked up, and out to sea. The bay was empty.

'Theo? What's the matter, boy? What's the matter? You can tell me.' Vincent continued to cup the water in his palms and bathe and clean the boy's body. Theo was looking up to the sky.

'What're you telling me Theo?' He stared into boy's face, into his eyes. Theo looked back at him. It was not for long, but his eyes did really meet those of Vincent's with a recognition which had not existed before, in any of their previous meetings.

It saddened Vincent that the boy had had to bring things to this extremity, for this to happen. But, it must mean something that he had decided, or had been driven to this, to make himself known.

He held the boy within his doctor's arms. He continued to clean him with a doctor's hands. The boy's nakedness was not something that was foreign to him. He had had to examine many children. It was not unusual for him to take the penis and wash it, to wipe between the buttocks. He performed this with understanding, as a professional. What astonished him, and made these gestures different, were the circumstances.

What surprised him at this moment, was seeing himself in the sea, fully dressed with the naked boy in his arms, looking out to the bay, to the gulf beyond.

Holding the boy, he surveyed the world: the high blue mountains beyond the port of Guira on the eastern coast of Venezuela; the empty distance of the gulf from this position in the sea; the bay itself with the white walled convent over the other side. When he turned and looked around him, he saw that the green hills behind the house, with the lilac shadows of the afternoon, and the light which the increasing sunset threw across the water and over the hills, were dissolving into flames. The house was a livid pink, its white lattice work gleamed. The fret work was like white lace. He and the boy were in the house which was in the water. The pillars and gables were sinewy in the water. They buckled and twisted, were narrowed and elongated. Their own reflections, just beneath them, were part of this insubstantiality, this variable, this changing possibility, which was now their lives.

Theo was content to float, held at the small of his back with Vincent's reassuring hand. As far as he knew, the boy could not swim. This was his daily fear, when he left him alone in the house with Beatrice. The boy floated above Vincent's steadying hand as he sat in the shallows feeling the pebbles moving under him. With each wave he had to work to regain his balance. The water was filling his pockets like balloons. Sand was getting between the seams of his pants and shirt. But he remained balanced. Quite imperceptibly, Theo moved his legs like fins, keeping himself afloat. He swam away from Vincent a small distance. 'Oh, he can swim,' Vincent thought.

He stripped off and flung his own clothes on to the rocks nearby. He and Theo swam naked the length between the beach and the point at Father Meyer's house.

Returning, they could hear that the gramophone had already been started up with the evening's Wagner. It would have to stop soon, because of the newly enforced curfew.

It seemed as if Theo and Vincent had been in the water a very long time. 'Theo, come boy.' Vincent grabbed up his own wet clothes. 'Race you up the beach, back to the house.' As he looked back, Theo was running out of the water, the waves breaking behind him.

They both stood on the kitchen floor, naked, panting. It was like he was taking care of a smaller child. 'Theo, wait here. I'll be back very soon. Let me get some dry clothes.'

He ran upstairs to his own room, dressed and came back with a towel to wipe Theo. He also brought one of his own white cotton shirts to dress the boy. Theo stood, transformed in the tails of a man's big shirt. It made him look smaller, like a very small boy, like a boy in his father's shirt.

The strangeness of what had happened dawned fully on Vincent now. He got the boy a clean pair of khaki pants. He paced around, tidying up. He stopped, abruptly. 'We're going to sit and have a cup of tea. We're going to have tea Theo, like I used to have tea in my mother's house.' Vincent looked at Theo, as he turned from the sink where he was washing his hands. He did not quite know why he was doing this. The moment called for something different. 'Now, you sit there. I'm going to get the tea.' He had been so distracted, so swept away by what he had found, by what he and the boy were doing in the sea. He stood looking at him, standing in his man's shirt. He stood there in the middle of the kitchen, staring at Vincent, looking down at the floor. 'Why don't you go and sit on the wall by the tank. I'll bring our tea out there.'

There was the big silver tea pot, the silver milk jug, and the matching bowl for sugar. He went back and forth between the kitchen and the dining room. He ransacked the packing case under the stairs for these essential elements of his mother's tea. The water was boiling on the kerosene stove. The green tea was in the pot. There was just enough milk left in the churn on top of the ice box, in the cool of the pantry.

Soon the tray was ready. He got some butter from the safe outside the kitchen door, put some of Beatrice's guava jelly in a bowl. All that was needed were the Crix biscuits. He rummaged in the barrel under the counter for the rations from the *commisserie*. He put a handful on a plate. He poured the water over the tea leaves. All was ready.

'Ah! One thing missing.' Vincent went back out to the safe by the kitchen door. 'Cheese! Rat cheese!' The big yellow cheddar block was discovered. It was what he and Bernard had christened rat cheese. You could not eat Crix biscuits and guava jelly without rat cheese. Setting the mousetraps with big chunks of yellow cheddar was a feature in this house as it had been at Versailles.

Vincent went out into the yard by the water tank, which was overflowing, because it had been filled to the very brim this afternoon, from the water boat. Theo was perched on the concrete wall looking out onto the bay.

The sunset was dying over the island rock, Patos. A haze was settling on the fractured glass of the sea. Through the haze, a fire of the sun was burning up the gulf, as if there had been an enormous explosion; orange and red and the sea in flames, as if oil had been poured over its waves.

'Theo, come, boy. Here.' Vincent poured the boy some tea, into one of his mother's, Madame Metivier's china cups, the white ones with the gold monogrammed crest of the Metivier family which he had also unpacked from the case, stored under the stairs. The old past glinted on the tray.

'Now, Theo, let's feast.' He buttered a Crix biscuit and cut a piece of cheese, spooned some guava jelly onto the cheese and offered Theo the childhood confection. Theo took a quick look at Vincent, as he accepted the gift, and bit into it, the crumbs falling onto the front of his clean white shirt.

This tea ceremony that Vincent had remembered since childhood enveloped him and the boy, as they both gorged themselves on rat cheese and guava jelly, sipping hot tea from Madame Metivier's white china cups.

The crisis of the afternoon dissolved. The boy and the doctor did not talk, but there was an unspoken communion that afternoon, as they munched away.

Vincent, eventually, cleared up the tea tray got the fishing rods from behind the kitchen door. With his hand on the boy's shoulder, they walked down to the jetty. 'We're going to catch our supper.' Vincent got some old bait he kept in the boathouse. They sat at the end of the jetty on the warm boards with their legs dangling over the edge. Theo followed, as Vincent threaded his rod and baited the hooks. With a deft flick of his wrist, he slung the line into the water. With luck, they might catch two small red fish.

It was Theo who got the first bite, and, in no time, they hauled in the first catch.

'Hold him, hold him, don't let him slip away.' Vincent was a boy again. Theo said it all with his eyes, and his following of everything that Vincent said to do, though he knew quite well how to fish. 'Theo, you carry on. I'm going up to the house.'

Before the light had gone completely, Vincent boiled a large bucket of water. With cloths, scrubbing brushes and carbolic soap, he cleaned out Theo's room, using disinfectant and leaving the windows open to dry the room. The sheets and mosquito nets he put into the barrel outside the kitchen, and burnt them. The smoke trailed out over the bay as the last of the sun went down.

The boy was still there at the end of the jetty, on his own, fishing.

Later, Theo and Vincent ate fish and bake. They washed up in the dark, behind the black-out curtains which had been issued that day, brought on the island steamer, and put up on the windows at the front of the house. Vincent lit one kerosene lamp. He erected a camp bed in his room for Theo. The house now smelt of Dettol.

There were no words spoken by Theo. Vincent talked his way through his actions. 'Now let us get you another mosquito net from the spare room.' Theo followed and watched. Vincent looked after the boy.

That night there were no stories. Doctor and boy slept soundly. Vincent thought he had woken at some time to the sound of a dull thunder. Then, later, there was the drone of an Albacore. But these sounds were becoming part of his dreams.

History Lesson

Vincent watched Theo absorbed in the four o'clock news. His first act, on returning from Saint Damian's, was to turn on the radio. He adjusted the knobs to get the clearest reception, munching Crix biscuits, cheese and guava jelly, now his favourite. This was their time together, silently, all ears for the advance of armies across borders and frontiers. Vincent sipped his tea.

They listened to Germany's attacks. Poland was caught between the Russians and the Germans. Theo had his atlas out. He had retrieved a globe from under the stairs which had been Vincent's and Bernard's as children. He spun it, searching and tracing with his finger the movement of troops.

Earlier today, they had stood and watched the last shipload of Jewish refugees come through the *boca,* to be quarantined on Nelson island. The fishermen sang the calypso of the day, describing the *Making of a New Jerusalem,* as they put out for the fishing banks.

Since dirtying himself, Theo's night calypso had subsided. But Vincent was always waiting for it to begin again. He dreaded its resumption. What more did the boy have to go through? What more had he been through?

The afternoon light slanted, yellow as the lances of the palms. Theo had moved to the jetty. The wake of a British destroyer swamped the sunbaked boards as it turned in the bay. He stared at the sleek, silver strip, HMS Liverpool, slipping out of the bay into the gulf, fluttering the Union Jack, as if it were a toy he himself had pushed out onto the waves, a carved cedar pod on the stream.

After the news, he was checking his log of barges and tugs of the British navy doing their exercises. This had been the first visible sign of the war. He kept a note of what he spotted. The low flying aircraft had joined the frigates, cormorants and diving pelicans.

Vincent watched the boy from the verandah. He was in another world altogether, different from the one at Pepper Hill or Father Dominic's friary, as he threw his line from the jetty, in the hope of a catch.

Darkness came suddenly after a green flash on the horizon as far as Guira on the eastern coast of Venezuela, bringing its gloom into the lamp-lit house. The generator had broken down again. Fireflies pulsed in the bushes.

Theo had earlier kneaded the dough for a bake which was now ready. He fried a supper of his red snapper catch for Vincent and himself which they ate with the bake in silence. Vincent thought he seemed as if he had sun stroke. He had caught the sun on his face and arms and bare back. He had noticed him bathing his head with water from the tap at the tank, outside the kitchen. The water darkened his Demerara-sugar-coloured hair. 'You must respect the sun on the island, Theo. Wear a cap. There's one under the stairs.'

Theo looked up for an instant. There was a flicker of recognition, then his eyelashes were lowered, shutting down the light of his green eyes.

Vincent followed him up the creaking stairs to bed. He let himself into his room, barely opening the door, sidling in, furtively. What secrets now? Vincent thought.

'Sleep tight, don't let mosquitoes bite.' Vincent retired, without receiving a response.

It must have been just after midnight when Vincent woke to one of the island's owls. The *jumbie* bird, as people called it, kept the night watch. It was between a hoot and a trill. It had its own Morse Code, transmitting its own messages. Then, there was the usual static and hum of the night.

The voice which had haunted him was barely audible as it began its story. It ran like a river. Vincent listened, dreading the long night. Theo sat stunned at the foot of his bed.

Coco Mama, Emelda, know more than Mister. She have history lesson too. She give it to her boy. What she know was from where she come from, down in the gully, in the barrack yard, below the big house on top of Pepper Hill. What she know was from the dolly house in which she and Coco live.

Coco? Hmm! That's not my name.

What she know was from the yard of she grandmother, Ma, who come out at specified hours of the morning and evening to rock back and forth on her teak rocker, make for her by Mr Cardinez in Guapo, and who rise only to

134

water her anthurium lilies, growing in cut-down kerosene tins on the ledge of the verandah, with a calabash dip in the bucket of water, and which have to always be on the verandah steps for this purpose. She carry in herself a long memory which take her, herself, back to herself, back to the young girl, Christina Dellacourt of the Dellacourts of Corinth, that fair estate in the soft undulations of sugar cane, which lie between Petit Morne and Golconda.

She come on the request of the then Madame de Marineaux, if not enslave, at least indenture still, or, at very least, feeling that the trip by buggy from Corinth to Pepper Hill, near Gran Couva, must be the longest trip she ever make in this life.

Is here, Ma Dellacourt say, that her daughter Alice leave and go to work as a servant in the big house on top of Pepper Hill, when the present Mister Pierre was a little boy. All called Pierre, like they don't have other name to call their children. Pierre de Marineaux!

Coco Mama, Emelda, was a little girl then, and the secret that the whole world know run through she vein and blossom on the red skin cheek of the little girl that Ma Dellacourt daughter, Alice, leave with she.

Child, what trouble you bring me? But leave the children them, Emelda and Louis, the twins, and go and do your work. Watch yourself, Alice.

Alice continue to please her Mistress and serve she Mister, a Mister that come from a line of misters since they start to come in 1820. That shameful time!

De Marineaux and then de Marineaux and more de Marineaux, the name they give the children born to the Mistress inside the house, the wife, the one who is bride since she is a child sheself, dress up in yards and yards of Chantilly lace and *broderie anglaise.* You does see that in them pretty pretty picture, yellow yellow, stun by the camera, wrap in torpor. That is Father Angel word. I get it in vocabulary lesson. TOR POR.

But, as time pass, de Marineaux is the name take by the outside children in the barrack yard. De Marineaux bloom like orange blossom on the slope of Pepper Hill. De Marineaux, ripe like purple governor plum, like *jolie* mango. Like rose, like mango *vert*. De Marineaux like red sorrel in the breeze Christmas time.

Child, what you telling people, Emelda say.

Is so, I hear my great-grandmammy say.

Vincent was transfixed. Theo threw back his head and laughed. Vincent listened to the tongues in which the boy spoke, not the tongues of Father Dominic's devil, those wild, priestly superstitions, but the troubled tongues of a troubled child. A great-grandmother's story. He must listen to the boy. He must keep awake. Theo looked straight at him, but did not seem to see him.

The entranced child sometimes lay across the end of his bed. Sometimes, he was at the window in the shadow of the blackout, sometimes walking about the room, gesticulating, or sitting in a chair, imitating an older person, a voice in the story. He was a mimic, sometimes standing close to the mosquito net and peering down at the doctor's face, or kneeling by the bedside to confess the story into his ear, as if to a priest in a confessional, or an accomplice in a crime, pouring his history into his ear.

Theo strode across the room delivering his history lesson in the learnt voice of an adult.

MA DELLACOURT daughter, Alice, not the first to get take, on a quiet afternoon, to the tune of the catechism class downstairs, under the house, teach by the mistress of the house, Ma Dellacourt tell me.

What must you take most care of, your body or your soul, children?

I must take most care of my soul because it is immortal and will never die.

The fine, high voices sing and repeat, they learn by heart. Ma Dellacourt daughter, Alice upstairs, think, never die? What a tribulation! Sometimes, more easy, just to die. And she say, she say to she self, let me die. Die, die, die.

Vincent listened to the boy telling this astonishing tale, as he unfolded the history of his grandmother, as told by his great-grandmother. The story possessed him, so that he told it as he had heard it, rendering the tones of the voices which possessed him. It was as if he had a fever. Vincent let him tell the story. No matter how painful, he had to listen to the boy he cared for. It frightened him how much he cared.

IS TO THESE catechism voices that the young girl, Alice, who know no better or, even if she do, unable to do anything about it, let the attention of her Mister, in those days still Master, seduce her into giving up her body. She let him take her body, hearing the sing-song children, with their young faith,

136

repeat time and time again, that it was her soul she must take most care of. What of the body?

Before that, the Monsieur de Marineaux of the time make his way into the body of Christina Dellacourt, Ma Dellacourt as she become. It begin an ancestry of such interference! All she think of was how far Corinth Estate is, and whether it better to stay there, to scrub floor.

What a danger in such simple work! To kneel on the ground and let the soapy water swamp her dress. She tell how a young son of the Corinth house take her, there, on the floor, in the soapy water flooding her dress, a twelve year old girl. He take her like she was a dog. He call her puppy, and come up behind, to lift her skirt. Puppy, Puppy, and before she can fight, she feel the pain of it, the push of his swelling into her.

And all the time, Christina, my great-grandmammy, say she hear the keskidee in the zaboca tree. But the one sound that she never forget is the sound of the blacksmith pounding iron far down in the estate yard. Clang, clang, clang.

That dry season, that crop time, trash blow in from them burning fields on a hot afternoon. The clanging sound fill the blue sky. It toll and toil like a bell at church. She cross sheself for the Angelus. *The Angel of the Lord declared unto Mary, and she conceive of the Holy Ghost.*

Hmm? This was no Holy Ghost, my great-grandmammy say, but it make Christina think even then, that this taking of young girls in these houses, always have to have the music of the church accompanying each push of the mister swelling. The tolling of bells, the repetition of the catechism, telling them that if they have to lose their bodies, is their souls that the church want to save. *Ka-ka, Kif-kif.*

Even now, Christina, my great-grandmammy, say she hear the laughter from the barrack rooms.

Vincent listened to the laughter in the voice of the boy, mimicking the laughter of his great-grandmother, and under that laughter, the sadness of the story of herself and her daughter Alice, the boy's grandmother.

The fever was rising. Vincent was sitting bolt upright, his eyes wide open, listening to Theo who sat on a rocker, poised like the Ma Dellacourt of his story. He had taken the counterpane and draped it about him, and held his head sideways, his hand on his chin, a little tilted up in a manner both superior and spurning of the time that he was describing. He topped off his costume with a turban made from a white towel, so that he looked like one of those Martiniquaise women who strolled on the quay in Fort-de-France.

Theo continued. The voice changed to something more sorrowful.

EACH WEEK, when she go up to the little cemetery, and through the gate to the ground outside, to put flowers on the grave of her daughter, Alice, Ma Dellacourt have the twins with her, Alice little ones, Emelda and Louis. She read the name, Alice, with a cross on a stone with writing she know she pay for already with she own body, what she give the cemetery man. Well pay for, Ma Dellacourt say, as she turn from the grave, as she tell me the story, no matter my Mama, Emelda, who tell me. Tell me when she not even know she telling me.

My Mama have story, *oui!*

But, great-grandmammy say, as she look out onto the soft rolling hills between the high ridges, hump like the back of an iguana, rich with the cocoa, that she see, on their wild savannahs, a cemetery nobody know is there. Big with ditches.

In the dead of night, the pilgrimage from the little board house is by one desperate girl, no more than a child herself, anxious to make her life more simple, to undo her life and start again, to smother that last one she called, Mercy, who she fear get damage between the sheets of the de Marineaux.

Vincent felt to restrain the boy from his painful story of his mother's younger sister, Mercy. But Theo, possessed, delirious, sped on, leading here and there, and then coming back to the main road with his family's secret.

ALICE, take by the pain of guilt, remorse and despair, go down the dark canal of trace, to the shady patch with a mango tree at the centre of the brilliant light. It low enough to sling a rope over a branch and swing, and high enough that she can't drag she foot on the ground, but allow for her dead weight to drop. Once that young girl, Alice, who learn from her brother at games to swing, hice sheself up, she let the rope take the full strain, once she have the noose tight around that little neck of hers, upon which a mother once hang a cheap silver chain for First Communion. The neck crack and she swing, till the odour of death and the buzzing of flies, till high in the blue air the soaring and circling of the corbeaux, bring some cocoa picker to look, and run and call people. Look, who child it is, hanging in the clear light of the afternoon, down by the *dou douce* mango tree? Maybe she try to climb the rope to save sheself in one last moment of hope, but reach up too late, so slip back, jerk, snap, and let her grazed and bloody fingers lose their hold, as she cry, Mercy.

Theo did not let up. The voice carried him.

WHAT PEOPLE remember out in the open, then, was not the reason for this death, the one responsible. They don't pick up sticks and stones and pieces of iron to march up to the big house on the hill, for retribution and reparation.

Instead, they wail all night at a wake, and take her down, such a sweet sweet child, and lay she out in the same white of her Confirmation dress, as white as sweet frangipani flowers; a girl as delicate as a butterfly on a hibiscus hedge, as fragile as those flowers which are the frills on their mothers' *broderie anglaise.*

They lay she out and crown her with sweet-lime flowers, and take her to the ground outside the cemetery, after the Shango people blessing, because the church, with its Abbe, betray her as the Judas, because of the hanging and the life-taking despair, casting her out from the sacred and consecrated ground, so that the women and the grave diggers had to heap up the grave in the dark of the night with the fireflies, one flambeaux on the ground, just beyond the cemetery the next side of the fence, with all the flower they could find to make wreath.

But the grave that that young girl make in a ditch far beyond the shade of the mango tree, which she choose for her secret, before she kill sheself, will go unattend, unmark and trampled by the cattle. Except that in the night, when people passing, they only hearing somebody calling, Mercy. And a next voice crying, Mammy.

Teacher Theo rose up to deliver the conclusion of his history lesson. It was as if the voice could not stop. It was the rhetoric of the rocker going back and forth on the verandah. Theo *was* his great-grandmother.

139

* * *

AFTER ALL THEM STORY, Ma Dellacourt give praise and thanks that she have the strength to endure and survive, so that others go do the same, though she know, too, that those who take to swinging on mango trees on splendid afternoons, is witness to survival and martyrdom of this same endurance.

Sweet Alice she say, she was a sweet child, *oui*. And Mercy, mercy.

Then there was a silence, and then only the sea. Its sigh, exhaled, as it dragged the shale up the beach, and let it go again to meet the next wave. Vincent opened his eyes and saw Theo leave the room with his history and a music which sounded like '*Sweet Chariot, coming to take me home, swing low sweet chariot, coming to take me home*,' sung by a child umbilically tied to a great-grandmother's story, a grandmother's story, a mother's story.

Was he aware of himself telling these stories? Was he sleepwalking, dreaming the past? He was drenched with his fever.

Vincent had listened to the tale of the Dellacourts, the generations of servants in the de Marineaux household, a name he knew well.

His own past began to creep close. He thought of Sybil in his own house on the estate at Versailles with its Le Petit Trianon, the little pavilion, at the bottom of the garden. *Folies de grandeurs.*

Did he know the full story of that time, in the house where he had grown up?

The boy's history lesson was teaching him something, reminding him of something he did not like to remember. Odetta came to rest in his arms, to lie beneath his body.

Vincent lay back, infected by the boy's fever.

Again, it came back to him. Always there was the turret room and the tall palmistes. He always thought that it must have been the palmistes that he must have first seen when he was born. Outside, in the gravelled yard, there were six tall, tall palmiste palms. Palms! The island winds tore at their crowns. It seemed that the sun had a green light which filtered through those lances. Green light, like green water.

Then a young girl's cry, and the sigh of the wind in an indigo sky.

Lying there in the darkness and stillness, left by Theo's departure, Vincent entered that past as if it were yesterday. The pitch pine floorboards of his parents' bedroom creaked. The jalousied window banged. Sybil's fingers smelt of onions. His mother smelt of *vertivert;* cool *colognes* for the heat. His father's pith hat had a band of sweat on the inside rim. It was wet and it smelt of him. The sun had made his arms the colour of a mule or the red tobacco which he smoked on the verandah in the evening.

At the end of the pasture, the barrack rooms laughed in the day when children had the run of the yard; elders in the hot fields, or under the shade of the cocoa and the *immortelle.* At night, he heard what sounded like murder.

Vincent found his memories tumbling out an ancestry, a shared legacy, grounded in the source of the wealth of the creoles, much like Theo had described on the same hillsides. Was this why he had taken the boy from Father Dominic's convent? Did he sense that some crime had been committed, and this boy carried in himself testimony to that? Struck dumb!

These voices from the past paraded themselves in the night. Were these the stories that Father Dominic could no longer listen to? Was this the reason why the boy had to be put somewhere else? What else was there to be said? What else did he have to tell? Tonight, he told more of others rather than of himself – what did Theo have to tell?

Then there were those nights, like a fever, when the drums did not stop. There was something in the insistence of the boy's voice, like the insistence of those drums. And from his bedroom window, Vincent saw Sybil going down the gap to the village the other side of the savannah, under tamarind trees. She was dressed in white and her head was tied with a white cloth. Then he knew that soon there would be clapping and singing, which sounded like wailing, chanting and lamenting; not like hymns in church in the Catholic chapel; not Latin hymns, not *Tantum Ergo,* or, *0 Salutaris* at Benediction, or, the favourite ones to Our Lady, *Ave Ave Ave Maria,* or to the Sacred heart, *Sweet Sacrament Divine,* but singing which was more rhythmic, more rocking, more hand clapping, sounding like somewhere else and yet sounding like it belonged right there in that village.

The palms sighed. The boy's stories stirred all of this in him, and more that he wished to forget.

When Vincent walked out onto the landing, he saw that the door of Theo's room opposite had been left wide open. He could not hear the boy downstairs. He had not looked out of his window onto the jetty. Theo had taken to going out early in the morning, before dawn even, and sitting at the end of the jetty.

Had he missed the news? Had the boy turned down the volume of the radio?

As he approached, the light in the room seemed different. Not its usual, bright, early morning dazzle. When he got to the door and looked in, he could see why. It was the reflection that the morning sun was making on the walls.

At first, Vincent was not quite sure what had happened. Then he saw the brown grip, which was open on the floor and left in the middle of the room. He recognised it as the brown grip that Theo had arrived with, that he had run down the corridor at Santa Ana to get. Vincent could see him now, so small then, the boy and his grip which he had imagined held his small number of clothes. Quite obviously, they had held newspapers as well. Cut up newspaper was strewn on the floor. Newspaper cuttings were stuck to every wall.

Vincent went up to the wall nearest the door. The paper was wet and smelt of that familiar glue, flour and water, he had used as a child sticking pictures into a scrap book. He walked around the room passing his hand over the moist, damp walls. Where the sunlight hit the wall directly, the paper was drying fast. Vincent noticed that it was the entire room, not a single inch of wall was not covered.

He was struck by this transformation of the room. It was only as he stood there, staring around, imagining that Theo might emerge from somewhere, that he began to remember that, of course, it was customary for poor people to cover the walls of their small board houses with newspaper. It kept the rooms warm and stopped rain coming in. It brightened them up as well, papered over cracks. He remembered walking through the barrack yards below Versailles, and seeing the interiors of the board houses and the barrack rooms. He remembered Sybil, hording newspaper.

He began to read where there was a picture that he recognised. When he looked at the date of the paper, he could see that plainly these were newspapers from a few years back. The boy had horded *The Gazette* and *The Guardian*.

He looked at the familiar photographs, and began reading the news below them. The photograph he settled on was one of a fire in Fyzabad in 1937, when the oilfield rioters had captured the fallen policeman, Corporal Charles King, who had had a leg injury. They had fallen on him and drenched him with kerosene and set him alight. The police were unable to get to the body in time. The well known story was there, pasted on the walls. All of this time Theo had horded these cuttings!

Vincent remembered him staring at the burnt body of Michael Johnson in the yard at Saint Damian's. He heard again Ti-Jean's rendering of the calypso, *When they beat him and they burn him in Fyzabad.* As he stared at the walls, Theo appeared at the door.

Vincent turned towards him. 'Theo, come here, boy.' He opened his arms. Theo ran and clung to him.

Agave

The pouis were golden on the hills. Where there had once been an old cocoa estate, Vincent could see, this morning, the tall *immortelle,* planted for shade, the colour of red coral, orangey and pink, changing in the light and high breeze at the end of the dry season in May, 1940. He watched the morning hills as the pirogue cut across Chac Chac Bay to La Chapelle Bay. Jonah had brought the message. It was a note from Mother Superior asking him to come to the convent before going to Saint Damian's.

He was met at the jetty by the infirmarian, Sister Luke, and taken to a cell separate from the others, off the infirmary.

'It's Sister Thérèse,' Sister Luke whispered as she opened the door of the dimly lit cell.

He followed the infirmarian into the gloom of the room with the white muslin curtains still closed. He surveyed the small room. Sister Luke pulled the curtains. There was a single iron bed and a *prie Dieu,* above which was a small wooden crucifix. In the corner, to the right of the door, was a small table on which stood a white enamel basin with a jug. The rim of the basin was blue, as was the lip and handle of the jug. A white cotton towel hung from a railing at the side of the table. Along the opposite wall was another small table and chair, used as a desk for reading and study. Lemon light flooded the room as the nun opened the curtains.

Sister Thérèse lay in bed, covered with a white cotton sheet drawn right up to her neck. Only her face was showing, looking out of the round of the white cotton skull cap, stretched around her face, and firmly buttoned under her chin, attached to a cotton shift. She was cocooned. She lay quite still, as Sister Luke ushered Vincent to the bedside with the firm whisper.

'Doctor?' Her statement was inflected like a question.

He made to sit at the edge of the bed, as was his bedside manner on the wards. The infirmarian restrained him, and without saying a word, brought the chair from the desk. She put it next to the bed, motioning him to sit, as she stood by the door with her arms in her sleeves and her head bowed.

Sister Thérèse lay with her eyes closed. Vincent leant towards her. 'Thérèse.' Sister Luke cleared her throat, disapprovingly. He was aware that he had been too familiar, omitting the title, 'Sister', as he was tempted to do when they worked together. Sister Thérèse opened her eyes. She moved her lips. He leant closer to hear and understand.

'Meuse.'

'Say it again.' He had not caught the word.

She raised her head to speak more clearly. 'Meuse.' She ran her fingers along the sheets, tracing a swerving line along the white cotton sheet. She kept on drawing the invisible line, repeating what he then understood was the course of the river. She crumpled the covering sheet, pinching it to make peaks. 'Ardennes, *les forêts, les montagnes.*' She pointed with her fingertips. He watched her fingers, the one with her gold ring, her bridal ring, dab at the sheets, then crumple them in her fist. She concluded her action with, 'Sedan.'

The infirmarian cleared her throat again, showing her irritation. Vincent pulled back from the bed. Sister Thérèse smoothed out the sheet, stretching her hand towards where his hand had been. 'Warm,' she whispered. He turned to Sister Luke as if to say something, then turned back to Sister Thérèse.

She began again, more violently, digging into the mattress with her fingers, drawing deep invisible lines, radiating out in all directions. She stabbed the sheets more deliberately. He could not understand what she was trying to tell him. He wished he was not being policed. She lay back again and closed her eyes, exhausted.

'Sister Marguerite found her in the chapel. She must've fainted, or fallen asleep at her vigil. She found her on the floor before the communion rails.' The infirmarian's whispers were sharply enunciated.

Vincent nodded.

She whispered again, close to his ear. 'She's been babbling incoherently since then,' she said dismissively.

He turned, still sitting, and looked up at her, speaking quietly, 'She's quite coherent, quite coherent.'

Sister Luke went back to her post. Her fingers worried her length of black rosary beads, the fifteen mysteries hanging at her side.

Under her breath, Vincent distinctly heard her ultimate dismissal. *'Les Juifs.'*

Vincent was startled. 'In the convent,' he thought.

Sister Thérèse opened her eyes and looked at Vincent. 'You see,' she said. 'Even here.' She had not missed the tone of prejudice.

He turned again to look at the infirmarian on guard.

In order to calm the furious illustrations, he put his hand over Sister Thérèse's. This had been his gesture before, a doctor's way. She opened her eyes, and raised her eyebrows. Vincent understood her frustration with the presence of the other nun.

The sun was up and it poured into the cell. The dry season was ticking in the bush. The *cigales* prayed for rain. Beyond the garden with the cemetery, the thunder of the waves breaking at Bande du Sud, was carried on the salty air. The peninsular, at this end of the island, ended in the mangroves and agaves around Salt Pond.

Vincent turned abruptly to face Sister Luke. 'I need you to go and call Mother Superior. You may still catch her before she leaves for Saint Damian's. If she's already left, I want a message sent to her to come at once. Doctor Metivier wants to see her. Do you understand?' He spoke in his most authoritative tone. 'I think you may find that she has already left for Saint Damian's.'

Sister Luke hesitated, and then left the cell, mumbling something about it being out of order, leaving him alone with a nun. The door of the cell was banged shut.

Then there was peace and the *cigales'* prayers were a lament.

'Thank you.' Sister Thérèse opened her eyes. Her hand closed over his.

'Tell me what happened.' He held her hand. He smelt her sweet breath. It was the smell of communion wafers.

His childhood flooded his mind, that sweet smell of communion, when he and Odetta were allowed to kneel next to each other at mass, giggling and squirming in their seats. He remembered his mother's voice, 'That child must sit at the back with Sybil.'

Sister Thérèse sat up and then leant over the edge of the bed, digging under the mattress for something. Vincent leaned over to help her. She extracted from inside the fibre mattress, where she had hidden them, a bundle of letters tied with brown string. He immediately recognised her father's handwriting. He remembered the letters she had brought to read to him at Saint Damian's two years ago. While they were consolation, they were also the source of her fear. Without opening them, she clasped them to her breasts, hugging them to her neck. Then, staring at the ceiling, she began, as if she were praying, to recite a litany.

'*Pogrom, ghetto.*' Then with her hand at her side, her finger tracing the course of rivers, the contours of hills, drawing the boundaries of maps which were learnt at school, she continued her litany. 'Meuse, Rhine, Verdun, Donaumont.' She rested and started again. 'Maginot, Petain, *le vainquer de Verdun, le medécin de l'Armée, Jeanne d'Arc.'* He listened to her bizarre recital.

He heard the words plucked from a childhood memory, a father's history and political lessons.

'*La der des ders.* Verdun!' She had learnt her First War. As she grew more quiet, she whispered, 'Dreyfus, *le juif.*' Her words disappeared with the breeze.

Each name conjured an epoch and an event, describing now what she was imagining would happen to these places, to that history, for her father and her beloved *France.* She riffled her father's letters, tearing them open for phrases which she spat out from her position, propped up now on her fibre pillow.

Vincent stared, distressed.

'*Mourir pour* Dantzig?' She snared, in the voice of another.

'Thérèse.' He tried to comfort, forgetting his decorum.

'Phoney war.' She twisted the word in a mock, posh English accent.

'Come Thérèse,' Vincent stretched to hold her hand, disentangle her fingers from the brown string, and the ripped, opened correspondence from her father.

But she continued her diatribe. Softly now, '*La Marne Blanche.*' Vincent did not know how to stem this flow, how to quieten this derangement. For some time, he had felt her father's letters were not good for her. The convent rules should have been followed. She should have got rid of these letters. But she had broken the rules. She hoarded his words and fed her fear with them. She plucked them from his historical analyses.

'*Nous somme dans un pot de chambre et nous y serons emmerdés.* Shit.'

He was shocked but listened. He wondered if Mother Superior was going to arrive. What would he tell her? What would be his advice, his diagnosis?

'Thérèse, let me give you something to calm you.' He did not know what. Maybe words were the best cure, this blood-letting of words.

It was as if she was having convulsions, as she spat out the names: 'Gamelin, Daladier, Weygand.' Her father's bitterness was like a blood transfusion. '*Skitzkrieg.*'

He heard the last twisted word. He got up and opened the door and looked down the corridor. No one was about. The sisters were at the hospital. Somewhere, he heard the clanging of a water bucket and the slop of a mop. In the haze at the end of the corridor, he saw a lay sister mopping the floor. Hunched over her work, she looked like a mirage; the morning sun flooding through the arch from the convent's cloister into the gloom of the corridor.

He returned to the cell and to her bedside. She cried out, the words sounding like the voices of those who had attacked in the streets on *Kristallnacht*. '*Klotzen nicht kleckern*'. He knew enough German to translate. 'Make waves not ripples.'

The room went silent after that. Then, like the very waters of those rivers she had dug out on her sheets, the words flowed.

Vincent had a vision, as he sat with his hands in hers, of the low-lying countryside of Hainault and Flanders, like the watercolours and oils of their artists, seen in galleries in London; low-lying fields, water meadows and poplars; clouds, windmills and the bridges over the rivers of her maps. Her voice was precise on each name. A toponymy, a poem of names: 'Meuse, Sambre, Schelde, Escaut, Scarpe, Lys.' These were arteries of invasion. She continued, 'Seine, Marne, Aisne, Oise.' Like a strategist, she was mapping the navigational routes to Paris. Then, she stopped abruptly. '*Non.*'

She was sitting up in bed. She had kicked off the white cotton sheet, and sat with her legs splayed. She pulled her shift above her knees. He did not know where to look. He stared at her in her cotton shift, her white cocoon, her head tightly bonnetted, her face encircled. He saw only her wide black eyes, those shining eyes. She flattened the surface between her legs and began another map, another route. 'Somme, Amiens, Seine, Rouen.' She looked up at Vincent and smiled. 'Let the last man brush the Channel with his sleeve.'

He listened, amazed. She lay back and slept. He got up from his chair and covered her with the sheet she had thrown off, pulling it right up over her bare legs and knees. He was relieved that Mother Superior had not come in at that moment.

The name letting had stopped. Peace reigned.

He sat and watched her. He listened to the sea, to the wind and the *cigales'* cries which never ceased.

Vincent was in the servants' room of the house at Versailles. Odetta was sick. Back from school, he had gone to visit her. He was allowed this one visit, because Odetta was going away. They did not tell him where she was going. His mother had said that they could not keep her here. He remembered her running her hand through his hair and saying, 'Go and say goodbye, darling. Don't stay long. She's not well. Tell Sybil to come upstairs afterwards.' His mother had always comforted him, despite her disapproval.

He kicked a stone across the gravelled yard. He arrived dusty and sweating. Sybil was sitting by the bed. 'You come to see her. Cheups.' She got up from the bedside.

Like everyone knew everything, but kept their silence. The door to the bedroom was ajar, and the lemon sunlight threw shadows on the pitch pine floor. Motes of dust hung in the bands of light. Odetta was sitting up in bed in a white cotton chemise with her legs apart, her small bare shoulders, her round stomach lifting the chemise. Her black hair was unplaited, and was a glistening nimbus of black net. It reminded him of his mother's lace mantilla which always looked as if it had tarantulas trapped in its embroidery.

At first, when they were small, she was the little girl in the turret room, showing him her spider. And then, that last August, when they were older, so quiet and alone, the rain drumming on the roof, as if no one else existed in the world, they stopped playing, and found that sweet pleasure, which still, always, reminded him of the fragrance of guavas. It was a moment he had never been able to recreate, but which, on every other occasion with a girl, there had been an attempt. He was trembling over her. But, finding her cunt, that word, had been easier than boys at school had said. He had had a childhood to discover the tight entrance to her wet flower. Her guiding fingers had helped with their knowing touch. He liked to smell and lick them when they had been there.

Right away, they knew that there would be consequences; his awful banishment once she was discovered making baby. 'Why she go lie? Why for? Is the Master. Is Master Vincent, Madam.'

149

It was the grown-ups who quarrelled, his mother with Sybil, 'Always bringing that child up to the house, what did I tell you?' They quarrelled about who had failed to instil the right ways in their children.

Then the words of Theo's stories, the history of the Dellacourts of Corinth, flooded Vincent's mind.

Vincent was startled out of his daydream. Thérèse had dozed. He thought he heard someone in the corridor. He thought it might be Mother Superior arriving at last. He put his head outside the door. It was the lay sister finishing her chores with her clanging bucket.

Thérèse lay quite still, as if she was sleeping. He went and stood at the window. Thoughts of Odetta had disturbed him.

'You not leaving me, are you, Doctor?' He turned back to the bed. She was sitting up on the side of the bed with her feet on the ground.

He stood next to the chair which Sister Luke had placed by the bed. 'No. I thought you were sleeping.'

'I feel as if I've not slept for years,' she sighed.

'Are you not sleeping well then? How long has this been going on?'

'The night is full of noises. The sea, the wind, the insects, the frogs.'

'You've not yet adapted to our tropics. *Triste tropique.*'

'I wake, and a ship is all lit up at my window, like a moving city, a deep drone. Then, in the early hours of the morning, before we're called for Matins, the fishermen are returning from the *bocas*. The night's busy. I'm tired when I first go to bed. So tired after the hospital. Then I wake and listen and listen. I hear their words, their bottle and spoon, their calypso tune, long after they've passed through the night: *Anywhere you go you can tell a Jew. The nose in their face not like me and you.* Then I can't sleep.'

Vincent watched her trying to touch the floor with her bare toes. He noticed the scar on her ankle from the cut when he had first attended to her. 'It's healed well. Not too bad a scar.'

She looked down. 'Oh, that. It seems such a long time now. *Kristallnacht.*' She looked at him.

He did not want to encourage her dwelling there.

'I'm so thirsty.'

'Let me get you some water.'

'There's a glass near the jug on the table.' She pointed.

He poured and then handed her the glass. She gulped the water and he got her some more.

'Take one of these after ten minutes and don't drink after that for another ten minutes. I got them in France, in a pharmacy in Paris, when I was a student. Kept them for a rainy day, as they say in England.' He shook out a small pill from a brown vial.

'Isn't that most days? *En Angleterre!*' They laughed.

Thérèse toyed with the small white pill.

'It's called Aconite. Lie back and I'll tell you a story.' She slung her feet back onto the bed, and tucked herself under the white cotton sheet. She lay like when Vincent first came into the room.

'Yes, tell me a story.' She held the small pill in the tips of her fingers, waiting for the seconds to tick by in her head. She looked like a child waiting for a bedtime story.

Vincent began. 'There's a blue flower, almost violet, which grows in the mountain regions of Europe and Asia. Each bloom is a hood which some call Monk's Hood. It's the way that it folds like the cowl of a monk.'

Thérèse was staring at the ceiling.

'It flowers along the tip of the lengthy and leafy plant which catches the wind in the mountains. The blue-violet *aconitum napellus*. But you must not be fooled by that beauty, by that monastic cloak which hides a poison.' He smiled.

Thérèse's eyes flickered and she turned them on Vincent. Then she put the pill on the tip of her tongue.

'Let it dissolve,' he said.

'Will there be a big change?'

'Gradual.'

'What's this one for?'

'For when you wake in the night and hear the big ships. It's for the fear which comes with the wind and the sea. It's for when you think you are going to faint in chapel, when you think you are going to die.'

'Will you stay and watch till I fall asleep?' She reached out to hold his hand. He thought he could pretend to be taking her pulse, if Mother Superior arrived at that moment. He let her hold his hand. When he thought she was sleeping, he let go of her hand and slipped out of the cell.

There was no one about. The convent was dead quiet except for the intermittent breaking of the waves under the cliff, which seemed as if they were rushing right under the very foundations of the convent. He thought he could hear the pillars buckling. He walked down the steps to the jetty. The place seemed abandoned as he looked out over the bay to Saint Damian's and his own house, a pink blur in the green shade. Chac Chac Bay was empty, but there was an oil tanker passing outside in the gulf, heading for the Boca de Navios. Sister Luke had not returned, and he now wondered why.

The morning had flown.

He was suddenly startled by the sound of the Angelus, with a clanging of bells on the cliff above. It was rung by the same lay sister who had the iron bucket, mopping in the corridor. She seemed to be the only soul about the place. Her noise was soon echoed by the ringing of the Angelus at Saint Damian's. Then the bells stopped, though still ringing in the hills, like a shower of rain in the distance. He would just have to wait for a boat.

Vincent returned to the infimary's cell. When he got there, he saw that the door was open. Thérèse was not in bed.

He followed a trail of bed linen along the floor into the small garden outside the infirmary. He was now quite worried. He climbed the hillock with the cacti and agaves above the old cemetery. This gave him a view of the peninsular, at the end of which was Salt Pond, and then further on, Bande du Sud. He had only been there once. It was an exposed and barren part of the island.

The midday sun was high in the sky. He was thirsty and hungry. The morning had been a strain. If he was feeling this way, what condition would Thérèse be in, by this time? He began the descent, along a small track through the scrub and agave. The waves were breaking like cannons. The wind had died down. The *cigales* were screaming. A *corbeau* circled overhead.

He thought he might see her veil in the wind, a white flag of surrender. But, then he remembered, she had not had her veil on. He doubted that she would have got fully dressed. She must be out there, barefoot, in the white cotton shift she had been wearing in bed.

Vincent's worse fears, as he descended the cliff, were that Thérèse might have stumbled and fallen over from any of the sheer heights on the way down to Salt Pond. Even worse, that she might have ventured along the coastal path above La Tinta, which overhung the rocky coves of the Boca Grande.

Then he found the clue that he was looking for. Thérèse had caught her white cotton shift on the thorns of a cactus. It had left a ribbon fluttering in the breeze, which now gave some relief from the heat. Vincent unpicked the torn hem of her skirt from the thorns. He held it like a holy relic.

When he came out of the shade of the mangroves on to the edge of Salt Pond, he found a margin of salt on the shore. He brushed aside the dangerous manchineel with its poisonous ooze. The light was blinding white on the aquamarine of the water, which reflected the succulents and sedge which bordered the pond. A haze shimmered. The rocks and stones were dusted with salt. Thérèse, in her white cotton shift and skull cap, stooping down near the edge of the water ahead of him, was almost indistinguishable from some of the larger whitened rocks. She was still. The place hummed. Only the white egrets stirred, settling on the green branches of the mangrove.

There was a shimmer of gauze, the zing of a *batimazelle,* like a sliver of glass; two dragonflies coupling on the wind, almost invisible, a zing, then gone on the wind.

A jade green lizard emerged from the cleft in a rock near his foot and scuttled into a dried moss fissure.

Vincent approached Thérèse quietly. A *jaune d'Abricot* pinned itself to a piece of driftwood. It startled him with its yellow flutter.

His footsteps crunched on the salt. He knelt by her stooping figure. He put his hand at the small of her back. 'Thérèse, it's okay now.' He noticed that her bare feet had been bruised on the shale and stones along the track where he himself had slipped more than once in pursuit of her.

She turned and looked over her shoulder. Her face was burnt. Her fingers were cut, and she had scratches on her arms. Her white cotton shift was stained with blood and dirt. She took up a small stick and began drawing on the entablature of caked mud. Her abstract hieroglyphs were accompanied once more by her litany of place names.

'No, Thérèse. Don't worry yourself now. Leave that now,' Vincent advised.

Beneath her breath, she was singing a snatch of the fishermen's calypso. *'Anywhere you go you can tell a Jew. The nose in their face not like me or you.'*

Then the thing he had not wanted to happen, happened without choice, as she turned to face to him more directly, and as he leant towards her. Their brows were beaded with sweat. Their lips were cracked. Their mouths were dry. But, with that first kiss, their dry lips resting there in the glare of the midday sun, they let the *cigales'* prayers for rain drown their fears. They kissed and kissed.

'Doctor,' she whispered.

'Vincent.'

'Vincent. Yes, Vincent.'

'Thérèse.'

'Say Madeleine.' The sea breeze stole her words.

'Madeleine.'

'Yes, I'm Madeleine now. I'm Madeleine Weil.'

'Madeleine Weil, yes,' he repeated.

What would they do?

Her stooping, bruised figure, her dry, cracked lips, the silence of the desert they inhabited on the salt margins of the pond, filled his mind to overwhelming, crowding out his sense of caution and the proper decorum of a doctor. But then he thought, what had he done? Again?

Rainy Season

The calypsonians kept their commentary going on the time; words for an era. The Doctor's House was a buzz of humming and singing, replacing the ban on carnival by the governor. Theo kept up with the calypsos of the day. '*Hand me the papers let me read the news, because ah puzzle and I'm so confused.*'

A month later, the first rains stitching the sky, veiling the hills, bringing the pouis' flowers to the ground, the almonds dropping fast, thudding on the sand along the beach at Saint Damian's, they heard the news on the BBC, that the Germans had entered Paris.

'*France after fighting desperately, Got retarded and surrendered to Germany.*' The fishermen were the calypsonians.

Over at the convent, the nuns processed to the chapel for special prayers. '*Custodi me Domine, de manu pecatoris.*' Keep me, O Lord, from the hand of the wicked.

The younger sisters cried openly at the hospital for days after the news of the invasion of France, and then after the fall of Paris. The patients now tried to comfort their nurses.

The advance of armies had the fourteen-year-old Theo racing up to his room. The black *Swastika* crayoned in its white circle, on its red background, was pinned to the wall, stuck in the centre of Paris.

Theo had a way of showing which countries had fallen under the Germans, by laying out their flags flat against the wall. The *Swastika* and Union Jack were erect. '*Blutfahne,*' he whispered adjusting the pin. Vincent could not believe, sometimes, the words he came out with. 'Blood banner.'

Instead of filling the night with his own stories, Vincent found him awake, torch under the blanket and earphones on, attached to his crystal set, absorbed by the language of war, the crackle of Morse. Then the *tricolore* was lain flat.

'*Run your run, Adolph Hitler, run your run...*' he whistled and buzzed about.

'Come Theo, we need to get off. Remember you promised to go by Singh today. You mustn't ride Cervantes hard. He's only a small donkey. 'Vincent watched him flying about the house.

He would not leave till he had done his chores. He busied himself while talking to Vincent. 'Who go clean this place, tell me.' He had refused to give up his household work, even on the days he was over at Saint Damian's.

Vincent had overheard him last week. 'We don't need servant here, Miss Beatrice.'

A lot of his time was taken up with the maintenance of the vast theatre of war in his room which was taking the place of the 1937 Riots. A collage of newspaper cuttings could be seen between the cracks of maps with intriguing juxtapositions: Marcus Garvey and Jesse Owens disappearing behind Abyssinia, while a boatload of Jewish refugees landed on the jetty at Nelson Island, on a torn photograph from the Porta España *Gazette*.

Over at Saint Damian's, Vincent stood outside on the verandah of the children's ward and smoked a Lucky Strike. Theo went off to Singh's. 'I going and learn some science today,' he proclaimed. Thoughts of his brother, Bernard, distracted Vincent, as an RAF surveillance plane circled far out into the gulf, and then became part of the haze along the eastern coast of Venezuela.

Somewhere, somewhere, would be Bernard, Vincent mused. His letters to his mother and Vincent were brief and jolly. They were less frequent now. The mail was held up. Bernard kept the horror to himself.

The clinic, where Vincent and Thérèse worked at their research, was quiet, except for the rain dripping into the drain below. She could see him out on the verandah smoking. His khaki figure stood, looking away from her, blowing the cigarette smoke out to the bay. They were embarrassed to meet each other.

She bent her head to the microscope, examining her latest cultures of *mycrobacterium leprae*. She worked now to forget their kiss at Salt Pond. She worked not to imagine what was happening to herself. She lost herself in the secret life of the *bacillii* which created so much havoc in her patients' lives.

A macabre silence surrounded her.

Vincent came in off the verandah.

'I expect there'll be no more letters now,' she said abruptly.

He looked at her, unable to offer reassurance, and at a loss about their newly declared feelings. She did not meet his eyes.

'I don't know what to say. I don't know.' He could not hold her now.

'Everything has changed,' she declared.

'Everything?' He was unsure whether she was referring to them or to her father.

Then she was distracted again. She continued with her research. 'Look.' She pointed far out into the gulf where there was a glimpse of Nelson Island. 'History, odd, called after a British Admiral, now a camp for my people. You, know what the calypsonians have been saying. *The way they are coming all of them, Will make Trinidad a new Jerusalem.*' Vincent smiled at her rendition of the calypso.

'You're still kept awake by the fishermen?' Vincent tried to catch her eye.

'I take my doctor's remedy. I take *aconitum nappellus* and sleep.'

'No matter the ships that pass in the night?' he asked.

Vincent's question reminded her of their intimacy. She pulled away. Could not allow herself to be reminded. He was the doctor, and she was again his research assistant.

Neither of them recalled their time at the edge of Salt Pond. That, too, became part of the present silence. She had not taken his hand. He had not folded his over hers.

The present silence became part of the darkness which descended with the monsoon. It became part of the great silence of the sea. '*Le silence de la mer,*' Thérèse said to herself.

'What?' Vincent asked, looking across from his desk. 'Did you say something?' Thérèse looked up. They both looked sad with longing.

She checked herself and repeated, '*Le silence de la mer.*' They both looked out over the bay, into the gulf.

She retreated, he guessed, into her worry about her father. He could almost imagine her reverie.

She sees him in a narrow room built between walls. She imagines him waiting for a knock on the door which then opens a crack for the food that is

157

placed on the floor. The tray is laid with pumpernickel, red onions, radishes, *challah* and that sweet butter her mother made an effort to procure. All that's left is food, he used to say. She thinks back to him raging, that it was his culture, his race, but not his religion. There are no windows in the room. A car stops outside the house. There is a knock on the door. Her Papa hears voices above him and in the corridor outside. He hardly breathes.

'Do you believe in evil?' Thérèse broke her silence, looking up from her microscope and the notes she was making on the pad beside her.

'Evil?' Vincent questioned. Where was this leading?

'Yes, an absolute source of evil, as there is an absolute source of good,' she elaborated.

'I'm not sure I understand that. If, as you argue, God is all powerful then he must be powerful over evil. Anyway, without getting into metaphysical tangles, no, I don't. Not sure I believe in an absolute source of good, anyway.' He did not want to be talking about this.

'How do you explain?'

Vincent moved to the door of the pharmacy and lit a cigarette. He felt he had to go out. He drew deeply, inhaled and blew the smoke into the distance. He turned at the door.

'I observe and believe that people commit bad acts, wrong acts. If we call them evil and monsters we give up the chance to understand why it is that people like ourselves commit these acts.' He could hear himself lecturing. What were they doing? Why was he saying all of this? 'We need to understand history. We need to understand nature. Charles Darwin, Karl Marx and Sigmund Freud? They describe Nature and there's no God and no Devil in Nature. We need to understand why we commit bad acts ourselves.'

'What is a bad act?' She was facing him now.

'What do you mean? One that harms ourselves and others.' He was impatient with this conversation.

'You're thinking of the children?' Thérèse looked to see the reaction on his face.

'I wasn't actually, at that moment. I was thinking... What were you thinking about anyway?

She blushed. 'A bad act could be...' she hesitated.

'But I've wondered,' he cut her off. 'Of course, of course, I've wondered more than once. How possibly even Ti-Jean could've stoked the fire.'

'There are other kinds of bad acts.'

'I thought you might be thinking of the war. Of your father.'

'I wasn't then. I was... I was earlier. Sounds like you think we're left to ourselves to sort things out.'

'Ourselves? Sort things out?' He looked at her. She lowered her eyes. They were skirting around each other. 'Pretty well. With history and nature and, of course, reason and science.'

'Yes. I know about all of that, but I also meant us.' She looked directly at him.

He stood next to her desk. He reached out to anchor some papers which were fluttering in the breeze. He could smell her. She put her hands into her sleeves.

Vincent started his lecture again. 'We need to find the reasons in history, in personal history, in political history. Science and nature guide us there. Not comfort ourselves with hypothetical absolutes which are responsible for how things are.' He could hear himself again. He wanted to kiss her.

'Personal history?' Thérèse broke off from her work abruptly. They were both feeling they did not know how to talk to each other.

The Angelus sounded. She stood and prayed. Vincent continued with his work, impatient. The bell for the sisters' lunch summoned her. She tidied her papers.

'Such order.' She turned at the door and looked at him.

'There's so much disorder.' There was longing in her eyes.

'Or it is just how things are?' he differed.

'We don't agree,' she said emphatically.

'We might? Will you be back after lunch?' He checked his wooing tone.

She smiled, brushing her veil from her face.

'This Chaulmoogra Oil, more headache than it worth.' Vincent had a view through the window from the verandah into the pharmacy. He waited for a moment before entering. Singh and Theo were sitting at the work counter. They had their backs to him. 'This have side effects.' Theo was looking on intently as Singh prepared the tray to be used for the afternoon's treatment.

'The skin get pulpy and inflamed, yes?' Theo repeated.

'That's right. You listen well.'

'You think the patients get some help, because it work like a placebo.' Theo went over his lesson.

'You have the correct terminology. You learning quick,' Singh praised the boy.

'I does pick up vocabulary fast.'

Vincent smiled at Theo's eagerness. He did not want to eavesdrop, but he did not want to interrupt the science lesson.

'What we want is new medicine.'

'I frighten when I look at them, you know. When they have sores, and deformed hands and feet.'

'You mustn't fear that, man.' Singh was talking as an equal to the boy. 'They will feel bad if you show that. As I tell you, you have to understand what you seeing.'

'So, if this not really helping them...' Theo pointed to the Chaulmoogra Oil preparations.

'Well, is what the doctor say. Hygiene and care. Clean bandages.'

'How that go help that look in their face. Those stumps? What you call it? Claw hands?' Theo began to bend his fingers to illustrate his horror. 'Short short fingers. The way they hand bend so. No thumb, bones sticking out. Septic wounds! You hear that! More vocabulary I learn.'

Vincent did not have the heart to walk in and interrupt. He left the verandah. As he did so, he heard Singh. 'Colonial contempt and religious superstition, too many documents and prayers.' He stopped in his tracks. He had to wait to hear what Theo was going to make of this first lesson in politics.

'Oh gawd! What's the time? I suppose to meet Doctor in the clinic for lunch,' Theo shouted.

'Go then. Come back after your lunch. I go teach you some more.'

Vincent returned to the door of the pharmacy and met Theo as he came out onto the verandah. 'Eh, eh, I was just coming to see what you were up to.'

Singh followed Theo out. 'Checking up on your boy. In case I lead him astray.' He put his hand on Theo's shoulder. 'Bright, you know?'

'I learn science and thing, you know,' Theo enthused.

'Good, good. Thought you must be starving.'

Theo went down into the yard.

160

'Easy on the politics, eh?' Vincent said to Singh as he walked off, following Theo.

'So you was really checking up on me.'

Vincent smiled. 'Keep to the science.'

'That alone not going to save us. You know that.'

'He's a vulnerable boy, Singh. Young.'

'You know what I was doing at fourteen. Lighting fire in the cane. Sabotage on the estate. Golconda had the record in the riots.'

Vincent looked to see if Theo was within earshot. 'You know what I mean. Take it easy. I'll deliver him safely after lunch.'

'You still have a lot to learn, Doc.' Singh looked at Vincent searchingly. 'I have more story.'

After lunch, Vincent and Thérèse were back in the clinic and Theo had rejoined Singh in the pharmacy.

Gertrude Palmer, one of the very needy patients, entered the clinic. Vincent could not contain himself as he saw her walking in. 'Gertrude, Gertrude! What're you doing?' He checked his irritable tone. Gertrude had walked in on the end of her tibia. When he examined her he found bits of gravel and leaves wedged in the marrow cavity. 'Gertrude, Gertrude!' His voice was more sympathetic.

He and Thérèse exchanged looks and smiled. Gertrude left happier for her new dressing. Vincent and Thérèse threw up their arms in despair.

'Totally anaesthetised!' Vincent screamed.

'A kind of amnesia, isn't it?'

'Those messages just not getting through.' Vincent paced the clinic.

'She sauntered in completely indifferent to pain.'

'Seemingly without any instinct for self-preservation.'

'Nerves, the peripheral nerves all gone!'

'He jests at scars who never felt a wound,' Vincent said.

Thérèse looked up, inquiringly. 'Yes?'

'Shakespeare, *Romeo and Juliet.*'

'Doctor,' she said teasingly. 'A literature scholar?'

'We've got to understand how these channels of transmission, how that wiring has been impaired. Otherwise, we're doomed to sores, ulcers, leaking blisters, sepsis, and necrotic tissue! A nursing and doctoring of bandages and more bandages. Chaulmoogra Oil for another century!' They both collapsed laughing into their chairs.

'Madeleine,' he leant over to take her hand. 'Sorry.'

'No, no, Vincent. What are we going to do?' She took his hand. They heard a sister passing in the corridor outside.

'We'll think of something,' they said together, encouraging each other.

'Something?' Thérèse, more serious, asked. 'Something?'

'You're the one with the faith, Sister.' Vincent smiled. They were talking about themselves and their research. 'We'll experiment. Science will work with nature.'

'Where has reason and science brought us?' she asked another kind of question.

Vincent knew that Thérèse had moved onto the war. She didn't really believe that. 'That's lunacy.'

'Yes, we think so. My father thought that. But look. A lot of science and culture, and philosophers of reason, are brought into the service of this vision, their lunatic vision.'

Vincent could see that Thérèse was getting sad again. 'Thérèse.' He was going to put his hand over hers, but restrained himself.

'I know.'

'Let's get back to work '

'Where were we?'

The afternoon had disappeared. 'I need to get Theo back. We'll continue later. Can you work late?'

'I'll see what Mother Superior says.' Her eyes said what her heart was telling her.

As Vincent approached Singh's pharmacy, he saw Theo leaving. He met him in the yard. 'Science lesson finished?'

'Mr Singh say he have to teach another lesson. He have another student.'

'Oh? I'll be late tonight. I'll ask Jonah to stay with you. Leave Cervantes for me.' They found Jonah on the jetty.

'Don't worry, Doc. We go do some fishing, eh Theo?'

Theo was already in the bow of the pirogue.

On the way back to the clinic. Vincent looked in on Singh. He entered the pharmacy without knocking. 'Oh, sorry, I forgot Theo said you had another student.' Singh and Christiana leapt to their feet as he entered. They had been sitting close to each other reading from a pharmaceutical manual. The girl hurried from the room. 'You don't have to go,' he called as she ran along the verandah.

'Come back later,' Singh called after her. 'She shy.' Singh stood at the door.

'I see. Well. How did it go with Theo?'

'Good man. He does learn fast.'

'Christiana? Not sure why she's still here. I haven't found any signs of the illness,' Vincent commented.

'She herself knows that, and is scared now.'

'Maybe we need to get her back home. How old is she?'

'Sixteen.' Singh looked embarrassed.

'Must get back to the clinic. Sister Thérèse is waiting.'

'Good. I'll see you tomorrow,' he said, relieved.

Back at the clinic Vincent and Thérèse picked up where they had left off. The evening came on quickly. The kerosene lamp hummed and spluttered, as moths torpedoed themselves at the glass lantern unable to learn a lesson in injury. 'We need to operate. I need to do an autopsy. I need hands,' Vincent was saying.

'Where'll we operate?'

'Here. Maybe in Porta España.'

'Will they let you take the body there? Will they bring the operating theatre here?'

'We could. I don't see why not. What a memorial to life if a patient's hands gave us the evidence we need.'

'It'll need to be a day on which the ice arrives. When we have plenty ice.'

'If I'm called right away, we can operate quickly, before putrefaction. But we're running before we can walk.' Vincent slowed himself down.

'What do you mean?'

'We need to look at hands. We need to examine many hands, before we can think of operating. What are we looking for?'

They were both exhausted. The night ticked outside beyond the hum of the kerosene lantern. Vincent watched Thérèse's hands on the desk. Then she put them under her scapular like a good nun. They sat in silence.

163

'Hmm,' Vincent sighed.

Thérèse looked up. Their eyes found each other's. They smiled. Thérèse got up and started tidying her desk.

Vincent went out the screen door onto the verandah and lit a cigarette. It glowed like a firefly. Thérèse could see his face in the glow when he pulled on it. It went dark again, as he flicked the ash on the zinnia beds.

They were both thinking that they should not find themselves like this, alone, alone at night with each other.

At the end of the verandah was the night sister in her cubicle, where Thérèse would be sleeping.

When Thérèse came onto the verandah, Vincent was almost in total darkness. She bumped into him.

'Off to bed?' he asked.

'Yes. I don't like not being at the convent. In my own cell.'

'Yes, I understand. I like to get home too.' He did not sound convincing. 'How long does it take?'

'Depends on Cervantes.'

'My father's favourite author.'

'He's a good donkey. Not sure how he got his name.'

'Take care.' She put her hand on the bannister of the verandah, and inadvertently touched his. 'Sorry.'

But she did not move it. Vincent removed his hand and placed it on top of hers. They stood like that for what seemed an eternity to both of them. They could hardly see themselves in the darkness.

Vincent had thrown away his cigarette. It smouldered on the ground. She smelt the tobacco on his breath.

Further away, they could hear the surf on the beach below.

Where was she? Vincent thought. As he pulled Thérèse towards him, he felt her voluminous sleeves, her scapular, her veil and the rosary hard at her side. His hands moved up to her face. He wanted to touch her body. The wildest thought was to get his hands under her skirt. She was running her hands up his arms.

She was giving into her passion, as she broke through the buttons of his shirt to his chest, running her hands through the hair there. Resting her head on his chest, smelling him. It made it easier for her that she could hardly see

164

him. They could both pretend that it wasn't happening, because they could not see each other.

'Madeleine,' Vincent whispered as he found her lips which were wet, and not cracked as they had been at Salt Pond.

'Vincent...'

A screen door opened at the end of the verandah, throwing a shaft of light along the floor. A ward nurse came out and stood in the light. Vincent and Thérèse could see her, but she could not see them. They remained absolutely still, in each others' arms. To break from each other would have disturbed the gloom, and the ward nurse might have seen the movement of shadows. She had come out for air. She returned and the screen door banged shut behind her.

'I must go,' said Thérèse.

'Yes, me too. I must go home.' He watched her disappear along the verandah. For how long could they continue with these kisses, this holding of hands? To talk about it would be to let it take a place alongside their work and the rest of their lives.

Mounting Cervantes, Vincent thought he saw Singh in the shadows behind the stores with someone else. He could not see who it was.

Feathers and Cocoyea Sticks

Theo was up even earlier than usual, adjusting his wall maps and collages according to the latest news last night, and at dawn. 'I looking after things here, Doc.' Vincent smiled at his familiarity. He worried that he was not getting enough sleep, plugged into his crystal set. At least the night-time stories had ended, he hoped. The boy seemed so much better. Just letting him be had proved a sensible line of action.

But Vincent could see that Saint Damian's was a struggle for Theo. The science lesson had gone well. But he was not altogether surprised when, over breakfast of *Crix* and *buljol*, the boy suddenly asked, 'I could get leprosy?' There was real fear in his eyes, as he heaped the saltfish onto his dry biscuit.

Vincent was blunt. 'Theoretically, yes. But it's highly unlikely, if you take care with your hygiene. What did you learn in your science lesson? You're in much less danger than me or Sister Thérèse, or Mr Singh. Only one of the sisters, after all their years of nursing, has contracted the disease.'

Theo listened intently. 'I see someone up Pepper Hill who skin turning white. One day, they find him rotting away in a hut up in the bush.'

'Yes, that can happen, if the disease is allowed to take hold, and the patient does not get the required care.' Vincent explained to Theo the theory that he had lectured about, and was constantly arguing on the wards.

'Yes, Mr Singh tell me. Well, maybe I go come a doctor too, or a pharmacist,' Theo said thoughtfully.

'Those are fine ambitions. Your schooling is going to have to be more important than ever.'

Later, Vincent noticed that Theo was at the jetty with him waiting for Jonah. He had elected to carry his doctor's bag to the pirogue.

Thérèse was already at her desk, making notes and continuing her research from the night before. Or so Vincent thought, as he stumped out his cigarette and entered the old clinic, and saw her bent over her desk. 'Morning,' his voice tried to give a normal ring to things as he entered the pharmacy.

He expected her to turn and smile. He expected some joy, some sense of the continuing excitement of the night before to exist between them.

He had hardly slept last night.

When she looked up, he saw that she had been crying. He stood over her, his hand touching her shoulder. It was all that he could allow himself. She was sobbing.

'Thérèse.' He noticed how he used her different names, depending on whether they were doctor and nurse, or lovers. The word had entered his imagination. Her hands pressed against the desk. He wanted to hold them, touch her face, kiss her eyes. He had felt her body under her habit last night, but then let her go. She had sought the warmth of his body.

Her right hand was clenched. It was holding something. He moved over to her right side, putting his hand over hers, as was now their way. He unclenched her hand. It was a soft yellow cloth, like a stuffed pocket, shaped like a star, a yellow star. Pinned to the back of it was a printed message, WEAR IT.

Even before the war had started, they knew that the German authorities required Jews to wear yellow stars when they walked in the streets.

'Who's doing this? Who hates me so much?'

Then, he used her other name. 'Madeleine, no one hates you. This is the action of a sick person. It must be one of the other sisters. You can see the work.' The nuns did embroidery in the evening, sitting around the common room, after their tiring day at the hospital.

'Surely not? She didn't do this while sitting among the other sisters,' Thérèse protested.

'She must've kept it hidden in her cell then, progressing each day with her hate,' Vincent speculated. 'Let's leave this, Thérèse.' He had switched back to her religious name. 'We've work to do. Hands. We're going to start on the hands.' Vincent tried to change the mood.

She got up and followed him out of the pharmacy towards the adult wards, as he explained the plan he had come up with. Their night-time encounter in the darkness on the verandah had stimulated him, so that, as he rode back in the dark, he had planned the research.

'Thérèse.' She had stuffed the yellow star deep into her pocket, as they

167

went down the steps to cross the yard. 'For too long we've been seeing everything as if we were dermatologists. You know, if we look at our notes over the months, certainly in the last year, you'll notice, as I'm sure you do.'

Vincent looked across to her. She had dried her tears, but her face was sad. What a terrible world they were making.

'You know, we've been making notes about colour and texture of the dry patches on the skin,' he continued.

'Yes. We've noted it all clearly, the different reactions in a macule and papule. We noted each and every infiltration of the dry skin.'

'A nodule and a plaque.'

'Yes, as you say, as if we were dermatologists.'

Vincent could see Mother Superior at the window of her office. He felt as if he and Thérèse were naked, walking across the yard. He tried to look business-like, and put a little more distance between himself and Thérèse, in case their arms knocked into each other. He noticed that he had quickened his stride, and that Thérèse had consequently done the same.

'Do you remember that day on the wards when... no, it was in the book binding shop. That young Indian fella. I've forgotten his name for the moment. You know?'

'Raj. Raj Jaikaransingh.'

'Yes, of course, Raj.'

'What about him?'

'Don't you remember? His hand. He had beautiful hands with long slim fingers, completely intact. They were soft and supple, not like fingers stiff with arthritis. But they were useless. He was trying to pull that string through the binding on the book. The thumb and four fingers of one hand were curved in, and pressing against each other, the classic claw hand.'

'Yes. I remember.' Thérèse was involved.

'But do you remember what our diagnosis was then?'

'Paralysis.'

'Yes, paralysis from nerve damage.'

'I wrote down what you said, because it tallied with what I remember my professor saying in Tulle when I was training. That's what this disease does, paralysis, plus complete anaesthesia. I can hear Professor Rothmann at this moment.'

'Yes, Raj couldn't feel the string, to pull it through the loop in the binding.'

'And then you asked him to shake your hand, and to press hard. You thought it might not have any strength. I remember you yelping, shocked, when he kept on squeezing.'

'Absolutely. I had to cry out, stop. That's exactly when I realised, as my hand lay between his bent thumb and fingers.'

'Raj was so surprised. He didn't understand you, because you asked him to squeeze and then you were telling him to stop.' Thérèse laughed.

'He had no idea how much he was hurting me. But it sent another kind of jolt right through me, that shock. I realised as I've gone over it many times in my mind since, that though his hand was useless, nevertheless, concealed there, in that apparent uselessness, were powerful muscles. This wasn't paralysis.'

'No?' Thérèse and Vincent had stopped at the foot of the stairs to the adult ward. They were transfixed by their debate. This was when everything else collapsed: the war far away, the absence of her father's letters, his concern for his brother Bernard, the war that was building here in the gulf, the yellow star. Above all, those kisses, and holding hands in the darkness, in the white light of the infirmary, out in the glare of Salt Pond. Those kisses on her cracked lips faded in the excitement of their work. Their work held them close.

At that moment, there was the drone of a surveillance plane disappearing behind Cabresse Point. They both looked up, and followed the direction of the flight with their eyes.

'The mystery was on Raj's face,' Vincent continued.

'Mystery?'

'Well, a question. Why were we treating this whole thing as if we were dermatologists? When what was staring us in the face, was an orthopaedic question. Look at the deformities we've got before us each day. Why had not medicine, my training, your training, not asked the orthopaedic question about leprosy?'

'Why do you think?' Thérèse was a student again.

'There are probably many reasons. But, a known one for sure, is that leprosy is not looked at like other diseases. We, in our profession, have put it continually in another category. At the worse end is the conviction that it is a curse from God. Many of our patients come with that view, pursued by the fear of their villages, terrified by priests, pandits, imans and obeah women.'

'Do you think so?'

'Yes, I do. When I spoke to my professor in London, he commented, when I told him that I wanted to work at this leprosarium, that only mad people, missionaries and priests worked in leprosariums. They never had good physicians and never a specialist in orthopaedics. I've had my hunch for a while that dermatology was not the only place where our answer lay.'

'So, is that what I am? A mad missionary?'

'Thérèse. You know...'

'And you?'

'You've got to admit. Dr Escalier! What did he do, but inject with Chaulmoogra Oil, while the nuns prayed, and the government banished the buggers to this island.' He smiled, checking his language. 'What's been going on here is an eternity of bandaging. You know exactly what I mean. A system in various degrees of neglect, by state and church. No one is thinking about doing the research. Not now, while we fight this confounded war. We do charity. But it isn't charity. Because, in the end, we affect very little.'

'I think you're unfair.' They were raising their voices at each other. A group of children were standing around them staring. 'I think you should credit the sisters with more. I know your differences. I know you. You're like my father. You're a Communist. That's what I think you are. You're a Communist. A Bolshevik. Quite soon you'll have us singing the *Internationale.*'

'Don't be ridiculous, Thérèse. What's this about? What's Communist got to do with it?'

'It has everything to to do with it. You think we don't know what Singh, Jonah and you are up to here. You mentioned Karl Marx the other day.'

'Thérèse, can you lower your voice! Whose voice are you speaking with, your superior's? Is that what you think of me? I thought we were the same.' He was almost touching her, in the full glare of the yard.

'Don't touch me,' she whispered sharply. The stooping children were giggling. 'Run along. The bell has gone. Recess is over.'

'Thérèse, listen to me. I want to tell you about my research.'

They mounted the stairs to the verandah outside the women's ward. The rain came down while the sun was still shining. 'God and the devil fighting. That's what the children say.' Thérèse was retreating.

'Yes, thinking of children. I need feathers and cocoyea sticks.'

From the verandah, Vincent noticed Theo on his own, gazing out onto the bay from outside the pharmacy. Then he saw Christiana leaving the pharmacy. Singh welcomed Theo back in, as he waved to the young girl.

'Science students!' Vincent said cynically.

'What?'

'Nothing.'

'Where were you?'

'Nothing. Theo. Singh.'

'Feathers and cocoyea sticks?' Thérèse interrupted. 'And come to think of it, you protest too much. I heard my mother tell my father that one day.' Then Thérèse started crying all of sudden. 'Sorbonne. They were the brightest pair that year. The Ecole Normale, Montmartre, the little squares with the artists and the musicians, the bars, the cafés. Poor Papa. I still haven't heard anything. No letters. There'll be no letters. Paris. They both loved Paris. The Seine, Notre Dame, and the little street *La Rue du Chat qui Pêche* on the left bank, near where they had a room. The narrowest street in Paris!'

'*La Rue du Chat qui Pêche?*'

'*Oui.* What is it?'

'*Non, non.*'

'No, tell me. What is it?' They were now both laughing at the name of the street and the coincidence. Vincent blushed. '*Non.* Ah, a girl I once knew. She told me about that street, as we walked by the river. Her father had lived near there once.'

'A girl?'

'Simone.'

'You remember her name?'

'Yes.' He remembered watching her closing the shutters and the room growing dark while the afternoon sunlight leaked through the jalousies, like the light in Pizzaro. Light from here and light from his island, he had thought then. He remembered her naked back, the nape of her neck, and the length of her legs. Her hands closed over his eyes, when she returned to the bed and kissed him all over, asking him if it was his first time. He had gone in his mind, from that room above the street in Paris, to the turret room at Versailles, where he had first lain with Odetta, and then to the cocoa house with the leaking light through the cracks above himself and Odetta under the rolling roof. He smiled, pretending that it was his first time, so Simone could have her fantasy and teach him to make love.

171

'It's a pretty name, Simone. I had a school friend called Simone.'

'Yes. And you?'

'What?'

'A boy friend?'

Thérèse looked up surprised, caught unawares by the question. 'Yes. *Oui*, of course, Marcel. He was the brother of my best friend Sophie-Marie.' She had not thought of him for ages. Questioned, she built his identity. 'He loved to hunt, with a sling shot when he was younger and then with a rifle. He once gave me a rabbit's paw for good luck.'

Vincent did not want to elaborate on Simone. He did not want to confess to Thérèse that this was an afternoon of love, in Paris, and that he had paid for it with the few francs he had had as a student, and could not really afford. But, to be in Paris and not be in love!

How could he tell Thérèse about all of that now? What was he doing? Would he tell her about Odetta...

What had they done last night, and before that at Salt Pond? And she, taking his hand more than a year ago, so impulsively? He could be sacked from his post and made a disgrace in the local press. He could hear the gossip of the chattering family on the verandahs of Versailles and the other estates.

When they entered the ward, everyone wanted to talk to the doctor. 'Okay, all of you'll have my attention. After the bandaging, I want all nurses to collect on the verandah.' Turning to Thérèse, 'Feathers and cocoyea sticks. Get the children to help you,' Vincent smiled. He loved to have her at his side.

'Let's have the nurses in rows.' Thérèse was organising. Each nurse brought a chair from the ward and placed it at intervals along the long verandah, outside the women's ward, as Thérèse instructed them.

There were a dozen chairs. This was what she wanted most, to be assisting him in his work. She watched Vincent working himself down the ward, examining hands and feet. There were one or two bad cases of eye injury and one patient had malaria. She was always at hand.

'We need new mosquito nets on this ward.'

'You right, Docta, I get bite, for so, last night. Some big big fellas,' one of the patients called out.

'I bet you one of them is *Anopheles*.'

'Yes, Docta, I hear his violin in my ears.' They liked the *ole talk*.

172

'Don't forget the dengue fella, *Aedes Aegypti*.'

'Gawd! He sounding bad!' the patient laughed.

Vincent smiled. He loved their spirit. Together, they would conquer this illness, no matter what superstitions their priests filled their heads with.

The patients liked to hear Vincent raging against the authorities on their behalf. This morning, Singh was coming down the ward the other way with the daily doses of cod liver oil, and dressings for those who were having clean bandages. Vincent noticed that he had Theo in attendance. He was wearing a white coat. He beamed at Vincent.

There was notice given of the dreaded Chaulmoogra Oil injections. Everyone still had a vivid memory of the meetings under the almond tree, or the riots as they were called. Between Singh and Vincent, the ward was in an uproar of laughter and revolt against the authorities. These were the moments when they could throw off their sorrows.

Theo was witnessing a new side to life on El Caracol.

Suddenly, there was a distinct quietening down at the end of the ward, near the ward-sister's cubicle. Some of the patients began mumbling, 'Good morning, Mother Superior, good morning, Mother.' There was a kind of trained sycophancy in their voices. She progressed down the centre of the ward, her veil billowing out behind her with her stride, her black rosary beads, the fifteen mysteries, clattering.

'Good morning, Mr Singh. Is everything in order here?'

'Perfectly, Mother Superior. Things have never been better.' There was often a trace of irony in Singh's tone, and Vincent smiled, taking the lead from him. Theo looked on eagerly.

When she came to Vincent, Mother Superior's voice was more challenging. 'Doctor Metivier. What is going on here?'

All the patients were sitting up in bed, even Mildred Yard with her malaria. All eyes were on these well known rivals for their well-being.

'Here, Mother Superior? The usual morning duties, plus a couple of miracles. Isn't that so, Hilda?' Vincent lifted Hilda Black's notes hanging off the railing at the bottom of her bed. 'Hilda's sores are almost completely healed, and soon she will be picking up her bed and walking out of here. Isn't that so Hilda? Right up to your hut and your garden.' Vincent stopped himself from concluding with, as Christ once instructed the leper of Galilee.

'You right, yes, Docta. Is garden I want to plant. You see *Corpus Christi* gone, and I ent plant corn this year.'

Mother Superior stopped him short with, 'Doctor, I mean, out there, on the verandah? What are all the ward nurses doing, standing in a row by chairs, rather than getting on with their duties? Sometimes, I just don't understand what is going on in this hospital.'

Thérèse left the ward. She did not like to witness the open rivalry between her superior and Vincent. It challenged too many conflicting beliefs, too many conflicting loyalties. She went and gathered up some of the children from the school. She recruited Theo, stealing him from Singh. He was delighted to do another new job. They needed a dozen good feathers and a similar number of sharp cocoyea sticks.

Theo was put in charge of some smaller girls and boys, stripping coconut palms for the seam of the leaf. And others, chasing around the yard near Ma Thorpe's chicken run for light fluffy feathers, were led by Ti-Jean. Both of the Doctor's boys had an important job to do. Thérèse had found a way to combat any rivalry between the boys.

Each nurse, sitting on the verandah, was then given one of the softest feathers and a sharp cocoyea stick, which had been sorted by the children from the bundles they had deposited on the verandah.

'I'm conducting an experiment, a piece of research, Mother.' Vincent was, at the same time, ushering Mother Superior onto the verandah. 'I need to do some tests on the hands of the patients. I've got a hunch.'

'A hunch?' She shook her head. 'I do not know that word.'

'An idea. A hypothetical theory, about hands.'

'Do you think that this is what we need at the moment, Doctor?'

'Well, we've nothing else. I cannot continue with this kind of nursing and doctoring. We're getting nowhere.'

Vincent often felt it was better to have things out with Mother Superior in public, rather than in the privacy of her office, where she could reign supreme. For instance, if he had gone and asked her permission to conduct this survey, she would have come down on it with a sledgehammer.

The truth was that she still missed Dr Escalier of the old school, the old order, when everyone knew their place. She had known where she was with him. Vincent was not sure what she imagined. Coupled with Mr Singh, she might as well have had her leprosarium run by Communists. There was some bit of Mother Superior which almost understood the Germans and their National Socialism. Vincent wondered whether she gave her sisters talks on the subject before Compline. Was her hero Petain?

'Nowhere? This is the path to heaven, Doctor. This is their cross and they are bearing it courageously to their Calvary. Everyone's Calvary is different.'

Vincent thought to himself, I've been here before. 'Well, I'm not challenging you, Mother Superior. I just have quite good evidence that there is something else going on here. We've been looking at this disease with blinkers on. We need to try another strategy, and I want to conduct these tests on hands and feet, to see whether we should pursue it further. Have faith.' Vincent smiled.

'Faith, Doctor? You wouldn't know the meaning of the word even if Karl Marx tried to persuade you of it. What would you know about it? Indeed.'

He did not know why he said it. It just came out. 'Sister Thérèse Weil is persuaded that we should try it.'

'I'm sure she is. Let me just say Doctor, that Sister Thérèse Weil, as you call her...'

'Isn't that her name?'

'You know exactly what I mean, Doctor Metivier. Don't pretend with me. You may think me some kind of religious fanatic. Some old, what do the English call it, fogey?'

'Fogey?' You know that word. "Hunch" not, but "fogey", Vincent thought. 'Dr Metivier.'

'Mother.'

'Listen to me.'

'Mother Superior, how could you think...'

'What I want to say is that that girl. For that is what she is, a bright girl. And willing as she maybe in her youthful enthusiasm, to be persuaded by you, precisely why, I'm not sure, is a religious first of all. Don't forget that, and don't put temptation in her way.'

Vincent could feel himself physically recoil at the word temptation. He felt again like the naughty boy he had always been made to feel by priests and their church. He hoped he was not blushing.

'Pride is one of the seven deadly sins, Doctor. I know that Sister Weil is from a medical family, may even have had a glittering career ahead of her in

175

research, as you call it, but she has chosen to serve as a religious, first and foremost.'

Vincent was relieved. It was the sin of pride that concerned the nun. He shook his head in grateful agreement. Mother Superior could not have doubted his approval of what she was saying.

'Come and see, Mother. You may yourself be persuaded.'

Thérèse had begun to line up the patients. While one Sister performed the test, another took notes. There were about twenty-four involved in all, two per patient, as they worked on twelve at a time.

Firstly, they tested with the feather and then with the sharp end of the cocoyea stick, using it like a pin, tracing the sensitivity to touch and pain in the different parts of the hand. They measured the range of movement in the thumb, fingers and wrist. Then they repeated this procedure for the toes and feet, keeping the precise measurement of the lengths of the toes and fingers, noting which digits had shortened and which muscles seemed to be paralysed. Any paralysis in the face was also noted.

After looking at the enterprise for a few minutes, Mother Superior asked, 'And how long will this take, Doctor? All this tickling.'

Singh was smiling in the background. Theo was back at his side in his white coat.

Mother Superior sighed and left.

Vincent went up and down the line, checking what the sisters were doing, assisted by Thérèse. Singh, Theo and Christiana helped with the patients on the ward. It took the rest of the afternoon to check all the patients in the women's ward. 'Tomorrow, the men's ward!' Vincent announced. The sisters gathered up their notes and bundled the feathers and cocoyea sticks for further use.

'You feel you're onto something here with this tickling?' Singh laughed and played at testing Theo, who held out his open hand, giggling. Christiana laughed. The two went off together.

'Boy, this might be the biggest revolution we're going to create here.' Vincent inspected some of the notes the nuns had made.

'What you mean?'

'This might be our the leap out of the dark ages, from a world with shunned lepers, the superstitions of medieval religions, the stigma's of society.'

'Science.'

'Yes, science, research. Do you know leprosy is responsible for the greatest number of cases of orthopaedic crippling? And, yet, the only known surgical procedure, so far, is amputation. Amputation!' Theo was back, his eyes moved between the two men. Then he went off to return his white coat at the pharmacy and join Jonah at the jetty.

Singh called after him. 'Tomorrow.' Theo waved. He noticed Christiana entering the pharmacy.

Thérèse joined Singh and Vincent. 'I want all the notes collated. We must go over them as soon as we can. Can you stay tonight at the hospital?' Vincent looked at Thérèse. 'I would like to see if there are any recognisable patterns before proceeding with the men's ward tomorrow.'

'I'll have to get permission. Mother Superior doesn't like me staying two nights in succession. But I'll ask.'

'Well. I had a little scene earlier.' Singh and Thérèse smiled. They had witnessed it.

'Little? Don't we know, Mr Singh?' Thérèse teased.

'So, can you be particularly humble when you make your request to stay over. You must check your pride!' There was a twinkle in Vincent's eyes as he looked at Singh and then at Thérèse. 'You don't want her thinking that you're in any way proud of what you do, or that what you do has anything whatsoever to do with yourself, your intelligence, the years of training you've had, your own efforts in the research. All that you are, is an instrument of God. Do you understand? I tell you, there've been too many blunt instruments recently about this place. God needs to sharpen up.'

Thérèse did not like Vincent teasing her in front of Singh. She felt that it made it visible what was happening to them. She suddenly was blushing.

'Lay off, man. Sister must have her beliefs.'

'She knows exactly what I mean.' Thérèse did what was her custom, folding her arms into her sleeves and turning away, bowing her head. He was in each and every way like her father, she thought. When he got hold of some idea, he did not let it go. She wished she could talk to the chaplain. There was no possibility that she could talk to any of the nuns. The community was too small. She would not be able to talk about Vincent with any sense of anonymity for him. The chaplain, what was she thinking? That would be like jumping from the frying pan into the fire.

'You teasing her too much, man. I might think you were flirting with her.'
Singh looked at Vincent.

'What you mean?' As he turned to leave, he said, 'By the way, I saw you last night. Out late? Who was that with you?'

'Last night? Just hanging out with the fellas.'

'Oh. See you tomorrow. You seem to have got Theo really interested.'

'Bright too bad. See you.'

Hurucan

Vincent returned to the clinic, just as the ward sister was leaving cups of hot cocoa sprinkled with vanilla for Thérèse and himself. 'Very kind of you, nurse,' Vincent smiled.

'I leave you to it.' The door banged behind her.

'What did she mean by that?' Vincent asked.

Thérèse did not answer. She continued going through the notes on her desk.

'Looking after my boy,' Vincent sighed, as he sat down at his desk alongside her.

'Your boy?'

'Theo, how he's getting on with Singh.'

'He was splendid this afternoon. Thought you were speaking about Ti-Jean.'

'I know. Ti-Jean's not well. He was putting a brave face on things today. His wound has opened again. I've not been to see him with all that's been going on. The place is not the same without him around. So, it was good he got involved today. Your doing.'

She smiled. 'They are both so fond of you.'

'If only we had Penicillin,' Vincent complained. 'Anyway, Theo. I can't leave him at night easily. I had to get Jonah to stay with him. He likes Jonah. They fish together. They go out in the pirogue as far as Point Girod.'

'Doctor and his boys.'

He looked up, sipped his cocoa and smiled.

'Would you like to have children? Would you like to be married? Why aren't you married?' She spilt out her questions.

'What's this, the inquisition? What kind of questions are these, Sister?' He put on his doctor's voice, his doctor-in-charge-of-the-leprosarium-voice. 'Out of the blue?'

'Out of the blue?'

'What did you say?' He was distracted.

'Out of the blue! Really, Doctor Metivier. Is this what you think this is? Out of the blue? We've kissed each other twice, Doctor.'

'Lower your voice. And don't call me doctor.'

'We've not told each other what it means.'

They suddenly found themselves sitting in darkness.

'I can't see a thing.' Vincent got up and lit the hurricane lantern. It spluttered, and then the blue flame grew steady.

When he sat back down to his desk, he asked, 'Do we have to say what everything means?'

Thérèse did not answer immediately. She carried on with her classifications. The lantern threw their shadows together on the ceiling, and along the cream wall of the old clinic.

'No. We don't know the meaning of everything. But you're the one always going on about reason, science,' Thérèse insisted.

'Certainly. There are mysteries in science also.'

'I don't know the meaning of these notes I'm reading right now, for instance,' she added.

'Yet.'

'Yes, not yet. Hopefully, I will.' She smiled.

'I'm sorry for what *I've* done.' He changed his tone.

'What you've done?' She looked up, surprised.

'Yes.'

'It's not like that.' She understood. 'You've not done something to me. We've done something together.'

'Do you want to talk about this?' Vincent hoped not.

'Isn't that what we're doing? Is that what you said to Simone? I'm sorry.'

'Why do you mention Simone?'

'Was she not a girlfriend of yours in Paris?'

'No.'

'Oh, I thought maybe you were in love with her?'

'In love?'

'Yes, in love.'

'What do you know of love, Sister?'

'Sister?'

'Sister. Indeed.'

'Indeed?'

Thérèse got up to close the window. There was a high wind. The lamp spluttered. The papers blew off her desk. 'The sea's rough.'

'It was choppy when Jonah left in the pirogue.'

'You think I'm not capable of falling in love, Doctor?'

'Don't call me doctor. This is not a consultation. You're not my patient. Of course, I think you are capable of falling in love. What a ridiculous thing to say. What're you asking me?'

'If it were a consultation, you might be kissing me again,' Thérèse teased.

'Thérèse.'

'Madeleine. It's Madeleine speaking.'

'Are you mad?'

'That's what some of the sisters think, I'm sure.'

Vincent had got up and was opening the window again. 'The heat in here is unbearable. It's so still. We should have ceiling fans. The generators never work. Another thing to think about.'

He rattled the window open. A gust of wind blew the papers off his desk. Thérèse held hers down. The sea crashed onto the jetty. There was the smell of salt and weed.

They could hear great waves breaking over the jetty, pounding against the sea wall on the beach. When the wind died down, they heard dogs barking in the hills. They heard the thud of a coconut fall to the ground, *b'dup*.

In the hills, there were voices crying out. They could hear the sound of the Demerara shutters in the wards being pulled down. Someone was running along the verandah above. The rain suddenly burst down heavily. Water was seeping under the door from the drain outside.

'We're getting flooded.' Vincent was stuffing old newspaper under the door. Thérèse hitched up her skirts.

They were both sitting at their desks again, trying to get on with the work of classification and collation; the results of the research with feathers and cocoyea sticks, when there was a thunder clap that shook the building and sounded like the island had exploded, followed immediately by the rain falling even harder. A huge wind broke into the room, as if trying to suck everything out of the clinic. The lantern went out. The thunder broke again, after a lightning fork grounded itself either side of the building. Thérèse put her head down on the desk. 'Mother of God.' Vincent pulled the windows shut.

'What are we going to do?'

'We can't go out in this.' She had not experienced a tropical storm before.

They could hear the wind buckling along the sides of the hospital buildings. There was a ripping noise on the roofs. Vincent caught sight of a sheet of galvanise being dumped under the window. It was still very difficult to see anything, because of the darkness and the heavy rain. They could hear the frightened shouts of patients and nurses above them. Vincent felt helpless.

He thought of Theo and Jonah alone in the Doctor's house. He trusted Jonah to know what to do, but he wanted to be with Theo.

'We're trapped.' Thérèse pulled her feet up onto the struts of her chair. She hugged her knees, tucking her skirts tightly about her. The water was still seeping under the newspaper. The newspaper was sodden.

'On our own, and nothing anyone can do about it,' she said with irony. 'Can we light the lantern again?'

'I'll try,' he said.

'The kerosene has spilt. Watch where you strike the match.'

The flame spluttered and smoked.

Great swathes of sheet lightening lit up the skies over the gulf.

'*Sons et lumière*!' Thérèse exclaimed.

'Nature's war?' Vincent mused.

'Nature's manifestation surely,' she corrected him.

'We make wars.'

'Yes. And yellow stars.' She was bitter.

'No letters?' He knew her father was on her mind.

'I wait for the mail boat each day.'

'I can't see how they can get through.'

'I know. I hope for a miracle. A coincidence.'

The rain water was coming in again. They were both on the floor stuffing newspapers.

'Are we a coincidence?' he asked. They were kneeling facing each other.

'I think so. I'm the coincidence.'

'You're the miracle.' He surprised himself.

'So, you're a romantic after all, Doctor Metivier.' She threw back her head and laughed. Then she giggled nervously.

182

'What do you tell your confessor?' he blurted out.

'My confessor?'

'Yes.'

'Well, I don't tell him about you.'

Vincent protested. 'No, I didn't mean it like that.'

'Well, it wouldn't be proper would it? How did you mean it?'

'I meant, how do you cope?'

'How do you cope?'

'I asked first.' He knew that she knew that they were playing a game.

Their nerves were stretched

A bolt of lightning broke right overhead. Then the thunder followed, echoing for seconds, as they both forgot their questions and and delayed their replies. Thérèse put her hands out, and fell against Vincent's chest. He held her fast.

'Does this frighten you?' he asked gently.

'What?'

'I don't know. The thunder, the lightning? This, us here, together, like this?'

'You know my fears, even unto death.'

'Even more reason for me not to take advantage.'

'Advantage. I choose to touch you. I could tell you to stop. Well, maybe I couldn't. You know what I mean. I'm allowing this, or at least...'

They realised that the rain had suddenly stopped. The silence staggered them. 'Come with me,' Vincent pleaded.

'Where?'

'Come, quickly. Pack these papers away safely. It's so dark we won't be seen. If we're questioned afterwards, we'll say we went to check the huts on the upper terraces.'

'Where are we going?'

'Let's take the donkey track to the Doctor's House.' He talked of his house as the Doctor's House, how everyone else referred to it. In doing so, it seemed as if he was renouncing his position. He was just himself now.

She was reluctant to follow him on this escapade. Who she was, and her duty, tied her down. 'Why?' She guessed why.

'We'll say we had to check the boy. Come, come quickly, trust me. There's a boathouse where we can shelter when we get there. You won't have to enter the house with Theo and Jonah. They won't know we're there.'

'Why?' She wanted to resist but could not.

'We can't stay here. Not here.' He looked around the room of the clinic. 'Look all this.' The smell of medécines, the dreaded Chaulmoogra Oil, seemed as intense as ever. He looked around him, as if to say, not here, meaning not only the room which had shrunk in the darkness to enclose them, but the yard, the hospital, the leprosarium, the place of their work, and their devotion as nurse and doctor. He wanted to be away from there with her, Madeleine. This was the place of Doctor Metivier and Sister Thérèse.

Should he desire this? he asked himself. A hideaway, like a turret room among the tip top palmistes? A cocoa house with the roof pulled over, like a reckless boy? Or like a young man in search of love on the streets? The intimacy of strangers, far away from home? A shuttered room near the *Rue du chat qui pêche*? What was he doing once more? Trespassing! Would he be prosecuted?

Thérèse was already collecting up her papers, and putting them in order. She slammed the drawer of her desk till the next day. She was hardly thinking that there would be a next day. Time, as she knew it, seemed to have collapsed, as they were already half way out the door and ducking through the darkness along the back tracks, between the outhouses of the hospital, and the beginning of the huts, to where the donkey track began into the hills. They would surely be seen, someone would notice them, and wonder at them, hurrying along in the darkness on such a night as this.

As they left the yards, Vincent saw Singh running across from the pharmacy towards his quarters with the girl, Christiana. What was Singh up to? There was something going on between this girl and Singh.

The rain had stopped, but the showers still fell from the bushes, as Vincent and Thérèse made their way along the muddy red dirt track. Thérèse hitched up her skirts, collecting handfuls of black rosary beads. He held her hand as they tried to find the firm ground beneath them.

They took the track which led straight down to the small beach, where the boathouse was. They would not have to go through the yard of the Doctor's House. The windows and shutters were closed. The house looked battened down, protected against the storm. Hopefully Theo and Jonah were asleep.

Inside the boathouse was the old launch which had been used by Dr Escalier, and which Vincent had never used, always preferring the companionship of

Jonah and his pirogue. There was a small cabin in the bow of the launch. This was the place that he had in mind for Madeleine and himself to spend an hour, or more, of this time, this night of the hurricane. A mad imagining!

The tide was right in and the launch rocked in its tight moorings, knocking the sides.

The boathouse stood under two spreading almond trees. Their large rusting leaves covered the roof and the walkway. As Madeleine and Vincent entered the dark enclosure, he helped her into the launch. They both wondered what they had done so suddenly to find themselves alone, hiding here.

Vincent led the way into the cabin. He knew there was a bunk with a fibre cushion. The place was musty and smelt of paint and engine oil, with whiffs of gasoline from a small can in the stern. They sat on the bunk, their heads just missing the roof of the cabin.

'The best I can offer you.' He reached out to touch her.

'I can hardly see you.' She put out her arms. They could barely avoid touching each other, every time they moved; he making the bunk ready, she standing, waiting. She could hear her heart pounding.

Their eyes grew accustomed to the dark. He now thought of the time that he had stitched the wound on her ankle; examining her head for splinters of glass, making her take off her veil to reveal her shorn head. He tried lifting her veil now, but it was pinned to her skull cap.

It was different now, as she unbuttoned and unpinned herself. He waited. She lifted the veils off herself, and unclasped her skull cap, the tiny hooks and fasteners, the minute mother of pearl buttons slipping through her nervous fingers. She was trembling.

He would not have known where to begin. It had been bad enough not knowing how to undo Simone's bra, how to unhitch her suspenders from her stockings, but easy enough to have them curl down her legs. With Odetta, there was so little to take off. It was like lifting air, her light cotton chemise.

As Madeleine lay back on the bunk, Vincent found the bottom of her skirts, and felt the surprising down on her legs, as if she were a young boy. Her girdle, with the black rosary beads, clattered to the floor of the cabin. The noise startled them, the beads slid along the floor.

Further up, under her skirts, his fingers recognised that soft mound above her cunt. The word came to his mind, like it did, when he talked with school boys about girls. It became a tender word.

185

Madeleine raised herself with her arms about his neck to find his mouth. They missed at first, and then found each other's lips. As Vincent's fingers searched, he heard the word hymen in his doctor's mind. Madeleine moaned. His fingers searched for another spot. She cried out when he touched it.

So quickly, they were now here, transported to the small dark cabin beneath the almond trees. Madeleine could hardly recognise what she was doing. Her heart pounded. Her lips trembled.

Sophie-Marie had told her not to let Marcel press his legs against her, tip her school hat off her face, when they were standing by the convent wall, put his tongue into her mouth, the fast river just beneath them. She was losing herself, losing herself in her mind.

'Hold me,' she whispered. 'Hold me.'

She had felt Marcel's everlasting sling-shot in his pocket. She and Sophie-Marie giggled when she told her. She had not thought of Marcel like this for a long time. Marcel, what would he be doing as the German armies threatened France? Laying his traps for rabbits, stoning them with his sling-shot? Now, he must have a rifle.

'Vincent.' She was undressing him.

'Madeleine.'

They felt their nakedness, as they pulled at buttons and straps.

It had begun raining again. The tide swelled beneath the boat. They felt that the moorings would break. The wind raced along the sides of the boathouse. The sides buckled.

'What time is it?' Madeleine asked suddenly.

Vincent lifted his father's pocket watch from his pants pocket. 'Just before midnight.'

'The storm has been raging for hours,' Madeleine reflected.

'Most unusual for this time of the year. My mother always says that the worse rains come up from the west, up from the Orinoco delta.' Their conversation saved them from their own storm.

They were now sitting up in each other's arms. Their first nervous, passion had subsided. They were in various stages of undressing; his shoes, Madeleine's sandals, his socks, her rosary beads and scapular were crumpled and scattered on the narrow strip of floor between the bunks.

Accustomed to the darkness, he found her face. She looked more Jewish like this. Was that his imagination? What was it, to look Jewish? She must

186

have just had her hair shorn. It felt like his shaving brush, when he ran his hand over her neat head and drew her close to rest on his chest.

From her bare shoulders, hung a cotton shift. He had not allowed himself to look at her breasts. She covered herself again now.

When he had first seen her in the infirmary at the convent in a similar shift, lying in bed, his hands had moved like a doctor's, his fingers pressed with diagnostic sensitivity. Now, they lifted the light cotton to hold her breasts in the palm of his hands. She did not resist. He could feel her body go taut, and then gradually relax, trembling in his arms. He pressed his mouth against her nipples and sucked, feeling like the young boy who had first done that when first in love. She cried out with pleasure.

The past filtered in like an intrusive pornography. Odetta, Simone.

Madeleine held his head in her hands and moaned, kissing the whorls of his ears with her warm lips and her wet tongue. Shy, she nuzzled, and then explored with her fingers and tongue, her hands and legs, her whole body slipping and moving beneath and above him. How did she know where to go? He led her and then she discovered her own way to pleasure him.

They were rocked by the sea. They almost fell off the bunk. It sounded like everything was crashing down around them outside. Their hideaway seemed even more necessary, an apt refuge.

There was no other place at this moment. There was no past, no future, only this moment. This would not last. They pressed each other further and further.

Their lips and cheeks were bruised. Their bodies ached where they had hurt them against each other, against the hard constraints of their love bed.

It would only be when they were alone, in another place, that they would inspect the scratches and bruises which they had not felt. They had been anaesthetised by the pleasure searing through their bodies in the darkness.

They were not who they were. Decorum slipped away.

They lay sweating and naked against each other.

How would their lives ever be the same again?

They forgot to think. Now, only taste, and smell. The darkness became their natural element. Their fingers read a braille of moles, rough and smooth skin, down and bristle.

Once more, Vincent climbed up, to enter Madeleine, and she pulled him into her, so that they might each steal, once more, from each other, what they had come here for, before they would have to scramble up the debris on the floor, find their old selves, the masks of their old selves, for a world they could not imagine they had ever inhabited differently from this one. Not that they thought of that in this last instant which lasted an eternity, and then was over in a flash.

Their cries reached a pitch, which was part of all the noise the firmament unleashed this night; this night of the strange and unexpected hurricane.

They suddenly drew up against each other in consternation. Waking as from a dream. They thought they had heard footsteps outside, but it was the almonds falling. Hidden between walls, they held on to what the world would call forbidden.

Vincent's mind ran to the house, through the sorrel bushes, to Theo, the boy, his responsibility; to Jonah, his *pardner*. How would he explain this?

Thérèse was waking in the convent with her fellow sisters for Matins. *Deus in adutorium meum intende, Domine, ad aduvandum me, festina.* Make haste, O Lord to help me! Make haste!

Their fingers were now expert at finding things in the dark, as they dressed themselves, eager not to leave any incriminating evidence of their presence, as they each silently began to reflect, too soon, upon the possible repercussions of their deeds that night.

The foreday morning light filtered through the shady branches of the almond trees. A strange peace welcomed them back into the ordinary world outside the boathouse. The salt air was fresh. The earth was renewed. The sea was unmuffled. The palms sang soft psalms.

But, as they climbed the track again, alongside the sorrel bushes, they began to see the devastation that the storm had wrought. The sea, through the bushes, was churned up with a muddy silt, the colour of cocoa. They hurried along the donkey track, having to crawl under uprooted trees and torn off branches.

As they reached the path to the upper terraces, they began to see what had occurred in the night while they were hidden in the cabin of the launch in the boathouse. Red-dirt water poured off the hillsides. Landslides had taken with them a number of the huts which lay dilapidated on their sides, their galvanise roofs peeled off by the wind. Patients covered in crocus bags, picked their way through the ruins of their homes for their few belongings which had not been made useless by the rain and the wind.

Vincent and Thérèse stood together, looking down on Saint Damian's.

'Hurucan,' Vincent pronounced.

'Hurucan?'

'A local god.'

'Hurucan, hurricane. Was it a hurricane?' Thérèse asked.

'Something as strong as.'

'*Mon Dieu!*'

'I hate to think what more we shall find.'

They gradually separated, assembling their official roles, as nurse and doctor, making their way down to the hospital, calling in on still standing huts, and helping patients in the broken-down ones, to retrieve their lives. They knew that they had a duty to do this, but they also knew that they had to look as if this was why they were here in the early morning, why they looked the way they did with wet clothes streaked with mud, shoes and sandals caked with debris.

The sisters from the convent would not be arriving for another two hours. Vincent and Thérèse had not agreed on a story, except that she remembered his first idea when they were leaving the clinic. They would pretend that they had gone up to the top huts; that they needed to go to see Theo.

Vincent met Mother Superior on his rounds. The children's ward was spared. 'Who would wish to harm these mites?' she said, inferring maybe, that there were others who deserved the destruction, and that the hurricane was an instrument of a vengeful God.

'Do you think some of us might've deserved destruction? Of all the places to choose?' Vincent inquired.

'Well, you know, Doctor, it must be more than coincidence. Have you noticed that it's the new married quarters which bore the brunt of the attack.'

'The attack, Mother? Who exactly is attacking whom and for what reason? Nature simply manifests itself for perfectly natural, though not immediately known reasons.'

'Well the reason is plain enough, Doctor. But it's a manner of speaking, as it were.'

Vincent's patience was failing him. All things were part of her God's

189

mysterious plan, even to have picked out those huts, the married quarters, on the middle terrace, for particular destruction. They had been part of Mother Superior's reluctant policy after the murder of Michael Johnson, and the drowning of Sonny Lal. Indeed, Vincent had heard the name of the policeman more than once on the lips of quite a few this morning.

'You see, Doctor, people can't do what they like and get away with it.'

Why not? He was hoping to get away with something himself. He hoped Thérèse would get away as well. There had not been time to really worry about what had taken place, and what they would do now. Even dealing with the peculiarities of Mother Superior's invisible God seemed an easier proposition.

At least Hurucan was plainly visible.

Ti-Jean beamed when Vincent entered the children's ward, happy to see him after the terrifying night, though he would not want to admit that he had been frightened, imprisoned on the ward for days. His wound was worse. The boy was weak. But it was Vincent's habit to encourage. 'You'll soon be out and about, old man.' Vincent put the last touches to his new dressing. 'That football team is missing their coach.'

Vincent was just finishing the first cigarette that he had had a chance to smoke that day, when Mother Superior was at his elbow again; not with some piece of her macabre theology, but indicating that they were bringing a body down from the married quarters. 'I hear the women in the kitchen saying that it's Mr Cardinez. His wife,' Mother Superior cleared her throat, 'his common-law wife, they say, is safe, but beside herself with grief.'

Vincent could not resist it. 'It seems that this precision attack, Mother, to separate out the common-law marriages from the religious, is ingenious.'

Mother Superior seemed not have got the ironic point, and was already down in the yard off the verandah, where they were laying out the body on the ground, so that the doctor could come and see. Vincent indicated that they should take the body to the small room which served as a mortuary behind the pharmacy.

Mrs Cardinez eventually arrived. She and her husband had both had remission for sometime. If only there were the Sulfa drugs, they might have regained their own look. While Mrs Cardinez wailed, Vincent could see in

190

her eyes, and in the eyes of the women who accompanied her, in their keening, that they too subscribed to the theology of the mysterious plan, though he was sure that they had not a jot of a thought that Mr Cardinez deserved this punishment.

A beam had fallen across his chest. Those who came to help when Mrs Cardinez called did not have any fingers, and hardly any hands to lift off the heavy weight.

'You would think that the unemployment on Sancta Trinidad could solve this problem,' Singh argued, looking at the devastation.

'The authorities do not see it that way. Anyway, too many people scared to work at Saint Damian's. By the way,' Vincent looked directly at Singh, 'were you alright in your quarters during the storm?'

'How you mean? Yea, yea. A few leaks nothing serious.'

'Good. I saw you running across the yard in the lull.'

'You saw me?'

'Yes, with that young girl? Your student, Christiana?'

'Oh, yea, we get trap in the pharmacy.'

'Late lessons?'

'She keen to study. But where were you? I didn't see you.'

'Trying to get back to Theo.'

'Working late? H'mm. I thought I saw Sister Thérèse was staying over.'

Vincent looked embarrassed

The two men circled each other with their suspicion and innuendo.

Vincent and Thérèse found themselves standing on the jetty, waiting for the respective ferries. He looked at her all veiled again and pinned up. Cocooned. He could still smell her.

They chatted about their work. The pharmacy had not suffered any damage. The papers containing their research from the day before were safe. She was flushed. They kept looking at each other as they talked about their work. Their eyes spoke the conversation of the boathouse. Their hands touched, their fingers entwined, as they both took the rope thrown by Jonah to tie up the pirogue alongside the jetty. They did not want to let go.

Theo was in the pirogue. Vincent was relieved to see him safe and well. How could he have doubted Jonah's care?

'Tomorrow, Sister.'

'Tomorrow.' Then she boarded the *Maria Concepción*.

She did not turn back to wave. Vincent watched her figure diminishing, as they reached the halfway mark between Saint Damian's and Embarcadère Corbeaux. The convent stood, resplendently white in the afternoon sun on the cliffs above La Chapelle Bay, awaiting her arrival, reclaiming her. When she did turn to look back, the figure of Vincent had disappeared.

By the end of July, they were back at their jobs, trying to revive their research on hands. Hands, all he had were hands and her face. She was the veiled nun again.

Vincent felt doomed. He was going to father another child, he was sure, who would be taken from him. He had begun to think about Odetta. Where was she? He had been looking for changes in Thérèse, but noticed nothing which might alarm him or her sister nuns.

A ray of hope had been lit for Thérèse, by a letter which had arrived mysteriously via a sister house in Montreal. A sister at Notre Dame du Lac had a brother with the Free French in London. The mail came down on the convoys after many delays. Her father's letters had ceased, once the occupation of France had taken place. Thérèse conveyed the news to Vincent, barely being able to contain herself. 'Look at this news.' He could never get her away from the fears for her father.

Mother Superior read the letters out in the Chapter House before Compline. There were deep sighs when they heard of the visit by Hitler to Paris. This was how they enlarged on the news of Petain's armistice, De Gaulle's broadcast from London.

The different sisters carried the legacies of the original political affiliations of their families. Somewhere in their midst was the embroiderer of the yellow stars.

They heard of the setting up of the Vichy government. Deep divides fractured the community when the news came through of the British sinking of the French navy at Mers-el-Kebir, on the 3rd July, 1940.

Jean Michel – no surname was ever given for their informant from London – told in a postscript of the banning of Jews, who had fled to the Southern Zone, prevented from returning to the Occupied Zone. All this talk of zones mystified the sisters. What had happened to their beloved

France? Towards the end of the year they heard of the *Statut de Juifs,* of the census according to the *Statut,* by which Jews were no longer allowed to hold public office. Thérèse feared for her father as a senior surgeon in the hospital in Avignon, where he had moved.

It was only just before Christmas, almost as an aside, that Thérèse said to Vincent, 'I'm not pregnant,' as they pored over their notebooks.

'Why've you not told me before?' All his fear spilled out.

'I could barely contemplate the possibility. I wanted to be absolutely sure. I've missed periods before, once, when I had Dengue fever, the radical change in temperature threw my cycle out.'

'Madeleine!'

'You never asked me. I didn't know what you thought. We didn't talk. We don't talk. What can we talk about?'

When would he tell her about his son? Could he? Vincent thought.

They had kept things strictly formal according to their duties and research, though he could see her passion in her eyes. He spoke with his.

Jean Michel's letters from London via Montreal, after their perilous journey south as part of the convoys, had given them something different to talk about. By the end of the year, Thérèse was fearful of who were agreeing with Petain's advocation of collaboration.

Mother Superior was censoring the letters from Montreal, and not reading out those parts of the letters which referred to 'Jewish Affairs', as she called them. Thérèse had overheard Mother Superior talking to Mother Hildegard about, 'Jewish affairs', how the news 'inflamed' the sisters.

But she heard of the second *Statut des Juifs,* excluding Jews from commerce and industry, requiring a census in the Southern Zone where Thérèse still believed her father to be. The letters contained news of the resistance, and of Germans being shot. For instance, in August of 1941, they heard of the shooting of a German by Colonel Fabien at the Metro, and of a German soldier shot at the Gare de L'Est.

Advent

'Cut the motor, Jonah.' Theo was poised in the bow. Since the night of the hurricane, Vincent noticed that the boy and Jonah were closer than ever. Theo needed no encouragement now. He was leaping from the bow, with the coiled rope, to tie up on the jetty, before Jonah had fully pulled in alongside. He was giving the instructions. 'Easy, easy!'

Jonah had his cuatro this afternoon. He sat on the jetty strumming, improvising a tune, instead of immediately departing for Saint Damian's. The Christmas season had started. He was picking out a *Parang* tune, the Venezuelan, Spanish rhythms tinkled at the end of the jetty, accompanied by his soft humming.

Vincent stood watching and listening. Theo had taken his doctor's bag and deposited it on the verandah. He was back quickly, down the steps, with his fishing rod.

Vincent lit a cigarette, leaning up against one of the benches at the end of the jetty. He was allowing the day at the hospital to fall away. But his gaze fell across the bay, to the convent at Embarcadère Corbeaux. His mind was on Thérèse. He had hardly let himself think of the child she might have been pregnant with. But, now, the possibility of what might develop for them began to consume him. What really would they do? Could he tell her about his son, the son he did not know?

Vincent smoked, watching Theo baiting his line. The smoke from his cigarette trailed off into the soft breeze of the afternoon. The boy was hunched, bare backed, at the edge of the jetty, holding his rod intently for a bite. The plate of bait was by his side. Flies buzzed.

Jonah's *Parang* increased the afternoon's harmony. No one spoke. He hummed, and his song began to build towards its chorus, '*Maria, Maria, Maria, Maria Magdalena.*' The folk carol brought an elation to a time that Vincent could dread, when he returned in the afternoon from a hard day at the hospital, to an evening alone with Theo. But, now, that was changing. He looked forward to coming home with the boy. He was pleased with his relationship with Jonah. His progress under Singh's tutelage was a good thing, despite Vincent's worry about Singh's politics, and his puzzlement over Christiana. What was Singh up to?

As he watched Theo fishing, Vincent reflected on the influences of the two men. Jonah was big and generous. Singh was serious and fastidious.

'Jonah, where you learn *Parang*, boy? I connect you with stick fight and the Shango, not with this *coco 'panol* thing.' Vincent interrupted the playing, offering Jonah a cigarette.

'You good, yes, Doc.' Jonah laughed, taking the cigarette and cupping his hands round Vincent's lighted match. 'I in all kind of thing since I is a boy. Is through my father that I in the stick fight. The *gayelle* right there behind our house. I hearing drum and stick fight in that arena since I born. I bring up in that challenge. The *Orisha* worship strong with my father mother, that grandmother who live by we since I small. So, it in my blood from long. We in the Catholic thing, but we also in the *Orisha*. But is my mother who give me this. She mother is a woman who come from Venezuela and was half Carib. Is she who teach me these tunes. Is so our village is.'

Theo picked up the tune and whistled it.

'Plenty religion, boy, but what about this politics thing?' Vincent was getting into the talk with his own questions.

'Politics? Well, what you calling politics is necessity, *oui.*'

'How you mean, necessity?'

'Look at where we is. When you bring up so, with all them kind of soul thing going for you since you small, you know you have to stand up and do something. You can't just let thing happen and you don't do nothing. I never did want to go in no *gayelle*. Since I small I see my father come home with a buss head. My mother nurse that. One time I hear her ask, 'Warner, all this bravery boy, for buss head in the ring? I need you for something else.' Not, that she go stop him. She can't stop him. Then one day, my father come back and he say he join the Oil Workers Trade Union. My father was a rough neck on them early rigs. So he right in the old and the new, modern things and things from long time.' Jonah laughed with his story. 'History, Doc!'

The sweet *Parang* tune brought the welcome of clapping and the shuffle of dancing feet to the boards of the jetty. It was like a breeze. It was the gentle breeze which the old people of the country villages always said came on these evenings before Christmas, the sweet season. It came with the wood smoke from the cooking fires. It came with the coo of the ground doves and the murmur of the pigeons. It came with the drum of wood being cut in the forest, *Gommier* for canoe. It came with the music that water made over small stones, under the bridge where the children fished for *guppies* and *wabeens*. It buckled in the kerosene tins a young girl was filling at a stand pipe in a village somewhere.

'What about this young girl Christiana, Jonah?'

'What you say, Doc?'

'The young girl, Christiana. Singh's student?'

'Student, you say, Doc?' Jonah laughed.

Jonah had moved on to another tune. *Feliz Navidad.* Vincent began, like in jazz, to improvise, picking up an old bottle and spoon from the jetty, with Jonah strumming the cuatro, giving voice.

Theo was on winds. His boy's voice was a flute. '*Feliz Navidad.*'

'*Feliz Navidad,*' Jonah's deep voice echoed.

'I get him. I get him. I catch him. I get him, yes.' Theo was flicking his rod over his head, catapulting his line into the air and scrambling with its length, as he hauled in the weight at its end. It finally emerged as a big red snapper. 'Is a red fish. I catch a red fish.'

Vincent and Jonah looked on, more in awe at the voice, the natural voice of the boy, than the red snapper which was jumping on the boards.

Theo got control of his fish and stunned it into submission. It lay still, blood oozing from its gills. He looked up at Jonah and Vincent. He held up the red snapper, allowing its length and weight full view. He smiled with his eyes, with his mouth, his whole face creased with joy and pride.

'Well done, Theo. Well done!' Vincent walked towards where he was sitting. He went to touch him on his shoulder, to put his arm around him. But, suddenly the new Theo retreated. A barrier went up.

Not even Jonah, jumping up and parodying the excitement of the child, 'Oh gawd boy, is real big red fish you catch there,' moved Theo into the physical contact of *pardners*.

He had left them. He had given them a glimpse of who he was, and who he could be fully, and then retreated behind the veil which seemed to hang

196

before his eyes, to mantle his face. He had once again coupled himself with his old *pardner*, melancholia.

'Theo, what happen, boy?' Jonah tried in a gentler tone. Theo turned away.

Then, as he reached the steps to the house, he turned and shouted. 'I know about Christiana. I know about them.'

Jonah was already pulling in the pirogue from its mooring. He straddled between the jetty and the bow of the pirogue, descending into the boat.

Theo put down his catch on the steps and came back.

'What you know, Theo?' Vincent came and stood behind him as he coiled the rope for Jonah. Theo did not answer immediately.

Jonah was preparing to row, rather than disturb the stillness with the sound of the motor which might alert the Coast Guard. Theo got up and made his way up to the dark and empty house. Vincent picked up the fishing tackle at the end of the jetty. He followed the boy. Theo stopped and turned to face him. 'I see them. I see them. I see what they does do with each other.' He stopped himself.

Jonah straddled the pirogue. 'What he say, Doc?'

'Tomorrow, Jonah.'

'We go talk.' He pushed off.

Theo went to the tap by the tank outside the kitchen to clean and gut his red fish. Then he came back into the kitchen and prepared to fry his fillets in hot oil. When he was ready, he served them with a bake he had made earlier. He and Vincent ate silently in the light of a hurricane lamp Vincent had pumped up. It was a silent communion.

Something new had happened, but something old remained.

'Theo, you want to talk about what you've seen?'

'No, no, leave me alone!'

No sooner had Vincent fallen asleep, than he was awakened. Theo was perched at the end of his bed like an owl, like a *jumbie* bird. All eyes.

THIS IS MY last Christmas in barrack yard up Pepper Hill. Even Mama say, Like is your last Christmas, darling. Sweetheart? Those words. Just so. What she feel? I has a feeling in my blood. I has that feeling sitting down right here, night before Christmas Eve in the dark by the window, leaning on the sill of the Demerara window, waiting for Mama.

A sweet breeze only rustling the leaves in the sappodlla tree outside. A sweet breeze coming over the cocoa hills from Montserrat. A sweet breeze cooling down the day. But, is a lonely breeze too.

Barrack yard tinkling. Barrack yard tinkling with Christmas time music. Right down by Chen Chiney shop I hear it. *Parang* band. Bottle and spoon, *tamboo bamboo*, cuatro strumming. *Maria Maria Maria Maria Magdalena* under the rum shop where Spanish and the big fellas playing cards, All Fours. Arnaldo Barradas, slapping down dominoes on the counter as he drink Chen rum. Wha dap! Like I hear a domino fly down. Is like when I go to shop for Mama late at night and the fellas in a huddle playing. Wha dap! And is only rum I smelling.

Emelda boy! Spanish say, when I come in the door. Spanish only calling me, Emelda boy! Like Spanish like my Mama? Calling my Mama name so, in the shop. Running his fingers through my hair.

Vincent propped a pillow behind his back.

MAMA WORKING in big house late.

The feeling that I go miss everything here in the barrack yard crawling over my skin. It burning my eye. My eye brim up full full. I leaning my head on my arm. I fall off. Then they open big and the immense sky above me, as I lean out over the windowsill and look up to the heavens.

I learning big vocabulary from Father Angel for Exhibition class.

Con stel la tions. Father Angel say the syllabic way is the best way to spell. I learning a little Latin too, and I know that *stella* is star and Mary the Virgin is *Stella Maris*, Star of the Sea, like in the hymn we does sing after Benediction by La Divina Pastora statue.

Where I was? Dreaming. Dreaming of Chantal. That is what happen when Mama late in big house.

How I know Mama safe? Mama not safe coming home in the pitch black night. Tonight is moonlight. She can see the road like a white satin ribbon down the hill, and the barrack yard glittering like Christmas time candle. Like yellow flower-candle.

Chantal!

Yes. Big house like a giant Chiney lantern hanging in the sky. White and shimmering, like it make of lace. Mama late late. Chantal in there. Sometimes I think I can see her.

198

Chantal. Chantal. I almost shouting loud loud. But is a whisper in truth. Chantal, Chantal, because I don't want neighbour to hear. I don't want neighbour to hear my business.

I don't want Popo teasing me and talking talking. What you like that girl for? What you like that girl for? You don't see is big people. Big white people! Whitey cockroach. Popo get vex too much. Like the big men in the rum shop.

Mama say is the times we living in. Father Angel say is living history. Men must fight for equal justice. I read it on *The Gazette* I stick up on the wall. Policeman Burn in Fyzabad. Spanish say one day they go burn down big house.

I listen to all that. But that is not how I see Chantal.

Sometimes, I sure I see she by the balustrade of the verandah. Hanging over, and her long blonde hair like Rapunzel in my Royal Reader. I have in my orange box in the corner. That is where I does learn vocabulary. Sit down in the corner on a little box stool and rest on turn up orange box. Keep my old red Primers and my brown Royal Readers in the box by my feet crunch up. The kerosene lamp burning burning till Mama come down from big house and catch me, wrap me up against she warm skin, and take me into her cosy bed. Mama.

Vincent echoed the child's word, 'Mama.' So that Theo's eyes darted like a distracted owl, like an agitated *jumbie* bird. But then he settled back into his staring. Vincent dared not move.

CHANTAL. Sometimes I think of she spinning spinning. Mama say they have a Singer sewing machine and Chantal does sew in the bedroom.

When I go up to big house with Mama I don't go inside. I does stop by the kitchen door and peep in through the pantry door into the dining room and into the drawing room and the other room deep inside where Chantal is.

That is when Chantal don't come out and play. Chantal must be making things for Christmas.

Wait nuh, I hear somebody in the yard.

And down the road they still singing: *Drink a rum and punch a creama, drink a rum, on a Christmas morning.*

Vincent could hear Jonah again on his cuatro on the jetty earlier in the afternoon.

* * *

SOMEBODY in the yard. Somebody outside the window.

Not exactly voices. Sounds. Wet sounds. Like how *crapeaux* does sound on the wet rocks by river pool. Sschupp! Sschupp! I bend down under the windowsill. Then I poke my head up little little. I peep through the crack of the jalousies. Moonlight milky in the yard. I wonder that nobody don't see me. It so bright. Moonlight flooding Mama and my little dolly.

Like a vision, as Father Angel say. Somewhere for the Virgin Mary, La Divina Pastora to appear in all her splendour. Jewels and lace and golden crown.

I see all Ma Procop flower garden. Red red poinsettia, red turning into black in the Christmas Eve night. Because I see on the clock on Mama cabinet that it late late. Is now early early morning. Christmas Eve.

What I doing up so late? Where time gone? And Mama not home. Big house light turn off, only one light above the steps to the verandah. I imagine Chantal in she bed, in she linen sheets. Under the mosquito net making shadows on shadows. Mama say Mistress and the whole family does sleep in linen sheets, white like milk, shiny like moonlight, and all Chantal golden hair failing over the side of the bed and falling down on the ground. Spinning spinning.

Schuup. Oh God, is Mama. I know my mama even if I see she out in the night when is bed she belong, hugging me up and resting her tired body. And she head not covered. She go get cold. She arms bare, and Mama. Oh Mama.

I know this thing. Not out in the moonlight for the whole yard to see. *Parang* singers coming home late to *maco* and abuse my Mama.

Because I know that is what in Spanish voice in the shop. Emelda boy, Emelda boy. Looking at me and rubbing my head and saying, sugar head, sugar head.

Yes, I know it a long time. Long time I looking in the mirror and seeing more than Mama in my face.

My mama black like glossy coral, she eyes like tamarind seeds, green like glass bottle at the bottom of the river. My skin red like mahogany. More like Spanish skin. *Coco 'pañol*. And me, when I look in the mirror, a real sugarhead. Brown sugar. That is why Spanish like to rub my head.

What else I see in that mirror with questions to ask my Mama?

200

Is only me and Mama living in this house. Was so from the beginning.

And he, Mister, kissing my Mama out in the yard, under the window, out in the moonlight. And more! I see his hands under she dress, playing with she silky petticoat, down inside she bosom.

And those words I know on her lips, Darling, Sweetheart. They pass them between them like sweets they sucking. Schupp. Mama. My Mama.

Yes, I hear Father Angel tell Mama, Emelda, you too pretty for your own good child.

Brown skin girl, go home and mine baby... calypso say.

Mister look up from his kisses, and I don't know whether is the moonlight, but I hear him, *Coco Coco Cocorito*, like he whispering in her ear, like a lizard in her ear. Looking over his shoulder at me. Like a bird on a branch at the window talking to me.

I crawl on my hands and knees like I don't hear. I crawl into Mama bed. I keep my eyes close and smell my Mama. Mama smell of vanilla and sweat. That other smell is *eau de Cologne*. He does put it on his face.

I don't hear her. I don't think I hear her closing the door soft soft and blowing him a kiss on the night breeze. I dream that.

Jonah's Parang had released the boy, not just to whistle but to amplify with story and song. Then Vincent thought of Singh and Christiana. What was it that Theo had seen them doing which had prompted this eavesdropper, this voyeur?

The bed creaked as Vincent moved. Theo jumped off the bed and was now perching on the chair, with his feet crouched beneath him. His head stuck out like a bird, all eyes. Only then did Vincent realise that he was naked.

Far away, the sea. Then further, thunder. Theo proceeded undeterred.

EVERYTHING get fill up. The big hole in my heart get fill up.

Busy with everyone in the yard on the verandah step Christmas Eve, cram up in the little house and the *Parang* singers going sweet sweet and people dancing. My favourite is still *Maria Maria Maria Maria Magdalena*. Everyone have bottle and spoon and Grenade bring the *tamboo bamboo*, and the cuatro players strumming like magic from down the Venezuela main.

Then I hear Popo say, licking ice cream cone, Theo, Theo. Watch! When

I look out the window is Chantal. Chantal in the yard. I catch her eye and she wave.

Coco. I hear the name she always calling me. Coco. Mister name for me. What Chantal know? Coco.

I go down in the yard. Then I have the hole in my heart. Coco. Like I does forget to be happy when she call me that name. Theo, Theo is my name, I say to myself.

Chantal.

Coco.

Look, she raise her hand. Is for you. I make it for you. I sew it. For Christmas.

All the time her hair in the breeze spun out like gold threads. Is for you. A dolly that look like you. Brown like you, like Papa's cocoa. And the green eyes, see the buttons. Is you Coco. She laugh.

I grab the doll and run inside. I look at it and wrench the head off, and throw it in the corner of the room.

When I look out of the window, I see Chantal going up the hill to big house.

Wait, wait, I shout. Chantal! I reach down under the bed.

Move, all you move. Don't touch. Don't touch. Chantal! I stand with the big windmill in my hand. It make with silver milk bottle top, and stick on copy book paper and *papier mâch*e newspaper. It paint up with red, orange and green. For you. She hold the windmill by the bamboo handle and blow on it, and it spin and spin and spin.

Feel the breeze on your face. Like Christmas breeze. I think of the Coco doll with its head pull off.

You going away. Papa say you going away. Chantal blow on the windmill.

Yes. I going town. Father Angel say he don't think I could make Exhibition Class again. But he say the big words will come in handy.

Coco.

Chantal, is Theo. My name is Theo. Call me Theo. I see in her face something I see in the mirror.

Theo.

Chantal.

I wave. She wave.

202

Theo hopped off his perch. In the shadows, Vincent watched him disappear through the door. A streak of moonlight coming from the skylight in the corridor, fell on his back, and Vincent saw the scar and wondered again how that story went. How did Mister, Chantal and Emelda enter that story?

In the morning, Vincent found Theo's pyjamas on the floor.

The boy got the news first on his crystal set, and by the time that Vincent had relayed it to Jonah, and they had arrived at Saint Damian's, they were just in time to see the children processing out of the church ahead of the statue of La Divina Pastora. The children were throwing frangipani petals, which they held in small aprons, onto the path of the procession.

Vincent noticed Singh and Christiana at the door of the pharmacy as he watched Theo run off to his science lesson. As Theo approached, Christiana walked away.

Acolytes were carrying lighted candles. Six of the most able-bodied of the male patients were carrying the canopy over La Divina Pastora, the Divine Shepherdess. The whole congregation of able walkers and those on crutches, together with the nuns and other Roman Catholic patients, were in full throat with *Ave Ave Ave Maria*. The Hindus also processed as fervent devotees of La Divina Pastora. Others lined the way. It was the Feast of the Immaculate Conception.

Vincent left Jonah to tie up at the jetty, and joined the procession just behind Thérèse. 'The Japs have bombed Pearl harbour. The Americans are in the war,' he whispered.

Thérèse turned around abruptly, 'Shoo,' gauging the reactions of the other sisters. Mother Superior was way ahead in the procession.

'America is in the war. With Britain, they have declared war on Japan.'

The news spread through the procession of nuns.

At the altar of Our Lady, which the children had decorated in the garden of the hospital, Vincent went and whispered the news to the chaplain. At the end of his homily, he announced the news to the congregation.

'Pearl harbour? Where is Pearl harbour?' people turned and asked each other.

Then, there was silence. The war suddenly seemed much closer.

By the end of the week, Germany had declared war on America.

* * *

As Christmas of 1941 approached, the news which was to transform life on El Caracol even more radically than the killing of Michael Johnson, alias 'Charlie King,' or the havoc of the hurricane, was announced at a special meeting by the Governor's representative who had come to see for himself the worsening conditions at Saint Damian's. Krishna Singh, Dr Vincent Metivier and Mother Superior sat and listened to him announce the new arrangements.

El Caracol
1942-1944

Rum and Coca-Cola

El Caracol had been transformed. Vincent had seen the map in Major McGill's office at the lighthouse, pinned to the wall, and described at his meeting with the Mother Superior. The line indicating the barbed wire fence, the boundary, the frontier, over which no one must trespass, looked like the knots in a line of stitches. It was a tight cordon around the leprosarium and convent. It was as if the map had been sewn together at that point, a zig zag over the contours of the island, a suture, a wound that needed time to heal.

The prohibited areas were clearly marked and were to be observed strictly by the nuns, staff of the hospital, and the patients of Saint Damian's. There was to be little or no consorting with the Marines and soldiers. 'It's forbidden,' said Major McGill, in a midwest accent. A seaplane, landing in the bay, drowned his monotonous voice. 'You cross the boundary, you're on American soil. You can be shot on sight.'

'These are patients, Major.' Singh's anger was rising.

'This is a war,' the major came back.

'Yes, but it's quite plain they're not Germans.'

'They're used to quarantine, should not be too difficult.'

'I don't expect to see a soldier attempting to shoot a patient,' Vincent said bluntly.

'They'll be *ole mas* in the place if you shoot a patient,' Singh added.

'*Ole mas?*' Major McGill queried.

'Riot!' Singh quickly exclaimed. 'Don't underestimate the people.'

'Whoa! Gentlemen, are you running a hospital or a revolution?'

'Well, Major, I've asked myself that question before.' Mother Superior seized her opportunity.

Major McGill folded his map. 'I'm sure good sense will prevail. My men will want to make their contribution.'

'We'll be very happy to allow them that opportunity,' Mother Superior concluded the meeting.

'*For fifty old destroyers,*' Singh sang as he descended the steps of the verandah, whistling the calypso tune.

Vincent smiled. 'Let's watch it, Singh. By the way, Krishna, I wanted to talk to you about something else.

'Not right now, Doc. Look, Theo coming.' Theo brought the news of all developments on the base, getting about the island on Cervantes. Somehow, the boy was able to travel the island, despite the 'Prohibited Area' and 'Trespassers Will be Prosecuted.' Vincent could hear him as he entered the yard '*For fifty old destroyers,*' a tune he had picked up from Singh, referring to the price the Americans had paid the British for the base.

'Our young revolutionary is learning his songs well,' Vincent smiled.

'My science student. I must go. My other student, Christiana, coming soon.' Singh moved off.

'I see. Okay. Later. But, you know the boy. He's vulnerable, he's very impressionable. Be careful with him.'

'I know where that boy come from.' Singh waved.

Across the yard, the young girl, Christiana, was at that moment climbing the steps to the pharmacy for her science lesson. Vincent watched Theo approach the pharmacy and then turn and leave, going off to the school.

'For we land!' Singh spat out, standing in the yard with Jonah below the window of the clinic. 'Theo, I go see you in the pharmacy soon.'

Vincent listened to the men. He felt cut off. He had felt hurt when Singh said, 'I know that boy', just now. Did he, though? He watched Theo ignore him and walk away.

Singh continued, 'Is oil, man, and the shipping lines from down south, the Yanks come to protect.' Singh and Jonah had started again to agitate about the fact that there had been none of the promised improvements since the hurricane.

'I know why they here. That's one thing. You think them Germans coming all this way for oil?' Jonah protested in disbelief.

'Coming? They here already, boy. You not hear the talk from them fellas going out in the *boca* to trawl. They going to put a stop to that trawling. I think they stop it already, but them fellas from Carenage way don't heed no instructions. The German's out in them seas. Fellas see them. And the Yanks building air bases on Sancta Trinidad, just like they doing here.'

'They taking over the whole place,' Jonah announced.

'Wallerfield and Carlsen Fields. North and Central. They defending oil refinery and sugar factory. Don't forget the sugar. Usine Sainte Madeleine, that is the biggest factory in the Empire. You know that!'

'Yes, all of that good, them fellas from Carenage could say what they like, but I still asking what they giving us. Because the Japs bomb they arse they decide to join the fight. But, what they giving us?' Jonah protested.

'Giving us, boy? Well you know what they giving us. They could tell you in town what they giving us. They all about town, you know, all down Wrightson Road, drunken sailor. What they giving us is what them girls on the corner getting, and is not only dollars that coming with the Yankee wood, eh. I tell you. You ent hear the calypso they bring, *Mother and daughter working for the Yankee dollar.*'

'Boy, is so?'

'Like you ent go in town for a long while. Well, you better watch what you catch. Listen to the tune. *They have young girls going mad.*'

'Is so, boy?'

'What happen Jonah, you getting old? Time to return to Moruga by that wife of yours.' Singh was jaunty today. *'The young girls say they treat them nice and they give them a better price.'*

'Boy, I tell you. No joking, Singh. These fellas can't come here just so. Look how people living! They getting to operate, take over the place, and make no contribution.'

'No, you right. We go have to start the movement again. The people quiet, because of the battering they take from the hurricane.'

'They ent even begin to regain themselves since then. Singh,' Jonah changed his tone, 'you know the Doc asking about Christiana. The boy say he see all yuh.'

'See what?'

'You know what I saying. Watch yourself.'

'You don't know what you talking about.' Singh was on the defensive.

'Still, watch yourself.'

'Jonah, you watch your own business. Where your wife? She gone down the main?' Singh broke into the popular calypso. *'Matilda, Matilda, Matilda she take me money and run Venezuela.'*

'Is a young girl you playing with, you know.'

'What you know? Mind your own business, man.'

Vincent could see that the garrisons he had noticed on Major McGill's map had been camouflaged by the thick forests, and the natural contours of the land. El Caracol was now a hidden fortress with its strategically placed guns at Point Girod and Point Romain, guarding the *bocas*. No one would know that there were two hundred American soldiers stationed here. The safety of Porta España and Sancta Trinidad depended on these fortifications.

As Vincent trailed his hands in the wake of Jonah's pirogue, he realised that in many ways their daily routines were unchanged by the presence of the Yankees.

He watched Theo in the bow. He had gone silent again. He had asked to return on the boat, leaving Cervantes to be grazed by Ti-Jean in the grass behind the children's ward. What had caused this? Vincent edged closer to where he sat in the bow looking ahead. The sea was choppy and the spray drizzled on their faces.

The *Maria Concepción* was crossing with the nuns. Vincent had not seen Thérèse that day. Jonah steered the pirogue carefully. A squall was building in the gulf.

Theo had changed, but something which had disturbed him was pulling him back into his old melancholia. His nocturnal stories seemed to have ceased, or been appeased. 'How was the science lesson today?' Vincent edged closer. Of course he knew that there had not been a lesson, but he wanted the boy to tell him himself. The boy's gaze remained fixed on the jetty ahead.

Then he turned to look at Vincent. At first it was just a glance, then he said quietly, 'I done with that. I don't want to go there again.'

'Why is that?'

Theo turned back to the sea and the approaching jetty.

'Theo. You must talk to me.'

'Why? Why I must go back there. Science?'

'Theo, what is it?'

Vincent waited. 'Them,' Theo sneered. 'Them in the back the whole time. I tell you I see them.'

'Who is them?'

'Christiana nuh, and Singh. I thought she was a friend. She is no friend. Not now. She not sick. I don't see why she here. Them.'

Vincent did not want to explore all of this now, on the boat, just as they were docking. 'Theo, we'll talk later. Get your fishing tackle and we'll talk, okay?'

In the end, Theo did not come down from his room, but stayed up with his maps, not coming down to fish or to have supper. Vincent put his head round the door as he was going off to bed. He crept towards the bed and blew out the candle's flame which was waving dangerously near the boy's mosquito net. 'Night Theo, night, don't let mosquitoes bite.'

Vincent woke to the smell of chewing gum. Theo was sitting at the end of his bed, perched there again, like the *jumbie* bird in the bush, making the sound of his ironic nickname, *'Coco, Coco, Cocorito.'* The boy stared at him. He was chewing gum.

'Where've you got chewing gum from, Theo?' Vincent wiped the sleep from his eyes. 'I don't mind you having it, but I just want to know where you could've got it from.' Theo was mute, unless this tale was his answer. He waited for Vincent to get comfortable, with a pillow behind his head.

THEY SAY they get this far to the edge of the rocks, then whoosh!

Theo made a flying motion with his arms, then adjusted his sitting position on the railings at the bottom of the bed, so that Vincent wondered whether he would topple off backwards.

HERE, THIS PLACE, where is a midden. I ent hear that word before, midden. Father Angel never teach me that word.

This fella have a funny accent like a cowboy in the pictures, when I went theatre with Spanish and Mama down in Couva.

One day we take the buggy, and Spanish get a horse borrow in the yard. He take Mama to the picture. Mama beg him to bring me.

This fella have the same accent and I think he have this accent because he always chewing when he speak.

211

Vincent wondered whom Theo was talking about.

MIDDEN, he say. Right here, is a midden. His jaws rolling. He move over his syllable, chewing them up.

All the time he slurring and chewing. And I know that lieutenant is different to how they say it in English proper, *lieutenant,* because Father Angel tell me that.

But he never stop talking, this fella, this GI. He say his name is Jesse. But first I don't believe he is any GI. Well, well, is because he's a black man. I don't know they have black GI. Then he joke and say, Jesse James, the famous outlaw.

He want to know my name, but I stand up so and watch him. He say, Cat bite you tongue, kid? Same question like others use to ask, but it sound different in his mouth with the chewing gum.

He chewing the whole time that he speaking and kneeling on the ground and picking up shell and saying, this is the midden. The Lieutenant tell them they must mind where they digging. But they don't seem to mind. And the tractor just moving earth and clearing trees. And in no time, the barracks going up, the posts and the barbed wire fence all the way down the road. Red dirt in the green hills. They dragging out tall tall trees. That's timber, man, another GI say. He chewing too.

And the parrots rise up and take off, screaming across Chac Chac Bay. Whoosh. *Les perruches.* The GI say the French sisters call them *les perruches.*

Theo had flown like the parrots, leaping off the railing of the bed to crouch on the floor, and then jump up to sit on the chest of drawers.

JESSE SAY TO ME to come with him down to the shore where the ocean come in. Come and see the ocean. There is a big O in his Ocean.

Theo chewed on his chewing gum, the whole time, getting his tongue around the words as he had heard them.

THE SHORE is hidden, tuck beneath us, under the thick green veils of lianas and vines with broad leaves. I never see the sea like that. So far, yet so near, like a bucket of water, brimful, swelling and overflowing.

Atlantic, Jesse say, trying to embrace the world. Is a wide expanse as far as I can see, swelling, glinting, making a tumult below in the bay. Making a tumult as of many voices speaking at once, like Father Angel say.

Now, I know my geography and I know they have ocean. We does say, come down by the sea, or just, come down by the water. Go by the beach.

Words have a history too, Father Angel say.

This was progress, Vincent thought. This was a story in the present. This was not something from Pepper Hill's past or from the friary's past. This was a recent past. Vincent did not worry about the fact that Theo seemed to have a life on the island that he did not know about. That he had not been attending his science lessons but meeting with GI's in the hills.

THE MIDDEN is down on the shore where there is a landslide, and all you seeing is shells. Jesse crouching there among the shells, raking through with his fingers. Shells. Chip chip, conch, oyster, all kind of shell. I can see the pink on the lip of the conch and purple on the mouth of the oyster. What is in shells?

Then he say, stooping down, picking up shells and dead coral, Maybe bones. Bones! Whose bones? Shells and bones like white porcelain.

I know porcelain from Father Angel's cabinet in the presbytery up Pepper Hill.

It fine so, the shells, the dead coral. Is then that my ears prick up. What kind of bones? He take up something which is not a shell. This is pottery, kid, he say. We does say *pottery* like *poetry*.

This here is part of a pot, and he hold it and show me how it is part of a vase or a drinking cup. For truth, yes, it look so.

He say, these are the first peoples on this island. More than five hundred years ago. They must've watched Columbus come up through the gulf from the Serpent's Mouth. Watched his caravels, the sails unfurl, and wonder if it was a whale or something from another world. He naming these people: Carib, Aruac, Taino. Ancient peoples, ancient civilisations.

They build in palms and bamboo. He talk so.

That is why there is nothing to see. They have no ruins. Is part of the palms

213

and bamboo that grow now, is part of the noise that the parrots make, is part of the music of the sea with the shells and bones and broken vases. All of that is part of the sighing of the sea. That is all what remain of their history, he tell me. Just so, chewing gum the whole time.

Theo looked up and paused for a moment, to take in how Vincent was himself taking in the story. Then, he was off again.

AND I WONDER that this black GI, this negro GI, know so much about the islands, as he call them, throwing his arms in the air, making an arc for an arc of islands he say, stretching from Florida to our eastern coasts, the beaches at Guayaguayare, which he say is the name give by those people that he speak of. I excited because I know a word he looking for but he don't seem to able to find.

Theo looked up, and announced the word:

ARCHI-PE-LA-GO. Syllabic way is the best way.

Vincent laughed. He was enjoying the telling of this story. He marvelled how the boy spoke in the accent of the GI.

HE SEE QUESTIONS all over my face, but he stop worrying about whether I have a tongue or not, and he just telling me everything. But he wondering what I doing there, and he ask whether I is from the hospital. But then he say, he could see I not from the hospital. He see the track I come out from, so he say that I come from the Doctor house. He seem to know the island and everybody who living on it. I leave him with his stories.

Long before Columbus, he say. I can't imagine it. But he say, Listen to the sea, and I go imagine it. He say, a bone might not look like a bone, because it become a fossil and look like a stone. The danger is that the tractors go make graves of these bones and we go lose the story of that time.

As he talking, I listen to the sea. I only seeing all these bodies bulldoze into big big graves. I see bones, thin thin flesh hanging from the hip bones and off the shoulders. Bodies rolling over and over in the waves, the bulldozer heaping the red dirt over the bodies, and the parrots screaming.

The GI saying that the French sisters call them *les perruches*. They speaking a language that is the language of the Caribs, the Aruacs and the Tainos.

Theo clutched a small, heart-shaped, biscuit-coloured, earthen piece of pottery. He offered it to Vincent. He took it from him and turned it in his fingers. He ran his fingers over the grain of the earthenware, assessing its authenticity. He had known of the midden, but had not explored there. The Americans had disturbed the site. He returned the heart-shaped piece of a vase to Theo.

AND THEN JESSE give me this chewing gum. He say, all the kids chew gum back home. Back home is South Carolina. And he start right there on a story of his Mama and Papa, only his Papa gone north and his Mama not see him for a long time, and he Jesse don't remember him for real. He's a man on a porch with a banjo on his knee, who gone Louisiana. He is a man with a song in his throat.

As we climb back from the shore, Jesse start to tell a story of the history of his people, which he say is the history of my people, except that, then he laugh, and rub his hands through my hair, and say I am a sandy kid. I must've get mixed up with some white people.

I watch him, and I slit my eyes, so.

I shrug him off. Because if he see my Mama, her skin like mahogany. If he see the beauty of it. If he see her skin that can go black as ebony. He laugh. He teasing me. That is part of our history. He prepare now to go on that path, but is a path I know well, from Mama and Mama's grandmother, my great-grandmammy, Ma Dellacourt. He say they have black people like me in South Carolina, and he going to tell me about that.

Vincent watched Theo. He longed to hear the small voice of the boy, the boy who shouted out on the jetty when he caught his red fish. How much longer could this go on, this language of astonishment?

WHEN WE REACH the top again, they already fix the artillery guns. We face the ocean, camouflage by the trees. I hear the other GI talking about the German U-Boats. They say these guns go take them out of the water. And if these don't get them, then the magnetic loop below the sea, between El Caracol and the

215

island of Huevos will catch them, by setting off a signal if they touch the cable.

I keep my ears prick and listen.

I see the island of Huevos between the trees, the other side of the Boca de Navios. Plenty ship passing through the channel.

But then, is what I going to tell you when I start.

They say they get this far to the edge of the rocks. Then they leap right out into the blue air above the tumult of the waves and the expanse of the ocean. This is where they get to when they running. All the people jump from the high rocks. They take off like birds in flight. They rather die than get capture by the Spaniards. That is why the place call Sauteurs. The place of the leap. They rather die than give themselves to the Spaniards.

As Jesse talk, I see them flying and then tumbling out of the sky. They was the colour of the parrots. Green, blue and yellow. And is their voices that you hear in the air.

When we climb the hill, we hear the shells on the shore and the tumult of the ocean. I thought it was shells and bones, and the vases and cups breaking with the force of the waves. And that other thing return, the bulldozers heaping the bodies one upon the other, dump into big big graves.

Then, Jesse say, we never know what the future go bring. He say he have another story to tell me, that will change my way of looking at history. He tell me that I must come again to that place where the midden is, and he go give me more chewing gum.

Theo was sweating, and lay back, exhausted with his visions and stories, told in tongues.

Then there was a sound like thunder which was quite close. It was not long before Albacores and Barracudas were in the air over El Caracol. Vincent parted the blackout curtains a crack. Chac Chac Bay heaved in the darkness, and broke on the beach and under the jetty. But through the bedroom door, and coming through the windows at the back from Theo's room, and along the corridor, were the flares Vincent had not seen before. Then, there was another kind of thunder which must have been the guns that Theo talked about, trained on the ocean.

They were there, just behind the house, in the back yard.

The Governor Haul 'e Arse

Theo had added gardening to his chores. The last of the sorrel bushes had been cut down and piled high like a pyre. He had been up before dawn. More than ever, Vincent was aware of creaking floorboards as the boy never stopped moving about the house.

'Theo take a rest, please,' Vincent called out.

His reclusiveness, since deciding that he was not returning to Singh's science lessons, was converted into hyperactivity.

Vincent smelt the pitch oil, and then the crackling fire, as soon as he came out onto the landing from his room. It was a golden rule that Theo should not play with fire. His only use of matches was to be in the kitchen, and even that made Vincent nervous. Something he had picked up from one of Father Dominic's letters a while ago alerted him to this. He had not learnt, even by now, to trust the boy in this regard. He called out from where he stood at the window. 'Theo, you have that fire under control, boy?'

At first, Theo did not hear him, and then he looked up and smiled, chucking more sorrel bushes into the blaze. Vincent called again, but Theo waved, cutting him short with, 'Under control, Doc,' giving a mock salute.

Spending too much time with his GI friends, Vincent thought. He had begun to notice this way Theo had of calling him, 'Doc,' like Jonah did, while he chewed his chewing gum. He allowed the familiarity, taking it as a sign of Theo's change and growth. After all, he allowed Ti-Jean as much rope as he liked to take, to the marked disapproval of some. But he did not want any rudeness from the young boy developing.

He was still worried at times about the arrangement he had made with Father Dominic who seemed to have forgotten about the boy altogether. The friar never answered his letters anymore and did not come to visit; always some excuse sent by the chaplain. He was obviously pleased to have got a load off his shoulders. A short letter had, in fact, come a few weeks back, making light of all of Vincent's queries, concluding with Father Dominic's flattery. 'You're a miracle worker, doctor,' as if that made everything fine, shifting the load.

With each stab of his fork, Theo sang, *'The Governor say no mas, the Governor haul 'e arse.'*

Vincent smiled. Just what he himself was feeling this morning, the day that the Governor's secretary was paying a visit to Saint Damian's with the Archbishop. Mother Superior did not want either himself, Singh or Jonah there. She wanted the visit to pass peacefully.

'With dignity, Doctor Metivier,' were her words. They had been asked to keep away.

Vincent was enjoying Theo's resistance and rebellion. It was because of his spending more and more time with Jonah, and the fishermen. This meant that he was in touch with the talk in town, singing one of Tiger's calypsos:

'But ah going to plant provision and fix my affairs
And let the white people fight for ten thousand years.'

Now it seemed that Theo had taken inspiration from this spirit of resistance with his gardening. He must have overheard Jonah and Singh talking about the programme for the restoration of the vegetable gardens at Saint Damian's, one of the few ways for the patients to supplement their menial allowances. 'I joining the revolution. We go feed we selves,' he proclaimed.

Vincent recognised the calypso tune from the meeting. Tiger's calypso was becoming an anthem of the movement. It expressed how people were feeling about the war, and especially about how little had been done to restore things at Saint Damian's since the hurricane. As they watched the generous supplies being off loaded for the American base at Perruquier Bay, where some of the more able-bodied patients were getting light casual labour, they sang Tiger's couplets with pride and iron:

'But ah want a piece o' land at Mount Hololo
So I could plant me dasheen, figs and ochro.'

Theo's bonfire had flared up, and the last of the bushes became the crimson colour of the sorrel flowers.

'Watch that fire don't reach the house, Theo.' The boy saluted smartly. He was a shimmer behind the haze of the fire.

The digging continued, fuelled by calypso. *'The Governor say no mas, the governor haul 'e arse.'* He was obviously enjoying the rudeness and zest in the couplets with each stab of his fork.

Vincent echoed him under his breath as he passed. *'The governor haul he arse.'* They were not being allowed to be there to put their demands today of all days. He was sure that they were heading for another flare-up soon.

'And now them Yankees adding to the trouble,' Jonah had said at the close of the meeting yesterday, where they had reluctantly agreed with Mother Superior's demand to remain absent. He had flung down his words as a threat.

Vincent was anxious about not seeing Thérèse. She had not been at the hospital yesterday. They had been managing to work with decorum. But, for how much longer?

A wild fantasy made him want to see her emerge from the bush, cross the dry, beaten, red dirt path to the house. She had not ever entered the house. He saw her with the crimson of the flowers which were burning, held in the folds of her white habit. Then she was part of the flames, dissolving, part of the ash which rose with the sea breeze.

Their fingers had almost touched the other day, standing next to each other at the door of Mother Superior's office, listening to the lunchtime news from the BBC, telling them that the allied bombing of France had begun with an RAF raid on the Renault works at Bellancourt. They had had to say it all with their eyes.

While the sisters thought of their beloved France and their families, Thérèse of her father, Vincent had wondered about Bernard. His mother had not had any news for a while. Could he have been part of that raid? Standing so close to each other with their own anxiety, it felt reckless to Vincent to want to touch Thérèse in public.

Like with the new barbed wire fences around the leprosarium, they had erected their own boundaries. But they were temptations, like the trespassing signs were for the patients, even the children, who were all the time being caught entering parts of the island they had never dreamt of venturing into before. The prosecution signs were a red cloth to a bull.

Theo had gone quiet. He had finished working out at the back. When Vincent went into the house to fetch a book in the study, he noticed him escaping behind a door into the kitchen, out to the water tank. He moved rapidly and quietly, barefoot, in just his khaki pants, no shirt. There was the sound of water running into a bucket, then the sweeping of a broom on the pitch pine floor. Vincent too was restless on his enforced day off.

'Theo, what's going on out there?' His frustration with himself and the boy mounted.

There was no reply, and then suddenly, Theo was back with bucket and mop. 'I doing my chores, Mister, go and take a rest on the verandah, nuh.'

'Mister? Who you calling Mister? I'm no Mister.' Vincent was horrified at being called Mister.

Theo was already away, looking over his shoulder with a glance that said it all. This was a game, but taken seriously. 'Is you day off, take a rest. You don't know how to do that.'

The boy was right, he did not know what to do with himself this morning. He should be at Saint Damian's. This was a mad agreement. He would just have to be patient. Let Theo have his way.

There was the smell of wax polish. The surfaces of the sideboard and dining room table were as luminous as mirrors. There was the sound of scrubbing. When he turned to look into the house from the verandah, Theo was on his knees, and the pitch pine floors were coming up a beautiful, silky white, as he scrubbed with blue soap, his scrubbing brushes dipped into a bucket with bicarbonate of soda. It clanged as he pushed it along in front of him. The water slopped and splashed, as he slapped the floor cloth down. The boy worked, pushing himself along on his knees, wiping the floorboards dry with another large cloth, tucked into the top of his khaki pants.

Vincent's patience did not last. 'Theo, you don't have to be doing all of this housework.'

Theo looked up and smiled. 'Tell me, who go do it, then, Mister?' The voice was from one of his nocturnal tales, which unnerved Vincent. It was the parody of a servant's voice. He could take this sort of thing at night, but not in the light of day. 'Tell, me nuh, cheups.' He sucked his teeth.

Vincent's ears jangled with the bracelets of Indian women scrubbing the floors at Versailles. His mother's floors had always been scrubbed by the women from the barracks. He heard their voices in Theo's voice, the voices of Calcutta.

He noticed that Theo was not coming to the front of the house when he was in the hammock on the verandah. He kept to the back of the house. He was playing the well observed game. Then, when he looked up, he noticed through the side window, that there were clothes, Vincent's white cotton shirts and his khaki pants, drying on the line. The laundry was also being done.

Vincent dozed in his hammock. He was aware of Theo creeping around him. Once, when he opened his eyes, he saw him escaping from the living room with a sheaf of old newspapers and copies of the *London Illustrated News* that Father Meyer had dropped off on his last visit. 'Keep you busy and out of trouble.' He wondered what he had meant at the time. He felt that he was referring to himself and Thérèse. What did he know?

A glass of iced lime juice had been left on a side table near to his hammock. Theo had been observing his naps. 'Thank you, Theo, just the thing for this heat,' he called out. But the boy had already scuttled upstairs with his armful of news. He could guess the outcome, more cuttings for the bedroom wall. He had not entered the room since first discovering the complex historical collage. He could smell the flour and water paste. He could hear the snipping of scissors. He dozed and woke again into one of Theo's tunes.

'*Time so hard you cannot deny that even salt fish and rice I can hardly buy*'.

The macabre game of servant and mister concealed Theo's glee in having Vincent to himself all day.

The midday Angelus from the convent jolted Vincent into the bright glare of noon.

Theo was standing behind him. Vincent knew that he was waiting for the midday news. The boy was obsessed with news. His room was testament to that. 'You switch it on. Come on, let's see what Mr Hitler is up to, where the Allies have advanced.'

The radio crackled with the tones of the BBC newsreader. Theo pursed his lips to imitate the plummy voice. He stood listening intently. Then he sped upstairs to his room. Each name, each raid, fuelled his own advancing armies.

As he returned to the verandah he shouted, 'Doc, look!' He pointed out into the bay. The destroyer, US Barney with a corvette US Surprise were passing one in front of the other, outside Chac Chac Bay. They gleamed in the hot sun, metallic on the crinkling sea. Their engines droned. Their Stars and Stripes fluttered furiously.

'It's the convoy preparing to leave.'

Theo quickly got out his notebook and added the ships' names to his log, singing all the while like a true blue calypsonian. *'Before the war I was living nice, hot potato with me bacon, stew pork and rice.'*

'You better enter the calypso competition this year, boy,' Vincent joked.

Theo smiled. He was himself again. For a while, at least.

'Ei! What boat is that?' Theo pointed.

Vincent looked up. Entering the bay was a coastguard launch. Vincent raised his binoculars. It was what he thought. It carried the Governor's ensign. The visit was about to begin. He knew he should be there. What was Mother Superior up to? They should never have agreed to her demand. He was the doctor of the leprosarium. He felt like leaving the house immediately and going to Saint Damian's along the back track.

Not long after, they heard the salvos of the welcoming gun salute. State and church had arrived. The parrots screamed. There was the sound of a bugle, the rattle of a drum on the wind.

Vincent could hear Theo in the kitchen. *'Toast bread with butter and jam, seven eggs in the morning with a junk o'ham'.*

'You wanting lunch now, Mister.' That servant's voice again as he entered the kitchen.

'Theo!' Vincent was more impatient than ever.

Then the boy was playing another role. He was chewing gum.

'You seeing that GI friend of yours again? You must bring him to the house.' Vincent had not heard of Jesse since the tale of the midden. He was aware that he was using material from the tales as a matter for daytime conversation. He did not usually refer to events which had come up in the night-time stories.

Theo looked up and smiled, knowingly, and carried on, *'Before the war I was living nice. Hot potato with me bacon, stew pork and rice.'* He could be cheeky.

The wake of the passing boats had reached the beach and the jetty, swamping the boards, breakers crashing one upon the other under the kitchen. 'Big wake, them boat have.' Then, he was gone again.

With a tap on his shoulder, Theo called Vincent to table. A single place was laid at table. There was a steaming plate of ground provisions.

'Yam, dasheen, cassava! Boy, what's this? *Sancoche?*'

There was a tall drinking glass of iced red sorrel. 'The last of the sorrel? Are you not eating with me, Theo?'

Theo was back in role. Mute. He pulled out Vincent's chair, and then hovered near the kitchen door, looking from afar at the event he had arranged. This was his drama, lunch at the dining room table for Mister. The game was becoming uncomfortable.

Vincent played along. 'The *sancoche*, good, Theo, the best I eat.'

Theo came to the door of the dining room, hovered for an instant, and then disappeared again. Vincent smiled to himself. What had brought this on? One moment he was the sophisticated follower of the war, another a child playing a sinister game. But he noticed when the games were more than just a game. They were never really just a game.

The house went silent. Vincent sipped on his *sancoche*.

Then, he noticed that there was a small brass bell on the table. He had not seen this bell in a long while. From where had Theo retrieved this relic? He could see his mother's hand hovering over the bell at Versailles, ringing it between courses for the table to be cleared, for the vegetables to be served. He had witnessed as a child the elaborate training that new servants went through when they first took up their posts. 'My dear,' his mother would say to a visiting aunt, 'it takes all my time to train them, *they* might as well pay *me*. Breaking in a new girl!'

Theo knew that he, Vincent, would know all about this. He, Theo, had been a witness. His mother had been such a servant. What he did not know was whether Vincent would play along. Would he be playing or acting *for truth*? He was expected to ring this bell when he had finished his *sancoche*, wanted some more, or was indicating that he was now awaiting the clearing of the table, and desiring his dessert. He presumed there was a dessert.

They were having the full works. Should he play along and ring the bell? Vincent's hand hovered like his mother's had done over the bell. No, he would give another signal.

'Theo, Theo, really good boy, *sancoche* real hot!'

At first there was no reply. Then, Theo suddenly marched out of the kitchen to the table, picked up the bell, and rang it. Its shrill noise had the parakeets going off in the cocorite palms. Then he slammed it down. 'Ring the blasted bell, nuh,' he screamed.

223

For a moment Vincent was stunned. Theo had cracked. What he saw in that instant were the tears welling up in the boy's eyes. 'Theo, Theo, you don't need to to do this.'

He stretched out to touch his arm. The boy moved away. Then, he returned to the kitchen and came back out again as if nothing had happened. In his arms was the large bowl of *sancoche* and a silver ladle that Vincent had never seen before. Where was he finding all these relics of Versailles? He stood at the side of Vincent to replenish his plate. He accepted graciously.

Finishing his second helping, he then rang the bell for the table to be cleared and for dessert to be served. Theo delivered orange and grapefruit salad. There was a splash of Angostura Bitters, which reddened the syrup. He played along. 'Boy, that was good!'

Theo cleared the dishes in silence. Vincent waited. He remembered his mother saying that his grandfather always said, 'One never grows old at table.'

The washing of wares clattered in the kitchen. Vincent dozed.

As he opened his eyes, the sea kept appearing and disappearing as the hammock dipped beneath the ledge. Theo must have lowered the blinds. The verandah was in shade. He was sitting at the top of the steps. There was the smell of silver and brass polish. Newspaper was laid out on the floor. He had all the cutlery from the sideboard drawers out. They sparkled in the sun. He was counting the forks, rubbing down the spoons.

Theo had discovered more relics of Versailles' past. These he was busy washing in a basin with gravel and sour oranges. He was leaning into the bowl as into a mirror. Vincent watched the boy. He had not stopped all day. He was used up. What had brought about this endless preoccupation with service? Did this have anything to do with what he had seen at Singh's. 'I see them in the back,' he had said. Vincent could guess. His own guilt made him more censorious. He would have to speak to Singh.

The day had seemed unreal. Everything that Theo had been doing had taken him back to Versailles. All this old silver and brass was from under the stairs. Then Vincent thought of how this boy had obviously gone with his mother to the house on Pepper Hill, the big house made of lace and hanging like a Chinese lantern in the night. 'Big house,' he had called it, in his story; a house like the house where Chantal lived with her long blonde hair.

He heard the deep sobbing coming from the boy where he sat on the steps. He got up and sat near to him. 'Come Theo. It's all been too much, hasn't it. We've taken it too far today. Let's stop this. Let's put these things away. Let me give you a hand.' Together they put away the relics of Versailles, the toys for these games, back under the stairs.

'Let's go for a swim.' Vincent was trying to jolly Theo out of his mood.

Down on the jetty, they saw the coastguard launch, which had brought the Archbishop and the Governor's secretary leaving on its return journey. Vincent wondered how things had gone. He and Theo dived and then swam the length to Father Meyer's jetty and back.

The spell of activity which had fallen over the day was broken.

The priest waved from his verandah, happy to be back from the detention centre for all Germans on Sancta Trinidad. Instead, he was now content to have the police launch calling every other day. There had been a rumour that he might have been interred.

He was shouting something. It was just audible. 'Bacchanal over there!' He was pointing to Saint Damian's.

Vincent waved. He did not want to hear Father Meyer's account of the day.

'Race,' cried Theo, as he kicked away. Vincent followed.

They clambered up onto the jetty by the ladder. They lay exhausted, laughing. Theo then ran up to the house and came back with two towels and the fishing rods.

They baited the hooks and fished for their supper.

The evening declined, leaving the jetty in shadow. The sunset burned a red hole in the sky over Venezuela. There was an unusual quiet.

It was when Vincent went back up to the dark house to light a lantern, and to draw the blackout curtains, that he saw her coming down through the bush and the razor grass. She was picking her way across the burnt ground, lifting her white skirts, where the sorrel bushes had grown. He saw her stockinged ankles. He met her at the door.

'Doctor?'

'Sister? The boy's on the jetty.'

'Vincent.'

'Madeleine.'

Then, she was in his arms, their mouths hungry for each other.

'I had to come and see you,' she said, between kisses.

The Visit

As Vincent held Madeleine in his arms, he looked over her shoulder down to the jetty. He did not think that Theo could see them from there, standing inside the darkness of the house. Folded together, they would appear as one person from that distance.

Suddenly, the boy jumped up, pulling in his line with great excitement and shouting out, 'Doc, Doc, I catch him. I catch him.' It was his favourite, a red snapper, he was sure. Red fish were Theo's favourite dish. That would be their supper tonight, like last night. You need to catch another, Vincent said to himself, relieved to see the boy return to his old self.

'Stay for supper?' he wooed her. He felt like he was asking her out to dinner. She clung to his shoulder. She tried to smile through her tears. There was a wisp of black hair escaping from beneath the tight skull cap under her veil. He tried to push it back, slipping his fingers beneath the cap near her temple. But his efforts only made more of her black hair escape. 'Oh, dear, I'm making a mess of this,' he said.

'No.' She slipped her fingers into the crevice, tidying away her hair, unpinning, and pinning again more securely her veil to her skull cap.

He had not been able to get a coherent word from Madeleine as they moved onto the verandah, where they now stood, so that he could see Theo, and decide what they would do when the boy came up to the house. Madeleine wanted to be held, but at the same time she wanted to break out of Vincent's arms.

'I had to come. I had to come. It's all getting out of hand. I wish you'd been there today.'

'What do you mean? What has happened?' Then he remembered Father Meyer calling out, bachannal.

It was like trying to hold a frightened bird. He wanted to kiss her again and then he did not, because he felt he would be taking advantage of her

227

mood. They had kept their hands off each other since the boathouse. But now they could not resist each other.

They heard the early fishermen passing just out in the bay. It was Atilla's latest, which seemed ironic at this moment in time:

'We shall extend to the Jews hospitality
As a monument to our ancestors' memory.'

Vincent hummed the new calypso as he looked at Madeleine. She pinched her brow. 'These calypsos, even when they're positive, disturb me.'

She had heard Singh speaking under the almond tree recently, linking the fate of the Jews in Europe, their enforced migration, with the enslaved Africans and indentured East Indians. There was controversy over Atilla's calypso in *The Gazette*. It was was being censored by the Governor. He did not like the idea of the British slave masters being compared to the Nazis.

'Madeleine, try and tell me what is distressing you so much this evening.' Vincent lifted her chin.

'This afternoon. It started this afternoon, up in Indian Valley. Drumming. At first, it was just the Indian patients, but then the African patients as well, started going up into Indian Valley, taking their drums, all the time, the drumming getting louder. How come you didn't hear it at your house? When they drum at night I can't sleep.'

'Must be the way the wind blows. The sound carries directly across the bay to you. I'm round the point, behind the hill. So, what then?'

'Well, we waited, tried to keep the small children on the ward happy, playing. The older ones, even Ti-Jean on his crutches, took off with the grown ups.'

'What's going on? I'm away for a day and this is what happens. Why did Jonah not come over and see me?'

'Maybe they took the opportunity of you not being there.'

'It's not like that. Not Jonah, maybe Singh. What then?'

'The rumour is that they're planning a march. The slogans, anti-American rather than anti-Mother Superior. They find it easier to attack the Americans. They don't like the prohibitions, the threats of shooting. The children are confused though, because they like the soldiers. There's an epidemic of chewing gum. They hand it through the barbed wire fences. With cigarettes sometimes. The children play all along the perimeter.'

'I know. Theo is always chewing now. Goes up to the gun station at the back of the house, has made friends with one of the Marines.'

She turned and followed his gaze onto the jetty and the boy fishing at the edge. 'We've missed him at the school recently. Singh was asking for him.'

'He's been caught up in his work here. You should see his room. I think he needs his freedom sometimes, both here, and getting about the island on Cervantes. It rescues him from his isolation. Perhaps not a bad idea to have a break from Singh.'

A bat swooped in from outside.

'Will you rescue me?' She turned and looked up into his face quickly and then turned away, not waiting for an answer, and gazed at the boy on the jetty in the fast-encroaching darkness.

'Is that what you want?'

A *mabouyan* lizard darted across the wall. '*Esprit marlin,*' Madeleine whispered in Vincent's ear.

'What?'

'Sister Marguerite. That's what she calls the *mabouyan.*'

'Old superstition. Evil spirits.'

'It's what people believe. You don't believe in evil?'

'How did all this start, the decision to go up to Indian Valley? I can't believe this has been going on without me. Ah Singh! He's sure to be behind it.'

'Some of the sisters say it started during the Archbishop's service, during the sermon. I had to leave to be on duty on the ward. In fact, I left earlier because I was so upset. Then the drumming started and the crowds going up into Indian Valley. I felt I had to come and tell you. But also...'

'What is it Madeleine? Tell me what has brought you over at this hour. Forbidden by the rules. Has something happened? Something I should know?'

'Questions? I almost got lost getting here. It looks so different since the Marines have dug up the track and put down their fences. And then I found myself going to the boathouse?' She looked at him from under her eyes, wiping a tear away.

'Madeleine, sweetheart.'

'I was not in yesterday. I could not leave my cell.'

'I did wonder where you were. I found it difficult to ask. Could not leave your cell? Why? Influenza?'

'No, I'm well. Not influenza, nothing like that.'

'What then?'

'Such a surprise for me. Singh and Jonah have been holding meetings. Everyone today so agitated, with the Governor's representative coming. And the Archbishop's secretary going to be there as well. So much white washing going on to get ready for the visit.'

'I thought this would happen. Mother Superior wanted me away from the hospital today. Jonah and Singh were supposed to be absent as well.'

Vincent could see that Theo was packing up. He was preparing to come up to the house. He was tidying up his rods and lines. 'The boy will be here any moment. Tell me what has happened. Stay for supper. We'll talk later.'

'I'm being shunned. I'm being persecuted' she blurted out. 'You remember the yellow star?'

'Of course.'

'I've a collection now. Each morning, one is deposited under the door of my cell. I wake to it there. Well made, stitched with care by the fingers of one who knows how to sew well, how to embroider. I can tell. The last one had the word *Juif* embroidered in its centre.'

'That's terrible.'

'I can't go on. I can't show my face. This is a community of nuns! What's going on in the world? And this morning, a message attached. "Join the vermin on Nelson Island." Can you imagine? I wake to that. I find them as I lie on the floor and curl my body, performing my *venia.*'

He imagined her religious observance, her foetus shape on the floor of her cell. 'I'm sorry.' He took her hand.

'It's why I left the service. It became overwhelming, sitting there praying with the community.'

'It's not your fault.' He stroked her arm.

There was a clatter as Theo dropped the fishing rods on the verandah floor.

'Theo, is that you? I've not lit the lanterns yet, nor drawn the blackouts. We're here,' Vincent called from the shadows. 'Come and meet Sister Thérèse from the hospital.'

'Theo.' Thérèse tried to compose herself.

Theo put out his hand to shake Thérèse's. 'Theophilus, Madame.' He was being gallant, welcoming her for the first time to the house.

'We've missed you at the school. The smaller children are missing your stories. And Mr Singh.'

Theo stopped in his tracks to the kitchen. He turned and faced Sister

230

Thérèse. His eyes grew large with interest. What did she know about Singh?

'Is there enough fish for Sister Thérèse, Theo?' Vincent called after the boy. 'Don't mention Singh,' Vincent whispered. Thérèse raised her eyebrows.

'Plenty. I catch two, you know? Two on one hook. Imagine that. And, I done bake this morning.' He had run back out onto the verandah. He smiled at Sister Thérèse. He was excited by her presence in the house. They did not have visitors, and when they did, not women. In a moment he was in the kitchen again.

'There's a problem with Singh,' Vincent explained. He lit the lantern and drew the blackouts. 'You wouldn't think we needed blackouts here. I'll let Theo have the lantern.'

They sat quietly, as they heard the Angelus being rung, the familiar sound taking Thérèse back to the convent.

'Have you told Mother Superior about the yellow stars?' Vincent took Thérèse's hand in the dim light.

'No! I can't. I can't expose myself like that. I try to ignore it once I'm at work. Today I made it to the ferry, just in time, the boatman had almost started moving away from the jetty. I had to jump on. I can't look into my sisters' faces. I keep asking myself, which one is it?'

'This can't go on. We'll have to think what we can do.'

'I'm having the most terrible dreams. Each night, the same dream. I'm much younger. Younger than the year when my mother died. I'm hiding between walls. There are no doors, no windows. I'm wearing my confirmation dress. A yellow star, like a brooch, shines on my white confirmation dress. There is just this narrow space between the walls. Right at the top of this tall narrow room is a little bit of blue sky, like through a skylight? A black bird is walking on the glass. *Tock tocking* on the glass, scratching, you know? I keep looking up at it. There's more to the dream, but this is the bit which stays with me in the morning.'

'I can hardly believe that one of the nuns can be doing this, but then, who else? No one else can have access to your cells.'

'Maybe it's my fault. I've been talking about the refugees on Nelson island. You know there are over five hundred, and they say three thousand have applied to come. Maybe already there, and on Sancta Trinidad. Such a strange coincidence. Me here and them, there. Imagine! I was saying at recreation that

231

I would like to go and see them. Maybe there's work to do. Cooking, feeding, looking after children, the old people and sick. For a short while, it was an idea. Maybe, this is what put the thought in her mind about vermin.' The tears were streaking Thérèse's face. 'I heard someone say, "Well, your name is Weil." But, when I turned, they all had their heads bowed, their fingers stitching away, maybe even a yellow star right under my eyes. I ignored it then.'

'Are any of the sisters German?' Vincent looked for some kind of logic.

'I'm not sure. I can't believe it, even so. This old thing, as Papa called it. I can't go to confession anymore to Father Meyer.'

'It's quite possible. You know this kind of thing goes right back into the history of Europe, you've heard some of the calypsos. It's part of our world.'

'But *you* don't think like that?'

'No, but I was brought up hearing similar things about negroes. You know the history of these islands. Here, on El Caracol itself, the ruins near Perruquier Bay, the great house, the cotton fields. Chac Chac Bay, the Carib word for cotton. The bay, Chac Chac. The story that Theo tells me in the night. You don't know those stories. Imagine them. You should hear him. You see a boy fishing, but to hear him in the night with his stories is to come near to that terror. A terror which went on here. Some would say not as bad as in other islands, but still terrible.Terrible things were done in these islands to the ancestors of our patients. You should know that story. It's their story.'

Thérèse looked at Vincent as he seemed to grow angry.

'They sing such contradictory words at times, sometimes insults, sometimes praise,' Thérèse explained.

'It's the nature of the calypso.'

Theo was flitting in and out of the kitchen. There was a guest. He was making a fuss.

'And what about tonight? Are you staying at the hospital?' Vincent was looking ahead.

'I'll have to. I've missed the boat.'

'We can get Jonah to take you. I'll row you, if you want.'

'But what will I say? I went to see the doctor, because he's my lover.'

'Your lover! Madeleine?'

'Vincent. Don't tease. We can't keep denying what has happened, is happening. Each day as we work alongside each other. I know you. We respect each other. We don't touch. But that doesn't mean...'

'I know.' At that moment, the small brass bell was rung at the table announcing supper. Theo smiled as they came in. Three places were laid. Vincent was relieved. He would not have been able to cope with Theo role playing again. He wouldn't do that in front of Thérèse. 'We can talk after supper,' he whispered as he helped Thérèse into her chair.

While Theo was not role-playing the servant, he was still up all the time, dashing back and forth to the kitchen, for the pepper and salt, for the hot sauce, 'Don't burn you mouth,' he giggled. Then, there was a glass he had forgotten. He hovered around Thérèse making sure that she had everything. At one point, straightening her veil which had got caught at the back of her chair. 'Sister? Everything fine?'

Then, there was his grand entry with the two red fish. 'Smelling good!' Vincent exclaimed.

'Absolutely delicious looking,' Thérèse added her praise.

Theo beamed. The fish were still sizzling in the gravy made with coconut oil. The flavours were of *chadon béni*. 'Like coriander,' she breathed in the flavours.

Vincent smiled. He was proud of the boy. He was grateful for him, taking the tension out of the moment.

'Yes, thank you, Theo,' he said formally.

Theo dropped his head.

Then, they ate their snapper and bake in silence, Theo looking to see their enjoyment of his dish, but looking also for reassurance, looking after everything. Vincent saw that flash in his eyes. The visit had definitely excited him.

'More fish, Sister? It sweet, eh?'

'Thank you, Theo.'

Then, she insisted on helping him clear the table, and chatted with him in the kitchen.

'I catch plenty fish yesterday! But I throw them back. Plenty *crapeau* fish. *Crapeau* fish not good to eat.'

Vincent marvelled at her ease with the boy, his with her. While Thérèse was in the kitchen and Theo was clearing away his glass and table mat, he said, 'You like she?' He said it in an impish way. Vincent was startled. Then Theo smiled.

'She's a good nurse.'

Theo smiled again, his impish smile. 'I see it since first day you carry me to Saint Damian's.' Nothing slipped his attention. They had been so careful. Maybe it was because he himself liked her, and wanted that to be connected with Vincent somehow.

Theo disappeared upstairs. Vincent called after him, 'Do you want to show Sister Thérèse your room?'

She raised her eyebrows. She did not know anything about the boy's room. Theo waited at the top of the stairs. Then he called down to her, 'You coming?' She went up and joined him.

The sea crashed in. The wind had picked up, stirring the hot night.

'This boy? His room. His room is our world,' Thérèse exclaimed coming into the drawing room.

'Yes, made up from the news bulletins. He's been having an education in history and geography.'

'The names made me homesick. The rivers are a bright blue on his maps,' she laughed.

'Of course, a completely imaginary world for him.'

'What am I doing here?'

'Here?'

'I mean here, here, this part of the world, so far away. Why did I come here?'

Vincent looked dismayed. He had lost her. 'Here?'

'Yes here, here tonight with you. But also here, El Caracol. Why did I leave him?'

Vincent knew that she was talking about her father. In the end, these crises always came back to him.

'If you had not left, your fate would now be as uncertain as his.'

'But I would be with him.'

'Perhaps not. Perhaps there would have been a cruel separation, you taken off to one place, him to another. Imagine that, unable to help each other then, and to know that you were both in desperate circumstances. But you don't really know that anything terrible has happened to him.'

'That's the position now. He must wonder what I know about him. I keep wondering about him without getting any news.'

'At least he knows that you are safe. He must be pleased now that you chose the missions in the end.'

'I suppose. Who knows?'

'Anyway, what's the worse thing that can happen as a consequence of you coming here, tonight?'

'Summoned to see Mother Superior, questioned, made to feel abominable.'

'There, that's not exactly the worse thing on earth.' They laughed.

'No, not the worse thing. But what about you?'

'What about me?'

'What will Mother Superior say to you? She might complain to the medical board, have you warned or censored for consorting improperly with one of the sisters in your home.'

'Well, we'll cross that bridge when we come to it. What's important is you and your position in the convent, at the moment, having to suffer these insults, this persecution.'

'It feels like that.'

Their voices were low. A bat swooped out of the almond tree.

'It's your father, isn't it, at the bottom of everything that's difficult for you. You would be able to cope with the yellow stars, everything else if you knew he was safe.'

'Papa. Yes.'

There was a silence as they looked at each other. Her face was like a moon to him, encircled with white. He saw her again in the boathouse. He tended her ankle. He wanted to kiss her. He went through the history of their love, the geography of it. He had to undress her. He had to keep uncovering her. Should he take her to the boathouse tonight?

Thérèse emerged from her cave. 'Yes. Papa. But what do you mean? It's more than my father. It's more. My father, like you, believed in the working class, in the international, not in tribes, not like his parents, solely in his own people. He belongs to everyone. But that can't be how it is now.'

Vincent emerged from his reverie. His passion and his guilt were partners again.

'The real worry is that you don't know and can't know what's happening to your father. We hear snatches of what the conditions are like, but until those very infrequent letters arrive, we've no sure knowledge of what's happening. Therefore our imaginations run riot. It's worse in a way, not knowing, don't you think? And yes, it's always more than the individual.' He tried to comfort her.

'I only have what I can remember. I'm worried about the work camp near Paris.'

'Drancy? Maybe he'll get a chance to do good for the other prisoners. You always need a doctor.'

'But why? What's this locking up of Jews? In Germany yes, even before the war, but in France.' She was terrified.

'The occupation. History.'

'History? One bit of news suggested it's our own soldiers who come to the door in the early morning. People open up because they see the *gendarmes*.'

'We know what has been taking place since 1933.'

'Yes, my father talked about it.'

'Was she, the embroiderer, the one who smashed my windows?'

'Sorry.'

'The one who stitches and embroiders my yellow stars, maybe she's been at it for a while. You know? My shattered window, my night of glass.'

In the distance, they heard thunder. It came from over the hills, out in the ocean. They sat without speaking, each in their own thoughts. The fishermen were bringing back their stories of German U-Boats in the waters off the islands.

Cannes Brulées

They heard a splashing noise coming over the water as they sat talking on the jetty. 'Like someone swimming,' Thérèse said.

'There, Madeleine.'

'Fish jumping, yes?'

They both strained their eyes.

'As large as a person,' Vincent exaggerated.

'There are sharks in the bay.'

'Barracudas under the jetty.'

'Urgh.' Madeleine squirmed.

'Dolphins in the gulf.'

'And whales.'

'Have you seen them?'

'From the hills once, behind the convent.'

They looked out across the dark bay.

'Do you know the story about the nun who drowned herself?' Vincent began in a storytelling tone.

Thérèse was sitting on the bench with her legs curled beneath her. She looked at Vincent. Why was he asking her this? What story was he about to tell her? 'No.'

'Don't you talk, you nuns, tell these stories about yourselves?'

'No one's told me. Why did she drown herself?'

'She was in love with one of the patients.'

'*Mon Dieu!* Poor girl.'

'He used to swim across the bay to be with her.'

'Like Sonny Lal?'

'Like Sonny Lal.' They echoed each other.

'One night he did not arrive. They found his body a few days later washed up on the beach at La Tinta,' Vincent continued. 'The currents had taken his body around the point, and out into the *boca,* and then cast him up on the beach. Some days later, one of the coast guard found him lodged in the rocks.'

'What about her?'

'She wished to join him. Her body was found in the rocks below the cliff at Embarcadère Corbeaux. She had thrown herself off.'

'No one talks about it. Convent secrets,' Thérèse mused.

'It happened a long time ago. She was about your age. She had just come from France, one of the original community.'

'Why are you telling me this?'

'At the autopsy they discovered that she was pregnant.'

'Why are you telling me this?' Thérèse repeated.

'The fishermen say they see her on the rocks. She's trying to get to La Tinta to lie with her lover. So the story goes.'

'These are fisherman's tales. This is, what do you call it? Bush rum. I hear the men on the wards talking. This is *babache.'*

'Maybe.'

'You trying to frighten me?'

'Maybe I'm trying to frighten myself.'

Fish were still jumping. There was another splash just off the jetty.

'Frighten yourself. What do you mean?' Thérèse asked.

'Might be tempted to swim the bay to the convent.'

'I can't see your eyes. Come closer. Let me see your eyes.' He moved nearer to her on the bench. 'What did you say?' She watched him intently.

'I might swim the bay to be with you in the night.'

'Would you die for me?' she asked.

'Die for you? I'm a strong swimmer. Sharks!' Vincent smiled.

'You don't have to, I'm here.'

'I didn't think you would come here.'

'Neither me.'

'Could swim the bay?' She imagined it now.

'I used to able to see your lights before the blackout restrictions.'

'I didn't know that.'

'I never told you.'

'I imagined you were always the one ringing the *Angelus,* your ballooning skirt, your feet lifted off the ground by the weight of the bell.'

Suddenly, there was the sound of someone shouting from the direction of Saint Damian's.

'What's that?' Vincent got up and stood at the edge of the jetty, straining his ears and eyes. The shouting died down.

Thérèse came and stood next to him at the edge of the jetty. They had grown accustomed to the darkness, and watched as the familiar contours of the island, now shadows, outlines. The geography of darkness, formed and reformed, pulsing.

They listened and stared.

Then, all of a sudden, tall flames leaping out of the darkness. They stared in amazement at this transformation. They heard shouts like they had done earlier. 'Fire! Fire!' The flames seemed to be near the hospital. There also seemed to be a huge fire on the jetty at Saint Damian's, and flames as low down as the sea grapes, at the edge of the water, beyond Father Meyer's house.

'The Yanks won't like this. Makes a nonsense of the blackout. There was a U-Boat off La Tinta night before last. Did you hear the Albacores?' Vincent grabbed Thérèse by the arm. 'Come, we've got to get to Saint Damian's. What do you think is going on?'

'What about the boy?' she asked, suddenly seeing him in his room with his maps.

'As we go up through the house, I'll peep in on him.' Then Vincent hesitated. 'I'm sure, yes, he'll be fine.' He was unsure.

'What is it?'

'It's a fear I have. Theo and fire.'

'Fire?'

'Some other time. We must get to the hospital. A fire would be the very worse thing. Can you imagine? Can you imagine our work with those burns.'

'Our records, research?'

Thérèse waited at the back door, while Vincent went upstairs to Theo.

Shouts could be heard in the distance. There was a glow in the sky, as if there was moonlight.

Vincent was back. 'I woke him. I didn't want him waking and coming into my room and finding that I'm not there. I've told him to try and get back to sleep.'

'Poor boy. Is that still going on?'

'Sleeptalking? From time to time.'

'Maybe we should take him with us.'

Vincent was trying to find a hurricane lantern. 'We must try not to light this, but just in case.'

They could hear an American jeep revving on the now enlarged donkey track the other side of the bush at the back.

'We can't go that way. Let's take the dinghy. I'll row.'

They returned to the jetty. Vincent pulled the dinghy towards the ladder. He jumped into the dinghy and began bailing out the water that had collected from a slow leak.

There were lights on in the convent. 'Look, the fire on the jetty is bigger.' There was panic in Thérèse's voice.

'You sit in the stern.' Vincent fitted the oars into the rollocks and heaved off, trying not to make too much of a splash. Their knees touched.

There was the hoot of a *jumbie* bird. Its flight ended in a shadow on the dogwood branch at the edge of the water. Vincent was rowing close to the shore. 'Are you okay?'

'Yes.' She put her hand on his leg.

The shouts from Saint Damian's were louder. Their heads brushed the low branches of the dogwood trees.

'Looks like we're going to find a riot when we arrive,' Vincent said, looking behind him, gauging his direction. He stopped rowing, pulling the dripping oars in. They rested in a cove just past Father Meyer's house.

They sat in silence, being rocked by the sea. He wanted to kiss her.

They were beginning to drift onto the rocks. Vincent pushed off with one of the oars. 'Must be the police launch, or Coast Guard further out in the bay creating this wake,' he explained.

Their situation began to seem absurd. What might they look like to anyone, adrift in a dinghy in Chac Chac Bay?

'Did you say she threw herself off the cliff at Embarcadère Corbeaux?'

'What? Who?'

'The nun who was in love and having a baby.'

'Just a story.'

'Was it? What an absurd flight to meet her lover!' She watched the changing shapes in the dark water, and thought of the men who swam across the bay to be with their women, lovers, risking the current, the sharks, and the *remous*; that dangerous vortex able to pull you under with its fast currents. She thought of Sonny Lal swimming to be with Leela.

'Look at where we are, Vincent. I'm afraid.'

He knew that she was not just talking about their present predicament. He saw the absurdity of their love. He thought of his patients. He thought of Theo, alone in the house. How to follow their obsession and carry out their responsibilities!

'I love you,' he said.

'Vincent.' She leant over and kissed him.

They could hear the Coast Guard before they saw it. It cast its beam long and low, scanning the shore. They ducked as the low beam crept towards them.

When the drone had faded, they pulled out from under the sea grape branches. They could hear shouting in the distance. The *tassa* drums beat in bursts, changing with the wind.

'Do you hear the drums now?' She kept her hand on his leg as he leant towards her pulling on the oars.

'There won't be sufficient local police to hold them back. And they'll be cautious given what happened last time.' Vincent's mind was back on Saint Damian's.

'What do you think will happen then?'

'The Americans will intervene. I'm sure that's what the Governor will agree to, what Mother Superior will ask for.'

'I hope not.'

'It looks like that, but we'll have to see. We must get there fast. You can stay by one of the women in the huts where we pull in. Say you've come to see how they are. Stay with the older women. They won't be joining the crowd. It'll be useful and will give you some cover. I'll make my way to the hospital and try and find Jonah and Singh.'

'Your hands must have blisters.'

Vincent paused, resting the oars on his knees. She held his hands.

'We'll soon be in sight of the women's huts. There's a small beach where Jonah keeps his fishing pots.'

'I should go to the children, Vincent.'

'No, keep low to begin with. I'll look in on the children's ward. I can be anywhere legitimately.'

'I can't put my own safety before the children's.'

They could hear the crackle of the fire, the smell of gasoline and burning rubber.

'I understand. Please let's see how things are at first. Remember there are other risks here. Risks for you and me. We must be careful about everything.' Vincent started rowing again the short way to the beach where they were going to disembark.

'I don't care about my safety in that way. I'm a nurse first of all.'

Vincent heard her make her choice, but he begged her to do what he asked. 'I'll come back for you when I see what is going on. We must not be seen arriving together.'

Now they could hear the voices of the people clearly. They could hear the slogans. They were singing Invader's calypso. *'Mother and daughter working for the Yankee dollar'.*

They were carrying *flambeaux*. It was the pitch oil flames they could smell.

When Vincent reached the yard in front of the hospital, he met Ma Cowey.

'What's going on?'

'They can't treat we so, Docta.'

There were a group of children banging biscuit tin covers with sticks and stones, carrying stakes of bamboo creating their own *tamboo bamboo* band, pounding the earth. Other children had smeared themselves with molasses from the stores and were playing *jab molassi* from carnival time. They mimed the gyrating carnival imps.

'Pay de devil, jab jab.'

Vincent ignored their terror. He was hailed from the crowd.

'Eh Docta, eh Docta!' Ma Taylor shouted. 'You see people? Come and join the people. Where you is when we looking for you? Jonah looking for you long time. Singh looking for you.'

Ma Taylor and the band of children were the vanguard. 'Is like *cannes brulées*, you remember *cannes brulées*, Doctor, long time on the sugar estate. I come from Harmony Hall, you know Doctor? We did have *cannes brulées* there.' All the patients were mixed together, Indian and African, children and grown-ups. He thought of Michael Johnson.

He looked for Ti-Jean. Then he saw him, as indomitable as ever on his crutches, despite his unhealing sores. He avoided him. He had to find Jonah and Krishna, particularly Jonah, whom he thought he might be able to speak to more easily. Thank God Theo was not here. 'Ma Taylor, where's Jonah? You say he looking for me?'

'He done gone, Docta. Gone long time. I ent see where he go. He say, "Where the docta? Docta Metivier should be here," he say.'

'Thank you, Ma Taylor.'

'The Lord bless you Docta and keep you safe.'

Vincent cut through behind the pharmacy to get to the almond tree. The crowd's anthem was, '*The Governor say no mas, the Governor haul 'he arse'.* What had happened to Mother Superior's peaceful day? He smelt the burning rubber.

The huge tyres which were slung alongside the jetty as fenders for the boats had been piled up and doused with gasoline and set alight. He could see another fire starting in the stores.

'This is irresponsible. Who started this?'

No one answered Vincent. Where were Jonah or Singh?

'Me ent see them since this afternoon, Docta,' someone took the care to answer as Vincent passed through the crowd.

He could not find anyone to tell him how the riot had started.

Off the jetty, two American water launches were pumping out and spraying sea water onto the jetty where the fires were threatening the the nearby stores. A line of Marines passed buckets along to where the hoses could not reach.

'Lal, what you doing here, man?' The old man was sitting nursing one of his sore feet. Vincent sat down next to him. 'Help me, Lal. How did this happen.'

'Is some of those young fellas who help Singh organise a meeting under the almond tree, after the Catholics have Benediction. The Archbishop preach. He preach about suffering, they say, and offering it up for their sins. The people who there say that is what spark the whole thing off. You know Basdeo and Ram. They come round the wards saying, safer for people to be outside because they might be fire. So, people get scared and come outside. People just massing and moving where they hear things going on. So, first they follow the drumming, up Indian Valley, then down here, because of the fire. You must know about these things, Doc?'

'Tell me what else you hear.'

'Doc, I wasn't there, but Jonah *pardner*, Aaron, he tell me the thing start with fellas pelting bottle and stone by Mother Superior office, late afternoon.'

'Pelting bottle and stone. Man, I think Singh had this thing under control. What else, Lal?'

'I only telling you what I hear. I ent see nothing.'

'Yes, I not blaming you, Lal.'

'There was a service. And when the archbishop walking back up to the Mother Superior office after the service, they say the children sing sweet. So Doris tell me. But anyway, is then some young fellas, they head hot, begin to pelt stones.'

'Pelting stones!'

'They have that new fella with them that just reach from Laventille, the one who playing one of them new steel pan, they say people up Laventille making out of the oil drum. They was to bring it out on the streets for carnival and the Governor ban the carnival. Anyway, they have this fella under the almond tree playing he ping pong.'

'So?'

'Well the local police, they tell him to stop, as they having service and he making too much noise.'

'And?'

'The fella say he not stopping. He say this is a free country and he playing he ping pong.'

'Just so.'

'Just so. You know how them young fellas stop! When the police move to push him on, right so the fight start. Then the fellas who start the marching earlier, come and join in, even more come and join in. They say they lucky to get the Archbishop and the governor secretary down to the jetty just in time to take them to the police launch that bring them, otherwise nobody know what might've happen to them. But that ent stop the pelting and the cussing. Mother Superior try and talk to some of the more reasonable ones, and then she take she boat for the convent. Is when it get dark that the real business start.'

'I tell Singh to take it easy. And now the Yanks involved with the fire fighting. We lucky for that,' Vincent said.

'Yea, but first they come in with guns, you know, walking around the place with guns, threatening to shoot poor people, yes. You should've be here, you know, Doc.'

'They can't shoot people. But we must put out the fires. This is one of the biggest risks for all of you, as you know, Lal.'

'I know what you saying Doc, but people ready to die, you know. Them young fellas ready to die.'

'Well, at least I hope they put out the fires.'

'Yes, but now they'll think the place is their responsibility. To come in here any time, like is their yard, and sort things out. They say the British Governor ask them to come in and deal with the matter. You know the British. Them is talk. But the Americans, since the Japs in their tail they ready to go anywhere they see trouble.'

'You take care of yourself, Lal.'

'Yes, but now they'll think the place is their responsibility, Doc.'

Vincent saw the dilemma.

'You can't do nothing, Doc.' That was Lalbeharry's verdict.

'There must be something Lal.' But where would he start.

Then he thought of the pharmacy, the records of their research, the painstaking records kept by Thérèse. Would they be going up in flames? He decided to leave Lal and go towards the hospital.

Many were afraid of fire and that was why they were out in the paths, and staying in the open. He had to agree that that was sensible.

If you abuse a people this much, they will abuse themselves and others. Vincent was encouraging some of the older patients to take the children with them to their huts. Of course, all the segregations which they had organised against the spread of the disease were now destroyed. Maybe this would prove something, that quarantines did not affect anything, which is what they thought anyway.

There were screams coming from the direction of the stores. While part of the building was in flames, other rooms were being looted. The screams were because the Marines from their launches were now turning the water hoses on the people rather than on the flames. They were landing on the shore, beneath the jetty, and aiming the powerful water hoses on the looters.

Vincent decided to intervene in this. For while he could see the point, it was dangerous. Patients would be killed, and he did not want this added intervention by the American Marines. He sought out the sergeant in charge of the operation. His pleas were ignored. In the end he had to enter among those being hosed down. He decided to stand at the front of the line, taking the brunt of the pressure, which was forcing him back.

It was then that Vincent saw Jonah coming from among the looters who had transported foodstuffs in a wheelbarrow away from the stores. There was Singh as well. If they were not leading the riot, they were at least supervising it.

'Jonah!' His voice was lost among the screams and the power of the water. He was helping up patients knocked to the ground, and single handedly trying to keep back the soldiers, telling them to concentrate on the fire and leave the patients alone. Eventually, Singh and Jonah saw him and joined his efforts. They were beginning to make some headway in their persuasion. The hoses stopped being trained on the patients.

'Everything gone ole *mas.*' That was Jonah's estimation. Singh looked worried, but kept silent.

'Why was I not called earlier?'

'There was no time to come by you, Doc. What? Get boat, get donkey? Things take off, and before you know it, the people rampaging around. Them children, they not easy, you know.'

'So what was it?'

'When people see the preparations for the Governor secretary and the Archbishop, they boil over. They see for themselves. They don't always understand the things that we does talk about. But when they see how the government and the church can make things happen for a visit, and they can't produce food and medicine, they boil over. Women and children the most violent. They pelt the Archbishop you know, right down to the jetty. As they singing *Come Holy Ghost Creator Come,* they pelt him with rock stone. They pelt the Governor secretary. They still keep some control when Mother Superior beg them to stop. We stay right out of it. She tells us to stay out of things today. We stay out.'

Vincent stared at his comrades gravely. He believed them. But he wished it had not happened. He wished that they were not now going to have to start all over again, with trying to get the supplies in medicine and food. But maybe this would do it. Otherwise, they should let the patients die.

'They should let we die, Doc.' He turned round. It was Ti-Jean on some self-made crutches from guava wood. He looked terrible. He had lost a lot of weight. Vincent could smell his putrefying sores. The poor child!

'Ti-Jean,' he stopped himself from reprimanding the boy. 'You look out for the smaller children. Then, I want to see you back at the ward. Do that for me.'

'Is that I doing the whole time. But.'

'But?'

'But pushing fire too. You see them big people, Doc? Where you is all day? We look for you. Someone say Sister Thérèse gone to look for you. She find you?'

Jonah and Singh, who were listening, looked at Vincent to see what he was going to say.

'Sister Thérèse?' Vincent sounded defensive.

'She take Elroy donkey and say she going to look for you. She take the back track. She get permission from one of the Yankee fellas,' Ti-Jean continued.

'I think he take a liking for her. I see him helping she up on the donkey.' Jonah laughed.

'Jonah.' Jonah loved the *picong*.

'Easy, Doc, you know is joke' I joking.'

He and Singh winked at each other. Vincent was examining Ti-Jean's crutches, ignoring the attention paid to Sister Thérèse. He did not want to have to lie that he had not seen her.

'So you see she?' Singh asked, casting a glance at Jonah.

Ti-Jean looked on.

'I think she's down by the lower huts with the older women.'

'Is so?'

'I rowed over, leaving the dinghy down by that small beach. I'm sure she's down there helping the older women.'

'You row?' Singh sounded surprised

'Yes.'

'Why you didn't come on the back track? So she didn't reach you with the donkey?' They were putting him through his paces.

'I'm sure she's by the huts. In fact, I think I'll go and see her, and see how the women are. Ti-Jean you come with me.'

Singh and Jonah watched Vincent, they smiled.

'Don't play with fire, Doc,' they called after him.

Vincent turned and waved. He knew what they were saying. He and Ti-Jean changed direction to visit the pharmacy. So Singh felt that he had something on him, Vincent thought. That was it. That was why he could be bold with Christiana. He had kept the girl on the island for love. She was ready to risk it.

As Vincent and Ti-Jean approached the pharmacy, they saw the light on. Vincent's heart leapt. Just what he had imagined, the place had been ransacked.

'Ti-Jean, you wait here.'

On entering, he discovered Thérèse.

'Madeleine!' he wanted to take her in his arms. Ti-Jean was at the door.

'We had the same thoughts.'

'Is everything alright? Let me have a look.' He joined her at the files with the results of their tests and their detailed records on all the patients.

'No one's been here, thank God. This has not been their target. This is not what they're against. We should've known that. They've sense. They know who's responsible for their plight and who wants to do something about it.'

'You're right, but sometimes I think we get identified with the authorities. We're on the front line.'

'Well, thank God everything is fine here.'

'Ti-Jean is outside, maybe we should go to the hospital together. Is everything okay with you, about being here? Or, are you feeling that you should be at the convent?'

'I stayed with the older women for a while, and then I got anxious about here. I got anxious just staying there, not knowing what was happening.'

'What will you do now?'

'I don't know. We'll have to wait for tomorrow. I don't know what this night will bring. What has been seen, what others know?' She knew the risks she had taken.

Once Vincent and Thérèse had got up to the hospital, they saw that the night's riots were quietening down.

The children were wandering back from the excitement to their beds. No curfew or blackout restrictions were in operation. This could have been the night for the German U-Boat invasion. Vincent and Thérèse went around the childrens' wards tucking up the boys and girls into bed. Thérèse read one of the children's stories. The lamps burnt in the huts on the hills.

She changed Ti-Jean's bandages. When Vincent went out onto the verandah to smoke a cigarette, she took over the nursing, soothing his brow with Limacol, giving him water to sip. He was becoming delirious with a very high temperature.

Vincent asked Jonah to go to the house to see how Theo had been. Then he came back onto the ward and sat with Ti-Jean again. He and Thérèse kept watch on the ward till dawn. He worried that the boy might develop an infection he could not fight. 'Oh Alexander Fleming!'

'What did you say?' Thérèse looked up. She had her eyes closed.

'Nothing.'

As quiet descended, a gunshot was heard detonating over the island, echoing across Chac Chac Bay.

Girl at the Window

The Wagnerian concert at Father Meyer's was blaring from the gramophone on the verandah. 'Like he going mad, Doc,' Jonah laughed aloud over the drone of the motor and the strains of the *Gotterdammerung!*

A mine-sweeper was passing just across the front of Chac Chac Bay. Never, now, could they delude themselves that they were not at war. The wake was flecked with flame.

Jonah was quiet, and Vincent remained with his own meditation, after an inconclusive meeting with Singh, Mother Superior and Major McGill over the shooting of Eldrige Padmore, one of the young patients. He had not heeded the warning not to trespass into the base. Because of the night of the riot, the troops were taking no chances. This was how the argument ran, as Major McGill described the circumstances of the shooting the night before. Some, thinking back to the burning of Michael Johnson, saw it as a life for a life.

Vincent was late for Theo whom he knew would be looking forward to swimming and fishing. His mind was now on the boy, who was still refusing to return to Singh for lessons. As he passed by the pharmacy, he had seen Christiana and Singh in the the back room. He was going to stop, but then the shutters were closed. How could he challenge Singh? He and Jonah suspected something about Thérèse.

'We'll win through, Jonah.' His mind was back on the shooting.

'We have to win, Doc. We have to win. I know that my father never go in the *gayelle* unless he think he going to win. But you can't have them Yanks shooting innocent people because they climbing a fence.'

'There's going to be an inquiry, and there has to be an apology to the family. There has to be compensation. Singh and myself will fight for that. He was a young fella with promise.'

'People not going to take that sitting down. They go remember that shot in the future. Things don't just go away so.'

Vincent was exhausted. The whole night had been taken up with nursing Ti-Jean's fever, bringing down the temperature. Ma Cowey and Sister Marie-Joseph attributed his recovery to their prayers. Vincent had seen these things happen. Sometimes, you were lucky. He thought he was losing Ti-Jean last night. If only he had that Penicillin they were talking about. They had stores of it for the Marines. That's what they needed from the Yanks and the British, rather than guns and water hoses. 'We need penicillin, instead of bullets!'

'What you say, Doc?'

'Penicillin!'

'I hear is a kind of miracle.'

They pulled along the jetty. 'Who's that at the window?' Vincent asked.

'Must be Theo.'

'Yes. Looked like a girl, though.'

Vincent and Jonah said their brief goodbyes, neither eager for much conversation or banter. 'I'll see you, man.'

Vincent patted Jonah on the shoulder as he raised himself out of the pirogue onto the jetty.

'Take it easy, Doc. In the morning, please God.'

The motor was running and the pirogue turned and headed off into the declining light, the shimmer of pink on the water.

Vincent waved. He read the pirogue's name; as always, *In God We Trust*, painted in yellow capitals on the side of the red bow.

There was no Theo on the jetty fishing. There was no boy in the window under the gable. The verandah was empty. The doors into the drawing room were open. There was a settled gloom in contrast to the brightness of outside.

There was a quiet overshadowing the house. Theo must be in his room. He must have had a day working at his walls. Must have been a day of cutting up newspapers. He smelt the flour and water paste.

Vincent put down his bag by the drawing room door. He called once, 'Theo,' but there was no answer. He flung his cream linen jacket over the back of a chair, tossed his Panama onto the side table. He flopped into one of the long chairs on the verandah. Soon, he had fallen off into a deep sleep.

When Vincent opened his eyes, he awoke into a lilac evening. The very last of the light hung over Patos. It took him more than a few seconds to realise what he was seeing in the chair opposite. His groggy mind had read the form as Theo. Now he sat up with a start.

'Hello, yes. Who are you? What are you doing here? How did you get here? Where've you come from?'

The questions tumbled out quickly, as Vincent tried to gain some sense of what was happening, clearing his eyes. The figure was still and silent. Then he turned and called into the house, 'Theo Theo!' He was desperate to see the boy, for the boy to come downstairs and put things right. But then, just as he thought that, he again turned back to the figure on the chair and stared intently. He took a long, careful look. 'My God, Theo, what've you done?'

There was no reply. 'Theo, Theo!' Vincent sat on the edge of the long chair and stared. He pleaded and stretched towards the figure, withdrawing his hand just before touching the silken knee.

Because of the smallness of his frame and his height, he could easily be mistaken for a girl. It was not the red satin dress and the high-heeled shoes and stockings. It was not the green scarf tied into a turban, which yes, did give an exotic impression. It was the face itself, heavily painted with lipstick and rouge and a sweet smelling powder. It was smeared on with a heavy hand. While it gave to the young face a macabre, perverse beauty, a carnival mask look, it mimicked someone older, someone more sophisticated and knowing, who knew what this painted face meant, who this painted face was. This was more than a child dressing up as some character, or a child making a mess of what could be better executed; a boy getting it wrong, not knowing how to apply lipstick and rouge, how to use powder. No, it was deliberate. The heavy hand had painted this lipstick on so that the lips looked fuller and the cheeks looked heightened. This was done by a knowing hand, a hand with intent; a mimic yes, but a mimicking which had a history, and which seemed perverse in one so young. Clearly the figure, as she sat and stared, was a courtesan. He did not think whore or prostitute. He thought courtesan, suggested by her poise, her sophistication, that made Vincent wonder how it was learnt.

Maybe it was the setting, the colonial architecture mimicking with its lacy fret work, the grandeur of older houses, those of an *ancien régime*, an order of the kind that Theo played at previously with masters and servants, now master and his mistress.

There was no conversation. He had the distinct feeling that the boy was doing this to entertain him, to titillate him. Where did all these clothes come from? Where had he got the lipstick and rouge and powder? Then he thought, the brown grip. How much more would be produced from that brown grip; a magician's chest. The boy was like a conjuror.

Had Theo put on this performance in the friary for Father Dominic? What were his words in that first letter? 'We need the boy out of the island for a number of reasons.' Could this be one of them?

Vincent wanted to touch the boy. Anything physical might give all the wrong messages. The thought frightened him. Thank God no one else was seeing this. What would they think? This was a preposterous scene. He was now fully awake.

There was still some grey, cloudy, shell-pink light.

Soon, he would have to go inside and draw the blackout curtains, and light the kerosene lantern. The generators had failed again today. Could not the Yankees, at least, get that to work? Killing a boy on a barbed wire fence! Vincent's anger returned.

The familiar tolls of the evening Angelus filled the air. The figure of the courtesan knelt and signed herself with the sign of the cross. She whispered the prayer, 'The angel of the Lord declared unto Mary and she conceived by the Holy Ghost.' Vincent watched and listened. He waited for the completion of each stage of the Marian prayer, his own lips moving unconsciously over the words he knew by heart.

Then he exclaimed, "Theo! Theo!" This was all that Vincent could manage. He leant over to the boy to take his hand. But, at that moment, the figure rose, and went and stood near the ledge of the verandah. He, she, looked out to sea, and then turned back, and looked at him over his, her shoulder.

The boy was like a young woman. The high-heeled shoes gave him more stature, stretched his legs, gave him hips, and made his bottom jut out. The green turban enhanced his height, elongating his neck. The fast encroaching darkness, the play of shadow and light, gave the sense that the figure was disappearing and then, suddenly again, appearing.

The courtesan draped herself on the ledge of the verandah.

The drone of an Albacore in the distance, then its twinkling lights, took Vincent away from the scene for a moment to a bomb-carrying Spitfire with Bernard, somewhere over Europe.

He had a brother somewhere with his load to drop. The newspaper

253

photographs of the bombed cities and the strafed fields startled the day with their grained memories. His father had talked of the poppies during the earlier war. Mud, shell holes, poppies. Images from far away. From trenches. Little things that bring things back. He could still hear his father dragging his leg along the verandah at Versailles. 'That poor man.' He heard Sybil's voice in the kitchen. His father! He used to peep at him, the weak man with his sick leg, through the jalousies of the gallery. Bernard's hero!

When Vincent turned from closing the doors onto the verandah, drawing the thin blackout curtains, the masquerade was leaning over the dining room table. As she moved away, the increasing glow of two candles which stood in silver candle sticks, revealed a dinner table laid for two. The table was covered with a white damask linen tablecloth. There was silver cutlery, laid for fish and meat. Crystal wine and water glasses twinkled. At the centre of the table was a cut glass bowl with wild white orchids.

More of Versailles had been unpacked from the trunks and packing cases under the stairs.

This was game number two. On what did the boy draw for this drama?

The courtesan emerged from the kitchen with a small kerosene lantern in one hand, and a tray of *hors d'oeuvres* in the other, *Coquille Saint Jacques* in scallop shells. Vincent remembered them, they were a familiar sight on his mother's dining room table. Theo placed one in front of him, and then the other, in the place reserved for himself, at the opposite end of the table.

The kerosene lantern's light flickered on the familiar vases, silver *entré* dishes, trays and crystal decanters which used to stand prominently on the sideboard at Versailles with rum, whisky and cherry. Theo had known how to place everything so expertly. His were eyes that had seen these things. As a child, he had observed another hand dusting and cleaning. He had heard a madam instructing her servant.

But where had he found the figure of the courtesan to accompany the drama of this interior? Yesterday, he might have worn a cap and apron to carry out the role of servant. Today he was not the madam. Who was he mimicking, from where did the history of this mimicry come? He had his Ma Dellacourt stories. Yes, but this performance had the characteristics of a closer observation.

The courtesan, at the opposite end of the table from him, surveyed the doctor eating while she forked a morsel of *Coquille Saint Jacques* into her red mouth. In the absence of wine, she got up and filled Vincent's wine glass with the red sorrel. In doing so, she rubbed her shoulders against his. Vincent froze. They ate in silence, knives and forks clicked on the scallop shells.

Coquille Saint Jacques was followed by chicken, rice and peas and yam. Vincent marvelled at Theo's ingenuity, creations out of nothing. The poultry was a mystery. But, a patch of chicken peas at the top of the yard behind the sorrel bushes accounted for the vegetable. He must have been going at this all day.

After dessert of home-made vanilla ice cream, churned in an old freezer, Theo went to wind up the gramophone and put on a record. The soft saxophone seeped through the room. He lit a cigarette for Vincent.

The table was cleared. Vincent wondered what would follow. Maybe, Salome and the dance of the seven veils! He was trying to be ridiculous to himself, to deal with the macabre nature of what was going on, engineer his own humour.

He sat and smoked. The scratchy blues seeped through the house; one of his records collected in London's Soho. Miss Billie Holliday played over the surfaces, nestled in the crevices of the room, flickered in the candle-lit shadows.

Theo went back and forth from the dining room into the kitchen, clearing the table. When he leant over the table to brush off the remaining crumbs, Vincent said, 'Thank you,' quietly blowing puffs of smoke into the haze of the room, the two candles burning down, the kerosene lantern, humming and flickering, 'Thank you. It was a delicious meal, a charming evening.' He chose his words carefully. He played his part.

The boy needed to be doing what he was doing, and he, Vincent, needed to play this part, so that Theo could in turn play his. If he stopped it, he might prevent some important retrieval. Vincent did not know now how far this game would go, when he would have to stop pretending, and what would be finally demanded. He needed to trust his instincts. This must have happened to poor Father Dominic. Had he been asked to witness something he could not accept, or participate in, something he could not be part of as a friar, something tempting, perhaps, and dangerous?

Theo stopped brushing the crumbs, leaning across the table. Vincent could see down into the dress, the small frame of the boy. He had not stuffed himself with false bosoms like a pantomime figure. It was the boy's chest, Theo's flat brown chest.

This was Theo, who was nearly always bare backed while he worked around the house, while he fished on the jetty. There was something poignant in seeing the boy's chest revealed beneath the red satin. He wanted him back. But it might only be possible by allowing this charade to continue to its conclusion.

The courtesan withdrew, taking with her the damask linen tablecloth, shaking it out, folding it and putting it into one of the drawers of the sideboard. Vincent sat back.

The music continued to its conclusion, the needle suddenly grating, suddenly discordant. Vincent got up and took the arm away. He replaced it. He went back to his seat and lit another cigarette.

The noises of the night joined the music of sad love. Fireflies blinked at the window. He got up again and poured himself a measure of rum from one of the decanters on the sideboard. He could hear the clearing up in the kitchen.

He must have dropped off. He woke with a start, nearly falling off the dining room chair. His cigarette had burnt down and fallen as ash to the floor. His finger hurt. At first he thought that he was on his own. The kitchen was quiet.

Then he saw that there was a trail of clothes and shoes from the kitchen. The red satin dress, the green scarf, the high-heeled shoes, the stockings like transparent skin, were left where they had been cast off. Vincent followed where the trail led. Theo was curled up in the old soft Morris chair whose fibre was bursting out from beneath the upholstery. Vincent took another sip of his rum. He dozed.

On waking, Vincent noticed that Theo, curled into the embrace of the Morris chair, was naked. His skin had a sheen taken from the amber light of the room. His head was pillowed by his arms curled under him. He looked like he was asleep. He was an exhausted child, finished with his play, his masquerade strewn across the floor.

A sudden rain announced a storm, brewing in that stillness and heat of the night. Theo jumped, and then settled back into his still curled up form. Vincent sat and sipped his rum and had another cigarette.

Gradually, the sea and the wind calmed down. The only sound was the drip drip of water off the roof onto the concrete drain.

In the quiet of that drip drip that night, Theo's voice began. Vincent sat up and listened.

HE HOLD ME close to his face, and she say, Go, go, go to Mister. Mister Coco.

They play with me.

Mama hand smooth and smell of soap, blue soap, slimy soap on the shelf by the scrubbing board under the house.

I smell onion and lime. In bed, under counterpane, sweet and milky, fishy and salty.

Is it one day when I come in the room and hear her, hear my Mama? Is it that way? Did I get to hear it that way?

Mama resting by the Demerara window. Mama speaking like she in confession, soft soft, that I stop by the door and turn and sit on the step outside. First, I wonder who she talking to. Who Mama go talk to like this? Not Ma Procop. This is not how she does talk to Mister. Not so. On a good day that is chirpy and giggly. On a bad day is tears, lash and Mister speaking hard. Then I don't go near that house. When I peep is nobody there.

Once before, I hear a talk like this and nobody there. That time, Mama on the big bed and she looking at the picture album Ma Dellacourt give her, and she tell me not to touch. I see the picture, but I don't to go in her press and take that out, where she have it bury under a dress. She say that Ma Dellacourt tell her is her mother dress. Her talk, sad sad. Is so Mama talk to sheself.

Look at where I find myself? And who I go talk to? A mother, I never remember, but who belly I jump in. Jump from the same seed from the same egg with Louis. The Mama who is this face here, in this young girl, take out in this picture. They get rid of he. Is Louis self I must talk to about this business. But the old mister get rid of him. The old Mister can't take two cock in the same yard. Not when one white and the next one brown.

Look at where I find myself! My brother have to leave the yard since he is a small boy. I abandon in this life by mother and father and dependent on the very thing that trap me. From so long, I trap in this. This is a trap you can't talk to people about. Is not just that one white and the other black. Is not that

257

one is a Mister and the other is servant in the house. People know well about them things, and they choose to either talk about it, shout it by the stand pipe for people to hear, or laugh about it on the counter when they buy sweet potato and rice, sneer about it over the stall in the market when they choosing tomato and ground provision to take for their *pickney* them.

People can choose to say things. But this is a mix up that have the things that people don't speak about. This have secret that does live under the floorboard in a family house. That does get whisper, maybe, in a confessional, wanting forgiveness, that does get carry as a secret never to be whispered in the minds of mothers and daughters.

Fathers never talk about these things. Fathers refuse to let these things enter into their mind. Where the fathers? And that boy of mine? The father? Who I could talk to about this, but you, Mother, my pretty mother. You know about this. You were there. You must've be there, Alice.

From what Ma Dellacourt say, is the same thing. All of we in the same thing. You would've know what to do. Maybe you would've stop this. Maybe we couldn't stop this. This is how it is. This is how the place make. This is what they does call family in this place. This is what we make, and this is what they make of us.

Ma Dellacourt was the first that was pure, till. But you, you with the old Mister, the young Pierre. You breed half with he, and me now, breed with the next one. That is what gnawing at Mister when he look at my boy. Is what eating him. Is what he have to accept, but is what he want to deny. Is what he want to destroy.

My Theo. What I bind you in, my child? What I bind you in? That is what the Mister see. No more girl child. Then, the little Pierre, watch how he looking sick. He have no girl child to punish. No little half-sister to make baby with. None to take in a bedroom when the train passing in the gully. He have none to take in the cocoa. He have none to desecrate on his mother and father bed with the crucifix knocking on the railing, the very crucified Lord witness the desecration of his parent bed.

This one have none. He have no little girl child to take while she scrubbing floor. No little girl child to wonder where the world is, when she alone under that man. I have no girl children. None to continue with what is going on. When Mister see Theo with Chantal his head does spin. That he not going to allow.

My little Theo, not a thought in his head. Is just friend, he friend with she. He not going to let it happen that way, the reverse way, he not going to let any brown, black child take he long blonde hair princess and make little baby with she.

There was no interruption in the story, no interruption in the roll of the sea, in the gentle caress that the breeze touched the house with as Theo's mama's voice inhabited the boy.

He sat there naked and shivering. Then he began to sob.

'What is it, Theo?'

The boy looked up with his sad face. 'He jook she. He jook she in the back.'

Vincent, for a moment, thought that he was speaking of his mother and Mister. And, maybe, he was.

But then he blurted out. 'Singh, he jook she in the back room. I see them and she crying all the time.'

'Come Theo, let me take you up to bed.' Vincent lifted Theo up from the chair and took him upstairs and laid him on the bed and pulled down the mosquito net. All around the room, the walls told the story of the world and its terrible, terrible torments.

The boy's story was going in his mind with the engine of the sea.

What did it look like to a child, this love making? When had he first seen that? In his mama's bed?

Jonah's Whale

The litter of last night's masquerade still lay strewn upon the floor. There was something, now, utterly ordinary about the red satin dress and the green scarf, the stockings and the high-heeled shoes. They no longer held the allure which they had possessed in the night. They were no longer the macabre. Now was more like Ash Wednesday than the *ole mas* of *J'ouvert* morning, Carnival Monday.

Theo came and stood by the kitchen door and watched Vincent pick up the clothes, and wrap them into a bundle. He handed them to the boy. He took them without any reaction, like a child asked to clear away his toys. He returned to his room to put away the costume. The door of the bedroom banged and he came leaping down the stairs like a happy child.

The smell of fresh coffee percolated through the house from the kitchen. Vincent walked down to the jetty with his tin mug.

Theo leapt down the steps from the house behind him, stopping to pick up stones on the way. He came and sat at the end of the jetty, with his feet dangling over the edge. His reflection curled in the oily water beneath him. He took aim, beginning to play tick tack toe, using the flat stones to skim the surface of the water.

Vincent put down his mug, picked up one of the stones near to Theo and had a go. 'Tick, tack, toe,' he said, as the flat stone skimmed the water, just hitting the surface three times, before being lost in the deep. The ripples grew wider and wider and then disappeared. Vincent laughed aloud, his laughter echoing across the empty bay.

'You good, man.' Theo giggled.

He was surprised by the naturalness of Theo's voice, after the masquerade of the night before. He enjoyed the casual, confident, slightly mocking, but companionable, complimentary tone. It was not the mimicry of the night-time stories, not their incantation, not the *mêlée* of voices, just a plain ordinary boy's voice.

'You, good too,' Vincent smiled, stooping down near to his shoulder. 'Give me another chance,' he said. He picked up one of the flat stones, bent his knees slightly, to get down more to the level of the water, and let his stone fly, 'Tick, tack, toe.'

Then Theo had another go, then Vincent again, till all the flat stones had been thrown. And they both laughed together, aloud, over and over, their laughter coming back to them from across the bay.

There was another silence. 'You won't have to go by Singh again till you want to.'

Theo did not reply. He kept on pretending to throw stones.

Vincent detected a difference in the sound of the motor, as if Jonah was racing, straining it, so that he could get up more speed. Must be because he is late, he thought. Before he had arrived, Jonah was waving and shouting something excitedly. He could not make out what he was saying. He thought it was their old joke, because he heard the word, whale. Theo turned his head to look in the direction of the gesticulating Jonah. Together they watched the pirogue come alongside the jetty.

'Catch the rope, boy.' Jonah was chattering away, repeating what he had been shouting out in the bay. 'A whale man, if you see a whale. It beach. It taking up the whole of La Tinta. You not see the corbeaux? The Marines say they think it must be dead. Maybe get wounded somehow, then it beach. It come in on the tide and it can't get off the beach till high tide, they say. Is a sight to see, boy. Let we go.' Jonah was excited by his story, nearly overbalancing, as he stood astride the pirogue.

Vincent turned to Theo. The boy was absorbed in Jonah's story. His eyes were wide and staring. A whale! This was something that belonged to tales, to myths, to the bible, to the ocean with a big O.

'So your whale has at last returned, to swallow you up again Jonah?' Vincent joked.

Theo laughed, knowing his Bible stories.

'Doc, if you see it. You could believe a man could live in there for nights and days.'

Jonah turned to Theo. 'You coming boy? You never see anything like this before.'

Theo looked at Vincent. He jumped to it and began untying the rope immediately.

'Steady the boat, Doc,' Jonah leant over to the edge of the jetty, keeping his balance in the pirogue, and lifted Theo off the boy's feet, off the jetty. With one sweeping movement, he put him to sit in the middle of the pirogue. In no time, Vincent was on board and Jonah was at the tiller turning the boat in the direction of Perruquier Bay. Vincent sat next to Theo. The outboard raced. There was the smell of gasoline. Theo clambered into the bow with the rusty anchor.

Just then, the *Maria Concepción,* was crossing from Embarcadère Corbeaux. 'Like the sisters late this morning too, Jonah?' Vincent wondered about Thérèse.

'Everybody late. Is the whale. Some fishermen bring the news. They see it even before the Yanks.'

Jonah had trouble navigating the pirogue through the bay, busy with American barges and launches.

As they entered Perruquier Bay, a couple of Marines saw them safely tied up at the jetty. Theo dropped the anchor. Then, they were onto the land. Jonah was hurrying them excitedly along the tracks through the sea grapes and manchineel. They left the hard path, and were wading in deep soft sand. It seemed like the entire population of Saint Damian's had come to La Tinta to see the whale.

Looking onto the beach, with the morning light beginning to break from behind the mildewed clouds, there was a dazzle of figures. The sisters, with their white veils flying, and their cotton skirts billowing, were trying to keep a check on the children. They were standing and staring out to the rocks with their hands shading their eyes. The children, on crutches, were getting up and falling down in the sand. Vincent kept an eye out for Ti-Jean. And, where was Thérèse?

As they drew closer onto the black sand making the water look like ink, they could see the stalking corbeaux flying up, and then resettling on their pincer legs. They were heaping themselves onto what seemed, at first sight, part of the undulation of the beach, a mound of rock, glistening and wet. People were shooing the corbeaux away.

'The whale!' Jonah pointed, leading the party.

Vincent encouraged Theo to move forward. The boy shook himself out of his amazement, and did not resist.

When they got close up, they could then appreciate the sheer magnitude of the mammoth mammal. They stood silently. Even Jonah was stunned into silence now, staring at the wet oily cliff of flesh which seemed to be written on with prehistoric runes, telling an ancient story of voyaging the deep ocean. The dorsal ridge rose above them. Stuck to it were barnacles, a mosaic of encrustations. The cliff side glistened with purple, pink and jade. It was festooned and draped with seaweed and slime. It freighted the Sargasso Sea, which it had delivered onto the beach at La Tinta. It was a mossed tumulus.

Theo, Jonah and Vincent stood and stared.

What silenced everyone the most was the stillness of this presence of power, its passivity, its helplessness without its element, water. The tide was way out.

A very high tide had brought it right up to the rocks. It was now itself part of the contour of the coast. The danger, lack of water, on this dry island, struck everyone.

A group of Marines were running hoses from their own water boat in Perruquier Bay, and spraying the fast drying out mound. They were being able to just spray the dome of the head and the strangely smiling face.

On each side, there was an eye which seemed uncannily human with its intimate, yet faraway, luminous stare. Even one of the small children noticed and pointed up, crying out, 'It smiling at me.'

Then, Sister Rita picked up the child to see from a height.

Vincent looked for Thérèse. They had not spoken since after the riot.

On the other side of the whale, some of the children were touching the flanks of flesh, others were shooing away the corbeaux which were settling on the great bloody gash which had ripped out a huge chasm, a black gorge, revealing a bewildering interior. Already, flies and ants were buzzing and crawling all over. The wound was festering in the heat, giving off an odour of fish oil, blubber, blood and salt.

One marine had organised a line of children to pass buckets of salt water to throw onto the sides of the whale. Someone had got a ladder, and was climbing up to one flank, pouring the salt water which seemed a trickle on a mountainside. Another child had slipped down and scratched herself, trying to climb the cliff of flesh.

No one knew if the whale was dead. The high tide was expected after lunch. They were debating whether a tug should come and drag it off the beach and nose it back into the deep. Marines were coming from their barracks at Perruquier Bay with cotton sheets, and draping the wet sheets over the full extent of the whale, to prevent it from drying out in the increasing hot sun of the morning.

The tail with the tail flukes lay exposed on the small rocks, which were usually covered by the sea except for this unusual tide. Many of the children were looking for crabs and conches in the rock pools. There was a yell. It was Ti-Jean, balancing precariously between rocks and weed and soft sand, helped by one of the other children. Vincent waved. 'Docta, Docta!' Ti-Jean's voice rose over the wind, and the confusion on the bay, with all the children and Marines.

Theo and Vincent stumbled across the beach towards where Ti-Jean was expertly leaping over rocks and seaweed with his crutches, looking like some strange, spider-like crab on stilts. When he eventually met up with Theo and Vincent, he fell flat on his face in the sand. Then, he looked up, laughing at himself and his antics.

'Come, boy, let's get you up, Ti-Jean.' Vincent knelt down in the sand next to Ti-Jean. While he lifted Ti-Jean, Theo collected the crutches and stood holding them out for Ti-Jean to take them again.

He paid little attention to his accident, or to the loss of his crutches. He did not at first seem to notice Theo holding them out. He was obsessed with the whale. He came up spluttering and wiping sand from his mouth and off his face. He pulled himself along on his belly, and then with a huge effort, turned over and sat up with his plaster-of Paris stumps in front of him, like a figure in the stocks. He was immediately in full flow.

'Is like a mountain, Doc, like an island that come out of the sea. I wish I could climb right to the top of it.'

Vincent, busy brushing him down and adjusting him in his awkward sitting position, asked, 'And what would you do on the summit of the whale, Ti-Jean?'

'I go look out over the world. '

Ti-Jean was immediate with his reply. It was as if he had been preparing his response to the extraordinary visitor to El Caracol for some time.

The ocean, from this angle, was mountainous in its green swells, as it came through the *bocas* with a seaplane tender's steep sides seeming closer and higher because of how far out the tide was today.

The sea was above the land.

Ti-Jean's visionary fantasy loosened Theo's tongue. Determined not to be outdone, Theo showed off one of the stories he had heard from Father Angel. Using Ti-Jean's crutches to dramatise width and height, he launched into part of the tale of Moby Dick.

'He tired, Father Angel say, the writer who write *Moby Dick*, or Ishmael, the character who do the talking, when he come to think about the origin of the Leviathan.'

Theo pointed with one of Ti-Jean's crutches at the steep cliffs of whale behind him, as if he were lecturing on the origin of the species. Then he began to quote from the book of Job. 'You know, Leviathan, upon the earth there is not his like who is made without fear. Will he speak soft words unto thee?' His tale was a mixture of the Bible and Herman Melville as transmitted through the vocabulary of the parish priest who had educated him, contributing to his fevered imagination.

'Sometimes, in the book, it say that when you come upon cliffs, in far away land, where rock throw down, you go see the petrified form of the Leviathan. You know that this is the Golfo de La Ballena, so no surprise to see this whale. Long ago you would've see more.

'It not unusual to see, when you look up at a cliff, or even higher, look up at a cloud, to see the shape of a whale. At night, when you look up in the sky you go see whale crossing the starry sky, Leviathan swimming through the milky way.'

Vincent could detect the mixture of Theo's sources as he interspersed his own fiction between paraphrases of the Bible and what he remembered of *Moby Dick*, read to him by Father Angel.

By now, the audience for the boy's tale had grown. There was a tight circle of faces which included Sister Rita's and several of the children who were in her care. This was not like reading from the *Royal Reader* in school.

He was now working to his climax, his large green eyes getting wider and wider.

'There is men, with anchor and harpoon, use this as a way to hack and climb to the summit of Leviathan, to reach the top of the sky. These is the very words I hear from Father Angel who teach me them. He want to see whether the fabled heavens with all their countless tents really lie encamped beyond mortal light.' He smiled with his recitation.

He had Ti-Jean in the palm of his hand, Vincent was amused to see. Everyone applauded, and some of the children who knew his storytelling from the school whistled their excitement and approval.

Theo was standing in the middle of a circle. He sank to the sand and laid Ti-Jean's crutches in front of the other boy, and then went silent. When he looked up he stared straight into the faces of Singh and Christiana who had joined the enraptured audience. They were all applauding.

'You could tell story, boy.' Singh came forward to pat him on the back. Theo shied away. Vincent noticed his unease. He was surprised to see Singh so openly with the girl, now that he knew what was going on, if he believed Theo.

Vincent approached. 'He gets shy. Let's leave him.'

Singh looked embarrassed.

'We still have to talk, Krishna,' Vincent said. Singh looked away.

Vincent for the first time really noticed Christiana's beauty. She was a *dougla* girl, the African and Indian in her blended into an unusual perfection. Sixteen, she looked more like eighteen. When she looked up at him, as he spoke to Singh, her eyes flashed. He could see that she would get her own way. He now saw it all quite plainly. He had been distracted by his own affairs, not least by his own clandestine relationship. He watched Singh and Christiana walk away towards the whale. He envied their boldness.

The sisters were beginning to round up the children in preparation for the walk back to Saint Damian's.

Vincent still could not see Thérèse anywhere. He had not wanted to ask Sister Rita in case she suspected something, so much was Thérèse's visit to the house, and the events that night, still in his mind.

There was reluctance to leave the beach. No one wanted to leave the whale. Everyone wanted to wait and see what would happen at high tide, and whether the whale would be successfully launched back into the ocean. Vincent could still see Jonah working with the Marines to keep it as wet as possible. Still more sheets were brought, soaked and draped over the sad creature.

'They say it must've happen last night, Doc. You heard the thunder and the guns?'

'Yes, Jonah. What're they saying?'

'It get hit with a torpedo.'

They both looked at Sister Rita. They did not want to alarm her, have her carrying news to the convent which would worry the sisters.

'They could come right in here you know, Doc.'

'That's why we have the Marines here. Why we have our fortifications. Our American base, the artillery guns.'

'You believe in all of that, Doc? I ent see what they could do if they decide to come in.'

'Let's not terrify ourselves Jonah.' Vincent looked at Sister Rita and then again at Jonah.

Vincent knew that it was not the idea of a U-Boat invasion which was making Sister Rita look agitated, go silent, seem far away. She was looking towards the sand dunes which were heaped up near the pass to the other side of the island, which led back to Perruquier Bay. She looked embarrassed. There was some commotion where the pass narrowed to an obstacle path of rocks, a rough track among the agave. The children, who had begun the trek back to Saint Damian's, were clambering up to get through the pass.

'*Oo la la!*' Sister Rita gathered up some crutches which had been abandoned on the beach by children who did not need them, finding it easier on this terrain to scramble as best they could without them. 'What's going on? I must go and see,' she called.

There was a lot of shouting and waving. Vincent thought perhaps he should also go and see what was happening, and get hold of Theo at the same time. He could not see the boy nor Ti-Jean anywhere.

As they both neared the sand dunes, they saw what the matter was. It was Sister Rita who first recognised her. Some of the other sisters were trying to prevent her from descending to the beach. The children were laughing and pointing. Vincent still could not make out exactly what the tumult was all about, till Sister Rita ran away from him in the direction of the crowd, crying, 'It's Sister Thérèse. I must go.' Vincent followed hastily.

At first he could not see Thérèse clearly. Then his heart leapt into his throat. 'Oh, no. My God!' He looked around for Theo. He wanted to have Theo at his side. What would he make of this?

The sun was now so hot that the distance shimmered in the heat. He looked for Thérèse's veil, and then he saw what all the children were laughing and pointing at. He saw her bald, shaven head. What he saw was a girl in a short cotton dress. She looked so much younger than she did in her habit, so much younger than she had in the boathouse, in the gloom of the boathouse and the confined cabin that held their passion that night. Still he felt the sea rocking the boat, heard the thud of the almonds on the galvanise roof. He had time for the memories, like the scent of the boathouse, her breath, pervading his mind, caressing his body.

For some reason, he focused on the dress. It was a white cotton dress dotted with small blue flowers. Like a meadow in Provence, he thought. It was odd. He wondered where she would have got it. Where would she have found a dress? Maybe they kept dresses for those who wanted to leave. It never occurred to him that anyone ever left. That she would ever leave. Is that what she was doing?

He remembered the story he was telling her a couple of nights before as they sat on the jetty of his house, of the nun who had drowned herself.

Vincent was falling over as he ran in the sand dunes. Every time he got up, and then looked ahead, he saw that she was closer, fighting her way through the children and some of the sisters, trying to hold her back, as she made for the open beach, for the whale.

He did not think that she had yet seen him. Why had she done this? What really had she done? Vincent felt compromised. Why come out here like this?

The other sisters had abandoned their attempts to restrain her. As she stumbled towards him, he saw her bare white legs and the brush of black hair. Then he saw her face with rouge and lipstick. Her lips were carmine. Her cheeks were raddled. Her head was so small, so small, he thought.

When he stood up from where he had fallen, she at last saw him. She called. She shrieked, 'Vincent!'

All those at the path among the agave turned back to look at her, running and falling, and getting up and running towards him. He stood and waited, their secret being proclaimed to all the sisters, Marines and children on the beach. When she reached him she stumbled and fell in front of him, at his feet, her face in the sand.

Vincent knelt down next to her. 'Madeleine.' He knew no one was near enough to hear him say her name. He repeated, 'Madeleine,' as if to wake her, as it were, from where she lay, face down. When he looked up he could see everyone else staring from a distance.

Quite close were Singh and Christiana, standing and staring. They both looked sad. They both understood, he felt. They were suspended in the haze of the heat, as if they were not really there, a kind of mirage. They waved and turned.

'Madeleine, come, sit up, stand up. What's happening? What has happened? Why are you dressed like this?'

He hoped people would see this as the distressed Thérèse coming to him, the doctor. He hoped Singh might see it like this, but he doubted that now. He could still hear his name, Vincent, shrieked across the beach, echoing from the cliffs, proclaiming their intimacy.

Vincent noticed that the sisters were turning the children away from the beach, moving them back to Saint Damian's. Jonah was helping. They were all leaving him.

The Marines were getting on with their rehabilitation of the beached whale. Vincent found himself using the presence of Theo's Leviathan to distract the distraught Thérèse. 'Look, the whale.'

The beach was suddenly deserted, except for the Marines continually working at protecting the razor back whale, sixty feet long, from drying out in the hot sun; hosing the flanks, covering them with wet sheets.

Rift

Vincent and Madeleine sat at the mouth of a small cave at the end of the La Tinta beach. Sand flies stung, mosquitoes hummed. Vincent poured citronella from a vial he carried in his pocket. He rubbed it into Madeleine's arms and along her legs. He applied the repellent to himself. They sat out of the sun, looking towards the beached whale. The tide was coming in. It was a gentle trickle over the rocks. High tide would be hours away.

This was not the time to interrogate her about what was going on, why she was dressed in the cotton frock with the blue flowers. Where was her nun's habit? Why was she here with her cropped hair, without a veil? He was shocked. He sat with her and waited. The sun had already burnt her face and arms. Sometimes she spoke, other times he guessed, from her single words, the state of her mind.

'Papa, Papa.' She was hardly audible.

'Have you had some news?' He held her hand.

'Drancy.'

'The workers camp?'

'Yes.'

He did not think she could have had specific news about her father being at the camp. Since they had heard of its existence, it had been a fear. The letters from Canada were far more general, never specific enough news. The rest was surmise.

'Here, pin it for me.' She handed him an embroidered yellow star she had received recently. 'Pin it to my lapel.'

'Madeleine! No!'

'Pin it. My brooch.'

He humoured her. He pinned the yellow star to her frock with the blue forget-me-nots. He wanted, above all, to keep her calm.

'Would you like to get closer to see the whale? What a wonder!' He hoped that this would distract her.

She stared as into a mirage, the whale shrouded with wet cotton sheets in the morning haze, the Marines' hoses playing over its flanks.

Then, more lucidly, she said, 'I heard the fisherman say the whale was torpedoed, by a German U-Boat.'

'Or it took a depth charge from the Americans.' He played with her curiosity and fear about the accident and the immediate war.

He could see that talk of the Germans brought into her mind only one thing, scenes which were never very far away, images that she could not really imagine. Yet it was this that was precisely the making of her fear, the unimaginable, and what she made of it. 'These letters you horde don't help you,' he advised.

She read and re-read them, he knew. 'By the way, are you any closer to knowing who embroiders your yellow stars?'

She stared at him vacantly. He felt her distress. He felt scared.

'*Rafle,* Drancy.' Her obsession guided her.

'Sister Thérèse.' He wanted to distance himself.

She stared at him. He had not called her by her formal title for ages.

She whispered, 'My name is Madeleine Weil.'

'But you are Sister Thérèse of the Order of Martha and Mary.'

'Is that right, Doctor Metivier?' She spat it out, quite uncharacteristically. 'Is that right, Doctor Metivier?'

Vincent felt a mixture of anger and embarrassment. He knew the moment that he saw her in her dress with the blue forget-me-nots, that it would have to stop. She could not just turn up like this, shrieking out his name. They could not continue. How would he stop it?

'*Pogrom!*' she intoned.

'Sister. You are deliberately distressing yourself. I won't listen to this. You have got to get a hold of yourself.' He was very nervous.

'Verdun.'

He could read from the fertile miscellany, the glossary of her mind, influenced by talks with her father, her father's letters. Her mind was a map of rivers. He knew this geography. He had entered this territory with her before. But now he felt he had lost her.

'Meuse, Rhine'. She knelt and drew a map of lines, boundaries. She built fortifications like a child building sandcastles. '*L'homme mort.*' She was reading for her *baccalauréat* as a young girl, '*La France. Ils ne passeront pas.*' Vincent could see what was happening to her mind, as she built the ring of hills scarred with shell craters, ditches, trenches. 'Verdun, Donaumont.' He knew enough of Mr Freud to sense what was happening.

More names raced through her mind: 'Petain, Maginot.'

She looked up at him from her sandcastle. '*Le vainquer de Verdun* or *le medécin de l'Armée*. General Petain?'

These names of places, heroes and villains were all that she had with which to think, to feel.

'*La der des ders.* The last of the last. Now this.' Standing up, she scrawled the dates 13th May and 14th of June 1940, the dates of the German entry into France, and into Paris. She squatted again to trace with her fingers the Meuse. She was herself, in the Ardennes, thought Vincent. He was out of his depth. Who was there, but himself, to help her?

Jonah came over to talk to Vincent about the whale. Thérèse continued to kneel in the sand. Some of the older children, still on the beach, crept close, playing, looking for *chip chip* shells. Thérèse played along with them. They were reluctant to leave the whale.

Vincent knelt close to her. 'Sister?' She looked at him vacantly as if he were not speaking to her.

Then, she said, 'Dreyfus.'

'Come, Sister.'

They were both interrupted by an American accent, a voice saying. 'Doctor Metivier? So, you're the father of this boy. This is your son?'

Vincent got up and turned to face the voice.

'Lieutenant Jesse Morrison.' They shook hands. He repeated his remark, standing between Theo and Ti-Jean with an arm on each of their shoulders.

'Well, yes, they're both my boys,' Vincent answered.

The boys were smiling at each other. Vincent was pleased that Theo seemed to be at ease with Ti-Jean. What had happened that night of the courtesan? What had been exorcised by the carnival, with the red satin dress, the green scarf, stockings, high-heeled shoes, lipstick and rouge? The two people could not be compared. Something had been laid to rest.

'But this one. This lover of God, Theophilus,' said Jesse.

'What's that you name him?' Ti-Jean was jumping around on his crutches. 'That is name pappy! The-who-of-a-who?'

Theo looked shy. Jesse was telling tales. It was not fair.

'This Theophilus, lover of God, who I've to say is a smart kid. The other day, as we investigated the midden behind your house, tells me that, yes, you're his father and he's your son.'

Theo was now trying to break away from Jesse's clasp, and run off with Ti-Jean over the beach, trying not to catch Vincent's eye. He had been telling tales.

'Well, if that is what he says, it must be so.' Vincent looked at Theo as he said this. 'As good a son as anyone would want to have.' He winked at the boy.

'And me?' Ti-Jean interjected, not to be outdone.

'Well, you've always been first, Ti-Jean.' Theo looked intently, taking that in. Vincent smiled at Jesse.

The boys were off, and the men were left looking at them. 'Hop Along Cassidy and Billy the Kid! Hi!' Jesse called after them. 'Hi, Theophilus!'

'You can call him Theo,' Vincent advised.

'Theo!' Jesse shouted.

The boys ran back, Ti-Jean stumbling on his crutches in the sand, Theo helping him. Thérèse assisted him as a nurse. Both boys stared at her in her new garb. Ti-Jean put out his hand to touch the yellow star. She pulled away. He looked at her, both knowing her and not knowing her.

'Let's see if you've kept your promise,' Jesse interrupted.

Theo put his hand into his pocket and brought out a piece of pottery, part of the lip of a vase, shaped like a heart.

'At least five hundred-years-old, from a midden, a grave of bones on the outer shore beyond Point Girod, near the ocean,' Jesse lectured.

Vincent passed it to Thérèse, trying to make things look normal. He was aware how bizarre she looked in her dress, her face smeared with rouge and lipstick. What would Jesse be making of this scene? What were the boys making of it? She held the fragment of fired clay up to the light.

'From a midden on the north coast,' Jesse filled in.

The piece of earthen biscuit-coloured pottery had a rough grain. Vincent remembered it in the light of the night in his room, as Theo told his story of the midden, and the graves and the bones, and bodies falling into the graves.

Just then there were parrots in the air, making for Monte de Botella with

273

their screams and their fire. Vincent remembered the words about the voices of the ones who had leapt at Sauteurs.

Thérèse turned the shard in her fingers. 'A piece of the past,' she whispered, almost inaudible, as she handed it back to Theo, smiling. 'Fired in ovens not unlike ones used on the island at the present time,' she contributed knowledgeably.

'Probably,' Jesse responded, taking in Thérèse in her unusual dress. 'There is more here, I understand. Did you know that, Doctor?'

'Apparently. There are layers of history just beneath our feet.' Then he looked to the Boca Grande, and the opening into the Golfo de Ballena. 'If the gulf could speak, it could tell of myriad periods of history that have used these waters for its ships. From the dugout canoes, the first pirogues, to these destroyers. This small corner of the world has been preyed upon. There is a line of conquering soldiers who stretch out behind you, Lieutenant.'

'We're here to defend you this time, Sir.'

'We hope so. But it makes us part of your battlefield.'

'There are your oil refineries and sugar factories.'

'They are not ours, Jesse. We're still part of an Empire,' Vincent explained.

'They is our land, our natural wealth,' Jonah burst forth.

'Well, you'll want them when you govern the place. I heard the speeches the other day. I saw you there.' Jesse turned to Jonah. 'And that Indian fella. A *commie* if ever I heard one. Is that possible? That you will govern here?'

'Mr Stalin's our ally now, you know?' Vincent smiled.

'Sure, it's possible,' said Jonah, who was watching and listening intently. 'You hear Atilla's calypso, *Shout the glad tidings, and urge the hero on, he's a David, a Goliath, and a Sampson all in one...* And you have your own battles up north, Lieutenant.'

'So we have an historian and a revolutionary here.'

'Me, is a fisherman, Sir. Jonah Le Roy from La Brea where the pitch lake is, that other wonder of the world.' Jonah glanced at the whale. 'Sir Walter Raleigh caulk his ships from there.'

'I've heard of your bottomless lake. That buccaneer who was a poet, seeking booty for his queen. So this is your whale? You've just been delivered back to life. Jonah, you must make for Niniveh.' Jesse mimicked a preacher's voice, 'Those people need converting.'

'That's what the Doc, here, is always joking about. We're into the business of delivering people into life, into the light. Not so, Doc?'

'We sure are, Jonah,' Vincent agreed.

'What we want to know is how you Yanks going to help this business?' Jonah said to Jesse.

'Well, that's obvious,' Jesse replied.

'Yes, the war is one thing, but here, you've seen our people. You see the conditions of our people.' Jonah looked behind him at the patients finding the path to Perruquier Bay. 'Watch them children. You ever see thing so. Imagine shooting one of them!'

Jesse fell silent. 'Let's leave the shooting to Major McGill and his inquiry. There'll be an inquest.'

'We'll be coming to you, or to your superiors with some ideas.' Vincent cut in. Then he paid attention to Thérèse again. She had calmed with the distraction of the boys and the discussion.

'Medicine, Major,' she said suddenly.

'Sorry, Mam, I didn't get your name.'

'Weil, Sister Thérèse Weil.'

'Jesse Morrison, Miss.' It was now that he stared at her with her cropped hair and her white skin freshly burnt, her distressed look, the yellow star burning on her lapel.

Jonah looked at Vincent, inquiringly. Vincent introduced Thérèse. Jesse looked more puzzled.

She went on. She was now lucid. 'Medicine, equipment, better conditions. That's what we need here for our work. You've seen the place.' She wanted to go on. She smiled and stopped. Then she began again, 'We need Penicillin, the new Sulfa drugs. Should not be only for soldiers in a war, but also for poor people.' Her eyes were wide and watery, staring beyond Jesse, to the whale and the ocean beyond.

'Yes, Mam. You've got a comrade here,' Jesse said to Jonah and Vincent.

The men smiled, but, embarrassed by her appearance, hoped that would be the end of Thérèse's speech.

Theo and Ti-Jean had been listening to the grown-ups, while Theo showed Ti-Jean his find from the midden. He returned the pottery piece to his pocket. Then he and Ti-Jean walked off. The grown-ups began to make their way towards the patients among the dunes.

'Friends for life,' Jesse said to Vincent, looking at the boys.

'The whale has brought us all together.'

'Boy, he's bright. Your son.' Jesse smiled. 'Questions! And talk, talk talk.'

'Really,' said Vincent.

'Yep, never stops.'

'Oh, I can believe that. But conversation?'

'Not really, kind of shuts you out with his stories. Though he's checking up that you are listening.' Jesse smiled.

As they walked on, Thérèse lagged behind. Vincent kept his eye on her. He was dying to ask what stories Theo had told Jesse. They could compare stories. But he restrained himself.

Thérèse caught them up.

They all began to walk to where the other sisters had gathered up the children for the trek back to Saint Damian's under the supervision of Mother Superior, who had not really wanted this expedition to see the whale. In the end, she had not been able to prevent it.

She had stood on a high sand dune, with one of the novices holding a parasol to shade her, while she attempted to direct events as far as possible. She had decided, that what with the other battles which she had to win, to let this one pass. She glanced censoriously at Thérèse and Vincent. This was something that she was going to have to deal with, but not publicly.

Thérèse pulled at Vincent's arm. 'I can't go with them. I'm not one of them anymore. I have nowhere to go. Where do I go?' she asked pleadingly.

'What do you want me to do?'

'Stay with me. I'm lost.'

Vincent was in a quandary. What could he do?

The tide was beginning to come in gently, seeping over the rocks. A tug had come around the point, and was waiting for the tide to rise before coming any further into La Tinta. A group of Marines were attaching ropes and chains to the tail flukes of the whale, to begin pulling it off the shore, when they thought they could catch the incoming tide, and hopefully float the mammal. It might just move off, though there was not much hope that it would eventually survive this ordeal.

The smaller children, on the higher ground, were waving back at the whale. The adult patients were speculating about what had happened. Many were fearful of the talk about the war. The fishermen who came into Coco

Bay told stories to the patients who fished off the side of the jetty. The stories spread like wildfire. They had stories of survivors in lifeboats on the north coast of Sancta Trinidad. Some claimed to have seen a submarine surfacing off Saut d'Eau Island, and others, who fished, to have seen one as close as Corozal Point, up the coast from the Boca de Monos.

Jesse kept trying to engage Vincent in small talk but he had his mind on Thérèse. She stuck to Vincent. He hated to think what kind of impression was being created. How were they going to handle what Thérèse had done. What had she done? She had so obviously chosen him. He hoped everyone saw it as choosing the doctor in her distress.

'There was a very old guy in our home town,' Jesse began telling a story. 'He had a wound on his back. Theo's wound reminds me of that, took me right back home. But that was something that happened in those bad days. You know, slavery days. In the warm weather he walked around bare backed showing it to everyone. Letting us see. His back was a kind of monument, a kind of way for everyone from those days, and I guess, for all of us youngsters, to remember something, something of that history. So my Mama said, anyway.'

'Lieutenant?' Vincent interrupted.

'Jesse, Sir, if you please.'

'Yes, of course, Jesse, your story.'

'I grown in South Carolina. Mama grown all her children there. We flourished like a field of corn. Papa, he took off North.'

'South Carolina?' Vincent was distracted.

'Yep, you know, Charleston. You must know Charleston. I bet you've danced that music with a pretty gal.'

At that moment, Jesse looked at Thérèse who had turned away, and was staring out towards the whale. Tears were streaming down her face, drying in the sun, smudging her cheeks.

Vincent went towards her. Jonah was looking on and said, 'Leave her be, Doc.' Jonah sounded wise about the matter.

Jesse continued, more now to fill the space with something else. 'The world dancing that music.'

'What did you say, Jesse?' Vincent asked.

'Well, that history in that music, in the playing. But don't mind me Doc, I see you've got your hands full.' He laughed nervously.

277

'No, Jesse go on. Your story is important.' Vincent went and stood behind Thérèse, and in full view of the men, Jonah and Jesse, and those who could see from afar, he put his hand on her shoulders from behind to calm her.

'It's okay now, Madeleine,' he whispered in her ear.

Jesse continued, more not to seem awkward than to continue with his conversation, 'The blues and jazz, and you know, like down here on the islands, with your calypso. I hear a little of that. I hear the fishermen coming over the bay in the early morning when I'm lying in my bunk. They sounds, as if they've real fun. We're going into Porta España soon, and I go find myself a gal and dance them rhythms.'

Jonah and Vincent turned to him and nodded. Jonah tried to joke. 'You go find them by the corner working for the Yankee dollar.'

Jesse got the point. 'Oh, yeh. *Rum and Coca-Cola.*'

'You got it, Lieutenant,' Jonah laughed.

Jesse changed the tone and directed his remark to include Thérèse who had rejoined the group. 'It seems that we're all far from home, with this war,' he said meaningfully.

'That's true, Lieutenant.' Thérèse came into the conversation, listening intently. She looked distraught. 'But then I've left home to find a new one. And, now, I'm alone.'

'Here?' Jesse asked.

'Yes, here. But now, where?' She looked into the faces of each of the men in turn. They stared, embarrassed.

Then, they all three looked at the pilgrimage of patients, higgledy piggledy, zig-zagging along the beach under the manchineel and almonds.

'You do good work, Sister. You do a good work,' Jesse said gallantly. He noticed Jonah's deference. He was still confused by the sister's dress. He left to join his fellow Marines at Perruquier Bay. Then he turned to Vincent, 'One last thing Doc, the boy, he talks a lot about Chantal. Has he talked to you about Chantal? A girlfriend?'

'Chantal? Yes, he's mentioned her.' Vincent answered without giving anything away.

Jesse smiled. 'I'm right behind your house,' he waved. 'Okay if I call with my banjo?' They all three looked ahead and waved him off.

Vincent asked Jonah to take care of Theo, and to take him to Saint Damian's. 'Keep him with you by the jetty, till I get back. He doesn't want to go by Singh.'

'I understand, Doc,' Jonah looked at the boy.

'Ti-Jean, you must get back to school,' Vincent added.

Thérèse stayed back and walked along the beach with Vincent. 'Well, what a day!' Vincent exclaimed.

'It's hardly begun. You have the children to inject with Chaulmoogra Oil today.' Thérèse was still thinking of her duties.

'Oh God.' Vincent hated the pain it gave the children.

'I know,' she said, almost her old self again.

'Hopefully we're going to be able to stop the use of Chaulmoogra. What you said about Sulfa drugs. That's what we want from the Americans. You're right. We must get our hands on that stuff. And the wonder drug, Penicillin. Our patients need them.' Vincent was continuing as if everything was as normal. Even his inquiry, 'Any news of your father?'

'No, only nightmares.'

'Nightmares?'

'Mine, made of nothing but what I don't know. And the letters that tell of Drancy.'

They looked at each other, avoiding the poisonous sap of the manchineel, as they stooped below the low trees. Vincent let their talk carry on in this vein as if nothing was amiss. They stopped in the shade of the sea grapes. It was only now that they were alone and Vincent looked again at Thérèse, and she became Madeleine, that the full impact of what she had done stunned both of them.

'Where on earth did you get this dress?' He flicked at her frilly sleeves with his fingers. 'These things!' He looked for the first time at her shoes, and a pathetic discarded handbag she had slung over her arm, that he had not noticed before, and seemed hooked there permanently.

Thérèse stood there and just looked at him as he looked at her, uncomprehendingly. 'Madeleine! Madeleine!' he repeated with sighs of bewilderment. Then, he said firmly, 'Sister, this can't go on.'

She stooped near where the water lapped beneath the hanging branches of the sea grape and logwood, cupping her hands in the gentle waves which chuckled over the sand and shells, like bones. She tried to wash off the rouge and lipstick from her face. As she bent there at the water's edge, he saw the notches of her spine, the stretched nape of her neck.

The others were now out of sight. They were alone, hidden beneath the

279

trees. She turned and their faces met. They kissed, their mouths dry and hot, tasting of salt. 'What've we done?' Vincent asked.

'What've we done?' Thérèse echoed him

'What will we do now?'

'I'm not going back.' Thérèse was adamant.

Her stark statement cut deep into Vincent's consciousness. He realised at once, without really knowing how he was going to respond, that she was his responsibility. 'Madeleine you have to go back.' He tried to speak bravely and decisively, but he felt like a coward and thought he sounded like a coward. He unpinned the yellow star from her lapel and threw it into the water, where it floated for a moment, and then became saturated and sank, looking like the poisonous sap of the manchineel.

They took their shoes off and walked in the shallows along the beach to Saint Damian's. They walked, dangling their shoes in one hand and holding hands with the other. Vincent felt pulled both ways. They kicked at the water. There was a sense in each of them that nothing mattered now as they came in sight of Saint Damian's. Thérèse reiterated, 'I'm not going back.' Vincent pulled away.

Earlier, hidden beneath the sea grapes and the manchineel, his mouth on her mouth, Vincent had seemed convinced that Madeleine was right, and that he would support her in her decision. He could have, just a moment ago, dashed with her along the beach into some other future.

'Madeleine. There's nowhere to go,' he said earnestly.

'I can be with you.'

Her words twisted his heart. 'No! No, you can't.'

The incongruity of Thérèse's appearance struck Vincent even more now as he saw Jonah waiting on the jetty with Theo and Ti-Jean who had not fol- lowed his instruction. Both boys waved ecstatically and called out, 'Docta, over here!'

Life was calling Vincent. He managed to wave back. Thérèse had been part of that life, veiled, sandalled, the nun who worked alongside him on the wards and in the pharmacy, her head bent over her microscope.

'Madeleine, you can't go any further like this. Let me get you something to change into, something to cover you up.'

'Cover me up. Is that what you want to do? Hide me away.'

'Madeleine!

'Yes, your Magdalene.' She stood facing him with her hands on her hips.

'Madeleine, trust me. This is not how we must go. We run the risk of losing everything.'

She looked at him questioningly. 'I've already lost everything.'

Back on the beach, Vincent was refusing to imagine what he had to do. He hoped that the nuns would deal with the situation, find some way to take her back to themselves. Because of the public nature of her behaviour, they had let it pass by as if nothing much was amiss. Even Sister Rita had not acted. Now, Vincent saw her coming along the beach as if she had guessed his thoughts.

When she arrived with a nun's white cape, Thérèse was sitting on the beach. She knelt next to her. 'Sister, come, come with me, come put this on,' and she began to drape the white cape of the Sisters of Martha and Mary over the shoulders of her sister, Thérèse.

Vincent felt relieved as Thérèse did not resist, but seemed strangely comforted by the act of Sister Rita. But at the same time, he felt guilty. He had not found a way to take her with him. He could not find the way to do it and keep his job, keep the trust of his patients, their struggle, and above all his credibility in the eyes of Mother Superior and the authorities.

'Thérèse, go with Sister Rita now. Later I'll come and visit. I will. I promise. Sister Rita, tell Mother Superior that I've spoken with Sister Thérèse and that I have recommended that she take some rest. She is under too much of a strain at the hospital, and would benefit from a rest. I'll come and see her later today.'

As Sister Rita went ahead, Vincent whispered, 'Madeleine, trust me. I won't abandon you.' She looked back with longing and disbelief.

Much later that day, away from what many had noticed about *the sister who break out of the convent*, when the evening burnt down with no one watching particularly, the tug pulled the whale off the rocks. It floated on the high tide and was borne away on the fast moving currents of the Boca Grande. Its dorsal ridge faded into the distance like a disappearing island in the haze.

In that same sunset, Vincent walked up from the jetty at Embarcadère Corbeaux to the nun's infirmary. He had a duty to perform. He had decided that this would be the end of the affair. How he would tell Thérèse this and make the visit one of a doctor concerned about a patient, he was not certain. She would surely see it as his abandonment of her. He was resolute.

Eggs

Saint Damian's was a prison while Vincent and Thérèse battled with the authorities of state and church. Vincent was called in to Mother Superior's office.

'This is a misunderstanding, Mother. Yes, Sister Thérèse Weil and I have grown close. You might say that's an indiscretion, but our research has made this possible. It's a professional relationship and she has grown to trust me in her distress.'

'That's just it. That's why I think it's better that Sister Thérèse change her duties. I want her to be in charge of the patients kept up in the hills, with those who find it difficult to come down to the hospital for treatment. Some of our worse cases.'

'Very hard for one sister. Very taxing work. Possibly dangerous, because of the unhygienic conditions.'

'That's what I think she needs, Doctor. Allow me, please, to make this judgment here. It'll remind her of the primary duties of her vocation. This will take her mind off all the other things, extraordinary things she fills her mind with. Yellow stars! And this research of yours must be put on hold.'

Thérèse was removed from Vincent's influence. He saw her trudging up to the hills. He looked out for her visits to the chapel. He had to be content with glimpses.

But Mother Superior was still gunning for the dismissal of, '*That* Doctor Metivier,' speaking to Father Meyer and the authorities in Porta España.

Vincent had got the support of Jonah who had organised the patients. They marched to Mother Superior's office. She heard their deputation. 'We can't risk another riot,' Major Mc Gill advised her. Elridge Padmore's inquest had brought back a verdict of accidental death by shooting. That night there were fires in the hills. Soldiers patrolled the perimeter fence.

The patients resented the Yanks. 'They kill Eldridge for nothing.' Their sabotage continued.

'You can't dismiss him now,' the Medical Board concluded, in their report to Mother Superior, knowing that they could not easily replace Vincent. They prevailed upon her to be patient.

'How can I have him working alongside my sisters? Think of the risk of scandal. Under my very nose!' she complained to Father Meyer. Her pride was hurt.

'Sister Thérèse cannot return to Europe at this time. We can't just throw her out,' Father Meyer counselled.

'I suppose I should get to the bottom of the matter of the yellow stars.'

Father Meyer advised her to ignore that matter.

It was at this time, in the middle of 1942, that the most certain news they had had for some time was smuggled in a letter by Sister Rita to Vincent, one day in the pharmacy. She had taken Thérèse's duties. She was her *confidante*, visiting her in the hills, becoming her go-between with Vincent.

The letter Sister Rita brought gave the clearest description of the *Grand Raffle* of that year in the middle of July, of Jews being deported from Drancy to a German camp across the border of Germany, just within the borders of Poland. They had heard the name in a previous letter: 'Auschwitz,' Sister Rita read. Another name for Thérèse to add to her litany of fear, Vincent thought.

In return, Sister Rita carried a message from Vincent. Jonah would be in a pirogue near the small jetty by the womens' huts at eight o'clock that night. The message joked that he had no intention of swimming across the bay to meet her. He wanted to be alive for her, not dead. But he was sending his boatman to bring her to him. Sister Rita buried the letter in the folds of her habit.

He knew he was playing on Thérèse's vulnerability. She would be disturbed by the recent news in the letter he had just received. But, maybe, she had wanted him to realise that.

Jonah entered willingly into the secrecy. For a long time, he had thought that the Doctor needed a woman. Theo had become such a permanent presence, he wanted to encourage a feminine and maternal influence upon the doctor's house. 'All kind of thing does happen in this life, Doc. You can't plan these things. You can't plan love.'

'I don't want Singh to know.'

'Doc, he done suspect.'

'Yes, I thought so.'

'Anyway, he and Christiana. You know?'

'No I don't know. I have left it so long to speak to him. Theo won't return to work in the pharmacy.'

'Well, she's a young woman now, Doc. But it going on a long time. Singh go understand. As I say, you can't plan love. He should know that.'

Vincent did not know whether Thérèse would come. In the end, waiting on the jetty, he thought she would not at the last minute. He had been wrong to try and persuade her. She would have the good sense to see that.

At first, Vincent did not see her in the approaching pirogue. Then, there she was, in the halo of the kerosene lantern. Under cover of his usual routines, Jonah had fetched Thérèse without any trouble.

She and Vincent stood awkwardly on the jetty.

She wore her cotton dress with the blue forget-me-nots which she had worn at La Tinta. Was that a sign of something? They were formal in front of the others. The men winked at each other. Theo noticed. Over her arm was her nun's white cloak which she had used for her escape.

Vincent explained that they were going on a fishing expedition to the island of Huevos. The crossing was short but hazardous, particularly at night, and because of the military restrictions.

Jonah navigated the boat in such a way that it did not run the risk of setting off any alarms. Theo was all eyes and ears in the bow. What was he making of the present company? Vincent had to talk to him about Singh and Christiana. He had to talk to him about himself and Thérèse. Maybe he had already sorted these things out in his own way.

The fishermen in another pirogue led the way, keeping a look out for the Coast Guard.

They had to be careful. The stories of more and more torpedoed ships off the coasts of the continent and the island of Sancta Trinidad, alarmed everyone. At times, the fishermen brought back more than fish with them, in their catch, from off the north coast. There were bodies found on the rocks, or tangled in their seines.

On the beach, around a cooking fire, Vincent and Thérèse listened to the fishermen, who had come to fish for cavalli, tell their tales

There were the natural comparisons with other wonders which had been experienced, like the whale at La Tinta. They shared their stories like food. 'Who ever see a *macajuel* with a cow inside it belly?' Jai Singh asked, jumping up all of a sudden. He was from the plains of Caroni near the mangrove swamps and the oyster beds where he had been with his father searching for conch, throwing seine for *cascadu,* scraping off the blue lipped oysters from the mangrove branches, when they had come upon the *macajuel* boa constrictor on the path between the canals. They had interrupted its digestion and disgorged it of the crushed cow. Eyes opened wide and some fellas joined in the chorus of exclamations, 'I never see thing so, boy. You ever see thing like that?'

Not to be outdone, Sunil Ramchand, in a small voice, just above the crash of the waves, said it was *Divali* time when he went by cousins down Manzanilla way to keep the celebration, and his uncle took them to a green pool which they got to by taking a boat up the brown Ortoire, and then paddling under the manchineel and the mangrove to where the giant manatee grazed along the edges of the river. Their shadows, just beneath the surface of the water, were like the shapes you see in the clouds. 'Them is shy animal, only the tip of the head and sometime the back you see, you know. Sometime, the shadow, or the tip of a baby head riding the back of the mother.' The others nodded with understanding, imagining his wonder. He had clearly seen something, without really seeing anything at all.

There was the dull thunder in the distance. A flare on the horizon prompted speculation. 'Them U-Boat out there, boy.'

Thérèse was beginning to fall off to sleep. She and Vincent were going to spend the night on the beach while the fishermen sank their seine for cavalli. Vincent suggested a walk.

Theo kept the fire going to ward off the sand flies and mosquitoes, but also to keep the fish broth simmering. The air was perfumed with citronella. He was happy to sit and listen to the stories, looking after the pot. He watched Vincent and Thérèse walk away down the beach.

They were stopped in their tracks. 'Look. Do you see her?' Vincent pointed out the turtle.

'Yes. Extraordinary, how she pulls her great weight through the surf.' Thérèse knelt in the sand.

As they sat on a high dune and watched, the turtle chose her path without being deterred. She scraped with her fins, heaving her weight up the beach for the safety of the sandy dunes. She was in search of a safe place to lay her eggs. This was an annual ritual, a pilgrimage repeated through instinct over centuries.

'Should we call the others? Theo would love to see this,' Vincent enthused.

'No, not just yet.' Thérèse put her hand on Vincent's knee. 'There'll be another one. Let's watch this one on our own.' They had hardly had any time together on their own. Invariably, Theo or Jonah were hovering. 'I nearly did not come.'

'You're here now, Madeleine.'

'Yes.'

'I missed you. I'm sorry.' Vincent felt guilty.

'I suppose I had to come. How could I not?' she reassured him.

'After all this while.'

'It must mean something,' Madeleine insisted.

They stared, leaning in on each other, wrapped in their own thoughts and in the spirit of the place, and what they were witnessing.

This had been happening before there were middens, when the only graves were the bones of coral and the sigh of shells.

The turtle was six feet long and four across. They watched and waited for her climb to end. At first, she went one way and then another, then choosing the highest dunes with the softest sand. When she had chosen a suitable spot, Vincent and Madeleine crept closer, knelt by her side, and read the ancient runes on her back. They were inscrutable. She circled the spot. She settled. They waited and watched and were patient with her patience.

Then her rear fins began to scrape and dig and scoop what was an ancient form of excavation. They were both aware they were witnessing something which had been going on for centuries, ever since there had been turtles. 'She's scooping out a womb in the sand to catch her eggs.' Madeleine was animated.

'Yes,' Vincent murmured. They hardly wanted to speak aloud.

'Look.' They watched the turtle's rear fins repeat their action again and again, until it instinctually felt the depth was sufficient to hold its horde of eggs.

'A safe place for incubation,' Madeleine commented scientifically.

Vincent watched Madeleine stooping, leaning towards the turtle and her excavation. The cotton frock with the blue forget-me-nots now as if in memory of her first rebellion. She had tucked her skirt between her legs to kneel more effectively. He saw the stretch of her back. He crept behind her, massaging her spine, his fingers kneading her back through the soft cotton, stroking her neck. Over her shoulder, he too stared at the turtle. He kissed the nape of Madeleine's neck.

'How still she is,' he whispered, licking the whorl of her ear.

'She's waiting to lay.'

Then they began to come, eggs, one, then two, followed by another, and then in quicker succession, the size of ping pong balls, soft and wet. As they continued to watch it seemed so quick, like ten, then hundreds of membranous moons caught in a stream of light from the now high moon, a glutinous milky way. 'Turtles' eggs. A miracle,' whispered Madeleine.

'Nature's way,' Vincent responded.

All the while the turtle stared implacably with the wisdom of time at the incoming tide she had to reach to leave, once she had buried her future. Tears seemed to ooze from her eyes. The stream of eggs stopped. Then, as methodically as she had dug and scooped, she began to fill the hole to cover the eggs. Madeleine and Vincent watched as she raked in the sand and began to pat it down, with one fin then another. When this was complete, she then circled the spot twice. Then she dragged herself across the same spot twice more. This was her last, camouflaging, caring act. Her mothering was now complete. She had done enough for survival.

'How long have we been here?' Madeleine asked.

'An hour, I think.'

'A solitary hour.'

They could hear the voices of the others down the beach. There were the inescapable cries of Theo's excitement. 'They must've found a turtle of their own,' Vincent commented. Before deciding to rejoin the party, they stayed to see their turtle return to the sea.

They watched her scrape her way back down the steep beach, while her tracks were erased, as quickly as she had made them, by the incoming tide. Her epic had been lost.

'Her legacy is now ours,' Vincent said philosophically.

'Yes, we must come back for the hatchlings.'

As they looked about them, dazed after their meditative witnessing of their first turtle, they thought they had been lucky at the end of the laying season to see one. Then they noticed that two others were on the beach performing the same ancient ceremony. 'Wonderful!' Madeleine exclaimed at the sight.

They had to pick their way back down the beach between the laying turtles. Theo came running up to them, 'Come and see!'

Vincent and Madeleine knelt beside him and watched a similar excavation. They stared without talking. Theo was all eyes. He pointed in amazement, as if he could not contain this on his own, had to show it to the others. At intervals, he would look up behind him to either Vincent or Madeleine and smile to confirm their joint experience.

'Doc, you ever see thing, so?' He tugged at Vincent's arm.

Theo had become exhausted with his watching and was sleeping by the fire which was a mound of glowing embers among hot stones, keeping the chill off in the damp hours of the very early morning. Jonah was also sleeping. The fishermen were testing the cavalli nets. All hands would be needed to pull seine before dawn.

Madeleine and Vincent had gone back to the end of the beach where they had seen their first turtle. They were stealing time. Jonah would have to get Madeleine back to the Saint Damian's before six o'clock, before the first stroke of the Angelus.

They had found a fisherman's shelter of coconut branches. As they lay against each other, they felt as if they were hammocked in the sway of the tide. It thundered beneath them. They heard the rhythmic flip flip of the sand being scooped and pitched by a nearby turtle. The sand fell onto their naked feet. Their own shifting against the sand joined them to this instinctual ceremony. Vincent's strivings and Madeleine's cries and sighs were their own belief against the odds.

They listened to the rattle of the shells and the dead corals. The heave and thud of the sea, which passed beneath the ground on which they lay, were voices sighing from within a sea midden. At times it sounded like sobbing, other times, like wailing.

In the far distance was the sound of thunder, the war they heard about, which delivered its dead sailors onto their shores, out of the very sea from which the turtles came to lay their future.

'I won't make a baby now,' Madeleine whispered.

'Madeleine?'

He wanted to contradict her irrational feeling. His fresh sperm was inside of her. She curled herself into a foetus on the ground which had become a vast womb to incubate the thousands of eggs which had been laid that season. If ever there was a place of fertility this would be it. He curled himself around her. He raked in their discarded clothes, pulling them about their nakedness. Then, he heard her sobbing. He gathered her up into his arms. 'Madeleine.'

A baby had been their fear after the time in the boathouse. She could not then leave the convent. He was the new doctor. But now he had brought her here. How much longer could they go on with their separation? Could they have another moment? Madeleine's declaration was the dread that they had missed their chance.

'Not all the eggs hatch. Not all the baby turtles reach the sea.' Vincent tried to find the right balancing words to whisper in her ear.

She got up suddenly, pushing him off, and walked out from the fisherman's *ajoupa*. Vincent watched her, naked in the mist and spray, go towards the sea, tripping over a birthing turtle, falling in the deep soft sand dunes where the eggs were buried, disappearing down the sheer sand cliff to the hard shale where the sea pounded the shore.

He followed, naked too, to the edge of the sand cliff. He watched her enter the sea. He fell down as he followed her to the hard shore. 'Madeleine, take care! Don't go in too far! Don't lose your foothold!' She continued into the sea. He picked himself up and ran and stumbled into the breaking waves. 'Madeleine!'

They lay on the beach watching a returning turtle. After washing off the sand, they got back to the fisherman's *ajoupa* and gathered up their clothes, trying to dry off in the soft breeze which stirred in the palms above.

The moon was a still mask behind the mist and spray.

Back at the fire, Jonah had roasted bake. Everyone was quiet and exhausted after the night of turtle watching. Theo lay on his belly blowing the embers of the fire into a new flame. Bake and black coffee soon gave them the energy they needed to go down to the shore to help Bolo, Elroy and Jai pull in the seine.

Vincent watched with satisfaction the result of his surgery and their care, on the hands of these men, so that they could clutch and pull effectively.

There was a strong wind blowing, the sea was getting rough. The pirogues rose and fell in the swell. The fishermen were in the water with the net. The others, with the excited Theo, waiting to take hold of it on the shore. Soon, everyone was heaving in the net which was jumping with cavalli. 'A good catch boy!' Jonah shouted over the crash of the sea onto the steep beach.

That light which is before the dawn, came through the mist and spray, as they all encouraged each other with the heaving of the seine out of the sea onto the beach. *Corbeaux* were landing to guzzle the dead pickings.

Suddenly, on the wind, was a squall blowing off the gulf, swirling into the bay, causing the sea to swell and crash. The pirogues were heaved up and then let down. The pullers of the seine were slipping in the sand and falling back onto the beach. They managed in time to haul in the seine and transfer the cavalli to the other pirogue which would take the fish back to El Caracol.

Madeleine was worried about the time. Would she get back to the convent before the Angelus?

The men were eager to save the boats from being dashed against the shore. They were heaving them up the steep beach, running them along on logs, winching them up.

Then the rain came in, lashing the coast. Rain and spray. With the dark and pulsing light before the dawn, they were completely cut off.

Bolo, Elroy and Jonah, with Theo in fast attendance, built a shelter of coconut palms raised by bamboo poles they found on the beach. Madeleine and Vincent retreated to the fisherman's ajoupa, their earlier haven.

Time ceased here, under the coconut palms and the drip of the rain in the bush. They sat huddled together, staring at nothing. They were all ears.

'Can you hear them growing?' Madeleine mused.

'Growing?' Vincent was astonished.

'The baby turtles. They grow with the waves pounding onto the beach. This is what they will know most of all, this beach and the sound of the sea. To get to the sea will be their strongest instinct. To return here, to lay their own eggs, will be their strongest instinct too, a generational cycle going on and on. A repeated journey,' Madeleine spoke amazedly.

Then, words ceased. And time also, as they knew it, stopped.

Madeleine was kneeling in the sand. Vincent came up behind her and cradled her. She leant back into him. Over her shoulder, he could see the task that she was engaged in. She had discovered some hatching turtles burrowing out of the sand in one of the earlier sites. She had decided to help them. 'Look,' she said, 'they'll never make it.'

Circling overhead, were the corbeaux and the gulls.

'It's a cruel outcome,' she lamented.

'Nature's way?' Vincent said philosophically.

'You always say that.'

'What else is there to say.'

'We could enable them to survive.'

'We could, but we couldn't save them all. And would that be the right thing?' Vincent looked back at the beach. 'If they were all saved!'

The beach was strewn with debris of birthing.

'It's the survival of the fittest,' Vincent concluded.

'It's a matter of luck,' Madeleine replied.

'Chance, maybe,' Vincent qualified.

'The fittest may die.'

'Yes, the fittest may die,' Vincent concluded.

He watched her kneeling in the sand digging, and then with her skirt full of baby turtles, hurrying to where the dunes slid to the hard shore. There she released them to make their own journey, the rest of the way into the water, shooing off the predatory corbeaux, the pecking gulls and inquisitive sandpipers.

'They know only the sea. Look, at how strong their small fins are.' He watched her freeing them from her skirts.

It seemed as if at one moment the gulf was empty, and in the next, it was filled with destroyers and mine sweepers. They were transported from a desert island to a theatre of war. A Barracuda reminded them of waking at night to the boom of thunder in the distance.

Thérèse slipped through the palms in her nun's cloak, up the steps from the jetty at the first toll of the Angelus. She did not turn to wave. She and Vincent had not decided what they would do next. She did not know if any of her sisters had been watching, and seen her naked ankles, as she gathered her nun's cloak over her cotton frock with the blue forget-me-nots.

The Thunder Again

Lieutenant Jesse Morrison walked out of the darkness at the back of the Doctor's House. He had come down the path where the sorrel bushes had grown at Christmas time, but which was now a dry bank of yellowing, scorched grass.

He entered by the back door. 'Hello, hello,' he called, carrying his saxophone. Its brass gleam glinted where it picked up the stuttering flame from the kerosene lantern.

The generators had just been turned off. This was part of the new curfew.

Madeleine was sitting at the dining-room table, bent over a microscope in the glow of the humming lantern. 'Oh, hello, we met on the beach, last August,' Jesse reminded her.

She looked up without answering. He stared at her now more than ever. 'This is a beauty.' He pointed at the microscope.

'My father's.' She stroked the stand. Vincent had brought it over for her use, now that she was stationed in the hills. She had arrived one night, and now slept in the Doctor's house.

Jesse remembered this bald nun at La Tinta, in her dress. Her hair had grown. It was not his business to judge.

'Good evening, Lieutenant.' She greeted him now without raising her head, keeping some of that composure which went with being a nun, despite her thin muslin dress, her bare arms, her black hair, growing by the minute it seemed, falling over her eyes; her naked feet tied in a knot under her chair. Her veil and habit were in the room upstairs.

'Hi yuh, there, Doc. Good evening to you, Sir,' Jesse called to Vincent whom he now noticed out on the verandah.

'Good night, Lieutenant. You come to entertain us?'

'Man, you hear those guys, those fishermen, like Jonah with their bottle and spoon, beating out those calypsos? That tune, man. Man, they got me itching to blow. I like their humour and their message. Those fellas are ready for carnival.'

'If you're off duty, why don't you stay and share our supper? Or, maybe, I should check with Theo. He's the cook tonight.'

'That's already checked. The boy was up at the Look Out this afternoon. I'm here on his invitation.' Jesse eased himself into a Morris chair, positioning the saxophone on his knee.

'Oh, I see. Well, it's not for me to interfere, then.' Vincent stubbed out his cigarette. A silence fell between the two men. Vincent lit another cigarette. Jesse noticed his nervousness. He looked over his shoulder to where Madeleine's bent back told a story of labour and research.

'She's moved in?' Jesse spoke quietly.

'She stays.' Vincent pulled on his cigarette.

Changing the subject, Vincent said, 'Just heard about the torpedoing of one of the ships on the bauxite run from British Guiana?'

'Yep. She went down in the seas off Galera Point, the most dangerous, they estimate.'

'All gone down to the bottom of the sea. No survivors,' Theo joined in, coming out from the kitchen.

The boy's stories were often a mixture of tragedy and excitement, as he made these announcements, faintly imitating the news announcer, but mixed with his own sense of ironic absurdity. Then he laughed at his imitative efforts. 'There were no survivors reported.' He pursed his lips to mimic a BBC accent. Then, he was gone, out of the room, back to the kitchen.

'They took her out of the water. The fireball could be seen at quite a distance. Some heard the explosion, even here,' Jesse said. He played softly on his sax.

Madeleine cleared her things from the dining-room table, making room for Theo to lay for supper.

The men glanced at each other as she passed through the verandah. They watched her descend the steps, reach the boardwalk and sit on the small wooden bench under the jetty house. She pulled her skirt about her legs as it blew up in the sea breeze. She pulled her fringe from her eyes. She scraped her jet black hair up from the nape of her neck. Then she let it fall thickly alongside her face.

Jesse had questions to ask, Vincent did not have the answers, but was looking for his reactions.

Jesse spoke first, calling after Madeleine. 'Take some fresh air, Sis.' He tried to break the ice. She did not acknowledge his voice. She was not in a mood for his familiarity.

Vincent had noticed the way she chose the end of the jetty. It had become her spot. She was tasting her freedom, or pretending to explore it, like using her name Madeleine while she was in the house. At dawn, she would be slipping away in her nun's habit, making sure her long hair was tidied away beneath her skull cap and veil. Then she would become Sister Thérèse again. How long could this secrecy continue?

'We'll be eating soon,' he called down to her. He was trying to understand her isolation, since she had come to stay in his house, to sleep in his room, in his bed. He wanted her to be free. The other spare room was hers. He wanted her to choose again, so that these nights might be spent on her own, or with him. He loved when she did choose him in the night, chose his bed, coming across the landing in her white cotton chemise, her bare feet on the pitch pine floor. She mostly began the night in her own room. That way she felt that she was fooling Theo.

It was like being at her improvised desk at the dining room table, her head bent over her microscope, magnifying the secret life of *mycrobacterium leprae*. She could pretend that nothing had changed as regards her research. She could feel less lost in the Doctor's House.

It was not sufficient to be Vincent's lover. Not that she would call herself that. Most of it was unsaid. There had not been much choice. Then she wondered what the alternatives could be, the ones put to her to threaten her. There was either the choice to live under a cloud in the community, as had started after the incident at La Tinta, or fending for herself in Porta España, while her papers were being processed, and that could take up to a year because of the poor communication in wartime.

The Archbishop had come up with a room in the Magdalen House for the naughty girls, which the sisters ran in the city, in Freetown, she had been told. That could have sealed her fate. Madeleine refused that option also.

Choosing this clandestine life meant that she had not had to make any choices, irrevocably. This of course could jeopardise Vincent's job. Once they could find a replacement for him, they would both have to choose. In the meantime, they both decided to push ahead with their research here at the Doctor's House. But Vincent missed her on the wards. The patients took a surprisingly neutral position on the matter. 'Say howdy to Sister Thérèse, Doctor.' What did they know? How careful they had to be. He smiled at their innocence. There was always rumour in a small place.

On the jetty, Madeleine could have a view of the convent, and behind her, the house, which was now a kind of new home, a half-way house. It was a place from which to look at where she had come from, and a place to wonder what her future would be.

The tune on Jesse's saxophone was a mournful tune of loss and abandonment. More than ever now, she felt like a motherless child. Separating herself from her sisters brought back thoughts of her mother, how much she felt her death, finding refuge with the sisters at her school, and then in the novitiate.

There was no moon, and the darkness swallowed her.

Jesse's playing conjured his story which Vincent had heard of from Theo, and which Jesse himself had begun to speak about at La Tinta. Sitting here on an island in the confines of a bay, a place with distances and horizons opened up. Theo came and stood by the verandah. Madeleine came up and sat on the steps. The music sang of the cotton and tobacco fields, about the crops in the spring and the fall. It was the wind among tobacco leaves in the spring, in the cotton ready for picking in the fall. It was the red of maple trees up north.

The saxophone moaned for the hot trumpet of the trains which travelled north, bawling in the fading distance.

'You blow that good, Jesse. You want a rum?'

'I won't say no, Doc.' There was a kind of distance that the men kept as they got closer. They felt more than they spoke.

'Theo, we got time for a rum? Or is that cocoa hot now? Are those bakes ready?'

'If all you ready, it ready. But, I can bring you a rum first. I still have to swizzle in the vanilla and cinnamon.' He turned into the house, returned with two glasses and a bottle of brown rum. He put them on the small table between the chairs of the two men. He opened the bottle, pouring a couple of drops to the floor for the spirits, then filling the two glasses.

'I like the way you do that, boy,' Jesse said admiringly.

'What you mean? When I throw it on the floor? Is so we does do it before I reach here. Is I who teach Doctor to pay observance. Mama say...' Then he stopped himself, looking at both men, from one to the other, as if he had slipped up, let the cat out of the bag.

Then he just let himself speak as if the music had loosed his tongue. 'That is a whole new geography, yes, pappy! I done leave Pepper Hill, Gran Couva, Tortuga up in the Montserrat Hills, beyond Brasso Pedro, with the *coco panol* music, bottle and spoon, cuatro. I done leave San Jose, La Vega, San Juan, Josefito. I with you Jesse, boy.' Theo had not shown quite this degree of familiarity before. 'I with you on them dusty plains with howling coyotes. It like film I see with Mama, and Spanish, in Couva. Them people does live in a big country, yes, man. That is what Spanish tell Mama when we walking home along the road to Pepper Hill.' Theo stopped. He looked about him astonished. Jesse, Vincent and Madeleine were staring up at him. 'Play Jesse, play, nuh, man.' He sped off to the kitchen.

'He's a great one at the repeated tale,' Vincent explained.

'Yes, Sir. Repeated journeys.'

'What's your repeated journey, Lieutenant?'

'Mine? Well, I guess, it's a dream I have.'

'A recurring dream?'

'Yeh, I had it as a boy. But it's coming back now, regular, since I'm in the forces. Since I went North to school, to do my training.'

'Leaving the familiar, you look back over the past,' Vincent reflected.

'Something like that. You're a philosophical guy, Doc. I'm down by Granma's homestead. That's in the Carolinas, and I go round the house to the back porch, where my Grandpa's chopping wood. That's my Ma's Pa. Sometimes it's just that. And I think, why do I keep dreaming of my Grandma's homestead, and my Grandpa's chopping wood outside the back porch?'

'That's quite innocent,' Vincent commented.

'Right.'

'So?' Vincent encouraged the retelling.

'But then it sometimes continues, and my Grandpa is sitting on the porch steps with a sax. He's blowing. I never get to hear the tune. Only, he got no fingers. Them keys is pressed invisibly. In another version it's the same. Only, the sax is bleeding.'

'Bleeding? What's behind that dream?'

'Well, I know that my Grandpa taught me to play the sax. My Grandma,

298

and my Ma before that, told me that he was a great player in his time, jumping tracks and going from town to town. He played in sets with some of the greatest. But, I remember once he told me that the guys used to call him No Fingers. "Hi there, No Fingers," they would say. He had a way of pressing down those keys with his knuckles. It was painful to watch and painful in truth. No one knew how he did that, and still play the music. Him got his fingers broken when he was a young boy, broken on some ranch he worked on. You know, deliberately. They smashed his fingers.'

'Who?' Vincent inquired.

'Him who owned the ranch. It was a ranch and a cotton mill. They jammed his fingers in some machinery, on purpose.'

'Who?'

'My Grandpa was an enslaved man.'

Vincent listened in awe, as the negro Lieutenant told the story of his dream and of his Grandpa's life, intermittently blowing on his saxophone, his fingers moving invisibly in the dark over the keys.

A silence ticked in the house, disturbed only by the sea, sucking on the rocks, gulping round the pylons of the jetty, where the shadow of Madeleine rustled the darkness, where she had continued to sit on the steps combing out her hair.

'Madeleine?' Vincent pulled her away from herself.

'What stories! I'm so moved by your story and Theo's story,' Madeleine looked up.

'You have a story, I bet.' Jesse stopped himself remembering their first meeting at La Tinta and wondering about this strange woman.

Vincent smiled and took her hand.

The night was close.

Theo came out of the kitchen, carrying a tray with hot bakes and a blue enamel jug of frothing cocoa. They all turned and saw him and got up off their chairs on the verandah, and went into the dining room.

'Your fingers are fine?' Vincent smiled, speaking to Jesse again.

'Yes, Sir, my fingers are the fingers they took from him. They're my Grandpa's fingers. My Mama always say that. "Son, she say, you've got them fingers, Mungo picked up from the yard." Mungo was a lad that worked with my Grandpa. He was there when my Grandpa's fingers got chopped. He held the bloody fingers in his hand, my Ma say. They hurried, and it was a Dr Du

Bois who stitched them back on. But they grow funny. Imagine, them two, Mungo and my Grandpa, hurrying down the dirt road to Dr Du Bois. Them red stumps jumping, Mungo careful they don't fall in the dirt again. My Ma say, she was a little girl at the time. She have all them stories, and more stories, she hear from my Grandma. It's so it goes, where I come from, Doc.' Jesse took a last blow on his sax as they came into the dining room.

'You play well.' Vincent did not know what to say about the story, so appalling in Jesse's matter of fact, comic telling, so awesome with the sax for accompaniment.

'Oh, I ent play yet.' Jesse laughed aloud.

Theo hovered, listening to the two men, and pulling out a chair for Madeleine.

'Those bakes smell good, Theo. Thank you.' Madeleine looked at the boy appreciatively, enjoying his attention. He stared and moved the jug of cocoa nearer to Vincent to pour for Jesse, Madeleine and himself.

'And you Theo, you joining us?' Jesse asked.

Theo hovered round the table making sure they all had what they wanted, and then went back into the kitchen without answering. He had overwhelmed himself talking out on the verandah.

'Theo, you going to learn sax?' Vincent called out. But it really was something said for Jesse to pick up on.

'I done ask him that. I would be pleased to pass on what I know about this instrument to so bright a boy.' Jesse looked at Vincent and smiled glowingly, speaking loudly, so that Theo was bound to hear from the kitchen.

'And what did he say?'

Theo re-entered the dining room.

'You learn what you want to, *mon garçon.*' Madeleine smiled at him when he gave her one of the few linen napkins from the Metivier trunk under the stairs.

Theo returned to the kitchen. He had no intention of joining the table this evening. But he was in and out, hovering round the shoulders of the diners. Everything had to be just so for Miss Madeleine, and there was Jesse from the Look Out, whom he was strangely ignoring, letting him speak for himself; something Jesse could do.

Madeleine had a new name now, and Theo was the first to give her that position, Vincent noticed. She was the mistress of the house, conferred by him.

Vincent and Madeleine exchanged glances, as Jesse carried on with his long tales. They could hear Theo clanging about in the kitchen. 'You not coming to eat, Theo?' Vincent called. There was a greater banging of pots and pans.

'I don't know what to believe when the boy is telling his stories,' Jesse continued.

Vincent and Madeleine smiled, trying to get a word in. But Jesse was in full flood. They looked embarrassed as the American GI went on and on. Madeleine looked towards the kitchen door, expecting Theo to re-enter the room at any moment.

'He seems to have infected you, Lieutenant,' Vincent laughed. They all three laughed together. Jesse realised that he had been going on and on, much like Theo. The boy was still out in the kitchen.

'Yes. No, I tell you. He talks, at the drop of a hat. Then he starts humming one of those calypso tunes that you hear the fishermen singing. He just makes me want to go to that island of Sancta Trinidad, up in those places that he makes sound so magical.' He laughed with his mouth full of bake.

Vincent and Madeleine smiled, a little embarrassed, and ate their bakes and drank their cocoa. Theo remained hidden in the gloom of the kitchen, listening to Jesse's voice.

It was then that they all heard the explosion. Theo ran in from the kitchen. Vincent, Madeleine and Jesse threw back their chairs and went out onto the verandah. The empty night sky over the gulf outside Chac Chac Bay flared up orange and red like a late sunset. It was as if the whole island shone. No one had seen light like that before, transfiguring the hills and the metallic sea. It was as if the archipelago were throwing up a new island from its volcanic ridge. 'Boy, what was that?' Vincent exclaimed. 'Take care, you fall, Theo, in the darkness.' Theo had sped out of the house, almost as quickly as he had heard the explosion, as if he had been waiting on his cue. He was on the jetty in a moment, skipping the steps and reaching the boards in no time.

'That was a fireball!' Jesse exclaimed. 'That's a ship, some ship, somewhere near, hit by a torpedo. Sounds real real close.' Jesse had climbed onto the banister of the verandah, to see if that could help his vision in any way. But they could not see around Point Girod to where the explosion and the light had come from.

'Must be out in the gulf, inside the *bocas*,' Vincent suggested. 'Inside the Boca del Drago.'

'Yep, sure sounds like that. You got a pirogue here?' Jesse had jumped into complete GI role. He was half figuring whether he should return to his station.

'Yes. Theo, untie the pirogue.' Vincent called, going down the steps to the jetty. Madeleine and Jesse followed him. Theo was thrilled with the excitement of being and moving with Vincent and Jesse.

'God, what was that? Take care, Theo,' Madeleine called with her caution. The bay lit up the open gulf for second, like an apparition.

'It's the flares to detect the casualities after a bombing. Let's go out to the entrance of the bay,' Jesse suggested.

They waited for Theo, by this time in the pirogue, pulling in the anchor. 'The flares have died down, but we should see some burning wreck, somewhere round that point. There must be men in life rafts in the water. It's so quiet. You'd expect to hear bombers in the air. Where are those Albacores, those Barracudas?' Jesse was explaining the routine.

They all got into the pirogue. Madeleine sat in the stern. Theo sat in the bow. Vincent positioned himself at the centre next to Jesse. They both took the oars, fitting them into the rollocks. They needed speed. The sound of the oars grinding in the rollocks, and the dip of the oars in the water, was an added music to the night. There was the plunge and then the grind. There was the heavy breathing of the men.

'Better put out the lantern,' Madeleine said, bending to snuff out the flame. There was a whiff of kerosene.

There were no lights on at the convent, or at Saint Damian's. Voices and cries came from the hospital. Vincent felt that he should be there. The children would be terrified. The nuns would be praying. The old folks would be battened down in their dark huts. Now and then there was the faint glow of a pitch oil flambeaux. Fear called for light, despite the regulations. The far thunder had not come this close before.

As they rounded Point Girod they could see the harbour of Porta España on fire. There was no moon, only the clear sky of stars and the milky way. As they grew accustomed to the darkness, they could see the outline of Sancta Trinidad, and then the other islands in the archipelago, like the backs of whales.

The sky became filled with the drone of bombers over the gulf. 'Here they come, at last!' Jesse cried out, shouting in jubilation, leaving his oar, and crouching behind Theo in the bow, to instruct the boy in the war planes. They could hear the faint wail of sirens.

'They're scanning the waters for targets.'

Jesse dropped the anchor. 'Should take a hold on the rocks. The water near the cove is shallow. We don't want to drift out into the boca or get thrown against the rocks.'

Theo was all eyes. Still perched in the bow, looking towards the burning harbour, he kept looking round to Vincent and Jesse for reassurance. He kept an eye on Madeleine, smiling at each other.

Jesse explained in low tones what might be happening. 'They're looking for signs of the enemy but also for casualities. Those are anti-submarine aircraft out on the gulf, and those ships are scanning the ocean floor with their Asdic sets for submarines. I bet there's been a U-Boat attack. Unbelievable! How could it have got through the bocas?' Jesse sounded uncomprehending.

The GI and the boy were caught up in the excitement of the moment. Theo was still keeping an eye on Madeleine.

'How it cross the magnetic loop?' Theo remembered his lesson at the Look Out. The loop lay on the ocean floor, between El Caracol and the island of Huevos.

'Yes, exactly. How could a U-Boat cross without the defences knowing?' Jesse repeated his lesson.

Madeleine sat without saying a word. Mention of a German U-Boat alarmed her. Vincent turned to look at her. All talk of the war fired her imagination, conjured her father.

They heard its engine before they saw it, moving nearby in the darkness. They could feel the pirogue rocking because of the wake that came in from the open sea, to rock them in the cove where they were hidden. They were hammocked in the swell.

It was Theo's young eyes. He whispered sharply, 'Look! Something, there, moving through the water. I can hardly see it,' he whispered. Vincent and Jesse followed the direction of his arm and the pointed finger, rigid with intent, with an accuracy with which it wanted to pin down the moving shape in the water. Madeleine crouched behind them, getting up from the stern. They were a tight group, staring into the darkness.

It was Jesse who recognised what it was. Accustomed to his watch at the Look Out, with the artillery guns trained on the sea, precisely for these targets, he recognised the conning tower, just above the dimly lit water.

'Look like a whale,' Theo whispered.

'I hope those guys have got it in their sights.' Jesse expressed the frustration of a soldier. The others watched with their own thoughts of disbelief. At first, it seemed to be coming straight at them. Then, it was making for the open ocean, through the Boca de Navios.

Escaping this way, it ran no danger of setting off signals. 'Those bombers have lost it. Jesus Christ!' Jesse was beside himself.

They held their breaths and watched. 'Look, do you see him?' It was Theo who first saw the figure, standing on the open deck below the coning tower. He was bending to fix something.

Madeleine crouched behind Vincent, staring over his shoulder. They were so close. She saw distinctly, the blond hair of the German sailor. As if from deep inside of her, she began to hear that love song she had heard that night, when she had looked from her cell at the convent, and saw the German sailor on the deck of the training ship. Instinctively she sung the words *'Ja, ja, die Liebe ist's allein, die Liebe, die Liebe ist's allein.* Yes, yes.'

'Shush, please, he'll hear.' Jesse was biting his lip in frustration.

Madeleine felt the love song flee across the water to the blond sailor.

'If I'd been at the Look Out, I'd have blown her out of the water.' Jesse changed the tone.

Vincent and Theo stared at him in shock. Vincent thought of the young man swinging his saxophone through the kitchen door earlier that evening. He too had his love songs.

Madeleine went back to her seat in the stern. The drone of the U-Boat grew fainter. They were left rocking in the swell of its wake.

Jesse lost the coning tower as the submarine dived just outside the *boca*, safe now, in the depths of the Atlantic.

Theo looked over his shoulder to where the U-Boat had dipped away. 'He reach the ocean,' he said, with a big O.

Voices In The Dark

Jesse could not wait to get back to the Look Out, to make his report. 'See you tomorrow, boy.' Then he hurried through the house, out the back, into the darkness, into the bush.

Vincent prepared to visit Saint Damian's, and decided he would row himself there. He did not like going out on his own, even into the bay. But he felt that if he hugged the shore closely, past the Chaplain's house, he would be safe.

'Theo, I want you to go to sleep now. I've got to go and check things at the hospital.'

'I can't sleep now, Doc.'

'I want you and Madeleine to look after each other.' As he left to go downstairs, he saw that the boy was already lying across his bed under the mosquito net, plugged into his crystal set. What a night he had had! Vincent stood for a moment at the door and watched Theo's breathing, as he had done so many times before. He stared at his naked back with its serrated scar; a story still to be told, or maybe never to be told.

Madeleine was waiting on the jetty. She had the dinghy ready for him. It was easier to row the smaller craft than the heavy pirogue. 'Let me come with you,' she pleaded.

'I need you to stay here with the boy. Would not be safe for us to arrive together in the middle of the night.'

'But, Vincent....'

He saw her distress, the reasons for it. He was caught between his responsibility for his patients, and her need. In the past, he would have wanted nothing more than to have her at his side. 'Madeleine, sweetheart.' He reached out, almost capsizing the dinghy.

Their changed circumstances did not allow for Madeleine to be at the hospital with him. They both knew that. Her fear, created by the explosion, and seeing the German U-Boat with the blond sailor, recalling her earlier experience just before the war, left her terrified. She crouched, and leaned forward to take his hand. Vincent caught his balance. 'I need you to be strong, to be here, for Theo. Go up to bed.'

'Yes, I understand. Take care. But they're my patients too.'

'I know. But it's better I go alone.'

Then he could not leave her, as he saw her eyes fill with tears. Her fear was more than she could cope with.

Vincent could see the terror on her face, hear the agitation in her voice, notice the darting of her eyes. She was overcome with her responsibility for Theo. Something that as a nurse would have seemed like routine had become overwhelming.

Then the memory, the image of the U-Boat moving through the black waters of the bocas, a hundred yards from where they were anchored, alarmed him more and he became infected with her fear.

He clambered back onto the jetty. Together, they looked out towards where more flares lit up the night sky, as the search for the U-Boat continued. In each other's arms, standing at the edge of the jetty, they listened to the drone of the anti-submarine bombers, which were still circling the gulf, now spreading their search further into the *bocas*.

'It's too late. They've escaped,' Vincent said.

'Who's escaped?'

'The Germans.'

'What do you mean?' She was puzzled.

'You know?'

It was as if she had suddenly banished the incident from her mind.

The men who manned the U-Boat would be the same men who occupied her country, her *France*. They would be the same men who were part of her nightmare in which her father was caught. They were the same men who drove through her French village, in those dreams, in fast black Citroens, with machine guns poking out of the windows. They were the same men, on whose straining leads barking Alsatians woke her in her hut in the hills, hounds which had caught the scent of their quarry, worrying it into the thicket of her dreams, where they had gone to earth. The same men gave out the statutory yellow stars.

In one dream, she had told him, it was Marcel, with a rifle at the door, with the *gendarmes*. He was not hunting rabbits anymore.

How could he know the images which besieged her mind? Where did the stories come from that she told herself?

Rising out of a wood, there was a clatter of rooks. There was a line of cypresses. She and a young boy running there, in their excitement at going into the woods, found that it was peopled with others who were hiding, resisting the advance of a terrible army. She heard the tramp of their boots across the fields, down the village lane.

As Vincent, again, entered with his imagination into the nightmares of Madeleine, he saw them in her face and eyes, in her fingers scraping the wall of the jetty house, digging into the pits of the broken masonry. He put his hands over hers to stop the fury. 'Madeleine, sweetheart.'

They stood like that, looking out to sea, in the darkness, with the flares still burning over Porta España. This was the nature of their love: passion and comfort. He comforted her.

Madeleine turned to look at him. 'Will we be safe?'

'I think so.'

'You saw that man on the U-Boat before it dived?'

'Yes, there was one, closing the hatch after him, disappearing, and then the sea closed over the deck.'

'You saw what he looked like?' she persisted

'It was difficult to see. It was dark.'

'You know, his uniform? A naval officer's hat? A face?'

'No, sorry. I hardly saw him.'

'How could you not see him? His blond hair, his blue eyes, his smile. He was the one, who sang to me beneath the window of my cell, at Embarcadère Corbeaux. *DIe Liebe, die Liebe ist's allein.*'

'You want some piece of reality, some evidence, something to tell you that your dreams are true.'

'Or not true. *C'est l'amour, c'est l'amour seul.*'

'I love you.'

She looked sad and then smiled. *'C'est l'amour seul.'*

They both looked to where the flares over Porta España were now a dull glow, beyond the island of Gasparee. The drone of the bombers had stopped. The frogs pinged and the insects sung.

In that moment, with the singing night around them, with the intermittent barking of a dog, Vincent and Madeleine turned towards each other. He held her. She was close to his chest, his beating heart, his bare arms, his open shirt, his naked neck. He was close to her face, no longer cocooned in cotton. There was her face and her hands, her arms and legs as he swooped up her flimsy skirt. There were her breasts, her new body. She called it that when she came to his bed. 'I bring you my new body.' They did not resist the moment now, as they made for the jetty house and lay on the hard bench. He felt her heavy black hair, her soft face, released from its taut constrictions. Madeleine felt the unshaven cheek of her doctor. Their moment was hesitant, even now, and then they chose their lips. His tongue found her open mouth, his fingers the salt of her wet flower, and then they forgot where they were.

Around them, the darkness. Out there, the war. Not far away, there were sounds which came from a world that they shared in their nursing and doctoring, a child's cry, the pain of the disfigured. Their world rearranged itself, and settled around them.

'Let me go now. Try and sleep.' Vincent lowered himself into the dinghy.

'I love you.' She watched him disappear into the darkness.

She sat at her dressing table brushing out her hair. There was a knock at the door. It was Theo. 'Can't you sleep? Come, sit. Tell me what you're thinking.'

'What you thinking? I watch you sitting, brushing your hair. You look lost.'

'Looking at myself in the mirror, I thought how much like my mother I was becoming. I'm becoming my mother.' She smiled at him in the mirror.

'What you mean? You're becoming your mother? You can't do that. You could do that?'

'You know what I mean. Not literally. Of course not.' He was staring intently at her.

'Where is your mother?' he asked.

'My mother? She's in heaven.' Then Madeleine thought she was patronising the boy. 'She's dead.'

Theo quickly changed the subject. 'So what else you thinking about?'

'I was back in the Place de la Mairie in the village of Saint Jacques de la Campagne, where we went in summer; my mother's parent's home. Behind the house, the village falls away into a gorge. Deep, over the flat rocks, the cold water hurtles down from the icy heights.'

'The Alps? Snow! I learn about that.'

'Beyond the steep gorge, above the rocky cliffs, are fields. I liked to sit and watch the sun go down on the evening from that window. The rows and rows of lavender, so purple in the light. A blue mist.'

Theo was looking at Madeleine as she brushed her hair. 'You miss that place. You mother bury there?'

'Yes. She's buried there. When I was a little girl, she used to stand behind me with a brush, telling me a story, brushing out my knots.'

'You want me to brush your hair?'

Madeleine giggled. 'Okay, if you want to try. Don't pull it hard.'

'I know how to do it. Watch.' Theo stood behind her and pulled the brush gently through Madeleine's hair.

'That's good.'

'I know how to do this thing. I used to do it so for girl I know.'

'A girlfriend?'

'Nah. Just a girl.'

'Christiana? Your school friend.'

'Not she. Not she.'

Madeleine realised her error. 'Well, did she have a name?' Madeleine looked at Theo behind her in the mirror.

'Chantal.'

'That's a pretty name.'

'She, yea, she pretty.'

'You don't sound sure.'

'Yes, she pretty. Man!' Then Theo seemed distracted. 'I tired do this. Anyway, it looking good now.'

'Okay.' She took the brush for him.

Theo walked over to the window and peeped through the blackouts.

'Maybe we should try and sleep now,' Madeleine suggested.

'I can't sleep.'

'I know. A lot has happened tonight.'

'I still seeing that submarine.'

'Try and sleep. My eyes are closing up.' She got up from the dressing table. 'Good night.'

'Don't let mosquitoes bite.' They laughed. Theo left her room.

Eventually, Madeleine slept, but was woken suddenly by the moan of a plane. She lay back and listened to the sea in the bay, then, again, fell asleep. Once, she thought she heard footsteps on the landing outside her room.

It did not take Vincent long to row, hugging the coast, below Father Meyer's house. He was careful not to show any light, mainly because of the military activity in the wake of the attack. He did not want the Coast Guard coming into the bay to caution him. The lap of the oars disturbed a *jumbie* bird. The feathery owl flapped away into the higher *gommier* trees off the wet branches of the sea grapes leaning into the water.

As he approached Saint Damian's, Vincent could see a figure standing at the end of the jetty. As he got closer, he realised it was Sister Rita. 'Sister.' Vincent threw the rope.

'I've got it.' The pirogue knocked the jetty, where there had been tyres to break the thud. They had all been burnt.

'Thanks, Sister.' Vincent heaved himself up to stand next to her. 'You've obviously been alerted to the attack?'

'Is that what it is? I woke with the explosion, and then lay awake listening for something else. There was silence in the convent, and then Mother Superior was knocking on the door of my cell. It was then that I could hear the cries coming from the hospital. Myself and Sister Marie-Paul were deployed to take the pirogue and row across the bay. There was no time to alert the boat man with the launch. Luckily, it is very calm tonight. We took it in turns to row. It can be choppy as you cross in front of La Tinta, as you know.'

Vincent watched her tell her story in a graphic, animated way, trying to control her fear. He admired these women and that confused him, because he did not believe in what they believed in, except their dedication to care and healing.

'Yes, it seems that a German U-Boat has attacked one or more vessels in the harbour at Porta España,' he said.

'We could see the flares, as we came into the open bay out of La Chapelle.' She turned and pointed to the open sea of the gulf. There was still burning like the last of a sunset.

'Where is Sister Marie-Paul now?' Vincent asked.

'She's with the children. I came down here to see if I could make out anymore about the disturbance. I've been up to the huts, and tried to quieten the fears of the women. I expected to see Sister Thérèse there.'

'You know she goes to the very farthest huts. She's got sleeping accommodation there,' Vincent explained.

'Yes, of course. I just thought, that with the disturbance, I would've seen her. Jonah and Mr Singh were checking the patients. The young girl Christiana was with them.'

'I see.' Vincent did not know what Sister Rita knew, if anything, about Thérèse sleeping over at the house.

'Docta, Sister.' Sister Rita and Vincent turned suddenly into the darkness behind, from where the voice had come. Rattling on the gravel, the figure of Ti-Jean, on his crutches, appeared out of the gloom.

'Ti-Jean, what are you doing out of bed?'

'I hear the bomb.'

'Is not a bomb, Ti-Jean.'

'I thought I see you come in a pirogue. I up on the verandah. Watching. Then, I ent see you. So, I come to look for you.'

'Did you? You saw me. You have eye like *jumbie* bird.' Vincent loved the boy.

'I come down the steps, and I thought I hear a voice, and then is you and Sister I see.'

'Did you?' Vincent pulled the boy towards him. He tottered on his crutches. But he could not quieten him, nor comfort him for the moment.

'Yes, I'fraid doctor. I'fraid too bad.'

'Come here, Ti-Jean.' His crutches clattered on the concrete path as Ti-Jean clung to him. 'Too bad, too bad, yes, doctor.' He was usually so fearless, Vincent thought.

'Okay, there's nothing to be afraid of.' Vincent hugged the boy. 'Here, take your crutches, let's all go up to the hospital and see how Sister Marie-Paul is getting on with the others.'

Vincent and Sister Rita walked up to the hospital with Ti-Jean between them. 'Come on, Hop-Along-Cassidy.' Ti-Jean's limp was worse than ever.

Vincent made all well. Or that is what he hoped, as he got Ti-Jean back to bed.

On his return to the house, after seeing that all was safe, Vincent found Theo at the window of his bedroom. 'Theo, have you managed to sleep?'

There was no reply. Vincent could see that the bed had been slept in. He

311

pulled up the mosquito net and lay back on the boy's bed. 'If you're not sleeping I'm going to drop off right here.'

He was woken by Theo's voice. Had he been sleeping a few minutes or an hour? Vincent could not tell. The boy was at the window with his back to him. It was not his usual tale telling voice. It was more straightforward. The scar on the boy's back was a ladder to the nape of his neck.

'Theo, you telling me something?'

It was like listening to sleep.

I TELL YOU, I see Achilles at the periscope. He have our island in his sight. He see us from where he is, under the ocean wave. He know the *boca*. He know the gulf. He give us the slip.

They get the signal when he cross the magnetic loop, deeper than the cold current. Deeper than a shoal of cavalli. He come to rest on the sea bed. He wait and wait all afternoon for the darkness of the night. He only hearing ping, ping.

Through the water, the sound of the anti-submarine trawling for his silver fish in Orinoco water. An iron killer whale!

They give up the search. They scan the sea from the sky.

I there when he reach the proper depth and send the periscope up. The coast clear. The darkness complete. He break the surface. I there too when he climb out of the hatch. The cool breeze in his face. I there. I see him. He tall and blond with blue eyes.

What he see is the Mokihana all the way from Baltimore in Maryland. She have cargo to unload before she sail for the East.

Achilles line up his ship with the Mokihana. She is his target. The sea calm like a pond. Darkness hide him. Fishing pirogues anchor in the gulf. *Flambeaux* burning so close, he smell the kerosene. The torpedo ready. She shake. He give an order to starboard, the rudder swing, and she shudder. She let loose another torpedo.

Now the Mokihana explode. Is a mountain of water in the air.

Siren bawl. Achilles dive. It too shallow. He get stick in the mud. He break the surface again. He run for the *bocas*.

I there, looking into his blue eye, and seeing his blond hair blowing in the breeze. He dive into the ocean.

Theo stopped his story exactly where Vincent could continue with what he himself had witnessed. Theo walked across the room, entered the bed and curled up next to the doctor and slept.

Madeleine watched them both from where she stood at the door, listening with her fear.

Vincent woke to Madeleine stroking his brow, humming a tune. '*Oui, oui, c'est seul, c'est l'amour, c'est l'amour seul.*' The room was flooded with sunlight, and then shadow; shadows of leaves, shadows of branches of leaves as the light cotton curtains lifted with the sea breeze.

A cock crowed in the distance.

She sat at the top of the bed, and raised Vincent's head onto her lap. The boy's body was flung sideways across the bed, having kicked off his pyjamas as usual. He lay on his stomach. She stared at his scar.

Listening to the boy's tale last night, the first she had heard, allowed her to dispel her fear, to rid herself, for the moment at least, of her panic and dread. The story had saved her. But the tune she hummed, as she got ready to leave, was still the love song of the blue-eyed, blond-haired sailor.

She rested Vincent's head on the pillow and left the room, got dressed in her religious habit. Then, she slipped out of the kitchen door, tucking her hair firmly beneath her skull cap and veil. She was now, again, Sister Thérèse, girdling herself with her rosary beads, as she crossed the scorched sorrel patch, and entered the bush for the hills.

The Last Things

What Theo had called Achilles' killer whale, the sleek silver fish which had nosed its way into the Porta España harbour, torpedoing the Mokihana from Maryland in Baltimore, had also blown a hole in the routines of Saint Damian's. This iron whale was now more famous than the first natural one, which had been beached at La Tinta. While that one had brought a sense of wonder into everyone's life, this one had brought a sense of danger, that the world could be toppled at any moment.

Stories and rumours flourished under the big almond tree. Jonah and Singh had to keep an eye out for trouble, their kind of trouble, for the peoples' politics, the barefooted troops of El Caracol's long revolution on the march, whenever given the moment; no other kind of trouble, sabotage on the Yankee fences.

The people had not forgotten Michael Johnson. They knew too well what even the innocence of children had managed here. These were the myths that warned. They needed others to comfort and to transform their lives.

Bolo and Elroy were called upon, yet again, to repeat their tales of the *macajuel* of Caroni and the turtles of Matura. Sunil Ramchand was encouraged to tell and retell of the visible, invisible *manates* of Manzanilla. 'All you ever see them thing, or the way a fella does throw out a net in the ponds for the *cascadu?*'

'Tell them Sunil, tell them.' That was Mohan, who people seldom saw, as he lived right at the top of Indian Valley, and hardly came down by the almond tree to be with people. He was one of those in the care of Sister Thérèse.

'He too ugly to show himself to the world,' a young brave said, refusing to believe that he himself could become like that within a year; have his face collapse, become that lion-face look, or his hands disappear.

This need for stories was a great hunger. Even the most disillusioned collected under the almond tree when the doctor's son, as Theo was now known to everyone, was among them. Those who wanted to be irreverent, like Robert *The Midnight Robber*, as he was known to the young girls, found himself elaborating, 'How the doctor have a son, so big, after such a short while with that woman living in his house?' Some laughed, but others reprimanded him.

Ma Cowey always chorused up with support for Doctor Metivier who had saved her leg from the gangrene. 'All you, watch what all you say about Docta Metivier. That is a good man, *oui*, some of all you wouldn't be here now to laugh, *kee kee*, if it wasn't for him.'

'Okay grandma, we ent doing the good doctor no harm. We joking. Is *ole talk.*'

'And don't talk so about Sister Thérèse. You know is she who bright bright, and does find out things when she looking in that microscope, that does help the doctor to heal we. Don't talk about sweet Sister Thérèse so.'

'She better watch she self with the likes of Mohan,' someone in the crowd shouted.

Everyone laughed at the suggestion, but the irony had not escaped all of those who knew that there were real dangers of infection among the worse of the patients. Sister Thérèse, in her short while in the hills, had already got a reputation for her unsparing dedication to the wretched of this earth, as some of the sisters thought of the poorest and worse affected of their patients.

'Is not Sister Thérèse you know, girl? Eh eh, you ent here how she is not Sister Thérèse no more. He does call she Madeleine. Jonah tell them. You in the doctor house everyday as if is yours. Tell them about how she is Miss Madeleine now.' Rumour had excited the young Jean Cordallo.

Jonah ignored the *ole* talk, but the knowing Jean, who knew her catechism and bible story well, continued, 'Madeleine, is Magdalen, in truth.' People looked puzzled. 'Magdalen, what wrong with all you? She was a Dorothy who Jesus forgive when she went with all them men.'

'Girl what wrong with you? You calling the woman a Dorothy because she love the doctor? Is love you know. You yourself would want to fall in love, like you see in them *flim*, nice nice love. Girl, have respect. Must because you jealous and can't get a man to fall in love with you, you so ugly like sin.'

'Don't talk so. Don't insult people. All of we in the same boat. You don't know beauty is within, and beauty is in the eyes of the beholder.' Lal brought some order to the talk.

'Tell them, Mr Lalbeharry. Tell them. Them young girl stupid yes. Anyway, why all you don't listen to good story instead of minding people business.' Everyone was contributing to the *ole talk.*

'What I want to say to all of you, is that you should know better not to *mauvais langue* we good doctor. Where some of all you would be without that man?' Lal concluded.

Theo, standing in the midst, from where Vincent could see him from the verandah of the children's ward, was talking quietly. He was transformed by his story. So quiet, that everyone was edging closer into a tight circle under the branching almond tree.

Apart from Theo's voice, everything was so quiet that you could hear the waves breaking on the beach down by the jetty. Vincent wondered at this development, Theo telling the story he had told him at the foot of his bed. He had made the bombing of the Mokihana into a myth which instilled fear, in order to dispel it.

Sancta Trinidad and El Caracol were now part of Mr Hitler's and Mr Churchill's World War. El Caracol was the front line. And Mr Truman had his Marines right in the backyard. Theo told them living history in a quiet voice.

There were cheers from one part of the crowd, the ones who believed that they did not want any Yankee soldiers on their island, when the Yankees were not giving anything in return that they could see, that made any real difference to their lives.

In fact, one of them had been killed and there was growing danger it might happen again. Those who spoke were the ones who had a fund of stories about what was happening to Dorothy, why Miss Mary Ann, down by the seaside everyday sifting sand, and why all the mothers and daughters of the land had to go down Point Cumana to make a living, as Calypso say.

The children in the hospital were strung out. Those in whom the disease was dormant were less affected. But the really sick children, less resilient, less secure, were constantly waking in the nights which immediately followed the attack on the Mokihana, screaming their nightmares. The story was that the children all had the same nightmare about the destruction of the world. In a sense it was an easier fear to express than the one which erupted in their skin.

It gave full permission for their fear, so that Sister Rita and Sister Marie-Paul took it in turns to bring the children down to the almond tree to join in the fun.

Thérèse had not been under the almond tree to hear Theo's living history. Now that she did not go to the hospital, but stayed in the hills, she was dependent on Theo and Vincent, and on Jonah's stories on the jetty in the evening, back at the Doctor's House, to learn what was going on in the world.

Now more than one of the sisters had to sleep over at the hospital, when before this duty was left to the nursing assistants and warders. The older patients were more philosophical, Jonah explained to her. But everyone was aware now that no matter how many Yankee soldiers there were on the island, no matter how many bombers surveyed the gulf, the Germans had given them the slip and come right into Porta España.

'They play *ole mas* with them ships in the harbour.' Now, the fishermen, including himself, Jonah explained, who had been more guarded with their stories before, told of many more explosions they had witnessed, sneaking their way up the north coast out of the sight of the Coast Guard and the navy, hiding in the coves as far Saut d'eau Island. Some of us even reach beyond Maracas, Miss Madeleine, and have to hide out in La Fillette.' Even Jonah used her new name, when she was not in her habit.

The names were places she did not know, places she had not gone to, on the big island of Sancta Trinidad.

Some days following the explosion in the Porta España harbour, Jonah and two of his *pardners* had found their cavalli net weighed down. When they managed to pull it to the side of the pirogue, they found the body of a sailor which had already been food to the sharks and barracudas; a skeleton as white as coral and dead flesh wavy like weed. Madeleine blanched at the story. Jonah held out his hand to her sitting on the jetty. 'Take care, Miss. Here, take a little drink of water. I mustn't tell you these things.'

'No, Jonah, you too kind. I want to know what's happening to us.'

Everything seemed now to be on alert. Theo was the swift messenger from the encampments of coastal artillery guns, going up faster than you could say

Uncle Sam, along the coast from Point Girod to the lighthouse at Cabresse Point. Because he had been all ears, tagging along behind Jesse whenever it was possible, he had positioned the new coastal artillery guns on his map along the coast of Sancta Trinidad at Point Liguore and at Point-à-Pierre. 'Them is to guard the oil refinery.' He explained to Madeleine as they stood before the new map that he had added to his wall display, a veritable Caribbean theatre of war.

They were together this afternoon for a lesson. Vincent had suggested that Madeleine give Theo French and Latin lessons. But it was Theo who was now taking the geography lesson, or the combined history and geography lesson. They were in Theo's room, a sanctuary never entered into without invitation.

The new map of Sancta Trinidad was beautifully drawn and crayoned, displaying the best work learnt at the hands of Father Angel. The outline was in black. The coastal contours were ochre and blue, with dashes of green, except for the swamp areas which were a khaki colour. 'This is the Caroni, the Oropuche and the Nariva swamp. Here, is mountain range.' These were a darker green, almost jade, crayoned with an intensity which made them shine like enamel, smooth to the touch where Madeleine stroked them with her finger, turning to smile at the boy who was enjoying her admiration for his artwork.

'Porta España, San Andres. Them is not the real colours.'

She laughed, throwing back her thick black hair, tidying it behind her ears, knowing exactly what he meant, imagining what he said about the colours of the rivers and the sea, the vast enclosing ocean, labelled prominently in black. He was a schoolmaster with his cane. 'East and south, Atlantic Ocean. North, Caribbean Sea. Continent, Port Guira, Golfo de Ballena on the west.'

The archipelago running from the north-western tip of Sancta Trinidad, each island and *boca* clearly there, ended dramatically with their very own island. 'El Caracol,' Theo concluded with a flourish and decisive tap of his cane, a well-wattled piece of guava wood. 'The snail of that fantasist, Columbus,' the boy declaimed, with a touch of his mentor Father Angel de la Bastide.

Madeleine threw back her head again and laughed, and then crouched to read something lower down the wall. Theo stood behind her, eager to see what she had noticed and which he had not yet explained. She was running ahead of him.

'Wait, Miss.' He enjoyed it when she made it back earlier than her usual arrival in the dark. He liked her transformation from nun to young girl.

The wall display had grown far beyond anything that even Vincent was up to date with: newspaper clippings from *The Gazette* in Sancta Trinidad, the *London Illustrated News* from Father Meyer, and the *New York Times* brought in by Jesse.

There was also a gigantic wall map of the continental coastline marked with the shipping lanes coming up from South America, and those advancing north to the American eastern seaboard. Theo had little pins stuck into the map, with fluttering labels, each one recording a torpedoing.

'Galera Point is the tip of the torpedo triangle.' Theo had it clearly illustrated. 'Achilles responsible for all of them there. Here, and here, other warriors, Ulysses,' he explained to Madeleine, as part of his lesson. Each pin, with a flag attached, carried the name of the warrior responsible.

Madeleine read the names, whispering them to herself, as she worked down the wall, Theo hovering at her shoulder, 'Patroculus, Philoctete.' Myths and histories of wars became echoed in this war. The Caribbean became the Aegean.

They broke to listen to the news on the World Service which crackled with the events in deserts, seas, mountains and cities across the world. These were instantly recorded on the upper reaches of the wall.

There were the campaigns of Montgomery. 'That is Monty, the Desert Rat,' Theo reached up with his cane.

The face of the fat man with the cigar was pinned up. 'Mr Churchill, he like a bulldog on the radio.' Madeleine enjoyed Theo's running commentary. She admired her pupil, who would rather take the class, than have her instruct him in irregular French verbs, or Latin conjugations and declensions. Though his love of learning did encompass those as well, at the appointed time.

Theo's general knowledge was expanding beyond anything that Father Angel had originally taught him. While life was giving him the education which Jesse thought he should have, and Vincent had desired for him, this was now being developed by Madeleine, with whom he was now having more formal classes, not only in French and Latin but also in the science that came out of her research. It had not been possible to get him back to Singh.

This was how lessons in geography and history were mostly conducted, and he was lapping up the stories in the book of Greek myths which Vincent had left lying around the house.

He got his maths from the talk on fathoms and sea miles, the fractions and diameters of guns, their shooting distances. Jesse was his master there, not to forget his lessons in archeology at the midden, and the history in the jazz, in the blues' laments, blown on Jesse's saxophone.

All this learning was making him ready for his life ahead.

'What is this here, Theo?'

Theo knelt next to Madeleine and looked over her shoulder where she was staring at what looked like the torn fragment of a letter, faded Antillean blue. It was pasted onto an old envelope, which carried a Canadian stamp. It was part of a paragraph, torn from its context....*news to London. The speculations of our agents in and around Paris is that the those transported to the work camp at Drancy are inevitably for transport to a work camp in Eastern Europe. The numbers reported are...*

Madeleine completed her whispered reading of the fragment. There were other short pieces torn from similar letters. 'Theo?'

'Yes, Miss.'

'Where did you get these?'

'I sure I see them in the waste paper basket. That's where I get them.'

'Theo.' Madeleine did not believe him.

'He leave them about the house, you know.'

'Letters, Theo. Other peoples' letters. Letters written not to you but to others.' Her voice had become agitated.

Theo lowered his eyes. He did not like to be criticised. He did not like to be out of favour. He continued to defend his position. 'Yes, but if I find them throw away, then they come like something I find on the midden. They belong to history. Not pre-history. But history. Living history. Is as if I dig them up. They is one of my find.'

'One of your finds?' Madeleine smiled. But she was angry, and deeply moved at seeing fragments of those letters which had worried her so much, caused her so much pain, been part of her secret meetings with Vincent over the last few years as they worked in the pharmacy, and then had been entrusted into his keeping.

Here they were now, enshrined, part of the boy's museum, because she had passed them onto Vincent, when she could not keep them in her cell, and because Vincent had forgotten to give them back to her.

'Theo.' She was about to tell the boy that these letters were part of her story, her personal story, the story of her father. Then she stopped herself.

For the first time she realised, profoundly, that this was not so. These were not personal letters to her, were not about her father. She did not know anything about her father. These were letters about other people, thousands of people. These were documents about the war. The boy was right. He had come across them, as he had come across pots and vases at the midden, the bones like coral, his shard of pottery. These were not part of any one person's particular history. They were part of a collective history. Taino, Aruac, Carib, French, German. Yet, they were once personal histories.

Madeleine stood up and rubbed her hips, and then knelt down again, pulling her skirt around her knees, continuing to read:

French time is now German time. This autumn the early mornings are long and dark...

When was that she wondered? When was that time? When did time change, that someone noted it down? Autumn. She said the word over and over in her mind. She had not heard the word autumn for a long time. No one talked of autumn here.

'Theo...'

'Yes. Miss.'

'What do you understand from these? How do you read these?' Madeleine lifted the curled edge with writing which carried over to the other side. She continued to read to herself while she talked to the boy. 'Do you know what autumn means, Theo?'

'Miss? Spring, summer, autumn, winter. The four season.' He looked surprised that she should ask him such a simple question.

'Whose seasons are those, Theo?'

'They are the season of a temperate climate.'

'A temperate climate?'

'Yes. A cold climate.'

'I see.'

By the tone of her voice, Theo was learning that there was something else to this questioning, to these repetitions. He was learning something about the emotions, about the rhetoric of emotions.

He himself repeated himself. 'Yes, Miss.'

'When is time personal, and when is time just time?' Madeleine wondered aloud.

The last Metro is like a Carnival.. Paris at night. Noises, rifle shots, hobnailed boots on the cobbled street …a black Citroen speeds past. You wake and it's the gendarmes at the door of the neighbours who are not there when you wake in the morning. The city gets emptier and emptier.

Madeleine read, wondering which country this was? When did it come into existence? Who lived in it?

All the trains go East.

It was as if she had not remembered these letters. They were telling her, in their disjointed way, about a country, a time, which had been once hers.

She could fill the gaps. Her love filled the gaps; the deep surging love which she always carried in her heart for her father, who increasingly she could no longer see, could no longer imagine, not knowing where to place him.

Theo stood up and began straightening labels and flags on the wall display. Madeleine remained on her knees, absorbed. As she knelt, there, reading, she could feel she was going to cry. She could not control her tears which were welling up in her eyes and brimming over and wetting her cheeks. She saw a tear fall on the floor, a stain which quickly dried in the heat. She did not want the boy to notice, so she kept her face close to the wall, reading through the blur of her tears. But she could also feel herself shaking now. She tried to steady herself, her emotions. She kept with her reading.

The queues continue as if for miles. Then there is very little to be had when you get to the counters.

Then there were single words which jumped out of their contexts, *Kommandantur,* contexts she began to find too difficult to read. They were contexts which brought back memories of her first reading of those letters. *Arrondissements.* There was a kind of poetic cadence to the ordinary words as she said them to herself, careful that the boy did not hear her tearful whisperings, *concierge, quartier.* Did the letter writer know how clearly he had conjured a world, another country, when read from here? *Carte d'identité, Ausweis, Laissez-passer, feuille de mobilisation.*

The poetry of displacement told the stories of zones, Vichy and the Occupied Zone, the country on the move, prevented from moving, moving illegally. Families were broken up, their homes usurped by the presence of a German soldier. Prisoners were deported to *Stalags* or *Offlags*. Two million had been taken prisoner.

The boy had his facts.

These were the figures after the Armistice. Madeleine read the old news as if it had just come through on the radio. She relived her pain. Through her tears, she smiled to herself, that she was told this story by a young boy who knew these stories as learnt, as overheard, as rifled from waste paper baskets, stolen from drawers, picked up from his foster father's dressing table; a boy on the prowl in a house by the sea on his own in the day, on the hunt for a story of origins and fulfilments.

These were his stories, stories he told, as she knew he had told the story of Moby Dick on the beach at La Tinta, and the stories that Jonah told her the boy repeated under the big almond tree of Achilles and his silver fish. There were the stories he told the doctor.

She felt the silence, the music of the sea, as the shale and sand and shells moved up and down the beach under the jetty. She was transfixed here.

Theo cleared his throat.

Madeleine turned round to face the boy, who was standing with one of his little flags in his fingers, ready to be pinned to the wall, to indicate the most recent torpedoing that he had been told about yesterday.

'Theo, what are you doing? Come, give me that.' Madeleine pulled herself up from the floor. She took the flag from him. 'What's this Theo? What's all of this?'

'Miss?'

'Tell me. Don't keep calling me Miss.' She took him into her ams, and embraced him generously. 'Theo, Theo, Theo.'

He let himself be embraced. His respect for Madeleine, her work with the microscope, his fascination with her change, the way she had transformed herself from that shorn figure, looking like a boy his own age, absorbed him. He had noticed it all since he had first seen her from the end of the jetty that fateful afternoon, coming to spend the night with the doctor and himself.

Now, her beauty filled his thoughts with the possibility of transformation, both for herself and his doctor for whom he had wanted something like this, seeing him on so many evenings on his own, not content to have a young boy to look after on his own. And yes, secretly he entertained thoughts of his own transformation. Theo was overcome by Madeleine's demonstrations of emotion.

When he released himself from her embrace, he looked at her closely. 'Everything alright?'

'Yes, Theo. In time.'

'I know a thing or two.'

'You do, Theo. You do. You surely do. What is this all about, Theo?'

'You mean you don't know? Is so they keep you in ignorance in the convent. Let me tell you. Where I go start?'

'No Theo. I know. You know I know. I mean, I mean what is it all about, in the end?'

'In the end, Miss? Well the prospect of an ally victory is still in the balance. Decided, if you listen to the rhetoric of Mr Churchill. But you know what leaders are. That is their role in history. You read Henry the Fifth? Think of Napoleon.'

'Henry the Fifth? Napoleon?'

'Shakespeare. "Once more unto the breach dear friends…" Father Angel make me learn all that speech when I study for Exhibition Class.'

'Oh yes, Theo, excellent! But no, Theo, all of this is wonderful and shows how good you are at geography and history. But mine is another kind of question.'

'A more fundamental kind of question? Father Angel does call them kind of question me-ta-phy-si-cal question. You mean, ul-ti-mate-ly, what is the meaning of all of this in the end? Father Angel, well as you know, is a priest, so he bound to have a religious kind of twist to thing. He does call that an es-cha-ta-lo-gi-cal question. A question that does concern the last things.'

'Does he, did he?' Madeleine's eyes grew larger with her listening, as she heard the boy. She wanted to still him, to still his mind, so that she could feel his feelings. She wished she could stop the stories.

'Vocabulary. He was always extending my vocabulary.'

'I can see that.' Madeleine smiled. Whatever Theo had done, he changed her mood from one of despair into one of wistful amusement, by his astonishing optimism. At least, that is how it seemed to her then, in the boy's room, the afternoon light piercing through the cracks in the wooden walls.

'Theo. This is enough of geography and history for one day. I've always wanted to learn how to fish. I want you to teach me this afternoon, before the light goes.'

Seine

Madeleine watched Theo intently, as he went back and forth, gathering up all his fishing tackle from the shed under the verandah steps, bringing it to the jetty and laying it out on the hot boards. He was more than a young boy now, he was growing fast into a young man. There was still a kind of innocence about him though, in his face, in his voice, she thought, which kept him as a young boy. But his body was now filling out, the muscles on his arms and legs, his back as he bent and stretched, his strong neck, the definite line of his jaw.

She watched him in his torn khaki pants, bare back in the sun, barefoot always. Had he ever worn shoes? His reddish hair glinted in the light, his green eyes smiled, as he darted a look at her, as he put down the fishing rods.

He noticed her looking at him.

She turned to look over her shoulder, as he put the hooks and lines down on the boards behind her. Everything he did, he did neatly, with precise movements. He ordered the world around him. She noticed that, this morning, in his room. She noticed it in the kitchen at lunch. She smiled at his manners. She looked at him differently.

This afternoon, something happened to her. He allowed her to see things differently.

Before he had taken her up to his room, just standing around in the kitchen, relaxing, eating salt fish *buljol* and *Crix*, he was different, he was growing fast. 'Come, try some pepper sauce.'

Now, in the full glare of the afternoon there was something altogether changed about him.

'Theo,' she called to him from the edge of the jetty where she was sitting, dangling her legs over the side, watching her reflection curl in the rusty water. 'Can I give you a hand with some of that?'

He stopped in his tracks and looked back at her. 'No thanks. Is okay. I've everything now, I think.'

His manners! She smiled. His charm. But what was that other thing about him? She could not put her finger on it.

Madeleine shaded her eyes. The bay was full of activity this afternoon. There were barges and tugs going back and forth from the base in Sancta Trinidad through the archipelago.

'*Oui* boy! That's a mine sweeper. You see she, just now, she just gone round the point, any moment now you go see she through the pass at La Tinta. Watch so. Watch, watch!' Theo was pointing and jumping up and down excitedly. 'There she is!'

Indeed they saw the huge apparition of the mine-sweeper, its grey hulk, passing through the Boca Grande.

'A few last things, and then we ready,' he said.

Madeleine noticed how suddenly, watching the boat, Theo had been transformed back again into the small boy, then as suddenly, the efficient organiser of the fishing lesson. She looked over to the convent and to Saint Damian's, worlds that she was now excluded from. She felt like a hermit in the hills with her patients, her wretched of this earth. Mother Superior had found a way to exclude her without actually throwing her out, using her for the most dangerous work.

Something in her grieved for how things had been, her simple desire for her vocation to be a nursing sister in the missions, with her fellow sisters about her. That was the bit she missed, a meaning to her life, which was made of service. Yet, now, her service was extreme with the patient in the hills.

She did not miss the convent, the communal prayers, the petty rules, the cruel actions of some of the embittered ones. Nor did she miss the authoritarianism of her superiors, their neglect, their narrow mindedness and lack of sympathy; their world ruled by the idea of sin.

Not even their hate, with the persistent production of the yellow stars, seemed as terrible as everything else. She had only pity for that lonely mind, those embroidering fingers. Before she left she had come upon Sister Hildergard, her lap full of the yellow stars. She had simply stared at her covering up her cruel creations. She did not even have the words. The nun had looked so absurd, so foolish, caught in the act.

But it had only needed an opportunity for these views, long ago held by her father, and resisted by herself and her mother, to come to the surface, and be the language which she possessed, in order to understand what had happened to her.

They rose in waves to consume her with a rage and a hatred of something that paraded itself with so much power, so many self-righteous opinions of what was good and what was evil, with its bishops and archbishops and priests, lording over people. She had borne the brunt of that. The thought that the archbishop had wanted to detain her in a house for wayward girls, filled her with almost uncontrollable rage.

She did not miss any of that. There were her once a week visits back to the convent to get a clean habit, to go through the pretence, as she saw it, of still being a sister. But she missed the life of the hospital, the children, the old people, her part in trying to find a cure, to make them well again, to give them back dignity. Some of that she had regained when Vincent brought her microscope to the house.

She looked over into the sun, crinkling the sea in Chac Chac Bay. Then she turned to Theo, making everything ready to teach her how to fish. She did not know how much longer she could take the banishment to the hills, and then this other life, here with Vincent and Theo. She was torn by the duplicity.

Suddenly, she missed Sister Rita. They had been real sisters, looking out for one another. She had experienced a glimpse of what community life sometimes had been, what friendship in the novitiate had been, which had given her the strength to leave her father and come out to the missions.

What had her life come to? Now, she had time to think of Vincent, living in his house most nights. She had never been as close as this to any man, apart from her father. She thought now, maybe, that was one point to her mother's death, strangely, to prepare her for this, to be living with Vincent, a man like her father, a dedicated doctor, a man almost like a priest in his service to Theo, to Ti-Jean, to his sons, as she saw them, and to all the patients young and old. In the midst of all of that, she had noticed his eyes, his hands and the way in which he talked to her and touched her at her elbow from the beginning, opening the door with his charm. And then how she had, without very much resistance, felt she was falling in love with him, and letting her vocation as a nun slip away.

In the hot afternoon sun, Madeleine passed through this reverie of conflicting thoughts.

* * *

'Madeleine.' She did not hear Theo at first, calling her to start the fishing lesson. A *batimamzelle* zinged close to the water, the dragon fly, glinting in the sun and absorbing her. 'Madeleine.' Theo persisted with his concerned voice. The sun drugged her. There was numbness in her fingers which was worrying her. She put it out of her mind.

Madeleine turned abruptly. 'Theo. Where was I?'

'I don't know.' He laughed. 'You seem to be far away. I call you, but you ent hear me. So I keep calling. That does happen to me sometimes. Doctor does call me, and then I don't hear, and then, he does say, Theo where were you? Always funny when he say that, where were you? When I standing right there in front of him.'

'Where did *you* go to, Theo?'

Theo looked at her. At first, there were questions, many questions in his face as he frowned. Then she saw that other thing which had been puzzling her about him, that something else she could not put her finger on. Now, she saw it. It was a look of utter sadness. An extreme sense of abandonment.

She had seen many children who were truly abandoned among her patients, and there was an obvious reason for their plight. But here was Theo, with his confidence and his brightness. It seemed to contradict this other look which came over his face. It was a paradoxical face.

But, as he knelt close to her, she was tempted to run her fingers down his spine. She wanted to stroke the pain she imagined had first accompanied this wound, stroke out the pain from it, with her gentle fingers, where it blistered in the sun. Then her words came out without a thought. She immediately regretted them, almost at the same time as she heard their utterance. 'Theo, what happened to your back?'

He looked up from his hooks and lines. 'Bait. I forget the bait. Jonah bring fresh bait this morning when he come for Doctor. Some nice little bait. Funny, eh? They does call that bait, Jonah. I've it in the ice box, otherwise it does stink in the hot sun. I go go and get it now.'

He had escaped her, running along the hot boards of the jetty, two, three steps at a time, up to the verandah and disappearing into the gloom of the house. Madeleine knew that she had overstepped the mark, ventured where she should not have gone. It was a mistake. She would have to leave it. She would not even apologise. That would be to bring it up again, to place him in a dilemma, pressuring him.

Theo seemed to be ages up at the house, then he waved from the kitchen window, 'Coming.' Madeleine waved back.

She got up and stretched. What kind of life was this? Fishing in the afternoon? She watched the barges and tugs. A lone sea plane circled and then landed like a giant pelican in Perruquier Bay.

Then it seemed, like in no time, Theo was back with the bait, smiling and encouraging her to join him, kneeling before his fishing rods, lines and hooks.

'Right. We go begin. You ever fish before?'

'Yes, of course. I've fished in the Seine. But that's different, yes?'

'You fish with seine. I don't believe that.'

'On the Seine, yes? You know the Seine?'

For a moment Theo was lost. And then he looked embarrassed that he had made a mistake like that, with his knowledge from Father Angel. He should not have made a mistake like that. Then he burst out laughing at himself. 'Seine, seine. Maybe that's where the word come from, or, maybe, that's why the river call so, because it like a seine, a net full of fish.'

'Maybe. There are stories in words,' Madeleine said.

'Ety-mo-lo-gy.'

'Yes, derivations.'

'Yes, I see the Seine which run through Paris.'

'Yes. That's it.'

'That's a big river, *oui*!' Theo was excited.

'Long and wide.'

'Tell me about it. I mean I know it. You know I know things I learn. But I never see it, like you. You have first-hand experience.'

'You know things that have happened to you too,' Madeleine added.

'Tell me.' Theo had a way of ignoring inferences he did not want to dwell on. He had a way of pressing ahead with the conversation in the direction that he wanted it to go. 'Tell me how it is when you fish on the Seine.'

Theo sat back on his heels, fixing with his fingers the finickety business of threading lines and baiting hooks, ready to start his lesson. He settled back to hear Madeleine's story, every now and then bending forward to cut his bait with his pen knife. She turned to face him more directly, pulling her legs up from dangling over the jetty, pulling her knees up, embracing them, tucking

329

in her skirts, resting her chin on her knees, gazing into her past, but also into Theo's face.

'What should I tell you?'

'Tell me a fishing story on the Seine.'

'Well,' Madeleine smiled at Theo, suddenly made self-conscious, by his precise request. 'Well, where should I start?'

'At the beginning?' Theo giggled.

'Not a bad place to start. Yes. No, where was I?'

They both laughed remembering their previous joke.

'Our house had a path that led down to the Seine. It was a stone path, and it led from a door at the side of the house, between the garden beds to a wrought iron gate. I remember it well. When you opened the gate it led down some stone steps to a landing stage on the river. There was a key to the gate, a big, cold iron key which hung inside the side door of the house. I remember now that over the gate was a tree. It was a tree that I loved very much. I could see it from the window of my bedroom.'

Madeleine looked up to see how Theo was taking her story. Her eyes met his staring at her, as he listened intently, as they both sat on the still jetty in the hot afternoon sun.

'What kind of tree?' Theo asked.

'What?'

'The name of the tree?'

'The name? I don't think you have this tree here. But yes, the flowers are tropical looking. Magnolia.'

'Magnolia. That's a wonderful name.'

'They flowered in the spring. Their flowers are like big cups, big fleshy cups, white, almost cream. There are different colours, purple as well. But this one was a white Magnolia, and it bloomed in the spring over the gate to the river. When it bloomed, it was heavy and weighed down with lots and lots of these cups of cream. It made me so happy to see it.

'When it came to the end of its bloom, the white petals fell over the garden path, and onto the steps to the landing stage, and then they were blown onto the river. I remember them floating down the river, white Magnolia petals.'

'Well, so that's the setting. A story needs a setting. But what about the fishing?'

'Well, first of all, I'll tell you a joke. Near to the street that we lived on is the narrowest street in Paris. It's called *Rue du Chat qui Pêche*.'

'*Oui*. The cat that does fish. That's funny, because, of course, cats like to eat fish.'

'*Absolument!* Your French is very good.'

'*Un peu.*' Theo smiled.

'Well, I never saw a cat fishing, but there were lots of fishermen along the banks of the Seine. And on a Saturday afternoon, because I did not have school then, my father would take me to the river bank under the landing stage, and there we would throw out a line.'

'Throw out a line. Line fishing?'

'I don't know. A rod. A rod with a line. It looked a bit like that.' Madeleine pointed to one of Theo's rods lying across the boards of the jetty.

'And what you use for bait.'

'Maggots.'

Theo looked puzzled.

'Little worms.'

'Worms, yes, we does use worm up Pepper Hill when we fishing in the river for *wabean*. Bread too. We does use stale bread.'

The hooks baited, the lines ready, and the story of Paris and the magnolia tree faded into the fast turning sepia light over Chac Chac Bay. They threw their lines together, and waited. Madeleine got the first bite, then Theo got a bite too. They pulled in a red snapper each.

'We've got dinner for tonight.'

'We sure do.'

Vincent was late that evening. Madeleine and Theo ate their supper in the kitchen without ceremony, Theo moving between the stove and the kitchen table with bakes, fried fish and a jug of cocoa sprinkled with cinnamon. They sat in the glow of the humming hurricane lantern.

As they finished, and were clearing up, Vincent arrived back. With the closed doors and the blackouts drawn shut, Theo and Madeleine had not heard the *put putting* of the pirogue's motor, rounding the point at Father Meyer's house. The first they heard was Vincent as he opened the door from the verandah. 'You two still up. I'm sorry I'm so late.'

He stood behind Madeleine. He did not touch her or bend to kiss her as he wanted to. His fingers, at the back of her chair, tickled the nape of her neck with his secret touch. He still felt shy with Theo there, nervous of Theo witnessing their physical love.

He lit a cigarette and stood watching them eating. 'My God!' Vincent exclaimed.

'What?' Madeleine looked up.

'What happen?' Theo joined in.

They both turned to look at Vincent.

'Theo, I'm so sorry. I'm so sorry. I meant to be here.' And, he went back onto the verandah. 'Theo, forgive me.'

Madeleine looked at Theo, to see if he could explain these apologies. Vincent came back in, holding a long parcel wrapped in brown paper and tied with brown twine. 'Theo. We've not done this before. I can't believe I've not done this before, that I've allowed these four years to pass by without ever doing this, without wishing you a happy birthday, without giving you a gift on that day. I can't believe I've allowed you to have that day pass, each year, without anything being done in this house, to celebrate and remember that day of yours, your special day.'

Theo and Madeleine sat turned in their chairs towards Vincent, who was standing in the middle of the room with his large parcel, giving his long speech. Madeleine motioned to Theo to go and receive his gift. Theo was suddenly shy, and looked overcome.

She watched him take the present from Vincent. The present was long and light, and he stood unwrapping the oddly shaped oblong.

Vincent broke in, 'I had it made by one of Lalbeharry's pupils in the work-shop. There's a boy there, Khan, he sewed the net and fitted it to the loop. The stick is young guava, strong, but pliant,' Vincent described, as a butter-fly net became visible, trailing on the floor. Theo made a feigned swoop at an invisible butterfly to show his pleasure in the present, as it emerged fully from its chrysalis of brown paper and twine.

Almost inaudibly, overcome, Theo said, 'Thank you, Doc. Thanks.' Then his voice grew stronger. 'I go use it. I go try it out tomorrow.'

Theo was a burgeoning lepidopterist. This new interest had begun with collecting dead butterflies. Vincent was not sure how Theo was going to take to catching them and pinning them to death with the already mounted spec-imens of *Bamboo Page*, *Cracker*, *Yellow Migrant* and *Small White*. There was a *Brown Biscuit* kept in a matchbox on the kitchen table, and some *Blue Brilliants* stuck with flour paste to the jalousies in his bedroom.

'Now, I want to say Theo, because I don't think Madeleine knows. This is Theo's sixteenth birthday.' Madeleine looked surprised, but also reassured, having noticed that the boy was changing.

It was suddenly all too much for Theo, and he was quickly up to his room and his crystal set for the news, uncharacteristically leaving the clearing up of the supper things to be done by Madeleine.

Afterwards, she and Vincent sat out on the dark verandah, and watched as the moon cut its path from Patos to the wide embrace of Chac Chac Bay.

Madeleine was woken just after midnight. She followed the voice, and came and stood at the door of Vincent's room. Theo was at the foot of Vincent's bed on his usual perch. Madeleine listened, looking at Vincent and then at Theo.

Bedtime Story

I CARRY my nightmare along these corridors, up and down these stairs, out into the kitchen, with bucket and mop and broom, into the library with dusty book, out into the vegetable garden. I carry my nightmare as I plant *melangene*, as I plant ochro, as I plant pumpkin vine and *christophine*. I carry my nightmare in bucket to water the vegetable garden. I carry nightmare. I carry them in my work in the sacristy. I rub them into the brass. I arrange them in the flower I pick in the flower garden. I polish them into the floor.

I see my face in the mirror, Mama face and another face.

Work take the pain away and take away the fear.

I carry the gloom at my window, the voice at my door, the hand under the sheet. Sin I can't confess, because they not commit by me, but by another. I learn not to tell the priest this sin. I confess my own sin. I learn not to tell that sin. No one go believe.

Bring down the Demerara shutter, keep the window stick by the bed, Father Dominic say. Is a dream that fright you? If the window stick make you feel better, put it by your bed. Say the rosary. *Pater Noster... Ave Maria...*

Yes, Father Dominic come when I cry out one night, but no one there. Father Dominic come like Mama and sit on the bed. He don't hold me, but his word caress. He smooth my forehead with his long slender finger. I never see finger so long. Like smooth ochro. Finger which turn the soft page of book in the library. Finger make for consecration, for the wafer and the chalice of wine at the elevation. Finger for washing in the cup of the Lord and drying on the linen towel. *Lavabo manus meas.*

All the time I say, Father? Wish I had a father.

Mama say, Spanish go protect you. I hear her say that one day. Spanish go take care of you. Eh, Spanish, and you go take care of my son, *oui*?

Yes, Emelda, he say, is now you come to me after the fire in you belly, after you done bake the bread. And he run his finger through my hair. Sugar head. Like he know something. Emelda boy, he does call me.

Father Dominic blow out the candle and take the matches away. Far away, I hear Mama, *Do do, petit popo.* I curl up like a cashew nut. Rock myself to sleep sucking on my thumb. I sucking thumb again. Mama big boy, sucking thumb!

Vincent looked at Madeleine. She had sunk to her knees and crouched by the door listening. She was strangely lulled by the boy's story, but also astonished, bewildered.

HE DOES COME in the night, scratching at the window, prizing with his finger at the jalousies, whispering my name, that name that sound like a bird, *Coco Coco Cocorito.*

He is a voice, is an eye at the keyhole, between the crack in the door.

He arrive on horseback in the courtyard. He move across the gravel like *chac chac,* like *jumbie* bead in a calabash.

The horse snort and neigh and jostle at the rein and tug at the bit in it mouth. *Ride a cock horse to Banbury Cross with rings on her fingers and bells on her toes.*

He come to sleep in my ear. Like a lizard in my ear. A tongue in my ear.

The horse sniff at the window, snort and smell like him who ride the back, who creep into this cell with bare wall. There is no match and I can't light a candle to see who it is that come to perform the ceremony, I know since I small. I can't light a candle to see the shadow, to see the shape of the shadow of the one who come. Phantom.

I believe that he invisible. Invisible with the touch which is like fire. *Socouyant,* sucker of blood, the fireball witch. Hot like ice. Tip of the finger, like tong to pick meat. Like gabilan, the hawk, I see high high high over the convent sky.

The voice sound like, *Coco Coco Cocorito.*

Who it is that ride a horse through the window, pawing at the floor, strutting across the cell, galloping into my bed?

I know that smell, the smell of a horse and *de l'eau* from the city of *Cologne* on Father Angel's map.

Get the *eau d'Cologne* for the child.

Limacol is better, *Oui*!

Where Mrs Goveia? Now she does always have Bay Rum ready to revive the child when he faint.

I must stop breathing. And sleep. And then, die.

Pretend I'm dead. That is what Mama say I must do. Pretend you dead. If you dead you can't do nothing, and nobody could do you nothing. You not there. You dead.

I dead, dead, dead, dead.

Playing a game I learn to play it better. Shut my eye and disappear.

Then the grave digger has his way with the dead.

Madeleine was all eyes and ears. She exchanged her own fear for the boy's. She and Vincent kept the vigil.

HE LEAVE before the bell for Matin in the little hour.

He leave the sheet scatter on the floor. Leave me in this corner to cry.

I get up from the dead and wash myself between the legs, and let the water fall over my chest, and fling it at my face and gargle, and scrub away the smell and taste of the dead on my mouth and under my breath. And I fling open the window to fly, fly up into the milky con stel la tions. And the perfume are lily flowers, funeral flowers in the garden below. Don't fly.

We done loss the science of flight.

I let the bell rope take me up up, the big heavy bell with a heavy tongue in its throat. Toll, toll, toll.

Then I see him leave the yard on his chestnut horse.

In the past, before they stopped, Vincent had always been pleased to receive Father Dominic's letters. They were long and sprawling. He always thought that the friar had been infected by Theo's storytelling.

"I have looked into this matter of the one who visits in the night. This question of nightly visitations is very upsetting. Another preposterous phenomenon to explain to Father Superior. It would mean that I would have to keep vigil every night, and be able to get up with strength for Matins, as early as we customarily do. I do not think I can manage that and carry out my duties to the community in the day. It would soon be evident that I was under a strain. Which I am. But at that moment I insisted on getting my night's sleep. I went to the boy when I heard his call. No one else had seemed to have heard the call, thank God. I do have so much to thank God for. But yes, there is the story of the one who comes into his room. There is the chestnut horse. There is the dying that he must do. His Mama told him to die. I do not understand any of this. This is beyond me. I had to wait for him to tell me more, to describe more. Some of this I did not want to hear. I was disturbed by what I heard."

This night was a busy night in the doctor's house. The drama moved from room to room. The boy moved quickly. Madeleine and Vincent moved fast to keep up. Now they were in his bedroom and then across the landing, then back to his perch on Vincent's bed.

BENEDICAMOUS DOMINO, is the knock on the door.
  Deo Gratias. I is a good boy. I get up.
  Is another day. The man-horse don't come every night. Sometime, only once a month. I don't know. I lose time when I dead. I don't mark it on the calender.
  I don't know when the horse go neigh. And I can't stop myself. I must go to the window and throw down the key.
  When this start?

All the time the sea was breathing just near the windowsill. And, in the distance, a thunder. Vincent was alert. Madeleine perched at the top of the bed, got down. She could not listen to any more. She went to sleep on the couch downstairs.

I COME INTO MY ROOM after Compline one night, and I feel this big key on the table by the window with the wash basin and the jug. I see the key and I wonder about it. But I sleepy. I say I go find out in the morning.
  I clean my teeth. I pick nice hibiscus twig to make a good brush. I pass the wash rag over my face. Sleep come heavy after the hot day.
  But it cross my mind, someone come in my room, when I not there, and leave this key. There is nothing to come in my room for. There is nothing in my room. This room more empty than Popo mother house up Pepper Hill.

This room have nothing. The crucifix with the crucified one. The five wounds. The crown of thorns. The ill-used head from the hymn. My conversation is only a prayer I don't understand.

Carry your cross, Father Dominic say.

Father Dominic must've come to see if I hiding matches under my mattress. He have fire on the brain. Leave the key by mistake.

In the dark there is nothing at all, my naked body standing in the middle of the room. There is the naked man on the cross.

He don't come for anything. He come for me. And I am nothing.

I hang my cassock and scapular on a rusty nail behind the door. I crawl into my flour bag nightie. It still smell of flour. Like flour bag at the back of Chen shop up Pepper Hill. I lie on the coconut fibre mattress and I look at the stars, peeping through the jalousies.

If is moonlight it flow onto the floor and I can see the table and chair. I can see the wash stand. I can see my white cassock and black scapular and leather belt and beads hanging on the rusty nail. And the whip, the discipline, I en't use yet. I hear the friars Friday night lashing their back. I can see in the moonlight.

But tonight is dark. No moonlight. I creep to the washstand and touch the iron key. I lift it, heavy, cold in my hand. Smell it. It smell of cold iron. Rust. It smell of lock and keyhole. It smell of oil someone rub on it, long ago to make it turn in the keyhole. It smell of mortice and latch. *Clacityclack.* It turn and squeak. It jam. Is a key to open some door. Heavy and cold. It belong in a hole in a door somewhere. My door to my cell don't lock. There is no key in my door. I don't have the key.

Father Dominic keep the matches and the keys.

I smell it, and then I don't know why, I lick it. In the dark I kneel by the wash stand and I hold the heavy cold key in my hand, and I lick it. It taste of rust and oil, and the taste of the metal stay on the tip of my tongue.

I heavy with sleep and I crawl back in my wooden bed. I hold the heavy cold key under my pillow. I wait for sleep with my eyes open and my heart beating.

Is worse than before.

Then, that night, I must've close my eyes and fall into a dream. The horse at the window neighing and jangling it reins. I not hear a horse in the friary before. I sleep walk to the window. I find myself there. I lift the latch and throw open the shutter them. The horse chestnut and sweating in the hot night under the stars.

I see the horse. It all one figure, the horse and the man on top of it. He come like *borokeet* carnival time.

It go back on its hind leg and start to climb to the window from the courtyard.

Is the body of the man, and is the man who say, Give me the key. Give me the key.

Then I understand. I run by my bed for the heavy, cold key under my pillow. I lean over the windowsill and let down the key.

It worse than ever.

Them divide them self and the man leave the horse, so that the horse alone as a horse. The chestnut horse, Mister tether near the mango tree in the backyard. We call him Prince.

He is the devil. Pay de devil.

Not the carnival passing with *jab molassi* and red devil and *moco jumbie*.

He is the devil. He get over the wall.

Pay de devil.

Spanish say, give the devil a baby for dinner.

Mama say, cheups!

He have the key for the door. The horse stamping on the courtyard. I crawl back in my bed. I curl up like a cashew nut.

I don't sleep. I dream. I call it that, or else I dead. Mama say, die, die. Be dead.

She say once, that she fear that she might have carry me dead in she belly. Curl there like a dead leaf. Then I trans-pa-rent, like light on a muslin curtain.

No branch from she body go get cut out.

Cut it out, child. Go by Ma Sidone at the bottom of the track, cut it out.

She hear them voices tell her that. She say no, she not cutting out the child.

And Abraham take a knife to slaughter his son Isaac. And I look around for an angel. No angel in that room that night. Unless this devil was an angel in masquerade.

No angel in that room that night. No angel in battle array. No guardian angel with their hand on your shoulder, looking over your shoulder to take

339

you down the path of darkness to goodness. Like the holy picture Mrs Goveia give me for my First Communion. No angel with fiery sword. No angel to cast Lucifer, carrier of light, from the height of heaven to the depth of hell. No Michael with a flaming sword. No Gabriel with annunciation. No seraphim, no cherubim. I find no one in that room that night. Not one of all the host of angel.

I wait, curl up like before I born. No match to light candle to see my way. I must wait in the dark. Above me on the bare wall he hang naked, crucified, the crucified one.

I taste rust in my mouth, the rust of the cold key, the metal of the bit in the chestnut horse mouth. The key is a bit in my mouth. Suck it, I tell myself.

Suck it, he say.

Don't hear no door open, no latch click, *Clacytyclack*!

Must be a beetle. A black backed beetle which drop from the ceiling. Or a cold *mabouyan* lizard drop on the floor from it hiding place behind the crucifix. That was the only sound. My eye squeeze up as I try to die.

Pretend you dead, Mama say. If you dead nothing can't happen to you. You can't do nothing. Nothing go do you. Is not you. You not there.

Suck it.

I can't breathe. I can't bawl.

No one can hear. No one go know. And no one go believe.

But then, no one know when I say no. No one know what happen then, no one know when I force his hand, and there and then I must go and get the switch.

Not now, because of the silence of God's place.

Out in the yard to find a nice smooth one on the guava tree, or a sweet wiry one on the tamarind tree, like it use to be on Pepper Hill, out into the silence of the Thursday afternoon, all the windows and doors of the little house in the yard shut up-and-peeping at me as I go down the silent trace to pick a switch for Mister in the bush.

Here, he bring them, their length lying against the length of his leg in his breeches, and now a clutter with all the heap of khaki on the floor behind the door where he kick them. Khaki. Stains of sweat in the armpits of his shirt, in the crotch of his pants, in the seat of his pants, where his bottom sweat. Where I must put my face. He kick them here where I kneel to find their treasure, treasure he call it.

Bring my treasure, in the bundle of clothes whose smell I know so well, so well, so long I find on the floor of his bedroom, but much longer find against my young skin in my Mama's bed.

Here they is, as I turn to find a glimmer on his face, a glint in his eye to tell me which one he prefer.

One tonight, the smooth one, marbled green and brown,the length of the guava *bois,* or the flexible sting of the tamarind snake.

Each one I hold up, each I test for him with my finger pull along the length, bend and test against my knee, or swish in the air to hear it sing, to show that I concern that he get the best, that he get the one he need, he think I need, he know I need, and I know them, for he train me so.

Then I kneel to offer the switch. I must kneel and I must bow with my bare bottom, my flour bag nightie curl round my ankle like a pool of moonlight, bow straight against the slat of the board bed with my face in the slat watching the cockroaches crawl on the floor.

I must wait. Wait and not know when it will hit, when it will hurt, when it will sting, when it will go on. If there is a pause, and I lose count and start again, so always it seem it is one, two, three till I reach ten. But I don't know how many decade I have whispered here, bow and bend over the wooden bed with my face in the slat in the dark with the cockroach which tickle my toe and creep up my leg to nest. A rat chew at my toe.

That is to get him start before the ride, and the gallop through the cane piece. I must turn this way or that way, depend on how he pull his rein, pull the bridle.

Some brother think that is my virtue, my fervour for beating. Is not Friday night.

He knock on the door and say, Sufficient.

Is this Father Dominic?

He sing a song to cheer me up. *Frère Jacques,domez vous... sonnez les Matinas, ding dong dong..*

Not a sin to tell in confession. Is not my sin.

No one go believe, no one go know, except the one who put the key in my room. So I is the one who let him in? I is the one who say, yes, to this.

After that tale, Theo lay in the corner of his bedroom. Vincent did not stop the drama as it unfolded. He watched the re-enactment. He was relieved that he had not been invited to participate in this one, as he had done with previous re-enactments. He watched to the very end after all the newspaper cuttings were torn off the wall to make a bed of newspaper in the corner for the boy to lie down, curled like a cashew nut, like a foetus. Like a baby to be born, like a baby in a ditch.

When it was perfectly quiet, when it showed absolutely no signs of starting up again, Vincent went over to Theo heaped upon the newspaper cuttings, sweating, in a fever of his story. His warm body was clammy with the sweat and the exertion of his memory.

The story was what it was, and it had to be told. The burden was the awful secret of it. That was the pain, the secret of it. Tell it to the world, and a kind of healing would come, retribution and forgiveness. Was that it?

This was the world that had been given to the boy: this doctor who must have reminded him of Mister, the Mister of his tale. When Vincent realised that, he felt so ashamed, so sorry, for what had been done to this son of Mister.

He wanted to go then and there find his own boy, his own son, in the arms of others, hold him and tell him that he was loved by him. He wanted to tell himself that he was loved by him. But why should he be? Why would he want to come to him now? Why would Odetta want him to come to her?

'Theo, come boy. Come let me hold you. Theo, you are a good boy, none of this is your fault.'

That morning, there was an unusual low tide, the kind of low tide that preceded a spring tide. It was as if all the sea had been sucked out of the bay. There was a dramatic sense of exposure in the naked seabed from where Vincent looked from the bedroom window.

'Come Theo, let's go and walk on the sands and see the low tide.' They walked out of the house hand in hand, passing Madeleine still asleep on the couch.

They came down the steps at the side of the jetty straight onto the sea floor. Vincent had not experienced this tide before.

Theo was amazed. 'The sea get take away!' They walked as far as they could, to where the waves were breaking in the warm shallows, alarming the sandpipers in a frenzy at the edge of the ocean.

They talked of tides and the power of the moon.

It was as if the world had changed to what it must have been like when Noah's flood had subsided. Vincent had not remembered a tide quite like this. The air busy with gulls, skimming over the sandbanks and mud flats. Egrets in flight from the mangroves around Salt Pond alighted on barnacled rocks, stalking and pecking, inquisitive, pedantic in their search.

The dawn had not yet broken.

They let the silence in the wind and the waves wash over them. It soothed the turmoil of the night. They stooped and collected shells. They found starfish and chip chips, snails and oyster shells. Blue and rust. White and pink. The snails were like white coral, like the bones Theo remembered in the midden.

When they returned to the house, Madeleine had already changed into Sister Thérèse, and left the house.

El Caracol
1942-1945

News From Abroad

With the mail boat that morning came a letter from Vincent's mother in town. Ti-Jean brought the mail to the door of the pharmacy, where Vincent was working that morning on his own. He had seen him struggling up from the jetty on his crutches. He took the mail, noticing that Ti-Jean's condition had regressed. It seemed like they were not winning that battle. Oh Alexander Fleming! If he only had the stuff, Vincent sighed. Ti-Jean hung back at the door. 'I can't see you now, Ti-Jean. Maybe this afternoon. Find Sister Rita, if you need attention.'

'Where Sister Thérèse?' The boy pestered like a child, though now, suddenly, he seemed older. Made old by sickness. Vincent thought how he had not noticed his growing up, like he had noticed Theo's.

'Ti Jean, you know Sister Thérèse is working up in Indian Valley now.'

'Magdalen!'

'What did you say, Ti-Jean?'

'Magdalen. Is so the fellas by the almond tree calling she.'

'Is that so?'

Ti-Jean hung his head. Vincent watched him and realised that he could not feel the pain that he should be feeling with his wounds and sores in that state. This fact always amazed him as he looked at his patients struggling. Half the battle was lost before they had started, because they were not receiving the signals. There was no pain like this body without pain.

'Come, Ti-Jean. I know you miss her. We'll talk later. Okay? I wouldn't bother with what the fellas under the almond tree say.'

'They say she get *cocobay*. She come like we.'

'What you mean, Ti-Jean? Come like we?'

'You know.'

'What I know Ti-Jean is that we're all the same, but some of us are ill. You have an illness.'

Ti-Jean lowered his head.

'We'll talk later.'

Vincent sat back at his desk by the window. Inserted with the letter was a telegram. He toyed with the letter and the telegram. The letter fluttered in the breeze. Magdalen, he heard Ti-Jean's voice again. He saw her black hair, falling over her naked shoulders. They would have to make a choice, make a choice and live with it. *Cocobay*, what was Ti-Jean talking about? An irrational fear gripped Vincent. The boy was talking nonsense. He must talk to Madeleine about it. What an idea!

He unfolded the already cut open telegram.

WE DEEPLY REGRET TO INFORM YOU THAT YOUR SON 129620 FLYING OFFICER METIVIER B M FAILED TO RETURN FROM AN OPERATIONAL FLIGHT THIS MORNING LETTER TO FOLLOW.

Vincent placed his mother's unread letter down on the desk, on his left side, with the telegram on his right. He rested his head in his hands for a moment, and then looked up and stared out over Chac Chac Bay. He watched Ti-Jean, the messenger of bad news, retracing his steps to the jetty.

Bernard was not dead. He was missing. 'Come on, come on.' Bernard was running away from him in the pasture at Versailles. Bernard was running fast, holding aloft a World War One plane, hurling his model aircraft into the air; the one his father and Bernard had made of balsa wood on the dining room table. What he always remembered was the sound emitted from his lungs, the terrible roar of the plane, and its eventual crash into the hibiscus hedge at the bottom of the pasture. What danger had Bernard gone into? He had been driven by a father who had returned from a previous war with shrapnel in his hip, his mind shattered, but transfigured sufficiently to be his son's hero, his model; the Empire's soldier.

Then the thought overwhelmed him. Bernard was missing and he had not got to know him. He had not got to really talk and share a life with his brother.

While he had followed his passion for Odetta, Bernard had dreamt of being an airman. He had sat for hours, it seemed, listening to stories of the

348

front, to stories of Verdun and the Somme. The very words sounded like the distant thunder of the guns. Foreign fields.

All these thoughts and feelings flooded Vincent's mind as he played with the pages of his mother's letter, and the stern impersonality of the telegram, telling him that his brother was missing somewhere in Europe.

As he sat there and watched the mail boat, *George the Vth,* leave the bay to return to town, he felt himself shaking uncontrollably. There was a terrible croak coming from his throat. There was a stifled sob wanting to break from his chest. His eyes filled with tears, flooded his cheeks, falling onto his mother's letter. Smudged Quink ink ran along the lined writing paper.

The telegram, with news of Bernard missing in action, fell from the desk in the breeze.

The bay was hot and bright. The coconut palms scratched the air. Cocks crowed and Vincent could hear the end of Singh's speech under the almond tree. 'Vote for your rights and your freedom. Tell them Yankees where to go.' The vote was unanimous. Singh would never give up. The banging of crutches confirmed their intent. 'Vote for Rehabilitation!' They would hold Mother Superior to her undertaking to get their wages increased, to get the huts repaired for the married quarters. She would have to get the money from the Colonial Office or from the Americans.

From the window of the clinic, Vincent was surprised to see Theo in the crowd standing next to Christiana. They were smiling and laughing. Then Singh joined them and they all three went off towards the pharmacy. When had the boy learnt about love and got rid of his fear? This must be the gradual, healing magic of his own stories.

The door opened. Vincent did not turn around until he had regained his composure. When he did, he saw that it was Madeleine. 'Why are you here? You know the rules.' She, also, held a letter in her hand. The envelope carried innumerable stamps, telling of its travels, its crossing of borders, getting by censors, approved by many different bureaucracies.

'There's been another deportation from Drancy to Auschwitz.'

She spoke the names as casually as if they were neighbouring islands. She announced it like it had happened yesterday, paying no attention to the interval between the occurrence of these events and the time it took for the news

349

to travel. She sounded unaware of all the things which could have happened since that news was sent. Time played its tricks with her hope and faith.

'A sister at Notre Dame du Lac, you remember, the Abbey near Montreal, has a brother in the Free French in London. They managed to get the message through on a convoy which made a safe crossing. He has written a letter, sending it through their organisation's underground, giving us the most vivid accounts we have yet had. Sister Rita brought it up to me this afternoon. She smuggled it out of Mother Superior's mail bag. My nightmares are true.' Madeleine stood at the open door transfixed, blurting out the account.

Drancy, Auschwitz: now the names came from another planet, another life. Thérèse's father, a prisoner of war, not because he had been fighting and captured, but just because of who he was, a Jew.

His brother Bernard, missing. He remembered a trip to Paris and a train journey through Normandy. Verdun, Somme. His father had said that he must visit those places. Constantly now, this sense of life here and life there, life elsewhere. The West Indian regiment, the Empire. The century was falling apart.

Singh had lectured this morning to his university of hunger of the great Labour Movement, the rights of workers. Vincent saw his patients under the almond tree listening patiently, their rotting limbs, their blind eyes, their legless bodies; casualties of a war that was fought along their nerve ends. This would be his war effort, the life and health of these patients, shunted onto this island with a voluntary nursing force. Who was the war for? Not them. Not Madeleine's father.

She came to stand at Vincent's side. She saw the open letter and the telegram on his desk. At any moment, someone else would enter, they thought. She stood with her hands under her scapular like a good nun, her fingers worrying the beads of her rosary which hung at her side, not in prayer, but in agitation. Once she had her habit on, she possessed a certain demeanour. She felt that if she did not hide her hands, occupy them, she would stroke the nape of Vincent's neck. She would bend and kiss that naked nape which she could see under the white collar of his shirt as she stood behind him. She could see down his brown back to a depth of three vertebrae. She now stood back from the chair.

Vincent continued to stare out to the bay and then down at his mother's letter and the telegram from the Colonial Office in London.

'You've had news?'

'Yes.'

She would have to extract it from him. She was so open with her terror, her news. He now felt so angry. He had had to keep back his tears when she entered the room, holding back his emotion. She with her own story, as ever, now irritated him. All these emotions were confused and confusing. He had better sit and not get up and look at her.

'Is it from England?'

'Yes, and a letter from my mother.'

Vincent began to fold the letter and the telegram back along their creases and put them into the envelope. 'Ti-Jean brought them up this morning.' It was something to say, to fill the silence. He could feel her behind him.

Their minds and hearts were somewhere else, hers with a father and his with a brother. He did not know where Bernard was missing, whether it was over Germany or France. A letter was following. It would take a while. His mother had hope, hope got her over this time. What would get him over this time? Vincent stood up and pushed back his chair. She moved to the door. Vincent turned and looked at her.

'Don't leave.'

She stood with her hands on the handle of the door.

'You are hurt. I can see that. Why don't you share with me what hurts you? I do.' She stood looking at him pleading with her eyes, her tears brimming and trickling out of her huge black eyes. The sound of the yard was coming through the open window. They could hear the other sisters and patients walking in the corridor above. Now, suddenly, it sounded as if someone wanted to come into the surgery. Thérèse held the door firmly. She raised one hand to wipe away a tear.

'It's my brother. Bernard. He's missing. My mother had the telegram yesterday.'

'I'm sorry. To imagine it, the danger of it, those flights. I look at the planes here and I think of the men in them. The body's so fragile.' She held up her hands and made as if examining them medically.

'He had always wanted to fly. Flying excited him. He would've been so excited when he went out.'

'He must've been afraid too? Yes?'

'Yes, I expect he was. No, he must've been. I would've been. But then

351

Bernard was different, is different. He wanted to go to the war. He was obsessed by my father's stories, when he told them, when he was capable of telling them.'

'My father wanted to save life,' Thérèse declared.

'I'm sure he will. That must be what he's doing.'

'It's a work camp they say, making the best use of people.' She comforted herself with her explanation.

Again, Vincent focused on the wisps of black hair straying from beneath her veil. He wanted to lean out and touch them, take them between his fingers. 'Some of your hair has escaped.' She had begun to stroke the nape of his neck. With his finger, he prized up the edges of the tight cotton cap beneath her veil, a surgeon's fingers tucking away, preparing to stitch it up. The palm of his hand brushed against her cheek. He held her hand. He was examining her skin. 'What's this I hear from Ti-Jean about you having *Cococbay*.'

'Nonsense. You know how rumour spreads. It's because of my work in the hills with the very bad patients. I'm fine. Look, look Doctor.' She held out her hands.

He pulled her close to him and kissed her.

Someone was just outside the door where there was a cupboard with fresh linen. They stood waiting. The cupboard was closed, and then the person retreated down the wooden floor of the corridor. They could tell it was one of the other sisters, by the swish of her habit, the click of her rosary beads. Why were they putting themselves through this?

'I'll see you later. You must take extreme care always.'

She smiled closing the door gently behind her.

Back at the house that evening, Vincent continued to think of Bernard. His fear had not hampered his desire to fly. It had propelled him. At that moment, he remembered one of Bernard's letters. He could not give much away about the actual operations. But he did talk about his feelings. Bernard's letters to Vincent were more explicit about mess life than the letters he wrote to his mother.

"After a flight I can't wait to get to the bar. The first pint is the best. I knock it back in one. I'm not complete again until I have that drink, chased by a scotch and then lots of cigs, and another pint and then it really gets going, the stories we tell each other. Some of the lads fight." He had become so English. "They have to fight to rid themselves of all the horrible feelings. They have to get something out of them. It's all that fear exploding, all that real pleasure."

Then, Vincent realised more profoundly that he might never see him again. He missed the life he had not had with his brother.

'Fear excited him.' Vincent was very close to Madeleine's face as she bent over his shoulder.

Transformed from a nun, she wore her forever-blue cotton dress with the forget-me-nots.

'My fear is in the pit of my stomach,' she held her hand there.

As if he were her doctor, Vincent turned towards her and pressed his hand on her stomach, pressing his hand, here and then there. 'Does that hurt?' he smiled.

'What're we doing?'

'I don't know.'

'Your brother, my father.'

'Us.'

'Us.' They echoed each other.

'Yes.'

'Kiss me.' He heard her soft invitation. He could hardly breathe. He had hardly room to move. They were already so close. He turned his head and touched her lips with his mouth. They each listened to the familiar world out there, conscious of the world beating in their chests. Vincent smelt the *vertivert* which she wore. He smelt the scent of the soap in which her under-clothes were washed. He smelt the smell of her sweat. As he kissed her, her body as a nun came back to him; the body he had so long desired. They were back at the boathouse that first time, as if they could not move from there. They rose. He took her dress off, as he had done her habit and her veil, and made a soft bed for them to lie down right there, on the floor of the drawing room. As they fucked hard against each other, a vision of her shaven head came to him as she fell to the floor under him. When they got up they were astonished at what they had done. They stood and looked at Theo, sitting on the jetty, fishing.

Some weeks later, there was another letter conveying the deepest regret and confirming that Bernard was considered missing, having failed to return from 'an operational sortie.'

They now knew that his aircraft had left to take part in an attack on the city of Hamburg, and that after take-off, there had been no further contact with the flight. They conveyed that they were of the opinion that the crew would have been able to make use of their parachutes in case of an emergency. The exact circumstances were not known. They were not advising that they should hold high hopes. They mentioned that Bernard was a keen officer, popular with his fellow officers and always ready and willing to get on with the job. They would pass on any other news immediately. Bernard's belongings were being kept at the Central Depository.

He was dead and not dead.

One afternoon, later that month, when he had returned to the doctor's house earlier than usual, Theo brought Vincent a cup of tea out on the verandah with a composition on "Catching Butterflies" that he had written the previous evening, with the help of Madeleine. Compositions and stories were proliferating. Vincent was re-reading and reflecting on the impersonality and particular poise of the official telegraphic prose, and then comparing it with Theo's descriptively charged words.

Theo sat opposite him and looked over the corrections that Vincent had made to his composition, in addition to those which Madeleine had made.

The night-time stories had subsided. There had not been any more for some time, since the one who came at night, galloping through the window on a horse. There was no more talk of the cold key.

Vincent was not reassured that this was the end. No. It was probably only a respite.

The quiet of the afternoon, and the reflections of the boy and the doctor on the different kinds of prose and their purposes, was interrupted by the sound of a pirogue coming into the bay.

Theo got up and went down to the jetty, as he often did when a boat came close to the house.

Vincent could see that it was not Jonah, nor any of the fishermen that he knew. Unusually, they looked like holidaymakers. There were many holiday homes on the archipelago. But it was very unusual to find holidaymakers down the islands at this time, with the restrictions made by the Americans. He got out his binoculars. It was a family group, possibly even a family that he knew, though he so seldom went into town now. He wondered who he would recognise.

The boat had come in quite close, but was not showing any signs of wanting to come into the jetty. Vincent took in the whole scene. An older woman sat in the middle under a parasol, and a man, who he presumed was her husband, was at the tiller. A young girl, about Theo's age, with long blonde hair blowing in the breeze, was sitting in the bow. A younger boy was next to the older woman. The man was the first to wave. Vincent waved back. The man kept on waving as if he had not got the attention that he sought.

Vincent looked at Theo on the jetty. He stood with his arms at his sides staring at the pirogue in the bay. They had come in so close. It was now very clear who they were.

They were a white creole family. Vincent was sure that he recognised them, but then he had not met them for a long time, since his family had moved into town, and he had gone away. Vincent heard quite distinctly the man call out, 'Coco!' Hearing the name from the tale shocked him. He looked for Theo's reactions.

The boy remained stone-still, staring out to sea. He did not respond to the waving, or to the man calling out. The man called again, 'Coco!' He cupped his hands to his mouth like blowing on a conch. The pirogue circled the bay once more, so at one point, the boat with the blonde girl in the bow came in very close to the jetty. 'Coco!' the man called again.

Vincent felt a chill down his spine.

Then there was the girl's voice, 'Theo,' and she waved.

At first, Theo did not respond. Then, as the pirogue raced off, leaving a wide wake, the girl stood in the bow, and over the head of her father, mother and brother, looking down the length of the boat, waved wildly. Vincent noticed Theo raise his arm and wave very deliberately, and then his arms dropped to his side.

'Theo! Theo!' she called again and again. The girl stood staring at the bow until the pirogue left the bay.

The sun was just beginning to set. The light caught the girl's blonde hair in the breeze, and the spray from the fast moving pirogue. She disappeared into the white light.

Madeleine had left her work and come out onto the verandah, having heard the voices calling. She looked at the scene: Vincent watching Theo waving, the girl waving from the fast disappearing boat. And the man, still with one last shout, calling out, 'Coco!'

Then Theo let out a piercing cry. 'Chantal!'

Mister

That night, Vincent noticed that Theo was like he had been when he first arrived at El Caracol. He was impenetrable. He knew that the cause was the appearance of Mister. He had never wanted to know the identity of the family that Theo always talked about. He knew the name well, Marieneaux. But he had lost touch with the families on the estates, particularly after being away for seven years in England. He had also agreed with Father Dominic that the whereabouts of the boy would not be disclosed to the family. Something had happened to break that promise.

This would put Theo back, maybe months. He feared most of all that the boy would think that he had betrayed him. What would Theo do? He recalled snippets from earlier tales, earlier nights spent with his turmoil.

AND NOW, I want to fly. I hear a woman in Chen shop tell Spanish one day that people uses to fly, just so. They see them over the hills Tortuga way. Just so, they take a hoe in the yard, in the cane piece, and fly. Fly away. They never come back.

Some say they yearn for Africa. Africa? Yearned?

Father Angel say, Catch the spirit.

Spanish say, That is a lot of stupidness.

What a wonder it would be to fly! Me, Popo, Chantal and Jai. Fly away.

Me, Popo, Chantal and Jai. Vincent grew sad for the loss of the boy's childhood. There she was, Chantal, on the bow of the boat this afternoon. Vincent had to confess to himself his interest in this girl, an emblematic interest in the destinies of this boy and this girl. For sometime he had noticed some concurrence with his own story. But theirs was a terrible fate. Chantal, a girlfriend! Vincent left that sad fate for the more urgent understanding of Theo's desire to fly. Then he remembered one of Father

Dominic's earlier accounts, before he had lost touch altogether, of what had been going on in the friary.

"One day, the boy tells me I'm not seeing what is under my nose. When I leave his cell I must check for matches. And when he tells me I am not seeing what is under my nose, I think that that is what he means. Being sacristan, he could easily have some which he brings to his cell. He smiles when he sees me looking. There is a sense of humour there, or something else. 'You think I go burn down the place, Father?' he laughs. Maybe, we're becoming friends."

Father Dominic had a definite fear that the boy would resort to fire. Vincent's mind was running. He could not put any boundaries on Theo. He was left all day alone. He had access to everything. He had complete freedom. Vincent believed that that trust was paramount in the regaining of the boy's full health. But, with this regression, what was he to do? Fire was apparently part of Theo's pattern in the past. Theo's voice from the past moved and frightened him.

Flying and fire!

That night Theo was at his bedside with a fleeting tale.

AU REVOIR! Adieu! Ba-bye!

I see Father Angel and Mrs Goveia. I see Ma Sybil and all the children. The yard standing out and waving. I see far up on the hill where the verandah use to be, where Chantal use to be. Nothing. There is nothing. Pillars, blackened pillars! There is nothing, nothing.

First the dolly house and then the big house.

The stories were catching fire in Vincent's mind, and his imagination was running away with him. He read through some of Father Dominic's other letters the next day.

"That particular morning is an example in question. How to pick up the pieces? I thought, Oh, Lord God, and I excuse myself to take the Lord's name in vain. It is a prayer. For I needed to have all the assistance, both divine and worldly to deal with what I had to deal with that particular morning. And I had to swear Brother Stephen into my confidence, that this was not a matter to trouble the Father Superior with at the present moment, But in good time, I would let it be known what had happened. As indeed, I had intended to do. This was not an untruth. I intended, once I had brought the boy some harmony, or he came to it himself, that I would give a full report to Father Superior about his state.

"Brother Theo rang the house bell for Matins, and then went out into the yard to ring the big bells. So he was up earlier than the rest of the community. I had arranged that my room be on the same corridor as his. Not next to him. That room was spare. It was used as a store room. But I had grown so used to my care of the boy that even in sleep I seemed to be vigilant. I woke usually about the time that he should wake, so I would hear him on his way down to the cloister with the hand bell. He would start at the other end of the cloister, and make his way back to where my room was.

"I thought it strange that I had not heard the bell that morning. For all his tortured life, when it came to his duties, he performed them very well, with punctuality and with great credit. Father Angel's Exhibition Class boy, he would say to me. Sadly, of course, it did not happen. I have not got to the bottom of that as yet. I expect it to be made visible, as a consequence of the more serious happenings. Father Superior's words, his notes, are so brief.

"I am not complaining, but at times I am so in the dark. Father Superior, suspecting that I thought this on one occasion, when he routinely asked about Brother Theo, said that I had to work with faith. At times we should perhaps assist faith with some reason. I dare not even think that.

"I needed all my faith on this particular morning, given what I found when I got out of bed and went down to the cloister, wondering why the bell had not yet been rung, worried that the community would be late for Matins, and consequently all the hours would be thrown into confusion.

"The boy was lying on the ground, if not fully unconscious, at least dazed, very dazed, seeming to be asleep. It took me a while to rouse him. I coaxed him with some assistance from water at the fountain near where he had fallen, it seemed. I checked from bruises and cuts. I attended to the abrasions on his hands and knees. There was a cut on his forehead.

"I don't know what made me look back and up, but I seemed to do so instinctively. There was all the evidence of bed clothes and pyjamas on the roof beneath the window of his cell, which was above this part of the cloister. I then discovered some shingles which had been displaced and fallen into the cloister. Also, the galvanise parapet was broken.

"How to attend to the boy and repair this damage before the community got up? I had to seek the assistance of someone, and that was when I took Brother Stephen into my confidence about this matter, only treating it as an isolated instance, not something that indicated anything. I think I said something stupid, like he must be a sleepwalker. Brother Stephen seemed to accept this, and was quickly repairing the damage to the roof, and dragging the bedclothes through the window. Then he had to rush to ring the bell to get the community up, while I attended to Brother Theo, taking him to the infirmary where I didn't imagine there would be any danger of being discovered at that hour of the morning.

"Once in the infirmary, Brother Stephen was miraculously able to give me a hand to lift the boy, who thank God was slight. I pleaded with him. Brother Theo, Brother Theo. What have you done? What has been done to you? I could not get him to talk. I checked his limbs. Mercifully, they seemed to be in order, though I don't know, given what I imagined had happened, that he had jumped from the window or slid on the parapet. But what was he doing out there?

"But, you see, flying. He insists that he tried to fly from the window. One can understand the desire for flight. I am seeing now that this boy is here by force, against his will, if he knows what his will is. He expresses his will in such childlike forms. To be reunited with his friends Popo and Jai and the girl, Chantal, to take his Mama from the yard. Again, I would like to be able to see these conditions which the boy describes. He has admirable sentiments for his parish priest, Father Angel, and his housekeeper Mrs Goveia. But what really is the will of someone in his present state?

"Some arrangement has been made with the Marineaux family. I don't at the moment have the facts, but I must get to the bottom of the question if I am to be of real assistance to this boy. Having to carry the personal responsibilities for these deliberations, I find this very burdensome. But I feel this would be betraying the boy to something worse, if I was to simply tell all that has been going on.

"This idea of flight has to be one of his fanciful stories. What did he say? That over the Tortuga hills people used to fly. Apparently he is alluding to some ancient custom going back to the dark days of slavery when it is said that African people had the power, the science, to fly back to Africa, to escape the terrible conditions of their enslavement.

"So, yes, this was his explanation, that he had tried to fly from his

360

window, out over the cloister to reach the sky. He had been testing the breeze with his sheets, to see if they would billow like sails. What state of mind was he in, that he could throw himself from a window, jump from the parapet over the cloister? Thankfully, it is not very high."

Between the fear of fire, and the possibility that Theo would want to fly again, Vincent could not sleep that night. He saw the friar's words in a new light. He would have to make new arrangements. He would not be able to let the boy out of his sight. He would have to take him to the hospital at all times. Singh, Jonah, Madeleine would have to keep an eye on him. He could not have the boy killing himself or burning down the place.

Vincent dozed. Then he woke, waking Madeleine. They sat and listened, as they saw and heard Theo at the window of their room.

THEN, HE THERE. Right at the window this time, a string of stars is his halter, the milky way his bridle. Orion is his stirrup. He is there at the window. And the horse speak to me.

Come, ride, ride with me, for you know you have ridden me in the past. You know you stole me for your canter over the cocoa hills. Come, lay your cheek on mine. Come and rest on my eyelids. Come, lie the length of your boy's body along my long neck. Come, press your knees into my flanks. Leave your moons there, leave your tattoos for me to carry them to glory. Crouch and hide in the dark, as I take you through the darkness which hangs with the purple cocoa pods. High is the sound of the rivers running over the blue stones, which is a chorus of bell frogs, a choir of crickets, a net of fireflies, to our hiding spot that no one know about, where they can't hear me neighing with the joy of you on my back. Can't hear you cry.

Theo was now kneeling at the bedside and speaking into Vincent's ear in urgent whispers, his horse music, as he might speak through the grille of a confessional.

Madeleine moved from the bed and sat in the rocker near the window. She needed air.

FATHER SUPERIOR leave no key this time. I don't have a key. He calling for the key to be let in. He say is under my pillow. He say is by the wash stand. He say is wrap in a towel. Look under the mattress. He say don't play those tricks. We have enough of tricks.

Then I see the chestnut horse. I holding the cold key. I have it in my mouth, as I curl on the bed waiting for the horse to come *clop clop* through the window. Waiting for the door, *clacketyclack*.

I wait for him. I know the smell of the *eau de Cologne*. I know the feel of khaki. I know the switch. I know the echo of the boot on the corridor. I know the scrape of the boot outside. I know these things before they happen.

I anticipate and then I experience. I experience twice. I am in a double terror, because I know my terror and my torture. And in this quiet place of God, I do not know how no one hears what goes on in the next room. I don't know how they don't hear till I call and then it is too late. Even when I sing *Frère Jacques, dormez -vous*.

Vincent woke with a jolt. He had nodded off. 'What's too late, Theo? Theo, you must tell me now, tell me all. I'm here. I'm hearing. Call out, Theo. Call out. Call out to me. I'm listening.'

'He says it's too late when no one comes when he calls.' Madeleine leant over towards the bed.

But Theo was all whispers. He could hardly talk.

BONE STICK in my throat. Fish bone in my gullet.

'Bread Theo, eat some bread. I'll get you some bread, some water to dislodge the bone in your throat. Wait Theo, wait there.'

Vincent jumped out of bed and ran downstairs to the kitchen. He returned with bread and a glass of water.

Theo was no longer kneeling at the bedside like a child at the confessional when Vincent returned with the bread and the glass of water. He was standing with his back to the door, as if he were looking out of the window, but the window still had its blackout curtains drawn. He was looking into that darkness. When Vincent's eyes grew accustomed to the darkness he could then see Theo turn and kneel.

He spoke in the same urgent whispers.

I READY.

Then Vincent and Madeleine heard from his stifled throat the words:

362

DIE, DIE DIE.

When there was no immediate response from Vincent, Theo's tone of voice changed. His demeanour was transformed into an authoritative one.

GET YOUR SWITCH. Do your work. *Bois, bois*. Give it to me.

He turned and offered his naked bottom. He bent over and invited Vincent to beat him with a switch.

'I can't stay and see this.' Madeleine fled from the room. She hesitated on the landing, and then sat at the top of the stairs outside the room, part listening, part not wanting to hear.

Then Vincent came close and touched Theo's back saying, 'Theo, Theo, come, drink some water, eat this bread.' Theo leapt up from his bending-over position and knelt in front of Vincent. He knelt with his mouth open like a child, waiting for the priest to place the host on his tongue at Holy Communion. He began to undo Vincent's pyjamas, to grab at his penis.

SUCK. I SUCK. I suck the cold key. You open the door. You come in. Take me. *Clacketyclack*. Gallop with me through the air. Ride me through the night.

He was off again on poetry. On fantasy.

He turned and bent over, offering his bottom to Vincent with his small hands stretching his buttocks apart and opening his anus.

USE THE KEY, OPEN THE DOOR.

Out of a pocket of the khaki pants on the floor, he took out a large iron key.

THIS IS THE COLD KEY. I keep it for Mister to open the door.

He began to force it into his anus, pushing the cold iron hard into his soft skin. Vincent took hold of his hand.

'Theo, Theo. Give me the key.'

YES, YES, YOU. You open the door.

'Yes, Theo, you give it to me. I hear what you say. I see what you do. It's all acknowledged now. It wont ever happen again. You are safe with me.' He spoke deliberately. He put the key on the bedside table.

He knelt on the floor. 'Theo, Theo. There's no need for this. You don't have to do this. You don't have to do this anymore. There's no Mister, no horse, no key, no gallop through the air. There's you Theo, and me, Doctor Metivier, Vincent, your friend. This is not what I want you to do. I want you to eat this bread, drink this water. I want you to go to bed and sleep, peacefully.'

363

But it was not that easy.

NO HORSE, no chestnut horse, no *clacketyclack*, no suck the key, no *bois, bois*. Take.

He turned in Vincent's arms offering his back for him to beat him. His familiar scar began to tell its full story that night in the darkness with the boy and the doctor kneeling on the ground.

Vincent knew that he might have to take part in the drama, or give some sense of taking part in a drama, without exactly doing so. To deny the boy this act, was to deny him the opportunity to come out of it, to stop it. It was his way of telling something that he had not been able to tell fully, to get anyone to believe, to see fully.

This was obviously what Father Dominic could not go through with, the boy in his nakedness offering the friar to beat him, to have the boy want to perform fellatio, to let him gallop around the room. If he had told the Father Superior, there would have been no alternative but exorcism. Had they tried that? This had to be the devil himself. That would have been their logical conclusion. There was a demon in him. Vincent knew how the friar felt. He himself had not told anyone about the dressing up, the excrement, the painting of the room. He had wanted to tell Madeleine, but she had her own demons. Demons? Whose language was that? Anyway, she had had to leave the room.

For Vincent it was a trauma, an illness, a sickness. He had to discover the fine line between the acts the boy wanted performed, and the semblance of them which Vincent felt he had to use.

While he was trying to think things through as quickly as possible, deciding what to do, Theo continued to offer him the choice of beating him or allowing him to perform fellatio. Previous dramas had not required Vincent to participate. He had simply been asked to observe, or participate in ways that would not have been harmful, would not perpetuate the trauma, compound its damage.

Vincent picked up a stick which he then noticed that Theo had brought into the room. Another of the contents of the brown grip?

GUAVA, from Pepper Hill. Mister send me to pick it myself. Sweet guava.

Then Theo turned and ran out of the room and down the stairs. Vincent heard the door beneath the stairs bang shut. When he got down stairs himself, he saw himself standing outside the cupboard under the stairs with a stick in his hand. Inside he heard the whimper of the boy.

PLEASE, PLEASE. Mister, don't lash me.

Vincent did not have the language for the reply. After some moments of silence, the boy provided the missing dialogue in the drama, with the appropriate voices.

COCO, you come here immediately.

Then he heard again the whimpering of the boy.

PLEASE, PLEASE, don't lash me.

Then in another voice, the voice of a man, Vincent heard:

COCO, you little coco, you little bastard. Come out here right now.

O PLEASE, PLEASE Mister, don't lash me.

RIGHT NOW this minute. Or you know what I'll have do to you. I'll come right in there, and you know, it will be worse, much worse.

Vincent looked at himself, a full grown man with a stick in his hand standing outside the door with the boy pleading to be spared.

Suddenly, a small moment, secreted somewhere deep in his past. almost forgotten, flashed through his mind. He is eight years old, must be just after his father came back from the war. He hears his voice, Bend over, take down your pants.

He sees himself jumping over the thorns in the pasture. *Ti-Marie* closes her leaves as he touches her, as he goes to pick a tamarind switch. He hears his mother's voice, Wait till your father comes home. He hears his father again, The best of six, bend over. He feels the stinging tamarind switch on his naked bottom. He does not cry. He does not make a sound. He knows there will be more, like last time. Do not cry. It angered his father more if he cried. It was almost a call to be beaten more. He had to learn not to cry.

Vincent stood with the switch in his hand and cried for himself. He cried for himself and Theo. The house went dead quiet. Theo had stopped his pleading.

Madeleine sat on the stairs and listened. There was a wind in the trees, a cool breeze came through the kitchen door. They heard the dead almond leaves scuttling like crabs on the steps. They heard the sea lap on the jetty.

Vincent was grateful for the peace. He sat on the floor by the door and waited to see what might happen next. He must have dozed off, water was splashing on the jetty. He went to the window of the drawing room, made a crack in the blackout curtain. A huge American destroyer was turning in the middle of the bay. The wake washed the boards of the jetty, splashed against the black rocks under the kitchen.

Vincent stared out and went back into the house with the vision and power of the destroyer.

In his mind a Spitfire was hurtling into a line of poplar trees. Floating down was a white parachute like a white moon, descending slowly to earth. Landing on green grass. It landed, dragging the parachuter along the ground. There was the sound of barking dogs. He heard his voice in the dark say, 'Bernard.'

Vincent heard the door of the under-the-stairs cupboard open and bang shut.

He returned to the stairs. Theo was standing against the door, naked, facing him. As Vincent approached, he knelt. Vincent knelt in front of him. There they were, the boy and the doctor, facing each other, kneeling in the darkness of the war's blackout.

'Ride-a-cock-horse.'

'Theo.'

'Coco.'

'Theo.'

'Coco, Cocorito.'

'Theo, that's not your name. That's Mister's name for you.'

'Yes, is he name for me.' Vincent noticed that for a moment they were having a conversation about the boy's state of mind. Then he was off again with a story, leaping naked onto the arms of the couch in the drawing room.

PRINCE come in the yard with Mister on his back. Mister riding out of the cocoa. Like he just appear from nowhere. Crisp white shirt and pressed khaki pants and cork hat. Tall brown shiny boots in the silver stirrups. Stirrups to dig Prince. And Mister holding Prince by the reins. Mister, coming out of the cocoa, not down the gravel road from the big house, but back track.

Who he think he could fool?

Prince have a white star in the middle of his brown forehead. He was chestnut, Chantal say. A brown I don't know. Red brown like your Mama skin, she say. Like mine, even when it in the sun long. Long days dry season gravel trace when there is no leaves for shade.

Mister tilt the brim of his cork hat where there is a band stain with the sweat from his brow. He see my escape into the bush now.

I hear his voice, the cry of a bird coaxing me. *Coco, Coco, Cocorito,* coming along with the *clop clop clop* of Prince.

But as I come out into the trace where I think I lose him, he is there, dismount from his chestnut horse. He is there, tall in khaki. And the trace narrow with the cocoa thick on either side. And the trace is long behind him and long behind me. The trace is a black canal. Cocoa picker deep in the cocoa, so we alone. I hear the water in the river running over the pebble, pulling at the fine gravel. I hear it where it fall over rock, as it take the bend to meet up with a next little river coming out of La Vega.

I think of where I am. Mister there, standing, staring at me, and he have his switch. He have his switch out, hanging down in his right hand along the length of his khaki, along the length of his breeches. He hitting his tall boot with his switch. He swiping at them, and there is the crack of the switch against the leather. There is the reek of leather. It is the sign of a master for his dog to kneel.

I hear the *cigale* singing. Sand fly and mosquito playing their tune, the afternoon heat high in the blue sky, where is one corbeaux circling high high. We alone, I see. This is how he does chose to do things, when he have me trap.

I can't run.

I think to run. I think to hide. But I stand still, until he tell me to come. He know that I know what I have to do, as he walk off the trace into the bush.

He take me by the neck and pull me down, so that I must try to touch the ground. I must touch my toes. Touch your toes. And while I bend I must wait for the switch. I must listen to his voice.

Who say you can play with Chantal? Who say you can come up in the house and go downstairs and play with Chantal? I tell you now you must leave her alone. She is not for you to play with. And the words come with the switch. Do what you have to do. And what I have to do is to drop my pants there in the light of the cocoa.

I stare at a cocoa pod. I stare at the purple of a cocoa pod. I enter the cocoa pod. But that don't take away the sting. I take the sting and I enter the cocoa pod. I enter behind the purple skin, and I open the pod and take out the bean in their fleshy cocoon. I must get close to softness. I must tear something soft to place between my fingers. I forget how long I there.

Only now I know is Chantal's soft hair in my face, Catechism class, that comfort me as I bend low to the ground and I smell the dead leaves and the fresh crushed grass and the little pink flowers that grow under the cocoa.

Who tell you to talk with her? Who tell you to play with her? She is nothing to do with you. You are nothing to do with her.

And now I near his leg. I staring at his boot. I near where he like to have me by his crotch. I am nothing to do with she. She is nothing to do with me. I must repeat. My repetition smell like his sweat. The sweat which drip from his forehead. The reek of the leather. The salt of the sweat. The stench of his crotch. I forget how long it take. The smell is the sweat of his crotch where he have me. And that is a kind of softness to be lying my head on his leg. That is something. I think he do not know what he want to do. Whether to hurt me, or to make me the gift of something soft.

Soft and hard. I pull my khaki pants up.

I catch myself and I alone. My back hurt me for so. The sound of the river in my ear. The hoot of an owl in the darkness of the cocoa. *Jumbie* bird! And in the sunlight on the trace a *keskidee* with his question. Each sound in itself shrill and loud in this moment, when I open my eyes, and I alone, and Mister have his way with me once more. My back hurting for so, must have burst open. I reach so, to feel where I feel it bleeding. I must go home and wash myself by the pipe near the house, or if water shut off I must use a calabash to dip in the barrel and splash some water on my skin, to clean and soothe. I must dip from the big oil drum which collect water from the spouting.

And the next day when I bring message for Mama, is the Mistress self who say, We not see you in the yard for a day or two, *Coco*. I hear her say, *Coco*. She must've get this name from Mister. And I lower my head. I shy. So one invite me and the other shoo me off. But I feel that it not so simple.

And where is Mama? Where is my Mama?

'Theo, let's leave these stories. Theo, it's time to leave all of that behind. Come with me.'

It was like a code buried in some far off moment, part of some part of the story, a trigger which immediately had Theo turning around, and bending over.

RIDE A COCK HORSE. Ride me, ride me to Banbury Cross.

Vincent now saw what had really frightened Father Dominic. This was where he had got to, and rather than deliver him to another bout of exorcism, he had decided to try the doctor whom he sensed had a gift of healing.

Vincent immediately, by some instinct for survival spoke authoritatively. *Coco*, get up, at once, and go to your room.'

There was a moment when nothing took place, and then Theo rose from his bending position and went up the stairs to his room. Vincent slumped against the door. Maybe, if the boy could sleep he might wake into a normal state, it would have been like a dream. Then he could assume his own self, Vincent, the Doctor.

'Vincent.' It was Madeleine. 'It's morning. Come, I've coffee out on the verandah. The boy is sleeping.'

'Is morning, already?'

'Yes, after a long night.'

'You still here?'

'Yes, I'm late. I'll risk it.'

Pierrot

Vincent was glued to the stories in *The Gazette* when he got home that afternoon. So much was going on since the D -Day Landings last June. There was high expectation in the air.

The development of the war had come to a halt on the walls of Theo's room, since the allies had landed at Anzio. The cutouts had yellowed, and were curling away from the dried-up flour paste. One last one stuck without much commitment: De Gaulle Heads Parade from Arc de Triomphe to Notre Dame, was old news now, as was Sister Rita's last message about the *Maquis* and the *Milice*.

The papers had been full of the Ardennes and the Meuse at the time of the Battle of the Bulge. The Soviet troops had entered the camp at Auschwitz. They remembered when they first had heard that name with the trainloads from Drancy.

One of the last letters from Montreal, enclosing Sister Rita's cousin's news, which was coming less and less, had told of a hurried last trainload from Drancy last August, a couple of days after the French and Allied troops had landed in Provence.

Just when Vincent thought Theo would be recording the victories, he had lost interest. Today's Allies Cross the Rhine and Allies Liberate Buchenwald and Belsen did not get cut out or stuck up.

The U-Boats had quietened down almost completely. Bits and pieces of ships still floated up onto the beach. Quite recently, parts of the corpse of a German sailor were found, caught in a fisherman's seine, a macabre reminder of their proximity to the war, and of the night Achilles entered the harbour of Porta España and torpedoed the Mokihana.

Headlines continued to tell the story of the end: Allies Liberate Dachau. Madeleine read the news and looked at the grainy photographs with horror and without words to say what she was feeling. The letters from Montreal had old news. Things had moved on. Petain had been arrested. Mussolini had been executed. The news from France was all about what to do with the collaborators.

Madeleine and Vincent sat on the verandah. She had learnt to make rum punch and was trying it out. 'One of bitter, two of sweet, three of strong, four of weak.' She mimicked Vincent, telling her his mother's recipe. 'Would your *Maman* approve?'

'Of you? Or, the rum punch?' They laughed. No, she had not been presented to Madame Metivier.

They heard Theo at the back of the house. 'What's he up to?' Madeleine asked.

'Let him be,' Vincent pleaded.

Earlier, Theo had gone straight up to his room on returning from one of his island hikes, and then out to the back of the house with his butterfly net. He had not returned till now, sun down, and then went straight to his room without supper. 'I must check on him,' Madeleine said to Vincent.

She knocked at his door. She could hardly enter the room for the weight against the door. 'Theo.' There was a faint murmur indicating for her to push the door harder.

In the faint light, she noticed that the walls were bare. The maps, newspaper reports, headlines, the advance of armies with their flags, the torpedoing of U-Boats, the sea lines, the myths, the facts, and the scraps of letters, had all been torn down and piled high in the middle of the room and behind the door. There was the faint smell of sulphur, the scent of a lit match. Theo was in the process of dampening down a small flame under the heap of paper at the centre of the room when Madeleine entered. There was a trail of smoke, rifling through the singed newspaper. The streets of Dresden and Hamburg smouldered.

'Theo!'

Theo looked up.

'What're you doing?'

'What you see me doing?' He was immediate and unusually aggressive.

'Theo.' Madeleine knelt next to him among the pile of newspaper cuttings. 'We can take these outside and burn them in the backyard, if you don't want them in here anymore.' She began collecting up the newspaper cuttings

371

in her arms. 'I'll help you. We'll get some kerosene. You bring the matches.' Theo followed reluctantly with a pile of paper.

Vincent came to the back door and looked on with concern while Madeleine and Theo coaxed the bonfire of paper cuttings in the middle of the sorrel patch.

'Don't let the flames get too near the bush,' Vincent cautioned.

Madeleine looked over to Vincent with restraint in her eyes. She knew his concern. But she wanted the boy to take care of the fire responsibly. She went over to the back door and stood with him, taking his hand in hers. Together they looked at Theo bring the last of the cuttings down and put them on the flames. The World War, as told by the boy, roared, then fizzled out. Ash floated up in the still evening air. They had the fire doused before the curfew.

Madeleine and Vincent followed Theo up to bed that night. In the early hours of the morning, Madeleine woke with a start. 'Vincent.' She shook him violently. 'Vincent, do you smell fire?' They both sat up, startled.

They saw him crouching on the floor at the foot of their bed. Theo was kneeling over a small heap of papers striking matches, trying to light them. They both leapt out of bed. Vincent quickly lit the kerosene lamp. Madeleine knelt next to Theo. 'Theo.' She restrained his hands.

FIRST THE big house, then the dolly house down in the gully.

'Theo?' Vincent knelt on the other side of the boy. 'Come, Theo, you don't want to do this here.'

FIRST THE big house, then the dolly house down in the gully.

Madeleine sat back on her legs. Vincent put his arms around Theo's shoulders.

'Do you want to tell us this story, Theo?'

Then there was that inimitable voice they had grown to know.

I TELL CHANTAL to go and sleep by her cousin that night. I alone. I have my plan. First is the big house, then the dolly house down in the gully.

I have two pan of kerosene. The flame only following me like a fiery snake, where I run right upstairs and through the bedroom. I throw the match. Mosquito net disappear just so.

And down in the gully I gone. Is there I go catch them.

All them little dolly furnitures. Like the house light up for a party. I see the light through the windows. I watch till the flame take the whole dolly house. I ent wait to see. I leave the whole place to burn

It burn, pretty, pretty pretty..

Theo sat staring at the floor silently.

'Come Theo, let me get you to bed. All that's over now.' Vincent led Theo to his room and sat by him while he fell back to sleep.

When he returned to his room, Madeleine was sitting on the side of the bed reading the cuttings that Theo had been trying to burn. The headline read: Young Boy in Pepper Hill Responsible for Mother's Death by Fire. Vincent took the singed cuttings and read the article. This was what Father Dominic could never bring himself to tell.

'Will telling the story be sufficient to free him from this trauma? Is this what was attempted in the cloister? Father Dominic had been explicit about the flying, but not about the fire. We need to watch the boy, Madeleine. I'll sleep next to him tonight.'

They each went to bed with heavy hearts, and minds stretched beyond their believing.

The news had caught like a fire in a cane piece crop time in the dry season. People way up in Indian Valley, the men and women in the huts along the coast, had heard the news before it even reached the quiet slumber of Father Meyer's presbytery on the point. He was late this morning for the nuns' morning mass. Not even the sisters, just coming out of Matins, over at the convent, were aware of the news.

Vincent, Madeleine and Theo were dead to the world, following Theo's revelation of his crime in the early hours of the morning.

Parrots, with their agitated green screams, caught the news and flung it loud across Chac Chac Bay.

No sooner had that British Bull Dog's voice crackled and growled over the radio early this morning, than the *tassa* drums, like at Hosay, had begun to use the opportunity for a kind of *Jour Ouvert* morning *ole mas*. People came out of their huts in nighties and pyjamas to see what had happened in the night, and was now being celebrated at dawn.

'Germany surrender!' One fella shouted to another, one woman knocked on the door of her neighbour to announce. It was the phrase on every lip.

'Germany surrender! Watch Mr Hitler moustache.' It was like every carnival which had been banned by the Governor because of the war, every calypso which had been censored for insurrection, got now an opportunity to come out onto the road, onto the mud tracks, the gravel paths, where the barefoot people of El Caracol had tread these weary years, to shake themself, sing themself, loud, loud!

Yes, it was the end of the war. In one sense, people sung about that, but it was a release for so much more that had been borne and suffered here, that they wanted to use the permission of the time to dissent.

The Angelus at Saint Damian's was never so joyously and wildly rung, school children taking turns at the tolling. Young fellas began to *buss* bamboo like it was the sweet Christmas season; the bamboo young and exploding in the hills.

It was Jonah who came down the road taking over from the *chantwell* and the old *tambour bamboo* band some fellas had collected: the bass bamboo, the cutters, chandlers and the *foule*, beating the music the people had to make when the skin music and the Shango drum get ban. People say the *tamboo bamboo* band as sweet as the John John *tamboo bamboo*, as sweet as the Belmont, Cadiz Road *tamboo bamboo*. Jonah had the voice of the Shango from down in Moruga. He raised his arms and then poured libations on the road, and called upon the Orishas: "*Ogun. Ye Manja!*" Plenty people beat their bottle and spoon.

But, suddenly, men, women and children were making their way along the mud paths, the gravel tracks and the red dirt ground, for a new sound; a kind of iron sound, the sound of iron beating on iron.

Olga Cardinez came out of one of the huts beating her soap box, while her neighbour, Marjorie Rojas, beat her bucket. One fella, John Mendes came out beating a sweet-oil pan. People pick up pitch oil pan, biscuit tin, and milk can. But the sound everyone was moving towards was a kind of *ping pong*, a sound that those who were lucky had heard once, or twice, when the young fella who had come from Laventille, that bad John place in Porta España, behind the bridge, over the Dry River; the one who came with the illness and was forging cut down oil drums in his back yard.

In the heat of his fire he was ponging out an instrument of music, sounding light and trembling: a little shy this music this first morning, as if all creation right here bow down and stop to listen to this new kind of *ping*, this new kind of *pong* which make the very palm trees pick up the music.

And, suddenly, it was as if people sensed that this belong to them, and they gathered behind the young fella from Laventille and some few fellas he had persuaded to join him. They followed behind him with pan that does make the *du dup* sound, a bass pan from a big oil drum. And one fella who they call Mauby, because of how he like the drink, beat a big Bermudez biscuit tin, slap bass. They replace the big bamboo bass, the one that does make the bass sound in the *tambour bamboo* band because too many people foot get hurt. Doctor Metivier would've be glad to see that as his patients dance their music.

They made their way down to the meeting place beneath the big almond tree where Krishna Singh greeted them with speeches of freedom, and where a set of Hindu people were chanting mantra like it Pagwa or Ramleela.

'Come people, come!' Krishna Singh shouted.

The whole place come out.

All the politics talk, all the cries for Justice, for Bread, for Rights and Wages, for Humanity, get turned into the music which was now filling the whole island of El Caracol, and waking those sleeping in the priest's house and the doctor's house with the *tintabulation* of the iron. People catch the rhythm, the semitone melody, jumping wild on the ground. The whole place was catching fire. People sense the beauty in the music in the ping pong, but they sense too, they feel too, a kind of violence which was the violence of the fire out of which this music was made, a kind of violence that was needed to burn that music out. They felt the hot iron in the fire, and with that they pick up sticks, to walk with sticks like fighters to the *gayelle*. With the iron and the trembling noise of the pan was the old time *lavway* that people sang, to make their life sweet and to take away the violence.

Suddenly, a child's voice drew attention to a figure coming down from right on top of the hill above the hospital. Those who knew this Anansi figure on crutches, who knew the trickster, Ti-Jean, the exuberant boy of the yard, laughed and pointed, 'Watch Ti-Jean, watch Petit Jean! Watch my boy!' Crutches going like the legs of a spider, Ti-Jean had decked himself out in rags, all kind of pieces of coloured cloth, to give himself the cloak of Pierrot, story-teller *extraordinaire*. He was descending to people with a long tamarind stick in his hand which was the wand that Pierrot does carry, and he was bowing and receiving the applause of the crowd who parted for the favourite of

375

the yard to make his Pierrot dance. As he descended, Ti-Jean was singing a *melée* of calypsos: '*I heard an ex soldier exclaim never me go fight again.*'

'Sing Ti-Jean, give us the melody!' people cried out.

And he continued with the songs of the time with broken lines, words from here and there as he came like a *moco jumbie* on stilts, as he manoeuvred his way over the rock stones and the red dirt paths to come and stand right there under the tall and broad almond tree. 'Petit Jean, Petit Jean,' the children cried, and the old women reached out to touch the hem of the Pierrot's cloak, worn by the wonder child who gave them all hope, as he buzzed about the yards. People joined in with the sweet sweet calypso which the *ping pong* pan was picking up and accompanying them, as they had never been accompanied before. 'All you hear the beat of the steel band. You hear the semitone melody, how it have people jumping in the street.'

Another calypso started up. *All day All night Miss Mary Ann down by the seaside sifting sand..*' People were crowded onto the beach below the jetty, the waves breaking and thundering, adding to the music of the *ping pong* pan and the sweet calypso coming from the mouths of children, old men, old women, and young fellas with their girlfriends, taking the opportunity to grab their sweethearts and chip down the road.

The *Maria Concepción* arrived from the convent. At the same time, Vincent and Madeleine, with Theo in the bow, arrived having rowed from the Doctor's House. Father Meyer had called to them and they had given the priest a ride. 'Well, this morning we must ride together.' Even now, Madeleine turned away from what she remembered of his disapproving stares and advice in the confessional. They were all disembarking at the jetty at the same time. In the confusion, Madeleine lost herself in the crowd so as not to have to encounter Mother Superior.

Suddenly, there was a cry which rose from the crowd, and the music died down. There was the wail of one woman's voice. 'Watch! He falling,' and those nearby surrounded the fallen Ti-Jean. His crutches had collapsed under him, and he had fallen unconscious to the ground. There was the soft movement of the palms and the breaking of the waves on the beach. A high wind caught the trees. One fella still played a gentle *ping pong, ping pong* until an old lady came and rested her hand on his playing hands, just able to clutch, and folded his *ping pong* sticks with the rubber tips.

'The child fall,' she said.

'Call the doctor! Call the doctor!' Vincent heard the cry and was running in the direction of the voice and people who made way for the doctor to come through the crowd, to where Ti-Jean had fallen on the ground. When they tried to give the boy some air, and took off his cloak of rags, they found that he had strapped the crutches to his body, because he could no longer clutch at them. He had used them like splints to walk and heave his way, make his nimble Anansi spider dance. They began to dismantle him, like he was a doll.

It was then that Vincent saw the extent of Ti-Jean's injuries, the state that his sores had become. His inability to feel pain had made him irresponsible. The infection had given the boy a raging temperature.

Theo crept through the crowd to be near to Vincent. Madeleine kept herself to the edges. Sister Rita had found her for a quick word, but then gone to Vincent's assistance. Jonah and Krishna were looking after the crowd of Saint Damians who were there this morning for VE Day, and for the freedom they wanted for themselves.

Some fellas helped to take Ti-Jean to the hospital. Some people did not have the heart now for the celebration, while other people stayed under the almond tree, not wanting to leave each other, because of the spirit that had risen among them.

The news began to spread like cane fire, that the wonder boy, Petit Jean, had passed away, just so, in the arms of Doctor Metivier. Women and children, boys and girls, old fellas and young fellas wept openly for Petit Jean.

Madeleine returned to the Doctor's House. She wanted to be with Vincent, but she dared not go the hospital. As she turned onto the back track, she caught sight of him on the verandah of the childrens' ward and waved. He waved back, reassured.

Jonah and Krishna went up to the ward to see Vincent. 'Like you lose your son, Doc.'

'Yes Jonah, he was a remarkable boy. He gave so many others hope, by his spirit.' Vincent wept openly.

'We'll bury him good, Doc,' Krishna joined in. 'Jonah and I, we'll see about the wake and the digging of the grave. Don't take it too hard, Doc.' Krishna put his hand on Vincent's shoulder.

They understood each other now. It was as Jonah had said to each of them,

'You can't plan love.' Theo looked on with Christiana. He too understood more about love, noticing Vincent and Thérèse, Singh and Christiana. As Vincent had thought before, there was a healing magic in his night calypso.

That night, all the drums beat for the wake of Petit Jean. They beat so hard and long that Madeleine heard them over in their bay. It brought her out again, along the back track to mingle in the crowd and the darkness for the wake. People stayed up outside the hospital and congregated under the almond tree. The sisters brought out jugs of coffee, and they passed around sweet biscuits for everyone. This gave Sister Rita a moment to talk with Madeleine. Theo had gone down to the jetty to be with Jonah.

'What a time!' Sister Rita took Madeleine's hand.

'I know. A time of joy and sadness.'

'All that has been going on, and discovered in Germany. What will you do?'

'I can only wait. I don't know how we'll get the names.'

'It's a matter of time. A strange time of waiting. While some rejoice, millions must wonder what now.'

'I read the reports of the camps, and I'm left numb. I look at the pictures. All the faces are faces that I know and do not know.'

'And what will happen here? This can't continue as it is.'

'Jonah and Krishna will not let this continue. Vincent won't remain silent, as you know.'

'But there have been some improvements.'

'Yes, Vincent tells me. But they want more for their patients, for the people. They want more and they won't let go. Nothing will deter Singh. I know now that those patients in the hills must not be left like that.'

While they talked, patients came up to greet Madeleine, not seeing her like they used to. 'We not forget you, Sister. You looking well. We does ask the docta for you.'

She smiled. 'Thank you, thank you. *I've* not forgotten you.'

Theo stood with Jonah and the young fellas, Bolo and Elroy. They passed around the rum they had got from the fishermen. 'Take a nip boy, take a nip for Petit Jean.' Theo took the bottle to his lips and swigged. He coughed and spat it out. 'Take a next one.' They sat on the benches, along the jetty, and on the sea wall.

No one went to their hut or to their ward. They played All Fours and Dominoes, slapping down their pieces hard on the wooden slats of the benches and on the concrete wall. They gambled away the little they had made. Jonah threw in some cents for Theo. He was a big boy now. The police tried to move them on. They were threatened by the Marines, called in to assist the police, but no one moved from the wake of Petit Jean. They stood their ground and the forces did not want to cause trouble this VE night, and at the wake of the wonder boy, Petit Jean.

Still, Madeleine had not met with Vincent. Then he suddenly appeared when she had finished talking to Sister Rita and whisked her off to the clinic where they used to work. They held on to each other in the darkness, not wanting to draw attention by lighting a lamp. 'I'm so sorry about Ti-Jean. What a thing!' Madeleine exclaimed.

'I'd seen it coming. I didn't know it would be like this.'

'You did all you could.'

'No. Not all. We don't do our all. Soldiers have Penicillin. They have the Sulfa drugs they can give us. Money is sloshing around Sancta Trinidad. Some get rich fast, but the poor remain poor. Our patients are the poorest of the poor.' Vincent was angry, angry in his grief.

'Singh and Jonah will demand more,' Madeleine reassured him.

'Yes, but I'm not convinced of where their way will lead. I worry about the safety of the patients.'

'What should I do now?'

'Stay here. I'll tell Sister Rita. The wake will go on all night. Theo will be fine with Jonah. I must be among the patients.'

Only in the very early hours of the morning did the drumming stop.

At six o'clock, as the Angelus was being rung, Joebell, from Indian Valley, who made all the coffins when they were needed, brought one down on his shoulders the size of the young fella. It was made of good, clean and fresh cedar wood. He put it down on the verandah of the childrens' ward. Inside, the sisters were cleaning up the children, putting on fresh bandages and then sending them off to the yard.

Eventually, the coffin was taken in for the laying out of Ti-Jean's body. Vincent was there to do it himself. They dressed the boy in the best white

379

shirt and pants they could fine. The coffin had been lined with the best white cloth they found in the sisters' sewing room. 'Give him the satin we were going make the new vestments with for Father Meyer.' Sister Rita put a First Communion chain around Ti-Jean's neck with a medal of the Immaculate Heart of Mary.

A small procession of children with the coffin, carried by the most able bodied boys, made its way down the steps into the yard. The smallest girls and boys stood in front of the coffin. They had collected all the white perfumed frangipani flowers they could get. As they began to walk in front of the coffin, they tore at the flowers, its milk staining their fingers, and sprinkled the petals along the path, tossing them above the open coffin, the petals falling over the face and body of Petit Jean in the open coffin. Sister Marie-Paul started the recitation of the rosary. 'The Five Glorious Mysteries. The First Mystery, The Resurrection of our Lord.' The only sound were the mass of feet, bare feet and the pound of crutches, of the people moving, who had collected from all corners of Saint Damian's, and had now joined the procession to the church, where Father Meyer was to conduct the service.

Vincent went and stood at the front of the church with Theo, next to Jonah and Singh. Thérèse had crept out of the clinic where she had spent the rest of the night, and entered the church at the side entrance.

Father Meyer intoned the Introit of the mass '*Requiem aeternam done eis Domine.*' His short sermon talked about the innocence of children and of how Jesus had asked the children to come close to him. Someone, at the back of the church, mumbled the name of Michael Johnson, the policeman who had been burnt before the war.

Everyone turned around with, 'Shhh!'

The sisters led the singing with, 'Sweet Sacrament Divine,' for the receiving of Holy Communion.

Rain caught people on the way to the cemetery as the sisters, led by Father Meyer, sang the *Dies Irae*. It continued a steady downpour as the young fellas lowered the coffin into the ground in the small cemetery outside the church. As the chaplain intoned '*In paradisum,*' asking for the angels to lead Ti-Jean into heaven, where he would be met by Lazarus, all remembered how he, Lazarus, had once had leprosy and had been healed by Jesus. Bolo, Elroy, Jonah and Singh accompanied by Vincent, began to fill in the grave, the priest continuing with, 'Dust to dust ashes to ashes.'

When Vincent looked up from his shovelling of the earth, he noticed Theo staring at him. 'Theo, come, come, boy, fill your first grave. You were a *pardner* of Ti-Jean's.' Theo took the spade and shovelled in the earth.

The Disappearance

'Theo's disappeared.' Madeleine stood in the doorway to the verandah. She had made herself a new dress out of some red curtain material, with an old Singer sewing machine she had found in the cupboard of the spare room. It was a desire for colour after all that white, her cocoon of a nun's habit. The straps of the red dress allowed her brown arms and back to continue getting the sun. She had emerged from her chrysalis. The breeze lifted her red flared skirt, pushed her black curls off her forehead.

'Oh,' Vincent continued to read *The Gazette*.

'Aren't you worried?'

'No, Madeleine.'

'He's not in his room, or at the back of the house. I was always so sure to see him on the jetty.'

Vincent looked up from his newspaper. 'Where've you been these days and weeks? He hardly ever fishes now. Probably up on the back track, or further afield with his butterfly net.'

Butterflies were Theo's new obsession; a solitary activity which took him away from the house for long periods into the hills, below the barbed wire fences of the American base, trespassing as far as the light house.

'No. He's not. I went to look for him,' Madeleine insisted.

'You're spying on him? What on earth for?'

'I'm worried. Haven't you noticed? He's not been in the house, or anywhere near the house since dawn. He had his breakfast early this morning, sitting out on the tank. Not seen him since then. He's not been to Saint Damian's, helping with the Rehabilitation Plan at Singh's.'

'He's a big boy now. He can look after himself.'

'A big boy? I see. He may be sixteen going on seventeen, but he is still that little boy we fear for.'

'His nights have been much quieter these last few weeks.'

'The calm before the storm.'

'Come and sit down, read the papers. Look at this.'

Madeleine read the news over Vincent's shoulder. There had been so much over the last year, months, weeks and almost everyday the fast unravelling of the most terrible things which had been going on. VE Day had come and gone. There were now the ongoing revelations. Vincent stroked Madeleine's arm over his shoulder. They both read an account by a European journalist quoted in the local *Gazette* on the liberation of the camps. *In the course of my travels into liberated territory, I have never seen such an abominable sight ... where more than half a million European men, women, and children were massacred ... this is not a concentration camp; it is a gigantic murder plant.*

'I can't read these accounts.' Yet she continued to read quietly.

'Maybe there'll be better news any day now.'

'Better? Why? How? With each revelation it gets worse.'

'What's happened? What've you heard?'

'Nothing. That's the problem. Nothing. There's nothing to say. Nothing to do. No news. No headlines: Papa Saved! There are just these big events.'

'I know how you must feel.' Vincent took her hand.

'I think only of myself.'

'No, you don't.'

'Yes, I do. I haven't asked you about Bernard for ages. What's his news? I haven't allowed myself to imagine what has happened to the world, as we continue to live in this small corner.'

Vincent put the paper down. 'Everywhere is a small corner. He's also disappeared. My mother has not had any more letters from the Admiralty.'

Suddenly, the bright morning had clouded over. The far southern coast of Sancta Trinidad had disappeared.

'Rain again,' they both said. It poured down, sweeping in off the gulf making them desert the verandah. They sat on the Morris chairs in the drawing room and looked out at the deluge.

'It'll fill the tank,' Vincent said.

'Such an August, for El Caracol!'

Then the downpour stopped, and the rain water dripped and dripped from the leak in the guttering.

The lunchtime news told of the relentless bombing of over sixty Japanese cities. The incendiary bombs which fired the cities had killed six hundred thousand people. Instead of calls for peace, the Japanese were displaying increased anger. The US Secretary of War Henry Stimson had one moral misgiving about the campaign, which was that the terror bombing might gain America the reputation of outdoing Hitler in atrocities.

Madeleine and Vincent sipped coffee, and talked about the news. There had been the raid of Tokyo earlier in the year, when one hundred and twenty thousand people had been killed, and one million were fleeing into the countryside. Numbers were beyond comprehension. The American crews in the bombers had to wear oxygen masks because of the stench of burning flesh. One report had told of people jumping into the river Simida to get away from the flames and being boiled to death.

Jesse had come over one night and spoke of the talk on the base being of early victory, but he and some of his friends had their doubts about what was seen by them as slaughter. They were unusual.

Theo had not appeared for lunch and was not there when Madeleine took a tray with tea down to the jetty. No one had seen him. His butterfly net was not in its usual place behind the door of his room. Madeleine had checked, looking for any other telltale evidence of his disappearance. They were like a couple with an only child, thought Vincent. That was his fantasy at the moment. He had told her about Odetta recently, but not about the baby. She was like a worried mother. What would be their future? How much longer could they stay here like this?

'Come, give me a kiss. Don't be so anxious.' She got up and stood between his legs and bowed her head towards him, her hair falling over his face, and kissed him wildly on the mouth.

'Vincent? What're we to do?'

'I've got to stay and see this thing through with Singh and Jonah.'

'How will that end?'

'I hope well, safe.' He held her as she continued to look down at him.

'You're right. You must stay and stand by Jonah and Singh. I think that with you there, things will work for the better,' she said supportively.

'Rehabilitation is vital. We're convinced that peoples' lives will be immeasurably better with a good rehabilitation programme, rather than living in this quarantine. Spend the money on that. I agree. Jonah and Singh in their own ways are set upon it above everything else.'

'What's the problem for you?' Madeleine asked.

'It is a matter of education. We've made strides here, but out there back on Sancta Trinidad, there will be need for education, so that people will accept our patients back. We need family programmes.'

'Well, you see, that's what I mean. Each of you has a different contribution to make.'

'I need to persuade the authorities to let me have that job of going around the villages and towns where our patients come from, to talk to people.'

'I'm keeping you back. You'd be better off without me.'

'No. I'm not saying that. I want you to work with me.'

'But what about my father?'

'We'll deal with that as well. I promise you.'

'Can we go to Europe?'

'That's possible. Once we settle things here first.'

'Everything is so uncertain. And Theo? We've got to see to Theo, now that we know the truth about the past.'

'We're not going to abandon Theo. This rehabilitation work with Singh will be a job for him. He's been in on it from the beginning.'

'Will he abandon us?' Madeleine asked anxiously.

'What do you mean?'

'Sometimes, I don't know what goes on in his mind. Like now. He's gone off. He's not told us a thing.'

'I think that's fine. He needs that kind of freedom.'

'I wish I could be that certain. I'm so anxious.'

The thunderhead cumuli had lifted off the gulf. There was a blinding white light and glare.

Theo could be anywhere on the island, Madeleine thought. The heavy rain, and then the sudden flood of light, had meant that there were an abundance of butterflies, which had spawned in thousands. Madeleine kept to the boundaries along the barbed wire fence. The butterflies were everywhere, trembling in the light. She followed them.

The razor grass had cut her legs. She was not dressed for this hike with her new red dress, and wearing her open sandals. A nun's habit might have been better, she laughed to herself. She took the path which descended the hill on the other side, going down towards the sea. She remembered that this must be the path to the midden that Theo and Jesse had talked of. This was a place that Theo might go to. She descended the steep slope, leaving the butterflies, who preferred the wild flowers along the road.

Very quickly, she was in the forest which was loud with small waterfalls. She saw what would be a prize for Theo, a *Mort Bleu*. It was large and dark blue, sailing down the valley, settling on ferns right in front of her, and then moving off to settle again further along.

Eventually, she was out into the light again, onto to what seemed an utterly deserted beach, with the relentless waves breaking, and the air suffused with the spray and sea mist, behind which was the overwhelming white light of the afternoon. She walked to where she thought the midden lay.

She sat on the high sands and stared. She began to dig, bringing up the fragments of coral, dead mens' bones, shells as delicate as porcelain, *chip chips* and oysters, conches and scallops. She dug up the bones of the sea, centuries of bones.

She thought of Theo's story, of those who had leapt to their death rather than be captured, those who had flown. *Sauteurs,* the place of the leap. Might he come here, or to the cliffs above, to throw himself off?

She imagined ochre bodies falling, falling before her eyes, against the white light and the pounding ocean, more bodies, rolling in, one on top of the other.

There was no Theo. Sitting there, hunched over her knees in her new red dress, she hugged herself warm. How little she was, against the immense sea. There was a sandpiper skittering along the hard shore. Such a small thing against such a great force.

Then her mind filled with stories she had been reading in the papers of the camps, things she could hardly imagine. It might be that they were not true.

On her return to the house, there still had not been any sign of Theo. Vincent said they should wait and see if the boy did not return in the night. He did not want to raise a search in the dark. In the morning, he would alert Jonah and Krishna if the boy had not returned.

Strangely, they slept soundly. On waking, they realised that they had not been wakened by Theo. They had come now to always expect to be woken. But also they had not heard him come back.

Madeleine was the first to look in on Theo's room. The bed was empty. She went downstairs and out to the verandah. The jetty was deserted, the water tank outside the kitchen was equally abandoned.

Vincent and Madeleine bundled into the dinghy. He had no fears to take her along with him. Not now, not today.

They were both alarmed. Theo had never stayed out all night. Where had he slept? But above all, what would the reason be? What was he saying to them by this action? 'He must've gone quite some way. I was down on the beach yesterday afternoon, the other side, and all along the back track. No sign of him,' Madeleine described.

'Well, who knows. He might be close. At least, we know that there's a reason for everything which has been happening. But I can't believe he will leave us now.'

'What do you mean? Leave? Fly? Fly away? That's what I thought down at the midden.' She sat in the bow while Vincent rowed.

'Well, we've had the attempt at fire. There's a kind of logic at work. There's a pattern. There's the repeated journey to be made. That's what I realise now. Over and over, till something breaks it. Till he decides, or it's decided for him to disrupt it.'

Father Meyer waved from his verandah. 'Have you seen Theo?' Vincent called out.

'Not this morning.' The priest cupped his hands. He had not seen him since yesterday. He was sure that he would be roaming with his butterfly net.

Vincent waved back. Madeleine ignored the conversation. 'That man, that man! I can't bring myself...' Then she broke off.

Vincent looked at her and smiled. He enjoyed her rebelliousness.

Saint Damian's came into view as a flight of pelicans landed in front of them.

At the jetty, there was the usual busy activity of loading and unloading. Vincent and Madeleine tied up, and made their way up to the pharmacy, where Vincent knew he would meet Sister Rita at least, and hopefully Singh, who might have some idea about the boy and know where Jonah was. Jonah would be able to organise a group of fellas who could do the walking which would be necessary to cover the island search.

Madeleine followed behind Vincent. She was wearing her red dress which made her conspicuous. Her hair was coiled into a *chignon*. Some patients greeted her, some turned away in embarrassment, as did some of the Sisters.

Mother Superior would be in her office. They would avoid her if it was possible.

There was some alarm, apparently, on the early morning news, about Japan. Vincent decided to catch the lunchtime news.

Hopefully, Theo would be found by then. There was a great deal of activity over at the main jetty in Perruquier Bay. And Chac Chac Bay had suddenly become full of barges and tugs, a destroyer and a mine sweeper.

It had turned out to be a blazing hot day, high, deep indigo skies, dazzling sea out on the gulf, and blistering heat. 'Make sure all the fellas have enough water. And good shoes!' No one had seen Vincent so agitated.

Jonah was overseeing one of groups that would take the road up to the lighthouse, from there they would send pairs to different parts of the north coast. Jonah would go up into Indian Valley with another group, Singh would lead another. They needed to question people whether they had seen the boy. They would fan out, covering the forest paths. Everyone would be strict about not including the Yankees.

'I've sent a message to Jesse for his assistance,' Vincent declared to Singh and Jonah.

'*You can never be in a financial jam when you working for Uncle Sam,*' Jonah teased cynically.

'*With France, Russia, Japan, Czech Slovakia, I think the safest place is to live is in America.*' Singh added to the *mamaguy*, with Tiger's calypso.

'And what about Atilla,' Jonah loved the excitement. '*The Yankees launched a real social invasion.*'

'We don't want any Yankee here. The dollar is one thing, but not the rest.' Singh was adamant.

Vincent ignored the joking.

Jonah's group would do a hut to hut search, questioning people of Theo's possible movements.

'Ask them all. You see the Doctor boy? Ask everybody that,' Vincent instructed.

Madeleine and Vincent, with some of the older boys taken out of the school, would make their way first to La Tinta and then to Salt Pond.

The groups would communicate with each other across the island by blowing the conch. One blow to gain attention, two blows a positive find, three if it turned out to be negative.

The search went on all morning to no avail. There was no sound of the conch from any part of the island. The heat grew with the approach of noon. The glare was blinding.

Madeleine and Vincent got the boys to search all the caves in La Tinta Bay and the surrounding cliffs. After Salt Pond they inspected the shoreline beneath the navigation light.

As they stood on the rocky cliffs, covered with agave and cacti, they looked down to the peninsular. It was just possible that Theo could be among the mangrove. But from where they stood, they saw nothing moving on the shores of the Salt Lake.

Suddenly, a wild cacophony, a huge pandemonium of hooters and sirens were heard coming from the bay. As they made their way back to Perruquier Bay, they could see the Stars and Stripes being run up the rigging and unfurling in the bright light. 'What's going on?' Vincent exclaimed.

When they arrived in the bay below, they went out to the jetty to get information from some of the Marines who were working there. This was when they heard the news. The Japanese city of Hiroshima had been bombed. The Atomic Bomb had been dropped on the city. 'That's all we know, Sir.' The G I turned away to his fellow soldiers.

Madeleine and Vincent met up with the boys who had gone to search La Tinta. They picked their way through the mangrove to Saint Damian's. The boys were running along with the excitement of the sirens and hooters which were still going. They met a Marine coming along the shore. 'They've dropped *Little Boy* on the Japs,' he shouted boastfully.

'What did you say?' Vincent stopped him as he was hurrying past.

'*Little Boy,* the Atomic Bomb.'

There was a strange ordinary reality about everything. Apart from the noise, everything seemed as usual and just itself. Nothing had changed, nothing was amiss. The Atomic Bomb had been dropped on Hiroshima. It was quite simple.

Back at Saint Damian's, they joined the crowd outside Mother Superior's office, where the radio was on loud, coming from the verandah. The news they had heard was repeated. It had occurred at 8.15 am Greenwich Mean Time that morning. It was a clear sky, said the news announcer, as if it were aweather report. Everyone stood silently, listening.

It was difficult for Vincent and Madeleine to get hold of the enormity of what had taken place. The search for Theo had to continue. The search parties regrouped under the almond tree. Everyone was to be fed properly, and then the search would be resumed. Elroy had one bit of news to report. An old woman in one of the huts had said that she thought she saw the boy climbing the barbed wire fence into the base yesterday. He was carrying a butterfly net and she had thought nothing of it at the time. 'So, he might be in the base?' Vincent said. 'Get hold of Jesse.' They could trust Jesse to be discreet, to conduct his own search within the base. What was Theo up to now? Jesse had grown fond of Theo and understood the need for discretion. He would keep Vincent informed.

Jonah and Singh reported a strange unease at Saint Damian's. The talk of atomic bombs, fired cities, spread its own terror among the patients. Not all the facts of the war on the Japanese side were at hand, and the soldiers at the base came under verbal attack from patients.

They did not like the boasting. Fellas who rowed at night to Carenage to go to the clubs in Porta España returned with stories of the sweet life, the money, the good time. People had work and good pay. They also told of the drunken sailors and how men were complaining that their women were going with the Yankees. This angered those who had been listening to Jonah's and Singh's arguments under the almond tree. One of the tunes people were singing now was from The Growling Tiger:

With the circulation of money
at the advent of the Yankee
Take this advice from me
Because I am sure that after the war

390

Things are not going to be as they were before.

The jokes and the carnival rhythm of the calypsos masked the anger and spoke the irony in the feelings of people. The drunken soldiers themselves laughed at the lines of *Rum and Coca-Cola, working for the Yankee dollar.*

The fellas under the almond tree were now singing another version. *Rum and Coca-Cola / Kill the Yankee soldier* '

When after two days there had been no news of Theo, Vincent and Madeleine remained at the house. Krishna and Jonah knew that they were there, and any news of Theo's presence was to be brought to them immediately. The search parties were combing the coasts for a washed up body. The fishermen were asked to be alert. Jesse had not reported back any evidence of Theo's presence on the base.

The days after the Hiroshima bombing continued to be blazing hot. The white light, the intense glare. It was unusual weather for early August.

On the morning of the 9th of August the sombre tones of the BBC announced that a second Plutonium-type bomb had been dropped on the city of Nagasaki. Vincent and Madeleine were up early having their coffee on the verandah. They listened in silence. Their hearts heavy at Theo's continued absence, they listened stunned by this enormous, far away event. Only this week they had been reading in the American papers, which Jesse had passed them, a press release which told of $2 billion dollars spent on the greatest scientific gamble in history which they, the Americans, had won. The article had continued with:

We are now prepared to obliterate more rapidly and completely every productive enterprise the Japanese have above ground in any city... If they do not now accept our terms, they may expect a rain of ruin from the air, the like of which has never been seen on this earth.

The bomb was nicknamed *Fat boy.*

In a later broadcast, they heard President Truman speaking. '*The Japanese began the war from the air at Pearl Harbour. They have been repaid many fold.*' He went on to describe the Atomic Bomb as a gift of God. '*We thank God it has come to us instead of to our enemies. May he guide us to use it in His ways and for His purpose.*'

Vincent walked to the edge of the verandah and looked out on the gulf.

'Who is this God? What are his purposes?'

* * *

Theo had been missing for nine days. Vincent and Madeleine had given him up as dead. They both went about the house trapped in their own grief. On the 15th of August, the Feast of the Assumption of Our Lady, the Japanese announced their surrender.

VJ Day was proclaimed, and another day of rejoicings began which allowed people to come out with the *tamboo bamboo* bands and the steel band. Madeleine and Vincent did not have the heart for the celebrations, though they were relieved that the fighting was over.

At Saint Damian's there was a red alert. They did not want the celebration to degenerate into a riot. More police were brought in, and the soldiers were on standby. That evening, the destroyers, barges, tugs and mine sweepers in Chac Chac Bay were lit up. There was a fire works display, and sirens and hooters blared across the bay and the hills of El Caracol.

Vincent and Madeleine sat on the jetty at the Doctor's House and watched the garish display which ran deeply counter to the feelings in their hearts and minds.

After the noise of celebration had died down on Chac Chac Bay, that night, the children were put to bed. The older patients made their weary way to their huts.

The following morning, on the crowded jetty, a witness told what she had seen in the night. She had seen a figure running in the night with a *flambeaux,* and what looked like a large tin of kerosene. As the figure darted in and out of the buildings, a trail of fire streamed out behind.

The fire had burnt all night. Every major building, except the huts and the childrens' hospital, had been torched. The fire had leapt over in places to the base. Fortunately, people were saying, the soldiers had been up and alert, so that the fire hoses were quickly brought into operation, otherwise all the huts and the hospital with the children would also have caught fire, and been burnt to the ground before the children and old people were brought out, They had been led down to the jetty, and put in almost every available boat in the bay. Some were ferried over to the convent and to the jetty at Perruquier Bay. The judgment was quickly made that Saint Damian's would have to be evacuated completely.

Vincent, Jonah and Krishna immediately discussed howe this could be the beginning of the rehabilitation that they had been planning. This was an ironic gift. It would now be forced on the authorities. All the patients, as far as the sisters had counted, had been brought down to the jetty area. There was a fear that not everyone had made it. But so far, only one or two people were possibly unaccounted for, and the sisters were following up the reports.

In the midst of all of this emergency and confusion, with Vincent fully occupied dealing with injuries and small burns, Madeleine at his side — openly now, no matter what Mother Superior thought — a young soldier found Vincent and told him that Theo's butterfly net had been discovered, caught on the barbed wire fence on the cliffs behind the convent, above Salt Pond.

This was the first real sign they had had in days. Vincent grabbed Madeleine and told Sister Rita to take over the treatment of burns and bandaging. They made their way, as fast as they could, with Jonah in the pirogue.

They arrived at the nuns' jetty. From there, they clambered up the slopes to the cliff path above Salt Pond. Vincent wanted to go alone with Madeleine. Jonah waited on the jetty. 'Take a conch with you, Doc. You could blow conch?'

Vincent took the conch. He smiled. 'Of course I can blow conch. Wait till you hear.'

There was the butterfly net which Vincent had given Theo as a birthday present, entangled on the barbed wire fence. The pole had got wedged in the ground. The net was torn. A bit of the gauze which was free of the barbs, fluttered in the breeze, like a cluster of butterflies. 'It's a flag!' Vincent exclaimed. Indeed it flew like an SOS. It signalled with its own peculiar kind of Morse. Vincent tried to disentangle it. It proved too difficult and time consuming. 'He's trying to tell us something.'

'Yes, he's leaving a clue, like children in a game, leaving a trail.' Madeleine followed behind Vincent along the path.

Together, they descended the track through the agave towards the lake. The same hot blistering weather had continued. The white light and glare was intense here, because of the sand and salt margins of the lake. In the distance, the heat shimmered and rose above water.

'Do you want to blow the conch to tell Jonah that we've found the butterfly net?'

'No,' Vincent said softly. 'Let's go it alone.'

They each picked their way carefully. Together they had their eyes peeled for clues of their dear boy, on the scuffed path, for any trace of him on this deserted, windswept landscape.

The salt margins of the lake drew them to the mirror of lucent water. The deserted place held its own peculiar kind of beauty. In front of them, there were a myriad *Yellow Migrants,* issuing as if from a funnel of swift air; the rate at which they were fluttering and flying forth. They crouched together and stared. White egrets looming on the higher branches were disturbed, and sailed off to the further end of the peninsular.

Looking into the distance, following their flight, Vincent and Madeleine noticed, at the same time, what looked like a crouching figure. How had they not seen him before, out in the open in the blinding light, but seeming like a mirage in the rising heat?

They continued to stare, drawing close to each other. They got up and began walking slowly towards the figure they now saw plainly as Theo, crouching over a log at the far end of the open spaces around the lake. They skirted the shore, their steps crunching on the salt. They did not want to frighten him. Their own feelings were a mixture of intense relief, and ecstatic excitement. But rising in Vincent was a kind of anger. Why had he done this to him? He controlled his anger. Who knew why this boy did what he did? Did he himself?

Vincent and Madeleine, with Theo now before them, utterly absorbed in something in front of him, both exclaimed, 'Theo!'

Theo turned and looked over his shoulder blankly at them.

They moved forward to kneel behind him. He continued to be absorbed by what they then saw was a chrysalis attached to the under part of a dry log.

The caterpillar had found this well camouflaged spot to spin, with its sticky saliva, its silken web. It had already purged itself of its intestines and entwined the hind part of its body to the web of silk. It had shrunk considerably. The caterpillar was now a chrysalis. A dry leaf like the other dry leaves on the salt shore. This was what Theo was staring at. How long had he been here, to catch the short moment from caterpillar to chrysalis, this metamorphosis?

The outline of the butterfly could be seen clearly beneath the chitinous outer shell which must have been here for three weeks at least. They had caught it on the last part of its journey. The top and sides of the chrysalis had popped, and the head and shoulders of the butterfly were emerging. The butterfly was pushing itself out on its wiry legs. It was now half-way out, the wings crinkled like colourful tissue paper.

Theo, Madeleine and Vincent knelt and stared at the wet abdomen, and then the still folded butterfly began to ease itself away. There were these little pumping motions. They could hardly see the huge transformations with the naked eye.

Time had ceased, it seemed, as they knelt, till the moment a fully extended butterfly let the morning breeze filter through its wings, strengthening them for imminent flight. Then, it was gone.

'Theo!' they exclaimed again together.

He turned towards them and stared.

'We've been looking for you for days,' Vincent said gently.

'For ten days,' Madeleine said softly.

Theo registered but remained mute. He seemed well, not dying of thirst or hunger. He was sunburnt, his brown sugar hair dry and matted.

'Theo, we can hardly believe that you are here and safe,' Vincent continued.

Theo smiled, faintly.

'Come, let us go. You can tell us what you want to tell us, later.' Madeleine encouraged him to rise.

For some time, as they were kneeling behind the boy, Vincent had smelt the kerosene and seen the stains on Theo's khaki pants. He said nothing to Madeleine, or to anyone else. He did not blow the conch. Jonah was surprised when he heard them coming down to the jetty. He waved and shouted. 'Theo, Theo, they find, you boy. They find you.' Surprisingly, Theo waved and smiled, as if suddenly realising the stir he had created.

Later Vincent was to hear from Jonah and Singh that they had heard from some of the fellas that the running figure, which had been seen with the kerosene tin and the *flambeaux* at Saint Damian's, had also been seen running between the barracks and the stores of the American base: a running figure bent low in the night, escaping the search lights and the intermittent beam of the now renewed lighthouse.

That evening, Jesse visited the Doctor's House. He came through the back door, carrying his saxophone.

Madeleine was cooking tonight, and Theo was out on the jetty, fishing with Vincent. When, in the past, Vincent had longed for the words as conversation, now there seemed to be no need. Everything had been said. They could feel close without words. They each caught a red snapper. Jesse came down the steps just as Theo landed his on the boards of the jetty.

'Hi, Theo.' It was if nothing unusual had occurred.

'How you going, Jesse?' The boy looked up.

Then Jesse spoke to Vincent. 'After this, the authorities are not going to sanction the continuance of the base or the leprosarium. Your case and the case of Jonah and Singh has been forced upon them by coincidence.' When he said that, he looked over to Theo who was still fishing, and then back at Vincent. 'The preparations are almost complete. The soldiers will be away in days. The patients are to have a half way house on the base at Chaguramas. It's the least we can do. They're abandoning camp fast.'

'I'll be there tomorrow to see the last of the patients off safely,' Vincent said. 'Today I was occupied elsewhere.'

'I understand.' Jesse smiled.

After Madeleine's supper, they all went out onto the verandah, relieved of having to have blackouts or restrictions on noise. Small freedoms. There was a full moon and Jesse played his saxophone. Madeleine and Vincent danced. Across the bay, Father Meyer still played his Wagner.

'Hi, Father, turn that thing off,' Jesse shouted.

At that moment Jonah and Singh arrived with a bottle of rum. Calypso, bottle and spoon filled the night air as they all said their farewells.

The following morning, the bay was alive with the double evacuation. Jonah had arrived at dawn like he had for years. Vincent, Madeleine and Theo went to Saint Damian's to help the patients with their safe boarding of every possible craft which was available. Singh and Christiana helped. They were a few who had spent such a long part of their life at the leprosaruium, that they were confused by the idea of leaving. Mr Lalbeharry was philosophical about the change.

While the patients knew that they were not going to their homes immediately, and to some that would have been a terrifying prospect, they were, on the whole, relieved to be leaving Saint Damian's. The nuns were resigned to whatever was the will of God, as they too helped. Sister Rita waved from their passing launch.

All could see that the American base was being evacuated as well, because of the damage which the fire had done. The theme song of the departure, sung as the patients boarded the old island steamer was:

'*For fifty old destroyers, so it was said,*
They sold those valuable bases over our head
And today we don't know who are masters in this land
If it's the English or the American...'

The fellas, who had kept the meeting going under the almond tree, jeered with their calypso the departure of the soldiers.

'Bolo, I sure you know who is master here now!' Elroy called.

'Boy, is we self!'

Versailles
1948

Le Petit Trianon

In the late afternoon, Theo left to go into town. Earlier in the day, under his supervision, they had installed Madeleine's father's old desk from France into the room off the verandah at Le Petit Trianon, their small house in the grounds of Versailles.

The desk had stood in the small room off the hall in the house at Saint Jacques de Compagne, where her father saw his patients when he was not working at the hospital. Madeleine could see it under the window with the lace curtain. They had gone to the empty house on her return in 1948 with Vincent. On the door, still the scrawl *Les Juifs*.

Everything had been put by neighbours into Emile's barn. She saw herself again among the packing cases, her father's books and papers.

All left that day. At first, no explanations, only those single words *'Ils'* and the more staccato, *'Le Gestapo.'* The shadow through the glass of the door. The two chairs in the hall, the stumped out cigarettes: *'So polite. But they never told you anything, the German soldiers.'* All the villagers had their stories for Doctor Weil's daughter.

Everyone was now in the resistance. She found that people looked over their shoulders, guarding their backs. Some bowed their heads when others spoke. There were those who had resisted and those who had collaborated. But publicly, she felt that all wanted to have resisted now, at least now. It was *their* pain. She would not be part of that settling of scores, that division and its aftermath. She had not been there. She had her husband with his island and their possibilities, their future.

They visited her father's grave with the lettering on the stone which read: *Disappeared at Auschwitz.*

After Theo's departure, Vincent and Madeleine took a stroll to the old Versailles house, at the top of the pasture, near the cocoa houses.

'Who works these now?' Their sliding roofs were pulled back. The beans were being sunned.

'Bosoon, the old overseer. He's a small-holding farmer. He was my father's groom.'

'That's good. The future will be different,' Madeleine stated.

'Not immediately.'

'We must make it happen,' she insisted.

'Yes.' Vincent watched her, and wondered how long it would take to fit in. They had their work. That would make a difference. It would take time to slip past without being noticed, for Madam and Boss to disappear.

'Here, let's go up the front steps.' They seemed sturdy enough and the verandah had a concrete floor. 'It was put in just before they left.'

They looked over the estate out from the ledge. where there always used to be pots of seed ferns. 'They used to tickle my face. I remember that,' Vincent said, folding his hand over Madeleine's.

'We're always looking back,' she said.

'Yes. Making the journey over and over again.'

'We must stop this.'

'Look, let me show you, take care, stand back.' They stood at the door looking into the house. The floorboards had been taken up. They could look up and down into the depths and the height of the house, as far as the turrets. There were no floors. The wood had all been ripped out, as well as the windows. The house was completely open to the wind and the rain, and the corruption of the light.

'Like the bomb sites in London and Berlin.'

'Only, it's time that has done this, time and thieves,' Vincent explained.

'Wind and rain. Thieves? An abandoned house? Where else would you get materials?' Just visible, beyond the pasture, were the barrack rooms with their poor.

'How long will they be there?' Vincent wondered.

'They cannot burn down their homes. For where will they go?' Madeleine made her point.

'Well, someone has stolen the wood. Someone has dismantled it. Time now will finish it off. See, over there, that's another estate, and they are all falling apart.'

'Where was Le Petit Paradis? These names that they chose,' Madeleine laughed.

'The Marineaux estate? Yes, where Theo was. At the top of Pepper Hill, you turn right by the Saint Joseph church and go along that road. We can go and see it if you like. They never rebuilt the house after the fire. We can go in the buggy. Bosoon still has the buggy. It'll be like when we were children.'

'And there?' Madeleine was pointing just beneath them at the back of the house. They looked right through the house, through a green light. The walls were cream and mildewed.

'The servant's room.' Vincent remembered every detail.

'Such a world. There is nothing back there, in Europe, for all of this to rest on now, and there is nothing here for them to take anymore. It's unsupportable. People must support themselves.'

'We need Singh and his revolution,' Madeleine said emphatically.

'I'm sure Krishna will do it. He won't disappear.'

'Nor Jonah. He can't do it without Jonah, not really, and the barefoot revolution marching and standing in Brunswick Square.'

'What are they calling it? Did you hear Theo speaking about the meeting. The University of Brunswick Square?'

Suddenly, there was a gust of wind taking a piece of cardboard and hurling it out into the yard where it flew and tumbled in the air over the pasture. 'My God!'

'What? A little hurricane?' Madeleine exclaimed.

'Bernard,' Vincent explained. 'That piece of cardboard, like his toy plane. The plane he built with my father, and they flew on the pasture. It crashed.'

They had had a letter from one of Bernard's RAF Fighter Pilot friends. He told his story:

"We flew together in one of those two-man bombers, nothing but plywood, fast and small. A Mosquito. Mostly low-level bombing. The Mosquito's speed made it possible to escape the *flak*, you know, the anti-aircraft fire. Too risky man, too blasted risky. The Germans soon learnt how to deal with the Mosquito. Later, most of the bombs we drop never reach their target. That's something to realise. Your brother loved flying. He was a sucker for it. Bernard love the Mosquito. After the Mosquito, we join the Pathfinder Force together. It was our job to guide the bombers. Boy that's when we did flights like peas over Berlin and Hamburg. You didn't have time to be 'fraid. Too much work. When you get coned, catch in a search light and the *flak* coming at you. Well then, you 'fraid no arse. Frighten no arse, but nothing to do about it. You just keep in there. To tell you the truth, that night I could see his aircraft coned, miles away. I saw him get hit. I was sure I saw a parachute. But you know, in the end, I wasn't sure. I wasn't sure. And we got back to base. They didn't come back. I found the grave in France. All you gone there, I expect?"

'*Chéri,* we're going to have to look after ourselves, and others, but always ourselves. You're going to have to look after me and I'll look after you. We can't go on like this. Always remembering the terror of everything. We can't keep burying the dead. I know. Me, I can't speak. I'm the worse. Your poor brother.' They held each other, teetering at the door of the house without any floors in the green light.

Back at Le Petit Trianon, that evening, over rum punch on the verandah, Vincent said, 'You know, there is something I have to tell you.'

'Something that you've not told me before?'

'Yes. Something that I've not told you before.'

'What could that be?'

'I mentioned the servant's room.'

'Yes.'

'Odetta?'

'Yes, you told me about Odetta a long time ago, on El Caracol. A childhood love. There was Odetta, and Simone in Paris. Yes?'

'Nothing is a long time ago.'

'Seems so.'

'She had our child. A boy.'

The wind sung in the palms far above them. It seemed to Vincent that a long time passed before Madeleine spoke.

'Ours?'

'Yes. Hers and mine. Not ours. You know what I mean.' Vincent was nervous.

Madeleine could not help herself, 'What are you saying?'

'That I've got a son.'

'Why've you not told me all this time. My God!'

He saw a kind of horror on her face. 'Trust me.' He touched her arm.

404

'Don't touch me. How can I?'

'Believe me.'

'Do you know your son?' Madeleine cut him off.

'I was not allowed to. I glimpsed him once, feeding at her breast. I was passing the house in the village.'

'He must look like you, be about Theo's age. Does Theo know about this?'

'Of course not. Would I tell him before I had told you?'

'Have you thought what it will mean to Theo, you having a son, another son?'

'I was a boy at the time,' Vincent protested like a child.

'That's not the point. You've not been a boy all these years that I've known you.'

'I'm telling you now.'

'Why now?'

'He lives in the village.'

'My God! Vincent!' Madeleine got up and went into the house.

At supper, Madeleine was silent.

'At least that was done,' Vincent turned to Madeleine.

'What? I didn't hear what you said?'

'I was just thinking. At least, my parents gave money to Odetta.'

'Oh, yes, that's good. But he's your son. You're his father. Are you not curious to see him?'

'I've missed him all my life.'

'Why did you not tell me. Do you not know? You must know what this means to me?' She bit her lip.

'Madeleine. I wish I could start all over again. When I came back, and then the war, it all receded into a past that I could not retrieve, or, tried to forget. Because a boy, he could be seen as an heir to the family inheritance. There was the question of the name, whether he would carry Metivier. I think that is what persuaded my parents to fix a once-and-for-all financial settlement with Sybil, and then to be passed onto Odetta when she came of age. This, they hoped, would keep the matter quiet. They didn't want to be pestered. They were paying her off. It allayed the shame they felt.'

'And it has worked? But that's how the family dealt with it. But what about you? What about you and me? What about you and your son?'

'Yes. Except that now we're back here, and I had to tell you.'

'So you have a son, whom you've not got the pleasure of enjoying, or being responsible for, and we're unable to have children now. You ask me how I feel? I wish I had become pregnant on El Caracol. But not now. It would not be right for me to have a child now. I wonder if I could conceive.'

'I'm sorry. I'm sorry, Madeleine.'

'No. I've thought about this.' She got up from the table. 'You didn't do this to me. It is a legacy of your past. You were young, for whatever reason. You must not punish yourself because of your past. We're punished by the past as it is. Too much punishment. We've both had too much punishment. At least we've learnt that from what we've been through.'

He saw in her eyes the story of her own mother's death, her father's disappearance.

'All of this must end. We have to find another way of living. Will you try and find Odetta? She'll be a woman now.'

'I think I must. How will you feel?'

'I think it's right. But you don't know what she'll want.'

'Does that bother you?' Vincent asked anxiously.

'I do trust you. Of course I trust you.'

'No more surprises,' Vincent added.

'Now I understand about Theo.'

'He's our responsibility.'

'Well, he's himself. We must not be romantic about him,' Madeleine said thoughtfully.

'He'll want you. '

'Yes, but there will be many children. Many children will be coming to the surgery. I hope he'll help me build the new school. Of course Theo is special. But you'll arrange to see your son? You must. Yes? And, tell Theo.'

'Yes,' Vincent said, with resignation.

Later that week, Sybil, the old Metivier servant, arrived with a young man, and waited on the verandah. Madeleine recognised the young man at once. He had the colouring of Theo, a mixed child, slightly reddish hair and green eyes, and Vincent's definite look. He was a Metivier, but there, beneath that family resemblance, was a lucent bright-eyed intelligence that Madeleine thought must be his mother's, the girl Odetta, her husband's childhood sweetheart.

'Yes, have a seat. One moment. I'll show you in to the doctor. He has a patient, right now.' Madeleine smiled. She could feel tears welling up in her eyes. What for she was not sure. For Vincent? For herself, for the young man, his grandmother, his mother? Where was she? For everything that had happened? For the child she herself had not had?

'Thanks, Miss.'

When the patient who had been with Vincent was finished, Madeleine went in to warn Vincent of whom he was to see next. 'I'll bring them in, and then, maybe, I'll get a drink, some lime juice.'

'Yes. Let me clean up, give me a few moments.'

Vincent appeared at the door of the verandah. The old woman and the young man turned and stood up.

'Sybil. Sybil, you look just the same. It so long.'

Sybil put out her hands and Vincent took them. 'So long, yes, so long, Mister Vincent.'

The young man stood to the side, smiling. Vincent did not look at him directly, only fleetingly.

'Sybil.' Vincent could not get over the old woman.

'Well you know, I hear you come back. I say to the boy I must go and look for Mister Vincent. Madam, son. Then I get your message.'

'Yes, Sybil.'

'I say, I must take him to meet Mister Vincent. Let Mister Vincent see him.' She put her hand on the young man's shoulder, ushering him in, as it were.

It was then that Vincent turned to the young man and looked directly at him. He saw the resemblance immediately, and the realisation caught the back of his throat. Without reserve, without thinking what it might have looked like, he reached out and took the young man by his shoulders and pulled him towards him, embracing him. He then held him at a distance. 'Let me have a good look at you.'

The young man let himself be treated like a child. In that first moment he seemed to speak like a child. 'Grandmammy say you is my father.' He was a confident eighteen-year-old.

Again, Vincent pulled the young man to him and embraced him. Then, he turned to Sybil. 'Sybil, you did right.'

Then, with his arm still around the young man's shoulder, he said, 'Yes, your grandmammy is right, I am your father. You are my son.'

The young man smiled. He looked thrilled. He laughed. He did not seem to have any of the sorrow that that secret had meant to Vincent. He did not have any of the stoic concealment that Sybil had carried.

'Your name?' Vincent asked.

'Vincent.'

'Vincent!'

'Yes. They call me Vin.'

'You christen him Vincent, Sybil?'

'Is the mother. She insist at the time. At the time, Odetta say, no matter what people say, she naming him Vincent. We does call him Vin.'

'Odetta? Where's Odetta?' Vincent looked at the young Vincent when he said his mother's name.

'She gone America. Is I that mind the boy. I tell her, girl go and get your future. I go stay here and mind the boy for you. And you know, Mister and Madam was good, eh?'

The information and the meeting began to overwhelm. Vincent turned to Madeleine, who had stood in her study and watched the scene, as if it were a play. He beckoned to her to join them. 'My wife, Madeleine.' Madeleine shook their hands and smiled. 'I've told Madeleine everything.'

'They say you is a good nurse. The people in the village, the women. They say you is a good nurse.'

'She's an excellent nurse.' Vincent pulled Madeleine to him. 'What're you doing now. School? Work?' Vincent turned to his son.

'I entering for the Island Schol at Immaculate Mary.'

'Wonderful. That's my old school.'

'I know. I see your name in the roll of honour.'

'In the roll of honour?' Vincent laughed, mocking himself.

Then the group on the verandah stood awkwardly, unsure of what to do next.

'Where are you living now, Sybil?'

'Two houses pass Le Poy shop. Is there you will find me. I ent move all these years. Where I is to go, but here? The boy home for holiday. But he does be boarding in town.'

Vincent shook his head, reflecting on a life that had flown by. An image of Odetta and himself in the cocoa house flashed through his mind. Here was his son. He saw the girl in the boy's face.

'You must come again. Sybil, I'll come and look for you. '

'Yes, Mister Vincent. I there. I not going nowhere.'

'We'll talk.'

'I know you'll take up your responsibility, Sir.' Vincent looked at Madeleine. She smiled reassuringly at him.

'Yes, Sybil. You did the right thing to come here this morning.'

'What you want to study?' Vincent turned to his son again.

'Medécine.'

'Well, we'll definitely have to talk.'

As Madeleine tidied up after the morning surgery, Vincent stood on the verandah looking at his son and his grandmother walking down the gap back to the village. He was now his responsibility.

Another life was beginning. The surgery, the school, the young boy, Vin, were all signs pointing to a hopeful future, an island and its people yearning for self government and independence. But Madeleine and Vincent knew that it was not going to happen tomorrow. The lessons of El Caracol had been well learnt.

Only this morning, they had been told that the two big trade unions had joined, led by Krishna Singh and Jonah Le Roy.

Theo was coming up on the train to Flanagin Town. Vincent went with the buggy to meet him. On the way back he told him about Vin, he told him about the talk that he and Madeleine had had. Theo listened in silence. 'It won't make any difference to what we feel about you Theo, about what you mean to us. You know that.' Theo looked across at Vincent, trying to smile. Then he looked away. 'Theo, you must know that.'

'I've got dust in my eyes.'

'Here take my handkerchief. It's the road, this dry season.'

Later, back at the house, Theo talked with Madeleine alone. He checked that she was all right. Then he went into a flood of stories at dinner about how he was in touch with Jonah and Krishna. And he told of a big political meeting in Brunswick Square the night before. 'Jonah's last big speech begin with, "Massa Day Done!" People say the crowds bawled the place down.' Theo ended by saying, 'We making history.' He told them about how his work with the rehabilitation of the patients was going, how he had met Mr Lalbeharry and Ma Cowey.

Theo went off to bed early.

'Still full of stories. I suppose it'll take time,' Madeleine said.

'Yes. He'll need time, a lot of time, a lifetime,' Vincent reflected.

'We all need time to tell our stories,' Madeleine added.

They stretched out to each other, standing and embracing.

**Porta España
1983**

Iguanas and Orchids

I wait for the other client this morning to leave. They always pass me on the steps, heads bowed, never a word, a smile, a hello or a good morning. I sit on the top step in the sun and watch and wait. I watch *congoree* worms. I watch ants with their umbrella of leaves. I always have to wait, because I always arrive early. The brightness is too shocking for the darkness in my mind!

An iguana has crept to the edge of the steps and grows green in the sun. Its look is the gaze of the Sphinx. Dry almond leaves scuttle like crabs, blown by the wind across the yard. Everywhere, I hear the rustle of palms. An orchid exudes its perfume.

Then, I know it's my turn, because she's come onto the verandah, pushing one of the French windows out. The long white muslin drapes soar to the ceiling and then settle again. She bends to secure the latch in a groove on the pitch pine floor. I look up, and she smiles, and I walk along the verandah towards her. She's still bending, her long body in a profound bow, a kind of swoon, draped by the soft cotton or linen she so often wears. As she rises, I catch a glimpse of the nape of her neck beneath her hair which is swept up into a roll, or a bun, and lies there on her smooth brown neck; a *chignon*. As she turns, she emits the scent of *vertivert*, an old fashioned scent, the sort Madeleine wore, the kind I smell when I remember Chantal, my sister.

Come on in.

It's her opening line. It's our weekly ritual. She hardly betrays any emotion, only the beginning of a smile at the corners of her mouth, trembling on her lips which she bites. It's not a pleasantry, it's a prompt to begin the week's work.

She motions me to the couch. I lie down. She sits behind me.

I pause and then begin. There is a chorus of *keskidees* from where they are perched on the electric wire out in the yard, puffed up with their questions. *Qu'est ce-qu'il dit?*

What *am* I saying? About myself. Where should I start?

Wherever you like.

I was a child then...

Yes.

There's an island blazing in my mind..

An island? The one you talked about last week?

Yes. I've got all these feelings and I don't know what to do with them.

H'mm.

I stare at the ceiling.

Is that why you're here?

I've got all these stories. I'm tired of stories. I could tell you so many stories. I could go on and on and on.

But maybe there is another story, another kind of story which you'll tell here, a new story. It might not be so coherent, so fluent and all there, ready to be told, but nevertheless, a story. Maybe, even the story which will tell us something new.

New?

Yes, maybe all the stories in your head conceal, rather than reveal what we're trying to get at.

What's that?

Well, we don't know, we don't know as yet, we'll have to wait and see.

I was helped by this doctor, when I was twelve, between twelve and sixteen. He said I used to tell these stories at night. Like as if in a dream, or nightmare, or sleep-walking ...during the war.

Do you remember anything about them?

Yes and no.

There is a war going on inside of you.

Well, there was the war.

Yes, but you said earlier you have all these feelings and you don't know what to do with them. There's a confusion, like confusion in war. Conflict, maybe.

I found the war exciting. Well, what I made of it.

Yes, you've told a lot of stories about what happened, but maybe you've not told how you feel about what happened. There's a kind of absence of feeling. You say, what you made of it. That's like making a story of it. You're good at that, making up stories. Maybe telling all these stories is your way of dealing with all these feelings you don't know what to do with.

I stare at the ceiling.

I was only a child then...

When?

I was a child. How could I be responsible? They made me... they hid me away afterwards. They should've punished me.

Punished you? You want to be punished?

No.

Well, that's what you said.

He punished me. Do you want me to show you. Do you want me to take my clothes off and show you? I've got a scar right down my back, and yet another scar you cannot see.

Is that what you feel like doing? Showing me your scars? You're telling me that you're scarred.

I am. He beat me. Beat me till I bled. He...

Who did this to you?

My father. Well, I knew he was my father, but it wasn't clear... I wasn't ever sure. I can't talk about this.

Don't tell me the story. Tell me how you feel.

Well, I could kill him. My body, it's *my* body...

What did you do?

What do you mean?

Well, did you kill him?

No, no! He died anyway. Mister.

What happened?

I killed her. I killed my mother. I was only a child. I wanted to kill them both. But, really I wanted to kill him. Punish her. She died. He wasn't there.

So, it was an accident?

No, yes and no. A fire. I know all about this. I know this story, but I don't know why I feel the way I feel.

Or, don't feel. You don't know what you feel. Maybe you're so angry. It's like the war, like the worse thing in the war which could destroy everything. Your anger, if you allowed yourself to feel it, might destroy everything. That's the confusion.

I destroyed my mother. I've already destroyed everything. I killed Mama.

You were a child. You were not responsible, this is what you say. You killed your mother and you're left to have a feeling about that, which you've not allowed yourself to feel.

I tried to kill myself once. I thought I might fly to freedom.

You could not live with yourself and feel what you feel.

Yes.

Maybe this is the story you'll tell here, how you feel about killing your mother, which seems like killing everything.

A new story, to save myself.

To live with yourself.

To live with myself. To live with my *own* body.

That's what we might do here, allow you to live with yourself. In time.

I have called it, my calypso.

What?

My story, my night calypso.

416

Acknowledgements

I acknowledge my indebtedness to the following writers and their books: Paul Brand with Philip Yancey, *Pain: The Gift Nobody Wants* (Marshall Pickering) and Phyllis Thompson's *Mister Leprosy* (Hodder & Stoughton); Ian Ousby's *Occupation* (Pimlico) and Joanna Bourke's *The Second World War* (OUP) for the response by journalists and writers signalled by quotations; Gordon Rohlehr's *Calypso and Society* (Gordon Rohlehr) from which quotes of many of the calypsonians of the Second World War, including Atilla, Beginner, Lord Caresser, Destroyer, The Growling Tiger, Lord Invader, Lord Kitchener, Radio, were made; Gaylord T.M. Kelshall's *The U-Boat War in the Caribbean* (Airlife Publishing Ltd); Sister Marie Thérèse Retout OP *Called to Serve* (Paria Publishing), (though, it must be said that the leprosarium and convent of this novel, with all its characters, is entirely fictional); Arthur Lewis's *Labour in the West Indies* (New Beacon Books) and Susan Craig's *Smiles and Blood* (New Beacon Books); Malcolm Barcant's *Butterflies of Trinidad & Tobago* (Collins) for the names and language of butterflies; Ulric Cross's account of being a member of the RAF (Trinidad Express). I wish to acknowledge the use of a quote from John Berger's, *Afterword, Nineteen Nineteen* (Faber & Faber). I also want to thank the staff of the Imperial War Museum's library; Gaylord T.M. Kelshall for an interview, and Sister Marie Thérèse Retout OP, and Matron Paul at Port-of Spain General Hospital for talking informally. I was very fortunate to be able to meet Simon Ramdeo and Joseph Suran, two members of the Trinidad & Tobago Hansen Society who were generous with their stories (whose confidences I've kept), and Inskip Andrews who organised the visits. I am also indebted to Wendy Hewing for providing materials and films on the occupation of France and heading me in the right direction. I wish to acknowledge the support of The Author's Foundation & K Blundell Trust for a research grant, and Ruth Bromley, the then Director of The Sixth Form Centre City & Islington College who allowed me to take the time out of teaching. Many friends were generous in the loan of their homes in the country as retreats: Chris and Robin Baron, Penny and Robin Bowen, Wendy and Bernie Hewing. I thank my agent Elizabeth Fairbairn at John Johnson Ltd. for her time, reading, and ever continuing interest; my new editor, David Shelley, for his keen judgement and encouraging, warm support; Debbie Hatfield for her careful and sensitive editing and Nemah Kamar, also at Allison & Busby, for her enthusiasm; Professor Ken Ramchand for his reading and discussion of a draft manuscript. Above all, I have to thank Jenny Green for her critical reading and discussion of the manuscript at all the vital stages.